ITALIAN ICE

EM LYNLEY

Dreamspinner Press

Published by
Dreamspinner Press
5032 Capital Circle SW
Ste 2, PMB# 279
Tallahassee, FL 32305-7886
USA
http://www.dreamspinnerpress.com/

Italian Ice

Cover Art by Anne Cain
annecain.art@gmail.com

ISBN: 978-1-61372-481-1

Printed in the United States of America
First Edition
July 2012

eBook edition available
eBook ISBN: 978-1-61372-482-8

For Susan, Pam, Alexi, Maya, and Emilie.
I could never have done it without you.

PROLOGUE

The cell vibrated in his pocket, and he pulled it out, moving away from his companion, who had his face buried in a guidebook.

"Tiger One," he whispered, suppressing a grin. *Stupid fucking code names.*

"One of the lions is missing. Hasn't checked in for more than twelve hours. We're in a code blue sit right now." *A missing agent?* This was serious. No wonder they were calling him when he was supposed to be on vacation.

"Where was he?" Tiger One glanced at his companion again. Still reading.

"Not sure."

"I can't talk here. Let me go somewhere private so you can fill me in on everything."

"Sure."

Tiger One snapped his phone shut. He'd need to come up with a good excuse to get out of the afternoon's plans. But it was a missing agent. Worth ruffling a few feathers for.

1

Una bugia tira l'altra.
One lie draws others after it.
    —Italian proverb

Rome

TRENT COPELAND had expected more from the Vatican Museums. He and Reed had waited in line for nearly two hours just to get in. Or at least Trent had. Reed had said he felt a little unwell—that seafood at dinner the night before, maybe—then gone back to lie down at their hotel.

But Trent couldn't enjoy the priceless treasures on his own. He didn't want to. He wanted to share the joy of these beautiful paintings and sculptures with Reed, not stare silently at them alone. He could have stayed home in LA and taken a virtual museum tour if that was all he wanted.

He moved through the ancient rooms, barely absorbing Etruscan art and gems of Greek sculpture. He wandered down the long corridor toward the Renaissance masterpieces, stopping occasionally to glance at floor-to-ceiling tapestries and delicate hand-colored maps of the Roman Empire in all its stages. Even the exquisite trompe l'oeil ceiling didn't give him any satisfaction as he shuffled toward the crowning glory contained by these walls.

A ceiling, to be more precise. But Trent wouldn't even venture into the Sistine Chapel. Something this spectacular couldn't be experienced alone. He wanted to share it with someone as special as the room itself: Reed.

And if Reed wasn't well, it was doubly difficult for Trent to enjoy the splendor.

But Reed never got ill. The man had a cast-iron stomach. He could probably out-eat a goat. It was one of the things they'd—well, he wouldn't say *argued*—differed over. Reed never took the same level of enjoyment in eating as Trent did. It had taken time, but lately Reed seemed more interested in eating, one of Trent's greatest joys in life.

So was Reed really under the weather, or had he made an excuse rather than traipse around another museum? Despite his knowledge of art and antiquities, Reed's tastes ran to the more austere Asian forms, rather than the elaborate Roman and European treasures at the Vatican. But he knew how much the Vatican and Sistine Chapel meant to Trent. He'd said he wanted to see them; had it only been to humor Trent?

And he certainly owed Trent. The previous day they'd gone to the Capuchin Crypt, a series of underground burial chambers—more like caves—filled with bones of dead monks and priests. It had creeped him out. It had been Reed's idea to go—one of the few places he'd seemed excited about visiting, so Trent didn't think twice about agreeing. But once they got in there with the heavy, dank air and all those bones decorating the walls around them, the ceiling seemed to lower down on them like in some Indiana Jones movie. The skulls laughed as cold sweat trickled down Trent's spine. Just thinking about it again made his skin crawl. He brushed away some creepy-crawlies from his left arm and took a calming breath.

Damned Reed had talked Trent into staying by promising him payback with lavish sexual favors. He hadn't paid the debt the previous night; now he'd run off feeling "unwell." Reed might not want to look at painted ceilings or eight zillion sculptures, but he wouldn't just leave Trent, not after the catacombs. Reed had a certain sense of duty Trent could always count on.

Reed must really be ill for him to have left, Trent concluded.

He took one last long glance up and down the corridor and pulled the guidebook out of his backpack. Not usually a "check-this-off-the-list" type of traveler, he shook off the guilt of consulting a list of "Vatican treasures not to be missed."

He'd at least looked at them all, except for the Sistine Chapel.

That he'd save for next time. With Reed.

"TIGER One here."

"You can cut that code name crap if you want, Reed."

"Thank God. You know how much I hate it." Reed chuckled as he settled on the edge of the bed.

"I do."

"So, fill me in."

"I've got one agent unaccounted for, but his partner has a coded message from him that he can't seem to crack."

"Where do I fit in?" Reed swiveled so he could lean back against the pillows arrayed along the headboard, stretching out on the comfortable bed. "What makes you think I can break this particular code?"

"The missing agent is Peter Isett."

Reed sat up with a jolt, heart racing. *Peter is missing?* "Still, why me? I'm on vacation. With Trent." How much did White know?

"Isett was your first partner in the Bureau, right?"

"Yeah...." Reed waited to see if White knew more than that.

"You guys used a private code?"

"Yeah." Lots of partners did. Apparently Peter still did, but why couldn't his new partner break it?

"Peter's working on an investigation into a shady auction house here in Rome. Rossetti's. Heard of it?"

"No." Reed doodled on a hotel notepad as he only half listened to White. Peter here in Rome, now? Was this a coincidence, or...? No, he was being ridiculous.

"...Tuesday." White paused. "You got that?"

"Yeah," Reed lied. White's call about Peter's absence still had him shaken. "We need to meet."

"Just what I was about to suggest. Can you be at Piazza della Rotonda in two hours? Get a table outside and I'll find you."

"See you later."

White disconnected, and Reed slammed the phone down.

This was the last thing he expected or wanted. How could he possibly explain any of this to Trent?

Truth was, Reed couldn't.

TRENT made his way back to the Hotel d'Inghilterra, one of Rome's most luxurious, on the Metro, getting off at Spagna, near the Spanish Steps, and walking the last part along the via dei Condotti, home of some of the most expensive shops, before he turned onto via Bocca di Leone—the lion's mouth street. He loved that name. Loved the whole exclusive, elegant neighborhood. He moved more quickly than the usual leisurely Roman pace, passing people but trying not to plow through clusters of slower-walking pedestrians.

This particular street was full of exclusive boutiques and plenty of window shoppers, both foreign tourists and monied locals. Trent glanced around with more than a tiny bit of regret that he couldn't enjoy the scenery any more than he had the exquisite museum pieces.

He strode thorough the beautifully appointed lobby of d'Inghilterra, past the sumptuous period furnishings fitting for its origins as a royal palazzo, and to the front desk, richly paneled in smooth dark wood, maybe walnut.

"Key for Room 27, please?" He didn't want to knock and disturb Reed if he were asleep.

The desk clerk, a young woman with short honey-blonde hair and friendly blue eyes ringed with carefully applied eyeliner, peered out from behind an enormous crystal vase of calla lilies and handed him the key with a smile. He took the stairs three at a time up to the third floor and let himself into the room as quietly as possible.

He glanced around the spacious room, but Reed wasn't there.

Instead, a brand-new suitcase sat open on the bed with part of the fabric lining pulled out. Trent peered in and saw a worn US passport tucked against the hard shell of the case. He picked it up.

A sound from the bathroom caught his attention. The shower.

Trent's heart beat like a timpani as he assessed the situation. Reed had bought a new suitcase and packed it while Trent was supposed to be wandering—out of Reed's way—around the Vatican Museums all afternoon.

Reed, naked, walked out of the bathroom, his short-cropped dark hair dripping onto his shoulders. He froze in his tracks as he spotted Trent staring at the suitcase on the bed.

"So, who's Michael Reade?" Trent held the passport up.

Reed kept his gaze fixed on Trent's hand as he let out a breath. "I am." His eyes narrowed slightly, and an unidentifiable expression flashed across his features.

Was that fear or relief? Or something else entirely?

"New cover identity for a guy who's supposedly retired?"

"Not exactly." Reed looked away.

Trent tapped his foot about twenty times before he realized and stopped. He exhaled slowly and stared at Reed.

"It's me. Another of my names."

"Your real name?" Trent waited for a reply, but Reed stayed silent. "Then Reed Acton is fake? The guy I fell in love with and have been living with for six months is just all made-up?"

"Not exactly."

"Then what exactly? Is anything you told me true?" Trent thought back to what Reed—Michael?—had told him. Very little. Trent hadn't asked many questions, but he'd believed Reed/Michael's answers.

Reed/Michael shrugged and stared at the floor some more. "Most of it." He paused. "Some of it."

"Are you really from New York?"

"No."

"Do you have two sisters and a dad who owns a shoe store?"

"No." Reed/Michael was getting more agitated, shuffling from foot to foot.

Trent wasn't too calm himself, but he thought he hid his anxiety better than Reed/Michael. "Let me stop guessing here. Why don't you tell me something—just one thing—that's actually true."

Trent silently prayed for Reed to say "I love you." Anything along those lines would work right now.

"That I never meant to hurt you."

Disappointment stung Trent, but he did his best not to show it. "Oh, well that makes all the difference. I forgive you! Let's hug and have some really hot make-up sex that I can put in my next book. Then we can just move on like this never happened."

Reed/Michael looked up at Trent, hope or something like it glinting in his eyes. "Really?"

"Of course not."

"Oh."

Trent hadn't expected to hear the pain in Reed's voice. He wished he didn't enjoy hearing it, but fuck yeah, he wanted to know Reed/Michael/whoever the hell this man really was felt as bad about this—no, *worse*—than Trent did.

He sat down on the edge of the bed and leaned forward, resting his arms on his thighs. He craned his neck to stare up at Reed. "Out with it. This is your one chance. Don't lie now unless you want this to be last conversation we ever have."

REED looked down at Trent. How much did he want to fix this? Did he love Trent? Had he ever loved Trent? Sometimes he wasn't sure, but at the moment he wished like hell they'd never met. Reed's world had been so simple before Trent Copeland had sauntered into his life in the Bangkok airport and walked off with a map leading to the Ruby Buddha. What had happened had strained even Trent's overactive imagination, but they'd lived through it all—kidnapping, Thai mobsters, Chinese triads—and somehow found common ground where they made each other happy.

"I wanted to be Reed Acton." Reed finally found the words. "I wanted to keep being Reed, for you." This wasn't going at all the way he expected. He was fucking the whole thing up. But it wasn't one of Trent's books where he could just scrap the first chapter and start over.

Trent picked at the edge of one sleeve, studiously avoiding looking at Reed. But Reed continued anyway.

"When we got back to the States, I was supposed to become Michael Reade. Reed Acton supposedly got killed when they took down Kao Lung. The Bureau needed to kill him off to protect me. But I liked Reed. I liked who I was when I was with you. So I kept being Reed. I didn't have his official ID anymore, but I wanted to be him, for you."

Trent looked up, suspicion evident in his gaze. "Isn't that dangerous?"

"Well, no. I got a driver's license, and since I wasn't working at a regular job, my real identity never mattered. The few jobs I did for the Bureau were under various names, but of course you never needed to know about that."

"You did jobs for the FBI in LA?"

Oh, fuck. Reed had let that slip.

"Just a couple."

Trent was halfway off the bed, and Reed held out a hand to stop him. "A couple of little things. Just simple information gathering, mostly local."

"Mostly? But you never left LA, except with me. On the book tour."

Reed kicked at an invisible spot on the plush carpeting. "Okay, one job used the book tour as cover. And I did travel to Rome as Michael Reade, but you didn't ever look at my ID, did you?"

"No. You made our plane reservations. I guess I was too trusting."

"No. You're just normal. Normal people don't check other people's IDs. They believe each other."

"Normal people are just suckers. I'm a normal sucker." Trent flashed a weak smile. "I feel so much better."

Reed heard Trent's voice nearly crack, and he sat down next to him on the bed. "No. You're not a sucker. But you are normal and trusting—"

"And look where it's gotten me." Trent pushed Reed away.

"It's what I like about you. I like that you're not suspicious of everyone. That you're not used to everyone lying, or expecting more lies. I like—love—that about you. You're real. *You're* not a lie."

"So you repaid my trust by lying? Nice. Irony or hypocrisy? Or both?" The bitterness in Trent's voice burned into Reed's heart.

"So you wanted to be him, keep being Reed Acton. Which means you aren't him. And you aren't the person I thought I was living with. Or the person I thought I loved. I don't know who you are at all."

"You're overreacting."

"How am I supposed to react to this kind of news? I'm thinking you're a person who doesn't exist except in my own imagination!" Trent stood up and pulled at his hair as he started to pace around the room. "I make this shit up for a living, but I don't want to find out you're only another person I'm making up. I want to be in a relationship with a real person. With a real name and their own fucking personality. Not my imagination!"

"I get it. I get it. Just... sit down. Please. Your pacing is driving me nuts."

"Join the club."

"DO YOU love me?" Trent wished he didn't have to ask outright. Why couldn't Reed just say it, damn him!

"Yes."

"How do I know you're telling the truth?" Trent stared at Reed, expecting to see flesh go up in flames. A whole new explanation for spontaneous human combustion occurred to him.

Reed smoothed a hand across his right shoulder, unconsciously moving to the knot of scarred flesh, a small indicator of far more extensive scars on his back. Maybe he could feel Trent's gaze burning into his skin.

"I have to go right now, but I'll be back. I promise. This is something I need to do."

"Something requiring a new suitcase and a new identity?"

"Yeah. I know this is a really fucked-up way to explain any of this to you, and if there was any other way, I would have. But there's an emergency. A job I have to help out with. It'll take a day, maybe two."

"Do I get a good-bye kiss?" Trent cocked his head and waited. He'd meant it as a joke. Not that he'd forgiven Reed/Michael for any of this.

Reed's gaze softened as he looked directly at Trent. "Okay."

"Hey, don't do anything you don't want to." Trent waved Reed toward the door, but instead of turning away, Reed moved forward, taking hold of Trent's elbow and pulling him in close.

Trent wished he didn't like Reed's strong grip on his arm. But he let Reed kiss him. At first Reed just pressed his lips against Trent's, and then the kiss hardened, becoming much hotter than he'd expected. Reed curved his other arm around Trent's waist, locking them together.

Unable to stop it and not particularly wanting to, Trent opened his mouth, and a tiny moan slipped out as Reed's tongue slipped in. The kiss continued, deepened. Reed pressed his naked body tight against Trent.

Damn, it felt good. Reed would be able to feel Trent's cock hardening.

But so was Reed's.

And Trent gave up the idea of putting a halt to anything.

They ended up on the bed, both naked, hands and mouths everywhere, giving and taking, taking and demanding more.

When Reed's cock slipped between Trent's legs, he pulled Reed tight, grabbing at his ass, encouraging him to hurry up.

"What're we doing?" Reed half groaned.

"I kind of thought you were going to fuck me now."

"Is that what you want?"

Trent lay on his back, legs spread, one knee hooked over Reed's shoulder. Of course that was what he wanted.

"Make it count, whoever you are."

"Trent—"

Trent stopped Reed's words with a rough kiss, and when he let go, Reed plunged in.

Trent didn't let go of his earlier anger at Reed. He used it.

Reed started out slow. But Trent grabbed Reed's hips and dragged him in deep and hard.

"Fast. Hard and fast."

Reed sped up his movements as Trent kept pulling at him. Soon Trent couldn't tell where he ended and Reed began. They tore and grabbed at each other, more a battle than anything to do with love. When Reed slowed or softened his movements, Trent demanded more.

"It's going to hurt you. I don't want to hurt you."

Yeah, right. "Just do what I want for now."

Trent didn't usually like it this rough, but he didn't let up, and soon his brain turned off, just his body making the decisions, with the occasional demand or direction for Reed. He raked his hands across Reed's back, fingertips tracing the scar tissue criss-crossing Reed's back and shoulders. The rough, angry ridges seemed deeper. Trent fought off the urge to scratch into them, to see if Reed had any real feeling after all, physical or emotional.

On top of him, Reed pounded away, grunting, hips stuttering, any rhythm long gone as his own animal instincts took over. He pulled and grabbed at any part of Trent his hands could reach as his cock dug in deep and hard and fast, each thrust rocking Trent's entire frame, setting every nerve ending on fire. Trent slipped a hand between their sweaty bodies and tugged at his cock, wanting to make this last but needing it to be finished. He didn't know what he said or did, was just incredibly aware of every inch of his body connected to Reed. Every thrust tore into him, rubbed him raw. Reed's grasp tightened, fingers ripping into the very fiber of Trent's muscles. Reed's head smacked Trent's chin, grazed his lip, and the pain echoed through Trent's entire body, but it still wasn't enough to drown out the pain screaming through his brain. It overwhelmed even the pleasure of his orgasm when it happened.

Reed barely seemed to notice as he took even more from Trent.

When Reed got very close, he made a choking grunt Trent had come to expect. Reed fastened his mouth against the flesh of Trent's chest, a couple of inches above his left nipple. The force of Reed's orgasm made his teeth snap shut, and Trent felt another slice of pain while Reed's cock spasmed and spurted inside him. He held Reed tight against him, their two bodies finally slowing from the frenzied pace of their fucking.

Reed's cock had barely stilled inside him when Trent rolled Reed off and pushed him away. "Get out of here, Reed."

"Wha?" Reed panted, barely able to form words. He peered at Trent.

Trent pushed at him again, but Reed didn't let go. Trent punched Reed's cheek—not full strength, just enough to get the message across.

Reed punched back, a hard right hook to the jaw that surprised Trent with its power and speed. He could see from the shock on Reed's on face that he hadn't intended to strike back, but Reed's reflexes were ingrained. They'd taken over even when he faced no real danger. If

Trent needed any more proof they didn't belong together, that Reed didn't want Trent around, he had it now.

Trent's head ached worse than ever, but he would gladly have taken a dozen hits to the body, instead of the one he'd taken to the heart.

"Take your stuff and leave." Trent climbed out of bed, his body aching, sore, battered, and bloody. His asshole was on fire. He'd never before felt this amount of pain, or this level of revulsion. He wanted Reed gone.

Trent didn't give Reed a chance to recover or respond. He pulled him off the bed with one arm and hauled him toward the door, each step triggering additional pain. He opened the door and pushed Reed out, then the suitcase. He slammed the door shut and sat back on the bed.

Even sitting hurt, and he rotated so he was leaning on one hip. He raked his fingers through his hair as Reed pounded on the door.

"Good-bye, Michael," Trent roared. "Go away!"

The pounding continued until Trent heard voices in the hallway, a woman's startled shriek. Then Reed/Michael was silent. Hopefully he was gone.

2

REED stood naked outside their hotel room. His cock was still at half-mast, slick with lube and come, but shriveling quickly after that unexpected fistfight. His stomach churned as he recalled what had just happened.

What the fuck had gotten into Trent?

They'd never fucked like that before. Reed had been surprised by Trent's arousal and had gone along unwillingly at first when Trent wanted it rough. But the more Trent wanted, the more Reed put his own initial revulsion aside and gave it to him. Still, he hadn't expected Trent's regret to come so suddenly and so violently.

Reed rubbed one hand along his aching jaw, pounding on the door with the other until a woman—another hotel guest—came around the corner and started screaming.

He *was* naked, and more than likely a bit battered.

Reed quickly pulled something out of the suitcase to cover himself as she ran—probably to complain to the hotel management. He banged on the door again, then listened. This time he heard the shower running. Trent wasn't going to let him back in.

Reed dressed himself in the first items he found and rolled the suitcase toward the mirror at the end of the hall. He cleaned himself up enough to head for the men's room located off the lobby. He'd finish the job there.

This was not at all how he'd pictured this going. But it was probably for the best. He had intended for Trent to wait for him at the hotel while he connected with White, just hadn't expected to leave Trent this broken.

Why had he wanted Reed to fuck him like that? At first it had been a real turn-on, with their argument leading to some hot sex—again, not what he'd planned, but nothing with Trent had ever gone to plan. It started out great, but in the middle Trent's entire mood shifted and he'd wanted things Reed didn't want to do. He might have taught Trent the joys of fucking, but this had gone far beyond that. Trent wanted—needed, perhaps—a level of hurt and pain Reed found unnerving but Trent kept demanding.

Now, as Reed splashed water on his face in the lobby men's room, clarity set in. Trent wanted to make that last experience for them as terrible as possible. With this as the most recent memory, they could walk away from each other more easily.

But it wasn't at all what Reed wanted. He hadn't lied when he said it was temporary and he fully intended to come back. He wanted to come back.

He loved Trent, didn't he? That was what he'd said when Trent asked, but Reed wasn't quite sure about the details or definitions. He knew he wanted Trent in his life. Maybe that was as close to love as Reed could admit—or permit himself to be.

And he had just fucked it all up beyond redemption.

Fuck.

TRENT lay on his back, staring up at the ceiling, for a few minutes after Reed stopped banging on the door, then dragged himself into the bathroom for a much-needed shower.

He let the water heat up until it was nearly scalding, and jumped in, welcoming the burn. If he could, he'd wash every single trace of Reed from his body and his memory, but hot water could only go so far. Trent glanced at his bottle of beloved bodywash. It would take the whole thing to wash away what had just happened, and Reed Acton—though that wasn't his name—wasn't worth the sacrifice.

Instead, Trent lathered up with the hotel's fancy soap and hoped for the best. The mirror was steamed up when he finished and the air heavy with warm mist. He didn't want to look at himself anyway and ran the plush towel quickly over his body.

He couldn't wait to get out of here, out of Rome. He reached for the phone to let the desk know he was leaving.

"Front desk."

"This is Trent Copeland in Room 27. I want to check—" He stopped and made a split-second decision. "I want to change rooms."

"Certainly, signore. Which floor would you prefer?"

The clerk didn't even care why he wanted to change. Trent couldn't decide whether that was good customer service or bad customer service. "Top floor, if you've got it."

A moment passed as she clicked her computer. "Yes, I have Room 80, and I can offer you the same rate."

"Done."

"I'll send the bellman to move your luggages."

He loved that word "luggages." Why was there no plural in English?

"Thank you."

He hung up. With his hair still wet, he dressed and quickly threw everything from the bathroom and bedroom into his suitcase. Some of it was Reed's—Michael's—but Trent tossed it all in and slammed the suitcase shut. He avoided looking at the bed, the scene of the crime. His body ached and his jaw hurt. His stomach roiled and he thought he might throw up. He was glad he hadn't looked in the mirror.

Ten minutes later, Trent settled into Room 80.

No bad memories here.

No memories of any kind.

Nothing at all.

REED checked into a small nondescript guesthouse between the Hotel d'Inghilterra and the closest Metro station. He tried to convince himself it wasn't so he might see Trent coming or going, but even he didn't believe it. It was much more than simply convenient, but it didn't really matter. Chances were Trent might head home to LA now Reed had ruined their long-planned trip. Reed knew that might even be for the best—for Trent's happiness—but he wished he'd thought things through more carefully.

He was out of practice. Six months in LA with Trent, living a safe, comfortable life had dulled his skills. He couldn't afford to let himself get distracted worrying about Trent or anything else if he was going to be any use in finding Peter Isett.

He'd only gotten the bare bones of the situation from White on the phone at the hotel. They'd both decided safety required they discuss specifics in person, no matter how secure the embassy phone line purported to be.

After a thorough shower, Reed donned a Yankees baseball cap and the most American of the clothing he'd packed, left the new hotel, and made his way to Piazza della Rotonda and one of the touristy cafés with tables spilling out onto the piazza itself.

He requested a table as far from the restaurant as possible. Less chance of anyone overhearing anything. Once seated, he ordered a bottle of Pellegrino and settled in to wait, watching the other café patrons and casual-looking tourists strolling around shooting photos from phones, high-end digital SLRs, or the occasional yellow cardboard disposable with old-fashioned film. He wished White hadn't suggested this particular spot, Piazza della Rotonda sprawled in front of the Pantheon.

A remarkable building built around the first century BC but damaged and restored multiple times since, the Pantheon had turned out to be one of Trent's favorite spots in Rome, though they'd only been there three days. Considering the vast array of impressive Roman architecture—from the Colosseum to St. Peter's and a million places in between—it was high praise.

And Reed had to agree. There was something thrilling about the building, which, at the time it was built and for more than a thousand years after, boasted the largest self-supporting dome in the world. Even Brunelleschi, architect of Florence's famous dome, had been inspired by the Pantheon's perfection in aesthetics as well as engineering.

One corner of Reed's brain—or his heart?—hoped Trent might wander by. But he didn't. Instead, the man Reed had come to meet arrived thirty seconds early by Reed's watch.

Reed stood and shook hands with the slim, balding American in a tan off-the-rack summer suit that must have made his Italian counterparts cringe. "Tom, good to see you."

"I'd expected you to look healthy and happy!" Tom White, Reed's former FBI boss, took a seat, frowning slightly as he gave Reed the once-over, eyes lingering on his battered face. "Not as relaxed as I'd hoped. Is that a shiner I see working its way to the surface?"

Reed ran his fingertips over the painful area on his jaw, realizing the swelling extended up to his eye. "Considering what you told me, how can you expect me to be relaxed?"

"Trent around?"

"He won't be an issue this time."

"Ah." White pursed his lips and motioned a waiter over. He ordered espresso and turned back to Reed. "Does he know?"

"No. I…." Reed paused, not sure how much to explain. "He knows it's something to do with the Bureau, but that's it. Even I don't really know what you need."

"That's not what I meant." White met Reed's gaze head-on, and the scrutiny set Reed's nerves on edge.

"Definitely not. He thought I was completely retired. He had no clue about any of the jobs I did back in LA. He doesn't even know I'm meeting you here, or why."

"I'm not sure whether I'm happy or not to hear that."

Reed stared at White. Was he allowed to tell Trent about his missions? Reed wasn't sure he wanted to, even if White approved.

"I guess I was hoping Trent might be a good thing for you. Seemed like just what you needed."

White had never gotten into Reed's personal life before, and Reed didn't particularly like what he thought White was implying. "Meaning?"

"Either you'd quit the Bureau for good after you met him, or you'd open up a little and let him know you're still working for us. Too many secrets are not the way to keep a relationship going."

In Reed's experience, secrets were necessary. Within a relationship and sometimes even about a relationship. With the latter, he was all too familiar. He wondered how much White knew about that and realized he might have brought up the topic for a reason.

"I didn't realize you were undercover yourself. As Dear-fucking-Abby."

White pursed his lips and narrowed his eyes, then let out a wry chuckle.

Reed relaxed a bit after he'd risked insulting his boss. "So, are we here to talk about Trent?"

"No. Let's get to business."

"Good." Reed didn't want to find out White didn't need him, now that he'd fucked things up with Trent. "You didn't say much on the phone. Fill me in."

White opened his mouth to speak, then closed it as the waiter came by with his coffee. He watched the man move to other tables, acting for all intents and purposes like a real waiter. White knocked back the contents of the small cup in one gulp and proceeded to inspect both the cup and the saucer on which it had been served. He managed to make the actions look natural and not like those of a trained agent checking for bugs.

"Don't worry, Tom." Reed gave a soft chuckle. "I checked the table before you got here. Completely random table. I waited for two sets of people to leave before I asked to be seated. No one's listening."

"Haven't lost it, then, have you?" White gave a half smile.

"Of course not." Reed ignored the implied criticism. "Let's get to business."

"Right. As I mentioned on the phone, Isett's partner, Brett Decker, hadn't heard from Peter in two reporting cycles, and all he had was some coded message."

"Hadn't? As in you have heard something since we last spoke?"

"Reported in an hour ago."

"So you don't need me after all?" Reed's heart skipped a few beats, and the bruises on his body throbbed as he thought of Trent. What had he done? He forced himself not to leap from the table and run back to their hotel.

"On the contrary, I absolutely need you. Peter's left Rome, following a lead to Sicily, so I need you to step into the local operation in his place."

"What?" Reed hadn't been expecting this. He came here to decipher some codes or do a little quick-and-dirty legwork. *Not* sign on for a full-fledged mission.

"Let me start from the beginning and tell you what we need from you."

Reed signaled the waiter for a menu and another Pellegrino. They were going to be here for a while. White ordered a *panino con prosciutto e formaggio*—an Italian-style ham and cheese.

"Never worry about your cholesterol, do you?" Reed asked after the waiter had left.

"Plenty of people doing that for me. This is the only chance I get to eat what I want." For the first time since he'd sat down, White came close to cracking a genuine smile.

"Fill me in."

TRENT hadn't believed a word of Reed's Michael Reade story. Well, not all of it, anyway. It had been mostly lies. They'd lived together for six months in LA, and while he didn't know everything about Reed— far from it—Trent did know when he was lying. Reed was trained in lies and subterfuge. There was no fucking way he would casually leave his secret passport out or let Trent catch him still in the shower. He would have been long gone before Trent showed up if that was what Reed wanted.

Not that Trent was an expert on spies either. Since he'd met Reed, he'd gotten very interested in the subject. Instead of his daily dose of two- or three-hanky tearjerkers on the classic film channel, Trent had secretly been devouring spy thrillers. Everything from Hitchcock's original 1940 *Foreign Correspondent* to Angelina Jolie's *Salt*. Trent had seen the best and worst of the genre.

He'd read plenty of spy novels as well: le Carré, Graham Greene, Ian Fleming, Tom Clancy. Purists would argue Clancy wasn't in the same league, but Trent found his books damned entertaining.

But his all-time favorite and new hero was to be found on *Burn Notice*, a cable television series about a spy who'd been fired from the CIA. Michael Westen wasn't just an über-cool customer played by the dashing Jeffrey Donovan (not Trent's type, but so much hotter in this role), but Westen gave awesome spy tips in every episode. Trent had a little notebook filled with advice.

If Reed ever found the notebook and asked, Trent would have claimed it was research for a new novel, but as far as he could tell, Reed hadn't discovered Trent's new fascination. They'd watched a few spy films together at first, and Trent could see Reed found the whole genre ridiculous and unrealistic, so he took his spy film watching underground and did it only when Reed wasn't at home.

With his albeit faux-spy training and personal knowledge of Reed, Trent knew Reed was lying about something, holding back information, and it had nothing to do with his real name.

So why had Reed put on that act?

He was hiding something else.

"THERE'S an antiquities auction house here in Rome, Rossetti's, which has branches in Palermo and Milan. About six months ago, a collector in the States alerted the Bureau's Art Crime Team he thought he had been sold a fake Cellini at one of Rossetti's auctions."

"You mentioned them earlier on the phone. So was it a fake?"

"Yes and no." White grinned. "It wasn't a Cellini at all. It was a Cennini."

Reed shook his head.

"Another artist who lived a century before Cellini and was vastly inferior. There was an error in authentication at the auction house—the seller had some dubious paperwork which Rossetti's interpreted rather loosely. They refunded the buyer's money once the error had been established. But it put Rossetti's on our radar for a few months while it was investigated, and the FBI formed a joint team with the local Carabinieri Art Squad."

"What about Interpol?"

"We want to do some more digging before bringing them in. That's why I contacted my counterpart in the Carabinieri Art Squad to help us with some background into the local players, as we discover who they are."

In Reed's experience, art-related crimes had a farther reach than just between two countries, and it was routine to run them through

Interpol, rather than a bilateral task force as White had set up in this case. But he waited to learn more before commenting further.

The waiter returned with White's sandwich. The aroma of warm prosciutto and crisp toasted bread made Reed's mouth water, and he ordered the same. He couldn't recall when he'd last eaten or guess when he'd get another chance.

White continued once the waiter had left. "A month later, another claim against Rossetti's came through Interpol from a collector in Prague, who complained he'd been outbid on an item and accused the auction house of inflating its prices. Most recently, a third client, in New York, ran into trouble when he tried to bring his purchase home. Some question about the export permissions."

Reed shook his head slightly.

"The Italian government is hard as nails when it comes to taking Italian art and artifacts out of the country. Permits are few and far between, and this collector claimed some sort of extortion scam on the part of Rossetti's, the Italian government, the fucking pope—though I don't know what he has to do with it."

Reed burst out laughing. "The pope?"

White nodded. "I know! But we did some research before sending Peter Isett out here three weeks ago."

"Were you able to clear the pope?" Reed grinned.

"The Italians are keeping mum on that part of the investigation."

"Were there other irregularities?" Reed got back on point.

"The first, as I mentioned, was an authentication error. Neither of the other two pieces had proper provenance and paperwork backing up identification, but there were the usual explanations, all of which seemed realistic, given the pieces themselves."

"Which were?"

"A Roman statue and an amphora of Greek origin from a shipwreck near Sicily. The statue had a spotty past, and it seems the auction house used the questionable status as a way to get around export laws. It was, in fact, genuine, but it wasn't what it said on the export papers."

"Is it about fakes or about export papers? And where does Peter fit into this?"

"Right. You asked for what we had so far. I can't answer those questions yet, but Peter might be able to."

"Fair enough."

"We had an analyst crunch some data—this guy Brett Decker—"

Reed interrupted. "Peter's partner?"

"Yes...."

"You sent a *number cruncher* into the field?"

White bobbed his head as he finished off his *panino*. "I know. It's his first big case abroad. But he did such a great job with the analysis, I wanted to throw him a bone. No one expected more than forged export licenses or faked antiquities. Seemed tame enough for a baby agent."

"So far it still sounds like that's what you're dealing with."

"Maybe. I need someone with finesse to handle the next aspect, and—"

"And with Peter in Sicily, you don't want Decker fucking it up."

White made another noncommittal movement with his head. "I think you're a better fit for this particular task." He gave Reed another once-over. "Or I did before you went a few rounds with—"

Reed waved his hand dismissively before White could speculate on who had damaged his face. "What do you need from me?" He wanted to get this discussion back on business. This had better be worth what he'd put Trent through so far.

"Brett's analysis found a strange pattern of items being sold far above their expected sale prices."

"Plenty of items sell for more than what the auction house expects."

"True. But not in this economy. All of these items were consigned by the same few Italian brokers. And all of these pieces were purchased by three different dealers, one in Amsterdam and two in New York. Probably not coincidentally, one of the New York brokers had a fire that destroyed part of their warehouse, including one of the disputed items and several boxes of records. This happened shortly after Peter started working on the case."

"And the other?"

"We've got an agent undercover there."

"What was Peter doing here?"

"Undercover in the guise of a rich, clueless American collector, friend of someone who purchased through Rossetti's in the past, so he had a decent introduction. He recently came into some money—won the lottery"—White flashed a genuine smile this time—"and wants to 'do up his house nice and classy-like', or so he told Rossetti's."

"I'm sure they were very willing to help him find just the right pieces."

"But our Peter's taste went all over the place. Including the same sort of pieces we spotted that fit the pattern. He made certain to show his interest in several other pieces, besides the ones being sold by the brokers under investigation."

Standard operating procedure. "So, what went wrong?"

"Nothing. Or so we think. Peter overheard that one of the collectors was in town and asked his contact at Rossetti's if he could meet the guy."

Reed sucked in a breath. "That doesn't sound good. Acting too eager gets you noticed, and that can get you caught."

"I agree. I advised him to back off, and that's when he went silent. I wasn't sure if he was purposely ignoring me or if something had happened."

"And now?"

"He seems to have made friends. The broker invited him to his estate in Sicily, outside of Palermo. He's on his way down there now. He's hoping to find out whether it's the broker who's involved or one of the collectors."

Reed got a bad feeling in his gut. That was far too easy. What auction house would let a buyer meet with a broker who would cut them out of the deal? "I don't like it. Let me go down after him and make sure—"

White put up a hand. "It's under control. Peter knows what he's doing."

"You think so?" The words came out more forcefully than Reed had intended. He hoped White didn't catch the flash of anger—or of personal involvement.

"Look, I know you two had some…." White paused, clearly searching for the appropriate word. "History. A *lot* of history."

Reed looked away, toward the Pantheon, and let his eyes roam the façade of the building while he slowed his heart rate. Try as he might, he couldn't make any of his previously successful Zen techniques work. What happened with Peter was bigger than Reed—or Buddha—could handle at the moment.

"Look, Tom, you called me in on this. I figured there was a reason."

"You're the closest agent. That's the main reason. The closest one who knows art and the sort of people we're dealing with. I know Europe isn't your comfort zone, but I figured you could step in."

"What do you need from me?"

"Like I said on the phone: Go to the auction on Tuesday, bid on a few pieces, including one of the questionable pieces from these target sellers. See what happens."

"I could be kicking a hornet's nest."

"It wouldn't be the first time. If someone reacts, we'll see it. We've got warrants in the works for half a dozen suspects around Italy. Including the guy who just invited Peter down for a visit."

"Please don't tell me Peter's staying at the guy's house?"

"No. I made sure he wouldn't. I'm talking to him later, and depending on the details he's used for his cover, we may even be able to play this as though you're his boyfriend—"

Reed nearly choked as a sip of fizzy Pellegrino went down the wrong pipe.

"—boyfriend from home who decided to fly to Rome to meet up with him in Sicily. That way you two can work together if necessary to wrap this up."

"Boyfriend?" Reed coughed out the words. Who had Peter told? "Why would you even suggest that, Tom?"

"Just thinking out of the box here." He pulled a small notepad from his jacket pocket and flipped through a few pages. "Never mind. Peter's cover bio says he's married, but it could explain why his wife isn't here and give you two a chance to work together. I'm sure with your combined experience you can wrap this up in no time. And I wouldn't have to worry about either one of you."

It wasn't like Tom White to forget the details of a cover story. Just how much did White actually know about Reed's past with Peter? *No one* knew. Reed had never told anyone. Not even Trent.

White shuffled in his chair, and Reed turned his thoughts to just how competent this Brett guy was. First UC assignment in a foreign country. White wouldn't normally take a chance like that. Unless it had been Peter's doing, getting Brett assigned with him on what might have been a cushy UC gig in Italy….

Reed stopped his wandering thoughts. He wouldn't let himself think about *that*. "Which cover do you want me to use for this?" He listed the passports he'd brought with him to Italy.

White nodded. "Michael Reade, at least for now. I've got a strange feeling on this one."

Reed sat back in his chair and looked directly at White. The man had been an agent for fifteen years and running agents since he quit doing field work a dozen years ago. His instincts were impeccable. There was big trouble somewhere. White wouldn't have called Reed in the middle of his vacation for something minor. He should have realized that sooner.

Something much bigger than fixed auction prices was going on.

3

ON THE top floor of the Hotel d'Inghilterra, Trent paced around his new room until the pain in his ass and elsewhere made him give up. Even the view didn't keep his interest past the first hour. He couldn't shake off the restlessness, though he had no desire to explore Rome on his own just yet.

He padded across the thick carpeting into the bathroom and stared at himself in the mirror.

Bruises had begun to form where Reed had clipped his chin, and his chest bore scratches and bite marks. He needed another long hot shower to wash away the disgust he felt with himself and with Reed for… for what?

Trent paused as he ran a fingertip across the raised welts left by Reed's teeth.

For being Reed? Had Trent ever doubted who or what Reed was from the moment they met in Thailand? He'd known Reed bent the truth for his own purposes, but that beneath every lie or half-truth, he wanted to keep Trent safe—from Thai mobsters after a secret treasure map and now, apparently, from Reed himself. Or from whatever he was involved in this time around.

Trent splashed cold water on his face, then wiped a towel across his neck and chest as he headed out of the bathroom. He stood at the window, looking out on the eternal city. Rome. It had been around for thousands of years, and it would be here for thousands more. Trent and Reed had no impact on anything here.

In the distance, Trent could see the edges of the enormous, lush urban park that contained Villa Borghese. He'd wanted to come here for years, and though he'd been to Venice and Milan, he'd never been to Rome. The other trip had been with Marc, his partner before Reed. Marc had died in a skydiving accident three years ago, and Trent had taken it hard. Retreated into a shell until his best friends, Beth and Mick, along with his literary agent, Cassandra, sent him on a surprise trip to Thailand. He'd met Reed in the airport, and his life had never been the same since.

Even this trip had been because of Reed. In Thailand, Trent had completely by chance come across clues that helped archaeologists discover a long-lost Buddha thought to exist only in legend. The Ruby Buddha belonged to the Thai government, but the reward had been substantial.

Reed had insisted Trent splurge on a trip, and given Trent's interest in food, fashion, history, and art, Italy seemed a natural choice. Reed suggested Venice, but Trent wanted to visit someplace brand new, with no memories for either of them. Trent had planned out which sights to visit, where to stay, what to eat, which clubs or bars were the trendiest. And, of course, where to shop.

The first two days had been wonderful, until yesterday. Trent grabbed his suitcase and rooted around for the itinerary he'd planned so meticulously.

He didn't want to do a single thing on it right now.

Trent paced between the bed and the bathroom, then made a loop toward the window and back again. He completed three circuits before giving up and flopping onto the bed. He considered crying but decided he would not feel sorry for himself. There were millions of things to do in Rome, and he could choose to do them or sit here alone.

He'd spent the afternoon in the Vatican Museums by himself, and he hadn't enjoyed it one bit.

He decided to stay in the room rather than subject himself to further disappointment.

This trip had been *one big disappointment.*

At least it hadn't been Venice. If he'd gone with Reed to Venice and been abandoned, that would be the end of everything between them. He couldn't bear the thought of being left alone in a place as romantic as Venice.

Was Reed coming back?

Trent racked his brain for what Reed had told him: White needed him for a short job. A one-day job.

But Trent had kicked Reed out.

Maybe Reed wasn't coming back.

Trent had also changed rooms. What the fuck had he been thinking? How could Reed find him now? He raced to the desk and grabbed the phone.

"Front desk, how may I help you?" an Italian-accented voice asked in well-rehearsed English.

"Hi, this is Trent Copeland, and I just changed rooms...."

"How is your new room, Signor Copelan'?" They never managed to pronounce the *d*, Trent noticed.

"It's terrible. I'd like to get back into my old room, please."

"Oh, I'm so sorry. Your previous room is assigned to another guest."

Already? It had been less than two hours. Nothing in Italy happened that fast. Was this hotel in some Italian version of the Twilight Zone?

"But no one could already have checked in there, could they?"

"The computer says it's not available. I don't have the authorization code...."

Trent barely listened to her excuse. He'd heard it a million times. "I was expecting a message, and they don't know my new room number." Wishful thinking never hurt anyone, did it?

"If you leave authorization, we can give them your new room number." Her accent made the word "authorization" sound incredibly exotic.

"Okay." Trent's mood brightened a fraction. "If Reed Acton calls, please put him through to this room."

"Yes, signore. I am making a note right here." Typing confirmed she was at least hitting keys if not actually putting a note into the system. "I'm sorry about the room."

"That's okay. Thanks." Trent could hardly blame her for his impetuous move, but he cursed his own impatience.

Reed would find him. He'd ridden a motorcycle halfway across Thailand to find Trent last time, hadn't he?

But in Thailand, Reed had really been after the treasure map, hadn't he? He wouldn't have gone after Trent otherwise, Trent reminded himself.

Aw. Fuck.

"ATTEND the auction Tuesday as Michael Reade." White pulled a brown envelope from his breast pocket and put it on the table.

Reed reached forward to retrieve it, but White stopped him by placing his own hand on the envelope.

"This is a completely new ID, just in case."

Reed didn't have to ask in case of what.

"This cover is off the grid as far as the local Interpol office knows."

Reed raised an eyebrow, but White's expression told him he wouldn't get more details on the topic.

"The background shows enough shady activity to pass yourself off as half a dozen different kinds of felon. I'll let you choose how to run it once you meet the players tomorrow. You can stay Michael Reade, or you can leave him, based on what happens tomorrow."

Reed's heart thrummed in his chest. He craved the thrill of a new assignment. He took two long, deep breaths before he allowed himself to reach for the packet again. *Never show too much excitement or enthusiasm.* He barely admitted to himself how much he'd missed this. It was the reason he'd taken on the jobs in LA, but he had no idea what White expected from him now. He'd do whatever it took.

He opened the packet and pulled out a summary sheet of the contents, then scanned the bio and bona fides.

"I need you to go to Rossetti's auction house and bid on the items Brett's program flagged as suspicious based on previous bidding and sales patterns. Report back to me the following morning."

Air rushed out of Reed's lungs. He was here to bid on some antiquities, deliberately lose, and then make a report? That was it?

"Just bid and observe?" He hid the disappointment.

"Yeah. Nothing elaborate. You're not to engage anyone except through bidding, just observe reactions. Don't ask questions. Don't mention you know Peter. Don't make a fuss about the target lots in the catalog."

"Report to you here?"

"No. Go to the Trevi Fountain. Toss a coin on the left side if you have nothing to report. Toss a coin on the right if you do."

Reed grinned. "Are we back to that Tiger One crap?"

"Maybe. But do as I ask. Make sure to look like a tourist. Back to the fountain, toss the coin over your shoulder." He demonstrated, then ignored Reed's loud groan and continued. "After you toss the coin, go to the Hard Rock Café. It's a five-minute walk. Take the alley, not the direct route, so you can see if you're followed."

"This isn't my first rodeo."

"Right. But your boots are a little dusty."

"Tom, dusty boots mean a guy's been wearing them. Clean boots would mean I've been out of practice."

"Rodeo analogies are not my strong suit."

"Clearly."

"I'll e-mail the rest of your alternate cover bio and the list of target items in the auction."

Reed knew White wouldn't put those in the same packet as the identification. No one kept their own autobiography with them.

White pulled his phone out of his breast pocket and clicked a few keys.

Reed's phone purred as it notified him of the incoming message. He skimmed the file and nodded. "Looks good. I'll head over this evening to see the preauction show and note anything suspicious. Then bid on the items you've marked in the catalog."

"Money's being wired to you at the Hotel Intown, in the name of Michael Reade. Become him before you check into the hotel or step foot in Rossetti's auction house. Change hotels in between if you need to."

"I traveled on Reade's passport. You know that."

White cocked his head a fraction of an inch.

Reed exhaled. "The hair?"

"The hair."

"Got it covered." Reed tugged on his baseball cap. He'd have to lighten his hair before he went to the auction house in case someone recognized him later and wondered about the hair color. He'd take care of that on the way back to the room. It was one of the reasons he'd been wearing the cap. Michael Reade's passport photo had light-brown hair, unlike Reed's natural dark brown, but airport security hadn't cared—if they'd even noticed. They were more concerned with what was in your shoes or underwear than whether you looked like your ID. But for a mission, it was key to match your identification, especially in a situation you might want to be noticed—and remembered. He certainly didn't want to be remembered for not looking like his ID when he checked in.

He glanced at the address written on the packet. *Hotel Intown, 7 via Bocca di Leone.* Reed didn't have Roman geography memorized, but he'd never forget the name of that street: it was where he and Trent had been staying. This new hotel was within walking distance of Trent. Reed's pulse raced.

White's voice cut through Reed's concern. "I've given you upper limits for bidding for each item Decker's program flagged as potentially part of the pattern, plus three pieces Peter didn't suspect. Do not exceed those limits when bidding."

"You want me to actually win any of these?"

"That depends. If you end up in a bidding war, let it go. I need you to identify suspicious behavior, not get involved just yet. Given your limits, go ahead and win one or two of the clean pieces, up to twice the expected sale price of the items. Based on the observed former pattern, your budget isn't enough to win one of the suspicious pieces, but it should cover one of the decoys."

"That's still more than any of it's worth, as far as I can tell."

"Not the point. You have your instructions and your limits."

"Unless someone else really wants them."

"They're all pretty fucking ugly. Hope your imagination can come up with a reason you'd want any of the items."

"I've got a helluvan imagination."

"That's what I'm counting on." White pulled a few bills out of his wallet and dropped them on the table. "Be careful not to attract the wrong kind of attention."

"Got it." Reed knew enough not to enter a cutthroat bidding war. He was there to get information, and simply bidding might be enough. He needed to observe the pattern and interpret the other bidders' behavior, not obtain the item. If necessary, there were other ways of making contact that wouldn't connect him, Michael Reade, or his new identity to any of the antiquities. Keeping the appropriate separation was key.

"Just reminding you. Haven't had anything this challenging in a while."

"It doesn't feel very challenging." Reed still didn't consider the assignment was worth the damage or White's suspicions.

"It doesn't at the moment. But we haven't even measured the tip of the iceberg. You won't know how deep it goes until you see what happens tomorrow. Start slow and report back, and we'll see what the next step is."

Reed nodded.

"If it's what I suspect, your job won't be finished after the auction."

Reed nodded, not sure whether that made him happy or not.

White stood, gave Reed a casual little salute, and headed into the piazza, toward the entrance to the Pantheon, glancing up in awe just as any real tourist might. Then again, it was the sort of building that inspired awe in anyone, maybe even Tom White.

Reed's heart fluttered a little when he saw a tall, well-built man in a pale-blue shirt nearly walk into White, but the clumsy, aloof guy wasn't Trent.

Reed's imagination was working overtime, but he'd need more than that to fix things with Trent.

In the meantime, he'd visit the auction house for a hard copy of the catalog, pore over that tonight, and get his cover story straight for his assignment the following day.

Work would keep his mind off what White knew of his past with Peter, and whether or not Peter was heading directly into harm's way with this ill-advised trip to Sicily.

AFTER Trent had kicked Reed out, he considered going home to LA. But he knew something was wrong. Not with Reed lying, because he certainly had lied, though not about his name. He'd lied about lying. For whatever reason, he wanted Trent out of the way. What was he up to? He'd been acting strangely lately, and then he'd gotten that call while they were in line at the Vatican Museums.

Reed had said he had to take care of something that would take a day or two. Why hadn't Trent just let him do that? Why had he let things escalate to the horrible confrontation? Trent didn't know any of the answers. His body was sore and his chest ached where Reed had bitten him. He went to the mirror in the luxurious marble-lined bathroom and pulled back his shirt, revealing a perfect bite mark about two inches above his left nipple. They could probably match that to Reed if this were an episode of *CSI*.

Trent laughed for the first time since Reed got that phone call early that morning.

He went back into the bedroom and sat on the bed. The nightstand drawer was partially open. He pushed it shut and it rolled back open again. He'd tossed his maps and guidebooks in there when he'd unpacked the mess inside his suitcase after he changed rooms. He noticed he'd managed to include the pad of hotel notepaper in the jumble. It was a typical five-by-eight-inch white pad sporting the hotel's embossed logo at the top. It gave him an idea. Writing usually relaxed him, allowed him to focus his thoughts, and he certainly could use that at the moment.

He retrieved the pad and dug around in the drawer for a pen, but he found only a pencil. He couldn't remember the last time he used a pencil. He rarely even used pen and paper except to scribble in his little notebooks. The last person to use this pad must have been frustrated, he thought, because they'd left deep marks in the lower sheets while writing on the pad. Trent's mind immediately shifted gears to something he'd seen or read a million times, and he got a crazy idea.

Using the pencil at an angle, he colored over the surface of the pad, coating it with enough graphite to reveal whatever had been written on the page above.

"Fuck." Trent was shocked that he could actually make out a few of the words, and he kept coloring until the entire surface was gray and indented ridges of words stood out clearly enough to read.

Peter   auction Rosset   Rotonda   amph   TW

Trent recognized Reed's handwriting.

Yahtzee!

Reed might once have been a great undercover agent, but now he sucked.

Trent scribbled farther down the page and found one word repeated several times: "Peter." Reed had doodled it over and over around the edges of the pad.

The knot in Trent's gut thickened as an even worse thought bounced around in his brain.

Who's Peter?

Trent's mind wandered far afield. Sometimes Reed talked in his sleep. Could what Trent had initially thought were incoherent ramblings actually have been Peter's name? He had wondered that for a while, after he heard Reed talking in his sleep. When they'd gotten back to LA, Reed had nightmares about once a week, but Trent had never mentioned them. He didn't want Reed to feel obligated to discuss anything that had happened to him before they met, like how he'd gotten those terrible scars on his back. Trent wondered—anyone would, especially a writer. How could he not imagine what situation had led Reed into the sort of danger where he'd been tortured for information? That was the most Reed had ever let on, and Trent wasn't in a hurry to get answers. When Reed was ready to talk, he would. And Trent had always assumed it was just a matter of time.

But Peter was part of Reed's past, and part of his nightmares. Or so Trent had thought. The nightmares had ebbed away to once a month. But apparently Peter was back.

Jealousy fought curiosity within Trent.

He wasn't ready to give up on Reed, even after what had happened between them today. Of course Trent felt better after kicking Reed out of their room. It wasn't over, though. Reed had banged on the door for a while. He hadn't just left. And that meant there was hope.

Trent was a romance writer, after all. There was always hope until the story was over. And this story wasn't finished.

4

AFTER White left, Reed took a quick turn inside the Pantheon, where he and Trent had spent a lovely afternoon just two days earlier. He hadn't handled things with Trent very well, and he hated lying. This case didn't seem particularly important, but when White said Peter hadn't checked in, Reed's radar and his sense of duty had kicked in. Now it felt like an overreaction, and most likely Peter was fine.

But neither Trent nor Reed was fine. Was White's simple assignment worth it?

As Reed entered the ancient building and glanced up at the opening in the ceiling—the sole source of natural light—he remembered none of the facts Trent had told him their previous visits. He walked toward the beam of sunlight filtering down onto the inlaid marble floor, seeking its warmth. The contrast of the bright light in the dim building momentarily blinded him, but it brought a flash of insight. For all the magnificence of the Pantheon, it remained a cold, lifeless pile of stones without Trent to bring the ancient wonder back to life.

However, he'd made a commitment to White, and Reed would carry out what he'd promised. But he'd also made a commitment to Trent, and he'd let Trent down terribly. Reed took one last look around before he walked back into the bright afternoon sunshine, but Trent wasn't anywhere nearby.

With a pain in his chest, Reed went back to his hotel, making a quick stop at a drug store blocks out of his way. He headed for the hair products aisle and grabbed a box of hair color in a shade called *caramello dorato*, which was indeed the color of caramel, just a shade or two paler than Trent's hair color. He paid cash and then, on a whim, stopped by the Hotel d'Inghilterra, where he and Trent had been staying.

He discovered Trent had changed rooms, and the clerk wouldn't give Reed the new room number since he wasn't on the registration. Against protocol, he decided to leave a message—*I'm sorry about everything. Let me explain tomorrow?*—and added that he would be staying at the Hotel Intown that night. He signed it with the initials "MR"—Michael Reade. It killed Reed to do that, but until he could give a full explanation, it seemed a suitable option.

Not certain whether or not Trent would accept his apology, Reed moved his belongings from the guesthouse and checked into the Hotel Intown—still wearing his Yankees cap until he could transform his appearance. He stopped at the hotel's business center to rent a laptop.

Once settled into his room—Trent would have been torn between loving the luxurious appointments and hating its modern sleekness— Reed spread the complimentary daily newspaper on the bathroom counter and guessed at how to prepare the hair dye from the illustrated instructions. It had been quite a while since he'd had to change his hair color, but he mixed it, assuming it functioned similarly to American brands. His small acquaintance with Italian sufficed to cover the rough details if not the nuances. He unbuttoned his shirt and was about to drape a towel across his shoulders when he realized the extent of the bruises he'd gotten from that rough sex with Trent. Dark shadows loomed over his ribcage and one hip, just visible at the waistband of his jeans. He pushed the jeans down to examine the damage. How could he not have felt the pain? Now it served to exacerbate the ache in his gut—and his heart. But he'd made the first step in repairing the damage in their relationship, and he hoped like hell it would be sorted out before the marks on his body healed.

He brushed away worries of Trent in order to focus on Michael Reade as he began to spread the white cream in his hair, burying the naturally dark-brown locks. The ammonia smell quickly became too much for the tiny bathroom, and he flipped on the ceiling fan, though it was more efficient at making noise than clearing the air. Once he'd covered all his hair, he checked his watch. The dye had to stay on twenty-five minutes. He cleaned up the bathroom and settled carefully back on the bed to wait.

He downloaded the files White had sent him and familiarized himself with the specifics of Peter's research, based on Decker's computer analysis. It was thorough and showed a clear pattern of odd transactions at Rossetti's. Peter laid out his theories about the intent: either the items in question were fakes, or there was another reason for the strange bidding behavior, such as using the antiquities as a cover for smuggling drugs or other contraband out of Italy.

Too many possibilities and no solid leads on any of them.

First things first: the auction.

Reed looked through a PDF of the auction catalog. It would suffice until he got a hard copy with glossy photographs. He marveled at the array of beautiful antiquities for sale and choked as he noted their anticipated sale prices: most were expected to go for 50,000 euros—as much as one million for a chess set supposedly traced back to Charlemagne. Many of the items were likely to stay in Italy because the government wouldn't issue export licenses for them, except perhaps to a select few world-class museums or ones that offered to repatriate another piece of Italian art in return.

The items Peter and White had their eye on weren't expected to bring in quite that level of bidding, and they represented a step down in quality and appeal. They occupied a middle range for price.

Brett's program had flagged four: an amphora of Greek origin found in a wreck off Sicily and traced to the fifth-century BC, similar to one sold under suspicious circumstances; a portion of reconstructed ancient mosaic from a courtyard in a ruin west of Rome at Ostia Antica; an absolutely hideous eighteenth century lacquered wood sculpture of Cupid that was expected to go for over 1,800 euros—Reed made a quick calculation: over $2,500 at current exchange rates; and an exquisite Tang dynasty miniature terracotta horse valued at over 35,000 euros or nearly $50,000. After years in Asia, Reed appreciated the mix of beauty and history the piece represented. It certainly didn't fit with the rest of the items Peter had flagged.

Had Peter's interest in it nothing to do with the case?

Which one of these was the key piece? Could they all be part of something larger of which Peter had only scratched the surface? Reed was so engrossed in even the online catalog with its tiny photos that he kept the dye on his hair ten minutes past the recommended time. He raced into the bathroom and into the shower to rinse, cursing when the mixture ran into his eyes, stinging. He scrubbed at his scalp to rinse away all the dye and towel-dried himself and his hair.

A quick glance in the mirror revealed a surprisingly large change in appearance. Still wet, his hair was darker brown that it would be dry, and he wouldn't know the extent of the damage until later. He noticed a hair dryer affixed to the wall near the light switch, and against his usual habits, he pulled it out and turned it on.

Too bad Trent wasn't here to help him with this. He would have loved doing Reed's hair—or more likely laughed his ass off at Reed's inexpert technique, which led to singeing his scalp in more than one place before he figured out how far away to hold the damn thing.

His short hair dried quickly, and the final result, while not a color he would otherwise have chosen, was fairly flattering to him. Lighter than he liked because he'd left it on too long, the shade resembled light butterscotch rather than golden caramel. Thank God this was only temporary.

Sufficiently coiffed and dressed, Reed took a look at Peter's report again, at what scams he thought might be going on: disguising one piece as another in order to avoid export restrictions; smuggling drugs; or simply faking fairly innocuous pieces no one would think to authenticate, such as the amphora. It wasn't particularly attractive, but it had an interesting provenance, having been found in a ship that sank on its way to a Roman colony in North Africa in the second century BC. Any history buff would love to have such a piece in their collection. Given its reasonable price—compared to the majority of other items in the catalog—it was an easy way to own a fascinating piece of history. Precisely what many collectors wanted to do.

Reed pored over the reports and catalog for another hour, until his eyes stung and the sun set, casting long rays through the window. Reed's stomach rumbled. All he'd eaten today was a sandwich with White.

He needed food.

He password protected all the documents he'd accessed, closed the laptop, and stowed it in the closet safe, then set the combination as the day he quit the army. It wasn't a particularly secure safe, but who was looking for him now anyway?

Not even Trent, Reed thought and immediately cursed himself for being melodramatic.

He found a pizzeria around the corner and grabbed a couple of slices—upmarket and pricy, given the location. He washed them down with some local draft beer, something called Super Baladin, which tasted better than it sounded. He sipped at a second glass while he sat at the table, watching people wander past on their way to or from somewhere more interesting. Either heading out to meet their friends or heading home after a long day at work. Couples strode by arm in arm, and Reed couldn't stop thinking about Trent. He went back to Trent's hotel, but Trent wasn't in his room or at least didn't answer when the front desk called him. Reed leaned over the counter, but he couldn't see the room number the clerk typed into the phone system. Fucking security. Maybe White was right about being out of practice.

He returned to his hotel and was approaching his own room when he heard the phone ringing. After scrambling for his plastic electronic key, he inserted it the wrong way and kept getting the little red light instead of the green one as the phone continued to ring on the other side of the door. Finally, on the third, try he got in and grabbed for the phone.

"Trent?" The word slipped out as he answered, but he heard only a dial tone. His heart pounded in his chest and ears, and he sat down on the bed, cradling the phone on his lap. He nearly jumped out of his skin when the phone beeped and the "message waiting" light began flashing.

He followed the instructions to retrieve the message, but it was only Tom White checking in to see if Reed had any questions about the following day.

Reed had plenty of questions, but none of them had to do with White. Or Peter. With relief, Reed realized he'd barely thought about Peter all day, just tangentially as he'd read the reports. The earlier anticipation had completely died away. Whatever remained of Reed's feelings for Peter was gone, replaced by even worse regret about Trent.

It was dark now, and Reed walked to the window to close the curtains. He could see the hotel he and Trent had stayed at half a block away. About three floors higher than Reed was a man sitting at a desk near his own window. It was too far to see clearly, but Reed thought it might be Trent. The man's build and coloring were similar, and he was wearing what looked to be a pistachio-green shirt. Trent loved pastels and had brought one that color on this trip. Reed kept staring, finally identifying with those stalkery characters in films who watched the goings-on of their neighbors. The man turned away from the window, got up, and walked farther into his room before opening the door. Reed couldn't see who entered, but the green-shirted guy pulled the person close and embraced them. The two figures fell together onto the bed, and then the light went out.

Someone was having a good time tonight. Reed hoped like hell that hadn't been Trent.

TRY as Trent might, he couldn't contain his curiosity about the cryptic message on the pad. He wanted to know what it meant, though part of him dreaded finding out.

Trent headed for his laptop. God, he loved free Wi-Fi. And Google. He didn't know who Peter was, so he searched for "auction" and "Ross." Whatever Reed was doing was in Rome, so he took a chance on putting "Rome" in the search box as well, and the fourth result he found was:

Rossetti's Auction House
www.asterossetti.it
Rome, Italy. "Rome's Most Trusted Fine Art Auction House"

That certainly fit, since the next word on the sheet could be "amphora." Further clicking revealed an amphora from Roman times would be auctioned the very next day at 2:00 p.m. All items for the following day's auction were available for viewing from noon to 1:00 p.m. Trent had never been to an art and antiquities auction before, so this could be fun. He read a bit more about auction policies on the English section of the website. Anyone was welcome to attend the showing and sale, but apparently in order to bid, he would need to register in advance with his banking details.

Trent's curiosity outweighed his fear of identity theft, and he filled in the brief online registration form. Banking information could be presented in person, and then he would receive a numbered paddle that would allow him to bid. He couldn't wait. It would be just like TV and movies, waving his paddle as he bid on some ancient relic... maybe even Charlemagne's chess set.

He still didn't know whether or not Reed would be there. But Peter might be. Not that Trent had any clue what this Peter might look like. No one named Peter worked for the auction house. Trent had already checked their personnel pages.

How could it hurt to show up?

Maybe Reed would be there. That had to be a good thing. They could talk over what happened. Trent had already forgiven Reed for keeping his continued FBI work a secret, and he wanted to let Reed know.

Trent looked over at the room phone on top of the nightstand. He couldn't help hoping the message light would blink, but it didn't. Why hadn't Reed called? Was he with Peter now? Maybe in Peter's arms or Peter's bed? Or worse, in Peter's ass?

The thought sent shivers through Trent. His own ass reminded him of their furious whatever-it-was earlier. More bruises had bloomed along his ribs, though the bite mark remained the most spectacular of the mementos. He traced his fingers along it, feeling the raised flesh, the painful throb when he touched it.

He let out a sigh, lay back on the bed, and stared at the ceiling.

Why did I push Reed away? Have I pushed him toward Peter?

5

REED got to the auction house early and took another look at the items White had flagged as being similar to ones that fit the patterns of irregular bid activity. He wandered through the room, watching the other patrons, noticing which of them paid particular attention to the items he had targeted. There were several people who made notes in their own catalogs while looking at the items, but no one paused for more than a brief glance at all four. Either he'd marked some that weren't part of the pattern, or the buyer was being careful.

Peter had identified three suspicious buyers and included their dossiers in his report, and one of them was here today, a dealer named Marconi who owned a shop near Milan. He only stopped to inspect three of the four items, so Reed gave those three a closer look.

The first one, the Chinese chest, didn't set off any warning bells. He'd quickly researched the specifics of it that morning, and this example wasn't particularly stellar. It was the sort of item that was easy for a professional forger to fake. Nothing special, just one of hundreds or thousands. The cost of the necessary tests to authenticate it wasn't borne out by the value of the piece itself, so an unwary collector might happily buy it and never know—or even care—it was counterfeit.

Of the remaining items, Reed only felt slightly concerned about the authenticity of the ugly Cupid, but he saw so much interest in the piece that he decided it was likely to go for much higher than the reserve price.

He took one last swing through the room just before auction house staff ushered browsers out so they could prepare items for the auction. He went over to the bar set up in the lobby and ordered a sparkling water as he continued to watch people arrive for the auction.

As soon as the room was opened, he took a seat in the last row and watched bidders file in.

As was typical at society events, many men wore well-tailored suits. But this was Italy, after all, and everyone appeared to dress an order of magnitude better than in LA, even when going for the casual look. He suspected some of the "less structured" jackets cost more than all of the clothing he owned put together. And the women far outdid the men. They were stunning, and several tried to catch his eye as they filed past into the room. One in particular, a tall, dark-haired woman whose eyeliner technique bordered on that of Cleopatra, actually sat down next to him and tried to make small talk for a few moments, first in Italian and then in French and finally in English. Reed got rid of her by speaking Chinese. She flounced away, clearly offended that he hadn't been interested, but he kept his eyes on everyone else.

He quickly spotted Marconi, and once the room started to fill up, Reed moved closer to the stage, better to both see the items and keep a closer watch on Marconi.

The room was about half full when the first lot went up for bid. Reed observed the rhythm of the auction, listening to the auctioneer's voice and watching how the bidders behaved. It was no different from any other auction he'd been to, though the auctioneer said the prices in both English and Italian and bidding was in euros.

He was getting bored with it all as the first item he'd tagged came up for bidding. No one bid on it at first. Not a huge surprise, as several other items had had no takers at the first bid. The auctioneer lowered his price and a balding man in his late forties bid. On the third pass, Marconi also bid, then the first man bid again, with Marconi taking the piece at just under the first bid. The gavel went down.

The second marked item came up for bid about twenty minutes later. Bidding was consistent, and numbers flew as a variety of bidders got into a real competition. In the end, the item went for three times the estimated sale price. Not of interest to Reed, since it didn't fit the pattern. Marconi had bid early on, been outbid, rebid, and then got out of the action.

The third item, the Cupid, got Reed's Spidey sense tingling. The first offer wasn't rewarded with a bid, so the auctioneer lowered the price. The first bid was slightly lower, again by that balding man. Marconi made a last-minute bid just as the auctioneer was ready to award the item, and the bid, rebid situation was played out again, almost identically to the first item.

Now Reed's attention was on the first man. Who was he? He wasn't in any of Peter's reports. Reed hadn't been paying much attention to him, but he didn't think the man had bid on anything else. Damn, now he was going to have to figure out who he was. He leaned over to the woman sitting next to him and whispered. She'd seen him here before, but she didn't know his name. She'd ask one of her friends if Reed wanted to know.

The next item Baldy bid on was the amphora recovered from the shipwreck.

Reed decided to get into the game. He bid on the second pass and noticed Baldy turned around to see who had bid. He shuffled in his seat and glanced around like a lost child. But Baldy didn't look in Marconi's direction. If there was anything between them, Baldy knew better than to give the connection away.

Too bad.

Marconi countered, and Baldy bid again. When Reed bid again, he noticed Marconi getting jumpy. He rebid, and Reed was going to let him have the item. He had the information he needed on the bidding patterns. But before the auctioneer finalized the bid and sale to Marconi, yet another bidder jumped into the action, paddle number 472.

Reed glanced over to see who had raised a paddle, and thought he'd have a heart attack.

Paddle 472 belonged to Trent.

6

Quando si è in ballo, bisogna ballare.
When you're at a ball, you have to dance.
        —Italian proverb

WHAT the fuck was Trent doing here? Not just at the auction, but bidding? How on earth had he found Reed? Worse, why hadn't Reed noticed him sooner?

A lively bidding war ensued between Trent and Marconi, Trent countering each of Marconi's bids. Finally Marconi, sweat visible on his brow from half a room away, shuffled in his seat and made the amateur move of looking directly at Baldy, then at Reed. He made one last-ditch bid, but Trent outbid him yet again. This time Marconi's shoulders sagged and he let Trent take the item.

Trent nodded as the auctioneer announced his paddle number and noted the final bid. It was a helluva lot more than Reed had been authorized to spend, but Trent could afford it. What he didn't understand was why Trent would bid on the damn thing in the first place.

Unless… unless he thought *Reed* wanted the item and couldn't afford it. That was just like Trent. And precisely why Reed had tried to keep him out of this in the first place. Reed's instincts had been right.

But the damage was done. As Trent grinned at his bidding success, Marconi raced out of the room, cell phone already to his ear. Probably reporting in that he'd lost the item. Baldy headed for another exit, also clutching a phone. For all Reed knew, they were talking to each other.

Trent had walked right into the middle of something he was wholly unprepared for. And Reed hadn't been able to stop it.

He jumped up and headed for Trent, who smiled as he saw Reed approach.

"What the fuck did you just do?" Reed didn't waste time on pleasantries.

"I—I thought you wanted the amphora. I can afford it."

"Trent, we have to get out of here. Now."

"I have to pay for it."

"No. You. Don't."

"Yeah, I do." Trent had that serious, law-abiding look on his face; then a crooked smile took over. "Well, they have my banking info. I guess they'll just deduct what I owe."

"Trent. *Now*." Reed didn't bother being nice. He had to get Trent out of here. He grabbed Trent's arm and hauled him toward the door, other bidders watching them sidelong, probably remarking at their unruly behavior: "*Americani*." As they neared the door, a security guard tried to block their way through the exit.

"He's not feeling so well," Reed said, motioning at Trent, and reached for the door. The guard moved away, but Reed saw Marconi standing just outside. Still hanging on to Trent, Reed hauled him back into the auction room and headed the other direction. They raced out a side door, auction house staff in pursuit of Trent, who hadn't signed the sale documents.

But Reed didn't care. They had to disappear and fast, even if it fucked up Trent's credit. When would he need to go to an auction house again? Never, if Reed had anything to say about it. Especially not in Italy.

"AREN'T you even glad to see me?" Trent asked when Reed finally stopped dragging him around and paused in a foul-smelling alley a block away from Rossetti's.

Reed looked around almost frantically and plastered himself against the wall near the corner of the building, tugging at Trent's arm to get him to stand behind him. Trent wondered why he was so worried.

"Stay out of sight." Reed's tone signaled danger.

"Oh." Trent pulled his arm away from Reed. "Why did you drag me out of the auction? I can afford what I spent, you know."

"I know." Reed was crouched low, alternately peering around the corner and scanning the area around them. It reminded Trent of when they'd been in Thailand. And it finally sank in, what was going on.

Reed had gone to the auction for White. This was FBI business, not a secret rendezvous with the mysterious Peter.

"What're you doing here, Reed? There. At the auction?" Trent couldn't stop himself from asking.

"Later. I'll explain it once I'm sure no one's following us."

Trent waited, hunkered behind Reed, heart pounding in his chest. At the same time, he was kind of excited, not only to see Reed again, but to see him in his James Bond action-hero mode. It had been a long time.

After several more minutes of surveillance, Reed stood up and brushed his clothes off, straightened his jacket, and shot his cuffs. He motioned for Trent to stand up. "Let's get out of this neighborhood." He flagged a cab going in the opposite direction of the auction house, and they sped off with Reed giving the driver directions in a mix of English, bad Italian, and hand gestures.

The driver wove in and out of traffic and around corners faster than Trent thought safe or even possible without serious violation of the laws of physics. Twenty minutes later, the taxi deposited them outside a small trattoria on a side street, next to a tiny church, far off the tourist track. Reed paid and then hustled Trent into the restaurant.

It was dark and cool inside, and Trent reached toward a chair, about to sit down, when Reed grabbed his arm and pulled him toward the back, into the kitchen, and then out into the alley. Half a block down, Reed let them into the rear of what turned out to be a furniture shop and then out the front, around the corner, and then into another taxi. Ten minutes later they got out and Reed strolled into a café. This time Trent kept walking toward the kitchen and Reed stopped him.

"We're staying here."

"You sure?"

"Yeah. Sit."

Trent did, waiting for further orders.

"Sorry about that." Reed looked at Trent for the first time since they'd met up at the auction house and he'd felt the need to drag Trent halfway across Rome.

"Are you ready to explain what's going on?"

Reed looked around for a few moments, then switched seats so he was near the far wall, facing the door. A teenage boy came by and Reed ordered Pellegrino. Trent ordered espresso. He was so on edge at this point it would probably calm his nerves more than fizzy water.

The boy brought their order, and even though Reed kept glancing toward the door, he seemed to relax a little. He sipped at his water and ripped a corner off the napkin before he met Trent's gaze.

"That call I got in the museum the other day? It was Tom White."

"White?" Trent had met Reed's former boss back in Thailand. "Why would he call you?"

"Because I'm here and one of his agents didn't check in."

Now Trent felt like he was being watched.

He turned toward the door slowly, expecting to see Tom White waltzing in, but no one entered. They were alone in the little café. "How did he know you were in Rome?"

"He's monitoring Michael Reade." Reed had the good sense to look away as he said the name.

Trent's blood sped up, but it wasn't due to the caffeine he'd just ingested. "What?"

"I'm traveling on a Bureau passport. Just in case."

"Just in case what? In case you get bored and want to do a quick job for them?" Trent's stomach churned. Maybe he hadn't been so wrong when he'd imagined the worst about Reed/Michael. He pushed his empty cup away so quickly it rattled on its saucer. "Never mind. I don't know why I went looking for you today. What was I thinking?"

Trent got up, but Reed grabbed at his wrist. He wished he didn't want Reed to want him to stay.

"How did you find me?" Reed met Trent's gaze head-on again and waited for a reply.

Knowing he'd surprised and stumped Reed brightened Trent's mood, and his stomach settled a bit. He took a swig of Reed's fizzy water. That would help.

Reed grinned, probably at the intimate gesture of drinking out of his glass. It was something they didn't do much of in general, and especially not after they'd been fighting.

A mild description of what had happened between them the previous day. Trent's ass still reminded him of that when he sat on it the wrong way. He used to like that feeling, but now…. Well, now he wasn't at all sure how he felt about anything. All he knew was his ass hurt and he didn't think it had been worth it. Unless Reed told him the truth.

"Okay, what is going on?"

"I'm doing a job for Tom White."

"Yeah, I got that part, but where does the auction fit in?"

"One of their agents was working on a case involving the auction house. Suspicious bids, patterns of sales, et cetera, and he's missing. Or he was."

"Was?" Trent noticed how Reed's posture changed as he mentioned this agent: neck and shoulders stiffening. He was pretty sure Reed knew the agent or knew more than he let on.

"He checked in late, which got White worried. We met yesterday. The agent—" again Trent noticed Reed's gaze shifting away as he spoke "—left Rome, but White didn't have anyone to observe the auction. So I went."

"What did you discover?"

"I saw the pattern, and you stepped right into the middle of it. The amphora you bought? It was supposed to go to our suspect. He's going to want it. And he's going to want to know who the fuck you are."

"Oh." Trent's stomach lurched. This didn't sound good. "But I don't have it. You wouldn't let me pay for it. It's okay, then, right?"

"Not if they just charge your account and hold the piece for you to pick up. In that case, if the guy—Marconi—can't get it, he's going to come after you."

"What is it?"

"We don't know yet. I was going to let him bid and win and then follow him or send another agent after him."

"And now?"

"Now? I don't know." Reed ordered another drink and gulped it down. Trent didn't know how Reed could gulp fizzy water that fast. It always hurt if he didn't sip. But Reed still didn't meet Trent's gaze.

Trent didn't know if it was because Reed was mad at him for fucking this up or whether there was something else. That agent. Someone else. Peter?

"So, where is Peter?"

Reed's head whipped around so fast Trent thought it might snap off. "Peter?" The word came out more like a gulp.

Bingo. If he hadn't just figured out Reed had something to do with this other guy, Trent would be feeling pretty fucking proud of himself right now. But he wasn't sure he wanted to know who Peter was. He waited to see what Reed would do or say.

After shuffling in his chair for a moment, Reed licked his lips. "Peter. It's a long story."

"I'm not in a hurry. As long as Marconi doesn't show up, I'm not going anywhere."

"He was my first partner. My old partner at the Bureau."

"Oh, well, why didn't you just say that? Why didn't you ever mention him before?"

"There wasn't anything to say." Reed got all shifty again. Trent wished he hadn't asked, because clearly there had been something Reed didn't want to say. "I haven't seen him in a pretty long time."

"You guys don't stay in touch?" Trent almost literally clamped his mouth shut as soon as the words were out. Why the fuck did he ask that?

"No." Reed's tone made it clear he didn't want to discuss the topic, and he shrugged one shoulder as if he were trying to get rid of something sitting there. Trent had seen Reed do that whenever the subject of the scars on his back came up in conversation.

Was there a connection? Peter had been Reed's partner before Trent had met him in Thailand, when Reed's scars were already at least a couple of years old. Did whatever had happened have something to do with Peter?

But Trent didn't think Reed was quite as sure as he should be. Or as sure as Trent wanted. He started ripping at his own napkin. This was worse than the fact that Marconi was probably looking for him.

"Well, then, okay." Trent finished destroying the napkin. He'd leave a big tip to make up for having to clean up after them. He needed gelato. That would cheer him up. He thought he'd seen a shop next door before they came in here.

"Look, it's a long story, and it's not the best time. But I'll tell you. I promise."

Trent shrugged, hoping he looked nonchalant. "Whenever you're ready."

"So we need to figure out what to do about Marconi."

"We?" Trent's mood lightened at Reed's use of that particular pronoun.

"I think you're in danger. And even after what happened yesterday...." Reed's complexion got paler, if that were even possible. "I mean... I hate what happened, and even if you're still mad at me, I'll make sure you're safe."

Safe. Trent wondered what Reed used for brains. Couldn't he tell Trent wasn't mad at him about any of that now? He'd gone to the fucking auction house looking for Reed, hadn't he? Jesus, Mary, and Joseph, but Reed was clueless.

No. He was just a guy. A guy who worried about secret agent stuff and keeping people safe, not about feelings. Feelings were Trent's job, and he figured he had enough for both of them. More than that, even. In a way, it was nice for the two of them to be doing what they each did best: Reed protected people and Trent had feelings. It worked fine when they had met in Thailand, or at least it worked out fine in the end.

"Yeah. Remember I just bought that stupid amphora for you. Do you think I'm still upset about yesterday?"

"Right. I forgot. About the amphora. Not about yesterday."

Trent shook his head. "I need some gelato."

Reed let out a laugh mixed with a sigh. His shoulders loosened a bit, and his posture returned to some degree of normalcy. "Me too."

NEXT door at the *gelateria*, Reed let Trent order for both of them. Reed's eyes nearly glazed over at the vast array of colored tubs overflowing with every flavor he'd ever imagined and even more that he never could have. But Trent was in seventh heaven. Maybe even eighth. Reed never really cared what he ate, except for two or three foods he hated with a passion. But he knew Trent had favorites, so at restaurants Trent ordered all his own favorites, and Reed was generally happy.

"*C'è all'asparago?*" Trent asked.

"What's that?" Reed asked before the bewildered gelato guy could answer.

"Asparagus." Trent grinned and gave Reed a half wink. Asparagus was on Reed's most-hated-vegetable list. Trent *was* still upset about the day before, clearly.

"Whoa. That's not fair. No asparagus."

"*No. Non c'è. Niente del genere.*" The guy behind the counter shook his head and wrinkled his nose.

"No such thing, apparently."

"Thank God for that."

"*Sì, sì disgustoso!*" Gelato-guy agreed.

Instead Trent chose *gianduia*—chocolate hazelnut. He'd practiced pronouncing it more times than Reed cared to count, but from the rapturous look on the gelato-guy's face, he'd done it properly. He ordered *pera*—pear—and some kind of creamy flavor for Reed.

They took their gelati and sat inside to enjoy the treat. As Reed's tongue twisted in the palest-green pear-flavored gelato, he admitted Trent had made a good decision. The flavor was so subtle, gradually deepening, just like a real pear. And after their escape, the cool sweetness was doubly refreshing and satisfying.

He watched Trent lick at the rich chocolate gelato for a few moments, tongue darting and flicking, and thought about how Trent's mouth would taste at this very minute. *Bad idea. Very bad idea.*

"Did you give your hotel or your home address when you registered for the auction house?" Reed shuffled in his seat to disrupt the makings of an erection and got back to business.

"I USED my hotel address."

"You need to move out of there. It may already be too late. They're probably already watching the room."

Trent scooped up some more gelato and let it melt on his tongue. "Don't worry. I have a plan."

"You have a plan." Reed's voice was full of sarcasm.

Trent let it pass. It was kind of nice to be almost back to normal. "Remember Thailand?"

"I remember plenty, but what in particular?"

"When I rescued you from the triad guards?"

"Rescue. Yeah. I remember."

It hadn't happened quite as Trent had planned, but this time he had Reed to help. "I dressed up in the hotel uniform. No one paid any attention to me."

Reed nodded, a smile playing across his lips. "That would work. But let me do it this time, okay? Maybe you should just stay here eating gelato and I'll get your suitcase."

"No. I want to go with you."

"It's too dangerous. You're so fucking tall they won't miss you again. I don't want them spotting you and following you to the new hotel."

"New hotel?"

"Yeah, you need to move to my hotel. It'll be safer."

"That's the only reason?"

"Of course that's not the only reason. But it's the most important one."

Maybe that was a good answer after all. Reed was worried about Trent. It was better than him not caring or wanting to get away. Trent wondered whether once they were safe they could start up their vacation again.

"Thanks."

"I don't want anything to happen to you, especially when it's my fault." Reed put his hand over Trent's and squeezed it.

Heat swam up Trent's arm and spread throughout the rest of his body. "Let's stop in your room first...."

7

TWO hours later, Reed locked the door behind himself as he left Trent in the room at Hotel Intown. He stopped at a souvenir stand nearby and bought a hat, then made his way toward the d'Inghilterra, where he spotted a couple of suspicious-looking characters in the lobby. While the rest of the hotel guests had the annoying air of the entitled, these two looked uncomfortable and out of place in the elegant surroundings. The tall one appeared afraid to sit on the silk-upholstered couch in the lobby. The other looked a bit like Marconi, probably a brother or cousin. That worried Reed—if a family member was involved, this could mean ties to the Mafia or a similar organization, many of which still operated in Italy.

After watching the watchers for a few minutes, he remembered his cell phone and snapped a few images of them, which he'd pass on to White as soon as he had Trent's belongings. After leaving the hotel again, he rounded the corner until he found the staff entrance and slipped inside. These doors never had as much security as the front entrance. It was far too easy to infiltrate a hotel through the staff entrance, whether you just waltzed in like Reed did or actually got a job with a false identity.

If Trent could do it, anyone could. Reed grinned at the memory of Trent wearing the too-small shorts of the hotel staff uniform at the Thai golf resort where Reed had been held captive by Kao Lung, triad leader and human trafficker. Trent really had come up with a good plan, considering he was just a romance writer.

Just a romance writer. Trent would kick his ass for a comment like that. And Reed deserved it. Trent was pretty fucking smart. He still hadn't explained how he found Reed at the auction. And how the fuck had he known about Peter? Reed wondered which of them was the real spy now.

It was late, and the place was pretty quiet. In American hotels, the staff were busy doing laundry this time of night, but not here. No one stopped Reed or questioned his presence. He came across two men playing cards in what appeared to be a break room, and they just waved casually and mumbled greetings. He found the room where uniforms were stored, slipped a hotel jacket over his own. He'd worn black pants, so he didn't need to change. He donned a bellman's hat and checked his appearance in a mirror. He looked good enough to pass for a hotel employee, and since it was late, he didn't expect any of the managers to be ordering him around. He slipped back into the lobby, grabbed a wheeled luggage rack, and headed for Trent's room. Using Trent's electronic room key, Reed slipped inside and quickly packed up Trent's belongings.

Damn the guy. He'd spent one night here and it looked like he'd moved in. Shampoo and hair stuff all over the bathroom counter! Reed let an amused curse escape when he heard rustling in the other room.

He turned and found himself face to face with a tall, thickset man with a neck like a bull—possibly another relative of Marconi's, from the looks of him. The guy threw a punch, but Reed was lighter and quicker on his feet and ducked, then came back at him with a fist to the gut followed up with a knee to the jewels.

He heard the guy grunt and go slack as he fell to the floor, clutching himself. Reed slammed his fist against the guy's head a couple of times until he was out cold, and then looked around for another goon.

He should have been more careful when he got here and searched the whole room before he started packing. At least this guy wouldn't necessarily recognize him from the auction house. No one else appeared to be in the room or in the hallway. Reed finished packing, which in this case meant dumping everything into the suitcase and cramming it shut as quickly as possible. He didn't want to waste time folding. Trent could fuss about the wrinkles later, in the safety of Reed's hotel room. Reed would even iron the fucking wrinkles out himself if it kept Trent safe.

With one last look around the room to be sure he hadn't left anything, Reed put the suitcase on the luggage cart and was about to leave when he noticed a pad of hotel notepaper on the desk. It was shaded with pencil. He took a precious moment to glance at the pad and realized just how Trent had found him.

REED took the freight elevator and slipped out the rear of the hotel, altering his original plan of wheeling the suitcase right out the front door. If anyone else was watching, they might follow him, and he couldn't risk it. Once in the alley, he checked carefully, but he was alone. He grabbed Trent's suitcase and made his way to the new hotel, keeping careful watch around him at all times. No one and nothing suspicious caught his eye. He purposely entered a different hotel two blocks away to see if he was followed, and went into the men's room on the ground floor, where he waited just inside, but no one came in.

The coast was clear for the time being. He went back to his own hotel but entered through the staff door. The employee area was even more deserted here than it had been at the d'Inghilterra. Italian hotels were definitely not up to par in terms of service. He rode up in the freight elevator, and when he got back to his room, he found Trent on the bed in tears.

"What happened?" Reed left the suitcase near the door and rushed over.

Trent sniffed a few times and blew his nose. "I can only understand half of it, but it's sooo sad." He motioned toward the television, where a black-and-white film flickered across the screen. Trent was crying over some TV movie?

Just like normal.

"You had me worried!" Reed fought to keep annoyance out of his voice. He went back to the door and fastened the lock, then put a chair against it so no one could enter. Or if they did, they'd make enough noise that he'd be ready for them. Unless they started shooting. He better get them the fuck out of there.

"We need to switch hotels again."

"Why?" Trent blew his nose into a wad of tissues.

"A guy was waiting for you back at the hotel."

"Did you kill him?"

"Of course not." Reed wasn't entirely sure he hadn't, but it bothered him that Trent immediately went there. "Just punched him enough that he won't remember even seeing me."

"I guess that's okay, then."

"You guess? If you'd walked in there, no telling what he would have done!" Reed realized he hadn't checked the guy for ID. "Marconi's guys, if that's who they are, are after you."

"You make a cute bellboy."

"Trent, focus!"

"Sorry. I'm just really freaked out now."

"I'm sorry too." Reed sat next to Trent, put an arm around him, and gave a reassuring squeeze. Trent seemed to relax at the touch. "I didn't mean for any of this to happen. I just needed to help White find—"

"Find Peter?"

"Yeah. And I do owe you that explanation."

"Later is fine. We just made up. No need to ruin it again right away."

Reed looked down. Why did Trent assume the worst? Not that he was far off, but how could Trent even sense Peter was unfinished business for Reed? Or was Reed unfinished business for Peter? He might find out sooner rather than later. Maybe it was just Trent's overactive romance writer's imagination that went directly to the worst-case scenario in every relationship. Given that Trent was batting a thousand here in Rome, Reed wondered whether he should just level with him about everything.

Maybe Trent could help him figure out what to do next.

Would wonders never cease?

"REED, I don't understand why White contacted you to go to some auction like that. What's that got to do with your old partner?" They lay in bed together in the third—or was it the fourth?—hotel room in Rome.

Reed hoped Trent hadn't detected any reaction when the subject of Peter came up. "Peter's current partner, Brett Decker, got a coded message he couldn't understand. A message from Peter."

"I still don't get it."

"Peter and I had a code, one we made up and no one else would be able to break. It couldn't be traced to anyone in particular if a message were found, so it worked well for UC—undercover—work. White assumed I would be able to decipher the message if it were built on the same pattern."

Trent didn't respond, probably turning over Reed's explanation. And coming up with twenty more questions, in typical Trent fashion.

"So why don't we have our own code?" Trent moved closer to Reed and laid his cheek against Reed's still-heaving chest.

Reed ran his fingers through Trent's hair, soft and sweet-smelling thanks to the shampoo he loved enough to bring halfway around the world. After inhaling the minty-herbal fragrance, Reed let out a sigh. "We don't need a secret code. We live in LA. Nice, easy, safe lives— most of the time."

"Sure, we don't need it, but you don't need blowjobs or foot massages, and I happen to know how much you enjoy both of those." Trent shifted position so he could look into Reed's eyes.

"True."

"Life would be just fine without both of those, right?" Trent's eyebrows emphasized the question.

Reed chuckled, causing Trent's head to bob slightly. "You're starting to drive the point home, but I still don't see why you want a secret code."

"Some little thing to say, you know, in public, that no one would understand. Just us."

"But we don't have to pretend about who we are to each other."

"Just for fun. Something that means 'I love you' or 'Let's go find somewhere to fuck.' That would have been useful that time at the dumpling restaurant, you know?"

"I remember." Reed grinned at the memory, glad that Trent recalled the experience as fondly as he did. He tugged at Trent's arm until he shifted his position and Reed could wrap both arms around him. He planted his lips against Trent's mouth and kissed until Trent opened to let Reed's tongue inside. He licked at Trent's tongue, tickled the roof of his mouth and the insides of his cheeks, and sucked briefly on Trent's lower lip before pulling back. "What kind of code did you have in mind?"

"What was your code with Peter?"

Reed looked into Trent's eyes, hoping to find out where this conversation was really leading, but Trent looked as sincere and open as ever. He'd never been devious before, and Reed saw no reason to expect an ulterior motive this time around, but he still didn't relish discussing Peter. Well, Trent hadn't asked about Peter, he'd asked about the code. Reed had promised himself never to lie to Trent, never refuse to answer an outright question. He might not tell Trent everything—those jobs he'd done for the Bureau back in LA, for example—but he'd answer anything Trent asked. Reed just hoped Trent wouldn't start asking the really tough questions, because quite honestly, Reed didn't know the answers to a lot of the ones he'd been asking himself lately.

"Well?"

"Right. Our code." Reed was playing with Trent's hair, and Trent's eyes took on that expression that said he'd purr if he could. Reed liked seeing that look on Trent's face. "It was a simple substitution code. Replace one letter for another."

"Couldn't anyone figure that out?"

"Sure, if they knew where to start. But we had a twist on it. If the day of the month was odd, we'd start with replacing *E* with the other one's first initial. If it was even, with the first letter of their last name."

"I don't get it."

"If I wrote Peter a coded message on the fifth of the month, I'd replace *E* with *P* and then F with *Q* and so on. If he wrote a message to me on the sixth, he'd replace *E* with—"

"Why *E*?"

"*E* is the most commonly used letter in the English language. And it's not either of our initials. If we started with *A*, he'd be replacing *A* with *A* on an even day, and that's no code."

"What if you don't know what day the message was written?"

"We had a way to denote that as well, but it only mattered for the writer, and after a while we memorized most of the substitutions—there were just two variations for each of us—and it was easy to figure out the gist of the message even with replacing only half the letters."

"Like Hebrew?"

"Hebrew?" Reed would never be able to figure out how Trent's mind worked, but this was farther afield than his usual segues.

"Most people don't write the vowels in Hebrew, just the consonants, when they're handwriting. But everyone knows what the word should be. They're printed, of course, like in a book or newspaper, but not for everyday notes, I guess."

"How on earth did you learn that?"

"Marc was Jewish, so I learned a few things like that from him."

Reed expected to see that faraway look Trent sometimes got when he talked about Marc, but there was no trace. Had Trent completely gotten over the death of his partner of four years? Trent had never mentioned Marc so casually. This was good news. Great news, in fact.

If Trent could do it, why couldn't Reed put his past with Peter to rest?

The scars tingled again, reminding Reed how difficult it would be to erase the memories of Peter.

8

"WHAT'S the next step?" Reed paced around the hotel room the following morning, watching Tom White think his way out of the situation. It wasn't really Reed's case but he—and now Trent—were inextricably caught up in it.

"I need to send someone to help Peter."

"Peter?" Trent's voice faltered, and Reed spun in his direction. Lines deepening around Trent's mouth and a puffy, lopsided look from their fight the other day made him appear ten years older.

"Peter went to Sicily to follow a lead. He sent Brett on ahead to one of the nearby islands to follow up on one of the guys who's been selling the suspicious pieces—using the Palermo broker as his agent to keep his distance from the auction-house shenanigans." White got up and poured himself a glass of water from a bottle on the desk. He drank it in three loud gulps before crushing the plastic cup in his hands, the crunching sound overwhelming in the taut silence of the room. "Brett hasn't been able to contact Peter since he got there."

"This gets better and better." Reed let out a snort. "Did you—"

White interrupted Reed. "Peter's last contact indicates we're dealing with a drug smuggling ring. Decker can't handle a delicate contact like this on his own. No experience." White looked down at his hands, then back at Reed. "Reed, I need for you to go and be prepared to make contact—unless we hear from Peter again before the window closes."

Reed nodded. He understood time was of the essence once initial contact with a suspect was made, especially when it came to drugs. Any delay would be seen as lack of interest and gave the mark time to either check you out or decline the deal, especially if he had other interested parties.

"But, why me? Don't you have any other agents on the ground here?"

"Yes, but something's fishy with this." White glanced over at Trent, then, apparently convinced he could be trusted, turned back to Reed. "I need to bring in someone from the outside, someone no one else here has had any contact with. I think it should be you." White stared Reed down with that "it's for the mission" expression, going for Reed's jugular, his sense of duty to the job. And possibly to Peter.

"You want Reed to go to some island after Peter's partner?" Trent asked. He looked over toward Reed, eyes wide, but not simply with concern.

What was Trent worried about, the mission—or the connection to Peter? Reed's stomach knotted. White needed him for this mission, but Trent needed him too, with Marconi's thugs still out there. It was Reed's fault Trent had gotten involved in the first place.

"What about Trent? I can't leave him." Reed settled next to Trent on the bed, but it didn't seem to relax Trent at all. His shoulders were nearly up around his ears, his posture rigid. "Marconi's guys have seen him. They know he bought the amphora, and even though he hasn't gone to pick it up yet, they've been following him."

"Someone has to go, and fast. I can't trust anyone else nearby for this, Reed. I'll have another team watch Trent until you get this wrapped up."

"How can you trust them?"

"Don't worry; I'll keep them isolated from your mission."

"Doesn't anyone care what Trent has to say about any of this?" Trent's bottom lip trembled as he spoke.

"Yeah, sure." Reed reached for Trent's hand, but Trent pulled away.

"I don't want some FBI or Interpol babysitters. And I don't want to go home—"

"That's not really an option either. This group has ties in the US and—" White started to reply before Trent cut him off.

"I want to finish my fucking vacation with my fucking boyfriend."

The stridency in Trent's voice surprised Reed and might even have frightened White. There was more than just the pressure that this group—tied to drugs, based on Peter's latest intel—might try to hurt or even kill Trent. Trent was clearly upset about something else. More than just his residual anger over Reed lying to him about still being part of the Bureau. They'd moved past their fight, made up, and Reed thought Trent was okay with his lack of honesty.

"It's probably just for a few days. The Bureau will even foot the bill, and once Reed's done, you can carry on with the trip. We haven't got nearly enough to take this group down on the smuggling charges without identifying more of the key players. Peter has solid leads on how they're moving the goods—the island suspect runs an international shipping company. We just need to verify the scope of the operation and his role before we can organize the sting and mop up. But I need Reed to go down there and head Brett off from that contact."

"I still don't like it."

"We know." Reed tried again for Trent's hand, this time with success. "I know. I'm sorry, but someone's life might be in danger."

"White just said my life's in danger too. Why aren't you going to stay here and protect me?"

"Aw, Tee, I want to. I do, but this other guy is in a lot more danger. If I stay here...." Reed hated himself for making the tradeoff sound so easy. But Trent would be fine eventually. Peter's idiot partner would probably get a demotion after this mission. He'd fucked things up from the get-go. Clearly he couldn't handle the operation and either needed more training or—

Reed interrupted his own thought with another that ripped through him. He decided to ask White straight out. "Why was this Decker guy even assigned this case when he didn't have the right stuff for it?"

"Peter requested him."

That explained everything. Reed's mind was made up.

"When do I leave?"

9

Meglio soli che male accompagnati.

Better be alone than in bad company.

    —Italian proverb

REED took an early afternoon flight to Messina in the northeast corner of Sicily, where he'd catch a ferry to Panarea, the island where Elvio Milacio, one of the shady collectors, lived. His items were on Decker's suspicious list. He was also the seller of the amphora Trent had acquired at Rossetti's, which Marconi had gone to great lengths to try to retrieve.

Tom White took Trent to a temporary safe house—more of a safe hovel, he mused when they arrived at the run-down hotel not far from Rome's Termini train station. Back home this would be called a fleabag: a malodorous, dilapidated structure with a cast of shady characters lounging around the entrance. It wasn't even fit to be called a lobby.

White escorted Trent to a room in the back, near the exit, which probably led to an even more disgusting alley, based on the odors coming in through the half-open door. Sun never shone on this place in the shadows of the older and more decrepit buildings on either side. Trent fondly recalled the marble bathtub back at d'Inghilterra and fantasized how Reed was going to make this up to him.

Trent waited, clutching the handle to his suitcase, as White banged on the door to Room 14—no secret coded knock. It swung open on creaking hinges to reveal a nondescript man of about forty.

"Trent Copeland, meet Jim Felton, another FBI/Interpol agent, and this is Caterina Verdi, their Carabinieri contact on the team."

The two agents shook Trent's hand, quick, businesslike shakes, neither cracking even the hint of a smile.

Trent looked around the room as his spirits reached subterranean level. Not even a decent desk for him to write at, and he suspected he'd need to completely wrap himself in plastic to avoid catching anything on the ratty twin bed. *This is going to be a long couple of days.*

"Trent, they'll take you to a hotel where you'll continue your trip, slightly undercover, with Caterina as your wife, girlfriend, whatever."

Reed had explained to Trent that the Carabinieri were part of the Italian military police, with powers that made them a bit like a combination of the FBI and the CIA. The Carabinieri had a special branch called the Art Squad, which investigated theft, forgery, and illicit trade in Italian art and artifacts. Even so, Caterina Verdi didn't look like any soldier Trent had ever met before.

Caterina turned on a smile that nearly blinded Trent. Until that moment she'd been stone-faced and all business, but once she smiled, Felton seemed unable to keep his eyes off her. She was beautiful, in the unobtainable, perfect way Trent noticed common with Roman women. Dressed to the nines—or tens, since Italy was at least a notch above everywhere else in fashion—perfectly arranged hair, and impeccable makeup job. She wore her hair sleek, smoothed back from her face like she belonged in a Lancôme ad, the better to show off a pair of diamond earrings that flashed and caught the light whenever she moved her head. Those rocks looked like they'd set someone back a pretty penny, Trent noted, wondering how much members of the Carabinieri Art Squad made. She probably had some sugar daddy paying her way, keeping her up to her perfectly formed ears in jewels, La Perla, Prada, Versace, and Armani.

Caterina appeared sharp in mind as well as dress, but she was exactly the opposite of what he'd look for in a woman, if he were looking for anything in a woman.

"And right, people are just going to buy that she's my girlfriend?" Trent waved a hand indicating himself. He wasn't even referring to being gay, just that he didn't even remotely look like the average Italian man, much less one who could attract a high-maintenance diva like Caterina appeared to be.

"Don't worry so, Trent!" Caterina's mouth smiled, but the charm didn't extend to her eyes, which were still cool blue, peering into Trent's. "Your average Italian might easily be mistaken for a gay man back in the USA. Here, they probably invented the term for—how you say—metrosexual." She laughed, a lovely sound at first, trailing off with a trace of coldness as it echoed around the dingy room.

After an inexplicable wait of two hours, Felton and Caterina shuttled Trent off to yet another hotel—was this his third or fourth room so far in Rome? Trent's mood brightened considerably as they drove away from the dingy hovel into the brighter and more fashionable streets. They wound up not far from d'Inghilterra. He recognized the new hotel immediately: five-star luxury digs Grand Hotel Via Veneto. Even more extravagant than d'Inghilterra, and Reed wouldn't let Trent splurge this much.

Trent's heart skipped a few beats as Felton and Caterina took Trent through the beautiful art-deco lobby, featuring even more elegant and ornate antique furniture than the d'Inghilterra, and into the equally impressive elevator.

As they ascended, they kept their eyes forward, with Trent between them. He felt like a kid, half expecting them to hold his hands to make sure he didn't run off on his own once they got to the top floor.

With an elegant ding, the elevator stopped, opened, and they stepped out onto thick cream-colored carpeting. Caterina turned toward the left, with Trent and Felton following. She waved a keycard in front of the door until it clicked open. She pulled a pistol out from under her Prada jacket, and Felton did the same. Hers was silver with an elegant pearl handle, probably Versace, if Versace made handguns.

They entered as a unit, Caterina clearing the room with Felton taking up the rear, backing into the room as his gaze swiveled to take in all the corners and potential hiding places. When they declared it "all clear," the two agents holstered their weapons and waved Trent in from the doorway. Of course, someone could have shot him dead out there while he stood waiting for them to clear the suite.

The Grand Hotel made the d'Inghilterra look like a Motel Six. Trent looked around at the unexpected luxury. Carpeting even thicker than in the hallway, silk damask draperies lining the floor-to-ceiling windows offering sweeping views of the Eternal City. The panorama drew Trent to the window, but Felton held him back with a tug at the elbow.

"Let's check the balcony." Felton pulled out his weapon again and made Trent wait until the necessary motions had been gone through. He wasn't really buying that he was in any danger up here. No one—not even Marconi—would expect to find him here, unless this ridiculous security detail had drawn more attention to him. With a sigh, Trent flopped onto the couch and took stock of the arrangements.

There were two bedrooms, each with its own bathroom, and a well-appointed and comfortable sitting room where his two babysitters took turns.

"Sweet suite." Felton let out a coarse laugh, and Trent did his best to ignore it. No wonder Tom White hadn't sent this guy to the auction or down to Sicily to look for Peter and Brett. Felton wouldn't know fine art unless it was painted on velvet. Suddenly Trent wasn't at all happy with the way his tax dollars were being spent.

"I'll order some food." Caterina, silent until now, let everyone know her priorities. "It's early, but we didn't have lunch, and I don't want poor Trent to feel we are mistreating him." She pulled a leather-bound menu out of the desk at the far end of the sitting room and flipped through the pages. "How about *carciofi alla romana* and some *saltimbocca*? They're Roman specialties." Artichokes stuffed with mint and parsley and prosciutto-wrapped veal.

Trent's mouth watered and he might have licked his lips involuntarily. His stomach rumbled softly in case his brain hadn't quite understood.

"And I think the black truffles are coming into season now. You simply must try them if you haven't, Trent."

"Sign me up for some of that! All of that!" Felton responded, grinning. Apparently he didn't normally eat that well. Neither did Trent, even so far on his Roman holiday with Reed. He wondered if Caterina genuinely wanted to make his stay pleasant or whether she simply had to have the best of everything. He took another look at her expensive designer clothing and even more exquisite accessories. Definitely the latter.

Caterina looked at Trent. "Such a sour face, Trent. You don't like this accommodation? Something else wrong?"

Trent hadn't realized his thoughts were so easy to read. He looked away.

"Don't worry, we won't charge you or your FBI."

"No?" Trent wondered what else she'd figured out.

"This suite is a permanent room for use of the Carabinieri or another department which needs it. No charge."

Trent considered what the hotel got in return. The government overlooking what went on here? What did go on here, Trent now wondered. Not that he'd have any chance of finding out if he was going to be shadowed by these babysitters. It seemed overkill unless the Carabinieri knew more about the danger than the FBI did. And perhaps more about the antiquities scam that Peter—and now Reed—had gotten involved with.

A cold shiver ran down Trent's spine, and he shook off the feeling of dread. He wasn't worried about Reed's safety, was he? Reed knew what he was doing. He'd be fine. Trent only hoped Caterina and Felton were as skilled as Reed.

While Trent's thoughts wandered, Felton investigated the suite, shouting his discoveries as he made them. Each bathroom was equipped with bidets, marble tubs, and gold-plated fixtures.

"No, not the toilets, but how cool would that be? Crapping into a gold john?" Felton's running commentary continued while Caterina ordered their dinner.

They made awkward small talk until a soft knock sounded at the door. A bellman brought Trent's suitcase, along with two smaller cases for the agents. Caterina tipped the man, and before she shut the door, room service arrived. The waiter wheeled in an elaborate cart with several dishes topped with the ubiquitous silver domes. It reminded Trent of the golf resort in Thailand. Would he lift one to find the remains of someone else's dinner?

With another tip, Caterina sent the waiter away, then examined the dishes one by one, giving each a taste before setting a small table in the sitting room. She hummed softly as she worked, pouring for each of them from an unopened bottle of *acqua minerale senza gas*—no bubbles. Trent preferred bubbles.

"Dinner!" she announced. "*Tutti a tavola*, as my mother used to say. Come to the table."

Trent couldn't suppress the sound of delight that escaped his mouth as he beheld their sumptuous meal: everything Caterina had promised and more. Felton was practically drooling.

Revise that, Trent thought. Felton *was* drooling.

Trent surreptitiously wiped the back of his hand across his mouth in case he'd done the same. Nope, he was clean.

"Go ahead, boys, dig in!" Caterina said with a low murmur that might not have been about just the food. She eyed Felton in a slightly predatory manner throughout the meal. She knew any attempt to flirt with Trent was wasted.

Felton couldn't get enough of the delectable food or Caterina's attention, and Trent sat back and watched the ridiculous dance between them. It wasn't just unprofessional; if there was any real danger, it meant their attention was diverted from him. He wished he was with Reed. Even chasing some drug-dealing mob guy in Sicily seemed better than being here.

After dinner, Trent went to his room. He debated unpacking and decided against it. He didn't know how long he'd be here, but he didn't want to settle in. That would be accepting the situation, and he hadn't yet. Instead, he pulled his laptop out of his suitcase and spent some time working on the outline of a new novel he was playing around with. He didn't have much of an idea of what he'd write or any of the characters, but he knew he wanted to set it in Italy. He spilled random thoughts and ideas out through the keyboard, one or two catching his imagination and sparking creativity. An hour later, he'd written a couple of scenes that might go somewhere. He was thirsty and padded to the door, intending to get some water from the sitting room. The refrigerator was stocked with plenty of beverages, and he'd bring a whole bottle in here so he wouldn't have to leave his room again.

He opened the door a crack and saw Caterina and Felton sitting close on the couch, their whispers barely loud enough for him to make out. He stopped and listened, hoping they wouldn't notice him eavesdropping.

"So why did his boyfriend leave him here in Rome? Or maybe I should ask why his boyfriend brought him in the first place if he's on a mission?"

"Maybe he's just that good in bed." Felton let out a laugh Trent had heard far too many times in his life. His stomach clenched, followed by both fists, but he forced himself to relax.

"Reed worked a few undercover jobs in LA after he 'retired'." Felton made quotey fingers, causing Trent's blood pressure to soar. How had Felton known what Reed was up to while Trent didn't have a clue? Did the whole fucking FBI know Reed had been lying to Trent?

10

REED sat on the ferry from Messina, on Sicily's north coast, toward the island of Panarea, where Elvio Milacio lived. Peter had flown down to Palermo, on the western end of Sicily, two days earlier and presumably would be catching a similar ferry. Reed's luggage was in the cargo area, and he wandered the deck, gazing out toward the horizon where he could already see—and smell—Vulcano, the first of the Aeolian Islands, coming into view. The ferry was large enough to take vehicles and cargo and rode smoothly if slowly through the Mediterranean. The water was choppy, and though the ferry cut through the small waves untouched, Reed imagined in a storm it would be an unpleasant journey. Now, in late September, Italy was recovering from the summer season, when most Italians fled their homes in the cities and headed for the sea or the mountains—*montagna o mare*, as the Italian couple he'd met on the plane had explained. Now the ferry to the islands was nearly empty.

Trent would love this place. He'd enjoy the ferry, absolutely fall in love with the scenery. Reed wished yet again Trent was with him, but knew he was safer back in Rome with the security team. How had Trent managed to stumble right into the middle of Reed's little part-time gig for White? Again. Not only had he followed Reed, but he'd gotten right into the thick of things when he'd bid on the amphora Marconi intended to buy.

Worse, at least for Reed, Trent seemed to pick up on something about Peter. Reed wasn't ready to have that discussion just yet. Too much unfinished business remained between him and Peter, though he hadn't been aware of it until they'd come to Rome and White had thrown Reed into Peter's investigation.

The scars on Reed's back stung and he scratched at his left shoulder, fingers digging into the flesh, bringing real pain to mask the phantom pain he felt when he remembered what had happened. What had Trent figured out? How close he and Peter had actually been?

They'd been partners in every sense of the word. At first Reed had thought he'd been imagining Peter's interest in him, but as the attraction grew mutual, Peter's overtures became less subtle. Reed had given in, told himself it strengthened their partnership. The closer they became, the better partners on the job. Peter had used that rationale, and Reed had believed it.

Reed recalled the look on Trent's face when he said they'd been partners. Had it been jealousy—or pain? He'd never seen that expression before, never considered that Trent would question Reed's commitment to him, despite the fight they'd had only days earlier. Reed's response had been a lightning flash of guilt blazing thorough his chest. Trent had acted oddly after that hurried conversation in the café where they'd run from the auction house, and despite their patching things up, Reed wasn't certain how Trent felt about him right now.

As Trent eavesdropped on Caterina and Felton, he attempted to remain calm. He couldn't worry about what had happened, he reminded himself. His concern was for Reed to get back from this mission alive so Trent could kill him if he still wanted to—later.

"…and they came to Rome before Reed got involved in this case," Felton continued. "Just like Reed, to get the cushy mission."

"This is cushy." Caterina took a sip of wine. Her pronunciation of "cushy" sounded like sex on toast.

Felton was nodding like a schoolboy about to lose his virginity. "Sure, this is nice. But nothing like Reed. Getting sent to the ritziest island… Pana—"

"Panarea?" Caterina prompted.

"Yeah. Way out of my price range."

"It's lovely."

"Wonder who Reed fucked to get sent down there." Felton took a gulp of wine, clearly not savoring its unique characteristics. "Well, maybe who didn't he fuck?" He chuckled and raised his eyebrows, indicating there was far more to the story than he'd already divulged.

Caterina nodded, seemingly hanging on every word and staring into Felton's eyes. "Tell me."

"Well, Peter, the mission lead—he's Reed's old *partner*—went incommunicado, so White contacted Reed to translate some coded message Peter had left."

Neither Trent nor Caterina failed to notice Felton's emphasis on "partner."

"Peter? He was Reed's old partner?"

"Oh yeah." Felton topped his smarmy tone with a smirk.

Trent really didn't like the tone Felton used, but he compelled himself to stay quiet because he really, really wanted to hear this.

"Reed's first partner." Felton nodded, and his eyebrows shot up with enough innuendo to knock the window out of its frame. "You know what first partners are like."

"Sì, sì." Caterina gave a conspiratorial nod accompanied by a charming Italian shrug. "I fell madly in love with mine. Ahh, Giancarlo…." She threw her head back, giving Trent and Felton a good look at her cleavage.

"So you can imagine Reed and Peter."

"Peter is gay too?"

"Peter is… omnivorous. He doesn't have rules except to get every partner into bed."

Trent's gut twisted, and he almost let out a shout. He'd suspected something more than simple partnership between Peter and Reed, but he hadn't expected this. Nor that whatever happened between Reed and Peter would be common knowledge in the FBI. Could Reed have had another "partner" in the past? Or did some relationship still exist between Reed and Peter? What Felton left unsaid implied any or all of these could be true.

Or, Felton could be spewing a bunch of lies to get Caterina's attention, Trent told himself.

No, it had to be more than lies or speculation. Felton knew Reed had been working for the Bureau in LA—something even Trent hadn't known—so he must be fairly well informed, Trent told himself back. White trusted Felton enough to have him watch Trent.

Shut up, Trent told himself. He didn't want to believe what Felton had said.

Did Reed know everyone else seemed to know about him and Peter?

Everyone but Trent.

"So? Reed and Peter slept together? Big deal. It happens all the time in Italy. Reed can't still be interested now, years later."

"Oh, there's more. Reed was really into Peter, and Peter acted like it might have been more than just physical, at least for a while."

"Then what?" Caterina spoke Trent's thoughts.

"They were on assignment in Asia, Laos or Myanmar. I don't know the details, but something went belly-up. Reed went missing, got himself captured. Peter came back on his own—saved the mission, apparently. Never again mentioned Reed, at least not in casual conversation. Reed eventually escaped and stayed in Asia, and as far as I know, they haven't been on the same continent since then. Till now."

"Captured? By whom?"

"Now I'm afraid I can't tell you that…." Felton's voice dropped low and he sort of purred the words against Caterina's ear, still loud enough for Trent to hear.

"But Reed showed up when Peter got assigned to my unit in Rome? A coincidence?" Caterina's tone turned conspiratorial, and one corner of her mouth turned up in a suggestive smile.

"Good question."

This time Felton read Trent's mind. Reed had been in contact with White, who knew where his agents were all the time. Reed had suggested Rome. Could he have planned the trip around Peter's mission? Trent refused to believe Reed could be so manipulative—or so cruel.

Felton didn't offer more dirt on Reed, and Caterina didn't ask any more questions. She poured more wine into their glasses and handed Felton his. "Let's not talk about work…."

"Fine with me." Felton took a large sip of wine, focusing his attention on Caterina's eyes and occasionally on her low-cut silk blouse.

Trent had heard enough—for the time being, anyway. He closed the bedroom door, grateful for well-oiled hinges. High marks to the maintenance crew. He plopped onto the bed, lay on his back, and stared up at the ceiling, his gaze playing over the lacy patterned molding as he tried to recall what Reed had said about Peter.

It wasn't so much *what* he'd said as how he'd acted. Kind of jumpy, nervous. Trent had written it off as being on his guard against Marconi's men or anyone who might be following them. But with new information, Trent found new meaning in every one of Reed's glances and gestures. Trent wasn't a particularly jealous type. He'd never had much reason to be. As far as he knew, none of his partners had cheated on him. Reed hadn't cheated while they were in LA. Trent might not have known he'd done a job for the Bureau, but he was pretty sure he'd know Reed had been with someone else. Whatever problems they had—and Trent knew something had been building between them lately—it wasn't about someone else, despite what happened the other day when they'd come to blows.

Trent tried to process Felton's revelations. He gave the impression Reed had been more interested in Peter than Peter had been in Reed. Could Reed's odd behavior be a result of something unresolved between them?

Peter wasn't the only thing triggering Trent's nerves. He didn't trust Caterina for some reason. He wondered if she and Felton were making out on the couch or whether they'd moved to the other bedroom. Spying on Felton's clumsy advances would prove more enjoyable than stressing over the fear of Reed being reunited with his former lover. Reed had enough to worry about without jumping into bed with an old flame.

Then again, Trent and Reed had met and ended up in bed together on Reed's mission in Thailand.

Clearly Reed could multitask, and for the first time, Trent wasn't particularly glad. But Reed had been single in Thailand, and now he was… what? For all intents and purposes, they'd broken up the other day, but they'd patched things up, right? Trent didn't think they'd actually split up, at least not to the point of being free to see other people, not yet. They'd spent the previous night making it up to each other.

But Trent also acknowledged the thrill of being in danger. It heightened all one's senses and reactions. It had made being together so much more exciting in Thailand and brought them close quickly.

Safe in LA, they'd had to backtrack on relationship things that most people dealt with before they moved in together. Reed and Trent had fast-forwarded into a full-blown relationship before they even knew much about each other. For Trent, it had been great to get to know Reed better, but in retrospect, maybe Reed had found life in LA with Trent anticlimactic and boring after the thrill of their whirlwind affair in Thailand.

Trent determined not to dwell on any of the ugly possibilities he'd imagined. Instead, he opened the door quietly, hoping to catch Felton and Caterina in a compromising position.

11

WITH nothing to do but watch the scenery, even Reed was moved to "ooh" and "ahh" along with his fellow passengers as the ferry approached Lìpari harbor, a semicircle of turquoise water surrounded by a cluster of whitewashed buildings, with an impressive walled citadel overlooking the entire area.

The juxtaposition of gorgeous architecture with the beautiful natural setting impressed him even more than anything he'd seen yet in Rome. Until a day earlier, he'd never heard of these fascinating islands, a string of natural gems resulting from millions of years of violent volcanic activity, according to the guidebook White had supplied.

Had Trent been here, Reed might have enjoyed his first experience on Lìpari as he walked from the small marina where the hydrofoils docked to the larger marina, where he could purchase a ticket for a ferry leaving within the hour. They would have lingered, exploring the tiny streets or relaxing at a sidewalk café with a coffee *granita*—a Sicilian specialty of crushed ice and coffee, the original Italian ice—which he'd been craving since hearing about the local treat from someone on the ferry.

The islands were so beautiful, such variation in scenery and terrain. How had he never heard of this area before? He didn't know much about Sicily at all. Like most Americans, his knowledge was colored by unrealistic and outdated ideas based on mob movies like the *Godfather* series.

After the short walk along the seaside, Reed easily found the ticket office for the ferry to Panarea. He forked over another ten euros—he'd happily pay ten times that just for the scenery—and shuffled onto a small ferry with what appeared to be mostly locals.

On the pier, a group of elegantly dressed people with a mound of Louis Vuitton suitcases was being escorted to a smaller private vessel, which sped off while the larger lumbering ferry idled, bobbing in the wake the speedboat produced.

Now, as Reed looked out over the ocean, gazing northeast in the general direction of Rome, he wondered what Trent was doing. If he was safe, if he was happy, or whether he'd had enough of Reed after the lies.

The lies had never been to hurt Trent, but to protect him. In the same way Trent wanted to give Reed gifts, Reed wanted to keep Trent safe, precisely the way he'd felt since the day he'd first seen Trent in the Bangkok airport.

Only instead of staying in Rome to protect Trent, here Reed was, on a ferry off the coast of Sicily, about to meet up with Peter, his ex-partner—in every way. What would Trent think if he knew the truth? Reed would have to tell him everything. After he sorted out his own feelings for Peter. There would be time for that later.

Much later.

AS TRENT expected, Caterina and Felton were in a passionate embrace when he opened the door. He hadn't been as quiet as he thought he was, and they pulled apart, though not particularly quickly.

"Oh, Trent." Caterina trilled a laugh and buttoned up two buttons on her blouse, still leaving a fair expanse of skin.

Felton just gave a typical guy grin and an "oops, you caught me" expression that was supposed to make Trent feel like they were buddies. "How's the writing?"

Trent forgot he'd told them he'd been writing so they'd leave him alone. "Uh, not going so well. Need a break."

"There's more wine!" Caterina said in an inviting singsong. She walked over to the table, which still held the remains of the dinner, and grabbed a glass, which she waved in Trent's direction. She came back toward the couch and filled it up. "Come, join us." She handed the glass to Trent and settled onto the larger couch, opposite of the one where Felton still sat.

"Sure." Trent sat next to her and took the glass. He sipped tentatively. Not bad. Probably better than what he usually ordered, though he felt guilty drinking wine while Reed was off facing danger, no matter who was paying. Clearly neither Caterina nor Felton felt a shred of guilt over drinking or snogging while they were supposedly on duty. Felton even had a smear of lipstick near the corner of his mouth. Trent expected better than that of Caterina. She should have used a smudge-proof brand, especially if she'd been planning to seduce Felton.

Trent didn't find Felton particularly seduction-worthy and wondered what Caterina was up to. Nearly from the beginning, he'd sensed something was off about her, and now her unprofessional behavior only reinforced the suspicion.

"Nice. What kind of wine is this?" Trent saw the bottle on the table between the two couches, and he recognized the label of high-end Chianti Classico. He took another sip.

"Oh, you need to take more than that to taste it correctly. Big sip!" Caterina encouraged him.

Trent knew that was true. He'd been to plenty of snobby wine-tasting events with Marc, and two more with Reed before Reed threatened to run away from home if forced to attend another—unless it was at a winery in Italy. That was on the agenda when they got to Tuscany. If they got to Tuscany.

He took a slightly larger sip but decided he wanted to keep a clear head, and something about Felton's increasingly blank gaze worried Trent. He pretended to swirl and sniff, examining the wine like a typical neophyte, but he was really checking to see if Caterina had put something in it. Before Trent could take another sip, Felton fell asleep—or passed out drugged, if Trent's imagination hadn't run away with him. Trent kept an eye on Caterina as he feigned enjoying the wine.

"Oh, he's a big man, but he can't hold his liquor very well." Caterina smiled. "You like this wine? It's Chianti Classico."

"Classico?"

"To denote it comes from one of the villages originally classified by the de' Medicis in the eighteenth century."

"Oh." Trent wished he hadn't asked. He was torn between finding her answer annoyingly erudite and precise and appreciating her deep knowledge of wine. Damn, did he sound this supercilious when he told Reed what he considered interesting little tidbits of information? He'd better work on that....

"I like it." Just in time, Trent remembered not to take a big gulp as she watched him too closely for comfort. "Looks like Felton really liked it."

"He has a big appetite. For everything." She emphasized the final word, none too subtly.

"Excuse me a minute." Trent picked up his glass, made a little toast toward her, and headed into his room and then the bathroom, where he shut the door behind him. He dumped out the wine and flushed the toilet, then ran water. He didn't rinse out the glass—that would give away that he'd dumped the contents. He didn't trust the wine. Unfortunately, the firm tannins and characteristic dark cherry aroma were too strong for him to smell any drug, and Trent wasn't exactly an expert on knockout drugs. He'd watched plenty of spy films back in LA; meeting Reed had triggered the interest, and he knew Reed wouldn't care for Trent's DVD library full of classic romance films. Despite Reed's usual disgust with spy flicks, they'd watched every Bond film multiple times, even the awful ones with Roger Moore and his increasingly ludicrous hairpieces. They argued over which Bond was the best, the sexiest, which they'd most like to fuck.

"Think I could be a Bond girl?" Trent had asked during a viewing of *The World is Not Enough*. He loved Pierce Brosnan, even if his turn at Bond had included some duds.

"First, you have to be a girl. And no one would ever mistake you for a girl."

"Well, if Bond was gay?"

"I think you'd be able to give every Bond a run for his money," Reed had said as he'd caressed one of Trent's biceps. "No self-respecting spy wants a sidekick who's in better shape than he is."

"Oh." Trent hadn't suppressed his hurt feelings at Reed's comment. "Not even you?"

"Trent, you aren't my sidekick. You're so much more. And you're deadly with a dinner cart." Reed had leaned close and kissed Trent, softly at first then increasingly convincingly, before caressing more than a bicep.

Trent reluctantly pulled his mind out of the very satisfying way that particular conversation had ended—film forgotten, along with Reed's existential snub—and wondered whether he was overreacting about Caterina.

He slowly opened the bedroom door and saw her standing across the room, talking on her cell phone, her back toward Trent. She spoke quietly, but he made out a few words, and his limited Italian vocabulary was sufficient to grasp the general concept.

"…wine … asleep… soon…. Peter… Panarea… Michael Reade… tomorrow…."

He slipped out of the bedroom and decided to pretend he hadn't been listening.

"There's some wine left. Help me finish this bottle." He moved toward the couch, reached down for the bottle, and held it up.

Caterina's shoulders shuddered as he spoke, and she spun around, deftly managing not to let on that he'd startled her by the time she faced him. "Yes, let's kill this army man!"

"What?" Trent's heart stopped beating. Felton had been in the army? And why did she think Trent would want to kill him?

"Isn't that how you call the empty bottles?"

"Dead soldiers." His heart started up again.

"Oh, yes. Dead soldiers." Caterina glanced toward Felton as she spoke, and the connection chilled Trent.

Trent leaned over to make sure Felton was still breathing, then let out a sigh of relief when he detected a pulse and heard a soft exhalation. He gave the sleeping man a shake, but it wasn't enough to wake him. Felton had to have ingested more than just wine to be so far out of it.

"Maybe we should try and get him into the bedroom or something, don't you think?"

"He looks too heavy, even for you and your big muscles." Caterina stroked one of Trent's biceps as she handed him the wine bottle.

He poured a little wine for himself and the rest into her glass. If she'd drugged the bottle, then it would be difficult for her to make a switch without being completely obvious. Hadn't Michael Westen given this advice? If she'd drugged the glass, hopefully most of it had gone down the drain in the bathroom. On the downside, if Trent had completely misunderstood the situation, he'd wasted a delicious bottle of wine. He hoped he could remember the name of it in order to buy a bottle to share with Reed once all this was over.

As long as he and Reed weren't over before then.

Trent was glad he'd taken his own precautions. He just wasn't sure what Caterina wanted. She'd been talking to someone on the phone about Reed's movements. It couldn't be coincidence; she'd been chosen to liaise with the Carabinieri and guard Trent. Could she be involved with the antiquities ring Peter had discovered?

If she was on the up-and-up, she wouldn't resort to drugging anyone. That was the big clue. Trent didn't think she'd actually kill them, since White knew she was here to protect them… or would she? She couldn't risk drawing attention to actual murders or other law enforcement would be alerted.

Thinking on his feet wasn't one of Trent's major skills. He liked to ruminate on a scene for a while before writing it, but he didn't have the luxury right now. Not with Caterina settling herself on the couch next to him.

"What did you want to do tomorrow, Trent? I can show you my own favorite places to visit in Rome. The historical ones as well as the secrets we Romans keep from the tourists."

"I'd like that," Trent said, momentarily thrown by her casual, friendly chatter despite the proximity of Felton's unconscious body. "I was thinking of doing a walking tour along the Appian Way." According to his tour book, it was a somewhat strenuous four-to-five hour trek, especially for someone in Prada boots with five-inch heels.

"Excellent choice. But I'll never wake up if I drink all this wine you poured me." Before Trent could stop her, she poured most of the contents of her glass into his.

That clinched it for him.

He expected she had put in enough drug to knock down a guy of his size, so he took a pretend sip as if he didn't suspect anything amiss, ingesting only a minute amount of liquid. Even that tasted pretty damn good. He smiled and let out a low "mmmmm" as he swallowed the potentially harmful liquid.

"What're your favorite places?" he asked and yawned. "Oh, I'm feeling awfully sleepy myself. It's been an eventful day."

"It has. Drink up and you'll sleep like a baby."

12

CATERINA smiled seductively, which was totally wasted on Trent, but he could certainly see why Felton had fallen for her.

Michael Westen had the perfect advice for Trent's situation: to drink without getting drunk (or drugged, as in Trent's case), spill.

Trent raised his glass, carefully bumping his elbow against Caterina's shoulder, and spilled most of the wine down his shirt, but plenty down hers. He hated destroying a gorgeous blouse, but he felt more than a twinge about his own loss: a new pale-blue shirt he'd bought at a fabulous little boutique on via dei Condotti the day before Reed had gotten that inconvenient phone call. Now his shirt was as completely ruined as his dream vacation with Reed. He blinked a couple of times, as if his eyelids were growing heavy.

"Oh, dear." He slumped against the couch, the empty wine glass falling from his fingers.

He felt her get up from the couch in a hurry, sensed her bending low, hair falling against his cheek as she must have been checking to see if he was really out. She muttered imprecations—at least Trent interpreted them as such, given her tone of voice—under her breath and moved off in the direction of the second bedroom, pressing buttons on her cell phone as she left Trent apparently slumbering on the couch.

He listened to her conversation through the open door. This time she made no attempt to lower her voice, and while Trent's Italian was more useful for cooking than planning black ops, he gathered she wanted someone to come pick Trent up and take him somewhere. He'd been there and done that, and it wasn't going to happen again. Not while he could still protect himself. He knew she had a gun, but would she risk attracting attention by firing it here in the hotel?

Trent had to bet she wouldn't as he planned his move.

He heard her turn the water on in the bathroom, and he couldn't make out the rest of her conversation, but the sound obscured his movements as he slowly rose from the couch. He looked around for a weapon, and his eye lit on the dinner cart. He knew from his experience in Thailand it contained weapons he could use if necessary. But he didn't want to be a one-trick pony. He'd use it only if he couldn't find something else.

Always a fan of irony, Trent chose to use Caterina's own weapon against her. He picked up the wine bottle—Chianti Classico was always packaged in good-quality bottles of thick glass. One smack would certainly knock her out. He didn't particularly want to hit a woman, but she was dangerous—and armed.

He found her sitting on the edge of the bathroom counter, wearing only a wine-stained bra edged with the most beautiful—though also now stained—cream lace and the tiniest pair of panties he could imagine—matching, of course—as she rinsed red wine from her blouse.

The gun sat on the counter next to the sink.

She looked up, eyes wide, as Trent lumbered into the room clutching the wine bottle like a baseball bat.

She started to laugh.

Trent stopped and gave her a sneer he'd learned from a Bond villain, which only made her laugh even more.

Let her underestimate him, Trent thought, pleased that she didn't reach for the gun. She didn't even glance at it. *Good.*

He took a step forward, unsteady on his long legs, and made a half-assed swipe at her with the bottle, missing by a mile. She was still laughing when he fell to one knee and nearly hit his head on the counter.

She kept laughing as he grabbed the gun and pointed it at her.

Trent stood, bringing himself to his full six feet, three-and-a-half inches. With completely steady hands, he aimed the gun at her face.

She stopped laughing. She looked around, but the only available weapon was the empty wine bottle on the floor. Trent kicked it back into the bedroom without taking his eyes off Caterina.

"Trent, that is not 'umorous." A note of concern had crept into her voice, and her eyes flashed dark with worry. She sat up on the counter, her posture wary. "I may have underestimated you."

Yes, she certainly had. "I know you drugged Felton."

"What are you talking about? I meant you've got quite a sense of 'umor."

She tried to play it cool and innocent, but Trent wasn't fooled. "You drugged the wine."

"Careful with the gun!"

"Don't worry. I know how to use one of these." Trent wondered how that had popped out. Maybe Michael Westen was rubbing off on him. About time, because he needed it. He knew diddly about guns, except for a little research he'd done for one of his novels.

"I did not drug the wine. Felton simply drank too much."

"Yeah? Then why were you so mad when I didn't drink my wine?"

"Because you spilled it all over me. You destroyed my beautiful new blouse." She shook the dripping silk, now mottled shades of pink and cream, at him, her voice rising. "And my bra! They probably cost more than all your clothes." Her chin jutted out in defiance, and she threw the wet blouse back into the sink, splashing water on Trent.

Trent shrugged. She was wrong about the clothes. He'd spent plenty on them. "I don't trust you." He waved the gun at her, this time in what he thought was a much more controlled fashion. "Do you have handcuffs?" he asked.

She looked confused at the question, hesitating before she replied, "Yes, in my suitcase on the bed, but you don't seem the type."

"You do." Trent brushed off her insult. "Get up and get them for me." He took a step back to let her stand up. As she moved past, he grabbed one of her wrists. He'd never done anything like this before, but her strength was no match for his, and she couldn't get away. He kept her at arm's length so her free hand couldn't do any damage while he figured out what to do next.

"Trent, you're hurting me. And you are making a big mistake."

"We'll see who's making the mistake." He tightened his grip on her wrist and moved up behind her so he could put a hand over her mouth. He wasn't sure how to hold onto her and the gun, so he stuck the gun into the waistband of his pants at the small of his back. She wouldn't be able to reach and get it even if one of her hands came loose.

He smiled to himself, pleased he'd been able to overpower her. He walked her into the bedroom, where he fished the cuffs—police issue, not the play kind—out of her suitcase.

"Put one on and lie down on the bed."

She gave him another seductive smile and lay down in what would have been an incredibly provocative way had he been straight. Hell, Trent admitted she would be pretty hot, even to him, if she hadn't tried to drug him or order her lackey to come take him somewhere. No wonder Felton had let his guard down. Trent couldn't afford to make the same mistake. He straddled Caterina on the bed to immobilize her and dug the barrel of the gun into her ribs. Her skin was smooth and taut, and despite her large breasts, she was on the skinny side. He wondered how she managed to stay thin considering how much she'd eaten at dinner.

"So you're not gay after all?" She cocked her head and smiled, reaching her uncuffed hand in the direction of Trent's crotch.

He caught the hand by the wrist before it could do any damage. "Oh, I am very definitely gay, but if I weren't, I still wouldn't touch you."

He really wished he had a third hand right now. He didn't know how to cuff her hands together while keeping hold of the gun. Must be in the advanced class, next season on *Burn Notice*.

At least her legs were immobilized with him sitting on them. He put the gun down on the bed, wedged under his thigh, and reached forward to thread the free cuff between the rails of the brass headboard. He snapped it shut on Caterina's left hand.

Whew. Trent wasn't quite sure how he managed to restrain her, but he had. He double-checked that both cuffs were shut, then retrieved the gun and got off the bed. He made sure she couldn't reach the phone, and brought her suitcase into the suite's main room, where Felton snored rhythmically on the couch, oblivious to everything around him.

"Trent!" Caterina shouted. "*Lasciami! Lasciami! Aiutami!*" *Let me go! Help*, Trent guessed from his Italian lessons.

Fuck! Even in this luxurious suite, if she raised her voice much louder, someone might hear. He dug into her suitcase for a suitable gag and came out with some flimsy panties that wouldn't muffle a mouse. He considered using some of Felton's socks or underwear—that would serve her right—but it seemed too cruel a punishment, even for what she'd done to Felton. He settled on a hand towel from the bathroom, which he shoved into her mouth. It did the trick.

Trent raced into his own bedroom, gathered up his belongings, and after checking that Felton was still okay, he slipped out of the suite and down to the hall to the elevator. He couldn't hear Caterina, though he figured sooner or later she'd manage to dislodge the towel. He wanted to be gone by then, but he didn't want to attract attention to himself. He stabbed at the elevator button a few more times, as if that would bring it more quickly, and as soon as it arrived, he got inside. He wheeled his suitcase through the lobby and into the street, bright lights glaring out of the evening. He moved quickly, not looking behind him until he was two blocks away.

Finally, he stopped. He sucked in air. Had he been holding his breath this whole time? He felt weak in the knees and thought he might throw up from pent-up tension. The whole thing with Caterina in the bathroom felt like it had happened in slow motion, as if it took forever, but he knew it was only a few minutes. Blood pounded in his ears, and he felt a little dizzy.

He had to warn Reed! Whoever Caterina had spoken to on the phone knew Reed, traveling as Michael Reade, was heading to Panarea. Trent didn't even know for certain if Reed was going to Panarea. Hell, he didn't even know where Panarea was.

But he knew he had to warn Reed.

He grabbed his cell phone and sent a Reed text saying the first thing that came into his mind:

Don't trust anyone

Time to sit down and think his next step through carefully. Trent glanced around, realizing he was still standing on a street corner in the middle of Rome with dozens of people walking past him, giving him barely a glance despite his wine-stained shirt and disheveled appearance. Just the way he wanted it.

Trent wheeled the suitcase down the first cross street and around another corner before settling into the first café he came across. He ordered a bottle of fizzy water even though he really wanted coffee. The last thing his nerves needed was more caffeine, but he didn't want to look like a stupid American by ordering decaf. He drank half the bottle before he calmed himself enough to take stock of his situation.

Should he call White? He had been the one to arrange for Caterina and the move to the "safe house" at the hotel. What if White was part of the smuggling ring and had sent Reed to a dangerous rendezvous in the middle of nowhere? Felton clearly couldn't be in on it. Trent doubted the man was a good enough actor to pretend to be drugged even if he was in on the game. That still didn't clear White, and even though Trent had known White since Thailand, he still didn't know if he could trust him. Not after finding out White had been in contact with Reed since they'd come back from Bangkok.

If drugs were involved, the amount of money could turn the most honest man into a dangerous criminal.

What would Reed do in a situation like this?

So Trent did exactly what Reed would do, exactly what Reed had done. He decided to go to Panarea.

13

PANAREA'S silhouette grew more distinct as the ferry approached. A few tall, densely wooded peaks loomed over the flatter harbor areas. It was near dusk, and to the west, the sun moved lower, setting the clouds ablaze and warming the surface of the sea with red-gold reflections. A breeze blew across the deck, and Reed shivered. By the time they got to Panarea, it would be dark. He wished he'd gotten his jacket out of the suitcase.

In order to really become the man Elvio Milacio expected to meet: wealthy, a bit flashy and more than a bit shady, Reed had spent a few hours shopping for a new look at the kind of boutiques his cover identity would frequent, and came away with a week's worth of new clothing that Trent would adore. Rich natural fabrics and even the off-the-rack clothing fit him nearly perfectly. Italian designers really *were* all they were cracked up to be, though it pained Reed to admit he'd noticed. The impeccably suited guy in the second shop nearly burst into tears when Reed said he didn't have time to wait to have each piece altered. Despite Reed's usual animosity for clothes shopping, he admitted he felt like a different person as he tried on the clothes suggested for him. They accentuated his best features and minimized flaws—though the boutique guy had said he was nearly the ideal. Reed wondered what the guy would have thought of Trent.

Reed had needed to dye his hair again in the airport men's room, where he'd also changed into new clothes and camouflaged his suitcase. Out of habit, he traveled with several suitcase covers, which could easily be used to turn a black suitcase into a red one, at least temporarily. Anyone who saw Michael Reade enter the men's room would not have recognized him emerge with a different suitcase, different clothing, and nearly black hair. Reed couldn't find the right shade at the airport drug store, but it beat being a redhead—the other available color—which didn't suit his coloring. Training and experience taught him mismatched hair and skin tone called unwanted attention to one's appearance. Even in a world where men and women routinely dyed their hair for fashion, a bad dye job was particularly noticeable. Unless he went undercover as a punk, and he most definitely was not trying to move in those circles. He needed to appear wealthy and unobtrusive, blend in with his all-new designer clothing. Trent would have loved that shopping trip.

Despite the new wardrobe, he wore the one item Reed kept of his own clothing, a shirt Trent had given him, which fit Reed's new image perfectly. Again Reed's thoughts turned to Trent. More specifically, to the many times they'd gone shopping in LA. Reed detested shopping, but Trent had an unnatural enthusiasm for the pastime. It was only when Reed complained to Beth, Trent's best friend, that he understood why.

"New shirt, Reed?" Beth had asked one day while they were waiting for Trent to arrive in some trendy eatery he'd been raving about since it opened. A dumpling restaurant. Back in Asia they were all over the fucking place, but in LA they acted like they'd invented the concept. It had taken three weeks to get a reservation, and now Trent was uncharacteristically late, given that he had made the arrangements.

"Yeah. From Stag Rag or Douchebag or something like that." He looked down at his clothing and frowned.

Beth laughed. "You mean Square Peg?"

"Maybe. I never remember the name of shops or restaurants. But it's near that florist over on Melrose, by the place with the fancy tea."

Beth grinned. "You can't remember the name of the shop but you can tell me everything else that's on the block?"

Reed shrugged. "I'm used to Asia still, I guess. There people go more by directions and landmarks than by names. Locals do, not tourists. Tourists always want addresses."

"That's so interesting. I hadn't really thought of all the ways it's different, the little things which make every place unique."

"It's all about the little things. A lot of the big things are depressingly similar."

"Oh." Beth let out a sigh. "But the shirt looks great on you."

"Well, Trent picked it out."

"You don't like it?"

"It's fine. It's nice. I didn't need a new shirt." He glanced down at the shirt again, the soft, smooth fabric that clung to his shape more than he generally liked and not particularly practical. Plus, it was mint green. "I just don't really shop, you know. Don't buy stuff much."

"Yeah, I know." She looked him in the eye and gave a nervous little shrug. "I guess given your old job, you were undercover a lot or running around. But this is LA and…."

"And I'm supposed to look presentable?" Reed hated doing anything just because it was expected of him. He'd spent his life avoiding expectations, sometimes paying for it in other ways, but he didn't see any reason to change now.

"That's not what I was going to say." She paused and sipped at a fancy cocktail garnished with three different kinds of vegetables, one of which Reed had never seen before. "It's more that your life has changed, and you're in a place with a lot of luxuries and convenience. Why not enjoy them? You've earned some relaxation after the kind of work you used to do."

She had a point, but Reed didn't feel like he deserved the luxuries. He hadn't earned them, and he wasn't entirely comfortable with Trent providing so much. "I like the color, though," he added, although even to him it sounded lame and ungrateful.

"You seem to be the kind of guy who'd go out and kill his food, but around here there are restaurants and supermarkets everywhere. You don't have to keep doing things the way you always have. You're in a rut almost as much as Trent was before his trip. Before he met you."

"A rut?" Reed considered what Beth had said. He had found it difficult to adjust to life in LA, to life with Trent. To *Trent's* life. It was so different from what Reed thought he'd be doing or how he'd be living. "Trent's changed a lot?"

"Oh, God, yeah. He's got so many ideas for books, and he's got a spark back. His characters are so much more alive, now that he's really living again." She took another sip of her drink. "It's because of you."

Reed finished his beer and ordered another with a wave of his hand. He watched Beth lick sugar from around the rim of her glass. He liked the way she didn't seem to be self-conscious about enjoying herself.

"I don't know if you realize, but that shirt—" she pointed "—it's Trent's way of saying thank you. He can't possibly express how grateful he is for having you in his life. Giving gifts is one thing he can do. He doesn't like *shopping*. He likes giving gifts. It just looks like shopping."

The bartender put a fresh beer down in front of Reed, and he nodded before picking up the bottle. He took a long drag at the cool, refreshing liquid and let it ice its way down his throat as he turned over Beth's comments in his head. It made sense. All of Trent's little surprises and gifts, the way he always asked Reed if he wanted this or that item when they were out, was just part of Trent giving back.

Not that Reed thought he deserved as much as Trent wanted to give. He'd pushed away Trent's gifts or hid them, not wanting to wear the clothes or the fancy watch and chafing at Trent's fussing. Reed never wanted to be a kept man, and Trent's generosity made him feel like some sort of courtesan. He'd begun to resent taking anything from Trent, and it wasn't until Beth explained that Reed understood Trent wasn't trying to control him or keep him in a box. Trent just didn't know how to express his feelings toward Reed any better than Reed could understand Trent's meaning.

Ironic, since Trent was the writer. A *romance* writer. It had never dawned on Reed that Trent could write dialogue for his characters better than he could think of what to say in his own life. As everything fell into place, Reed's heart fluttered, partly in fear he'd offended Trent by not wanting all these *things* and partly with deeper feelings than he already felt for Trent.

Now he understood why Trent loved Beth so much. And he knew he wanted to spend more time with her to get to know her—and Trent—better.

"Oh, here he is." Beth startled Reed out of his musings.

He looked toward the bar entrance to see Trent coming in, a head taller than nearly everyone else, the usual eager grin on his face, his backpack slung over one shoulder. Reed's heart melted a little now that he saw Trent in a different light, though he berated himself for not figuring it out on his own.

"Hey, guys, sorry I'm late, I was just totally into this chapter and I didn't realize what time it was and—"

Reed interrupted Trent's characteristic run-on greeting by kissing him full on the mouth, pulling him close by a tug at one elbow. Trent's eyes widened, but he relaxed into the kiss. Reed let his tongue explore Trent's lips and push inside, and he heard Trent let out a little sigh. Reed kissed long enough to convey how glad he was to see Trent, and then a bit longer.

"Whoa, that's a helluva greeting," Trent said once Reed let go of him and he caught his breath. "Almost makes me want to skip dinner."

Beth punched Trent, but she caught Reed's eye and gave him a knowing smile and a quick wink. "Better not, because I'm starving."

"And it's all about you?" Trent teased.

"Me too. We've been waiting to get a reservation here for ages." Reed surprised himself, but the words sort of slipped out on their own. When he saw the expression of surprise and happiness on Trent's face, Reed realized he'd meant what he'd just said. Somehow he'd learned something not only about Trent, but about himself.

"Yeah, we have. But I didn't think you paid attention to things like that." Trent cocked his head slightly as he spoke.

"I do." Reed grinned at Trent, then gave Beth a little wink of gratitude.

The meal was one of the best Reed had eaten, and he'd wondered whether it was because the food was so delicious and well prepared or if it were something else. He'd gone to the men's room and was washing his hands when he saw Trent looming behind him in the mirror. Reed turned.

"What's up with you?" Trent asked, clearly not there to use the facilities.

"What do you mean?" Reed tossed the towel—a small one embroidered with the restaurant's logo—into a wicker basket on the counter.

"That kiss. Saying how great the food is. Not rolling your eyes whenever Mick opens his mouth. Where's Reed Acton?"

"Can't I be happy to see you or in a good mood?" Reed leaned against the marble countertop and stared at Trent. Usually Reed and Mick, one of Trent's closest friends, got along like oil and water, but tonight even Mick's presence—he'd invited himself along to dinner unasked—hadn't dampened Reed's enjoyment. He'd really only had eyes for Trent.

"Sure, but I don't want to get too used to it." Trent looked around and seemed nervous.

"Don't worry." Reed moved close and put his arms around Trent. He brushed his lips against Trent's cheek, then kissed his mouth softly when Trent didn't pull away.

This time, Trent gave in to the kiss and wrapped his arms around Reed.

Reed felt himself responding to Trent. "Want some privacy?"

"Yeah."

Reed took Trent's hand and led him into one of the stalls. It was more like a small private room. Reed decided he liked overpriced restaurants—they had such nice bathrooms.

Trent shut the door behind them and wrapped himself around Reed, their mouths coming together in a rough, deep kiss.

"We've never done this before…," Trent said against Reed's lips.

"I wonder why not."

Trent undid Reed's belt and pants and slipped them down his hips. He slid down Reed's body, tugging his shorts down, freeing Reed's cock.

"Mmm." Reed watched Trent take his cock into his mouth, felt the warm wet suction overwhelming his senses.

Trent grabbed Reed's ass with both hands and took him deep, throat working.

Reed didn't bother to hold back. "Now…."

Their gazes locked, Trent looking up, eyes wide beneath his long lashes.

As he came, Reed threaded his fingers through Trent's soft hair. He closed his eyes and let his body carry him through. When he opened them again, Trent knelt, looking up, licking his lower lip.

A tiny drop of come trickled down Trent's chin, and Reed leaned down and kissed it away.

"That was quick." There was more than a hint of disappointment in Trent's tone.

"Your turn."

"I thought you were going to fuck me in here…."

"I don't want to fuck you." Reed tugged at Trent's chin until he stood.

"You don't?"

"Yeah. I do." Reed kissed Trent hard, slipping his hand into Trent's pants and feeling his cock harden. "But not here. At home, when we've got lots of time."

"Then it's not fucking." Mischief flashed again in Trent's eyes.

Reed slid to his knees and tugged open Trent's button-fly jeans.

Pop. Pop. Pop.

"Where did you learn so much about fucking?"

Trent's cock sprang free. "I had a very good teacher." With that, Trent put one hand on Reed's head and pulled him close, the other hand guiding his cock between Reed's lips.

Clearly Trent was a very fast learner. He gave Reed a moment to adjust, then began to slide his cock farther in.

Reed reached between Trent's legs and cupped his balls, noticing that Trent closed his eyes. He rocked back and forth, hips stuttering as he fucked Reed's mouth. After a few gentle strokes, he increased intensity, and Reed's head smacked against the wall. Trent repositioned his hand between Reed and the wall and kept going.

Reed relaxed his jaw and throat and took as much of Trent as he could. He loved the feel of the hard flesh pressing against his lips, the smell of Trent, a combination of his crazy bodywash and his own pure essence. Soft moans morphed into breathless grunts, and Trent's grip on Reed's head tightened.

"Reed. Reed." Trent pulled most of the way out, and hot jets of come shot against the back of Reed's throat.

Reed held on to Trent's hips, sucking in more of his cock, careful not to let anything spill on his new shirt. Trent's cock continued to spasm in Reed's mouth as, above him, Trent groaned and shuddered. When the last tremor passed, Trent pulled out. Reed wiped the back of his hand across his lips, then took Trent's cock into his mouth for one last cleansing suck before pulling Trent's boxers and pants back up.

They checked each other's clothing, making sure everything was correctly buttoned and buckled before leaving the stall and washing up at the sink.

When they got back to their table, Beth flashed a bashful smile, but Mick's usual smirk deepened.

"Gee, that was subtle, guys."

"Shut up, Mick," Trent shot back as he sat down, grinning at Reed.

This was new. It wasn't the wittiest rejoinder, but Trent never stood up to Mick's taunts, so it took on epic proportions. Reed liked this new version of Trent, daring, sexy, and confident.

He couldn't wait till they got home that night.

As Reed remembered that night, he felt closer to Trent, even as he moved farther away in reality. He'd be on Panarea soon, planning his meeting with Elvio Milacio and looking for Peter and Brett. For the moment, Reed could relax and enjoy himself, experiencing the journey as Trent might see it.

Was Trent thinking of Reed right now, or enjoying a night out on the town in Rome?

Reed chuckled out loud at the unexpected reversal of roles.

Trent was in good hands with White's team.

TRENT couldn't get a flight to Sicily that night, and he was leery of flying anyway because he needed to show his passport. Instead, he took an overnight train. He would arrive at nearly the same time as a morning flight, with little or no risk of Caterina and her phone buddy tracing his movements. He made sure to pay for everything in cash, just for that reason.

Little did he realize train travel in Italy rarely resembled the timetables. His journey was fine until Napoli, when some mechanical problem caused a delay. Intent on reaching Reed as quickly as possible, Trent asked at the ticket window about getting on the next train to Milazzo.

"*Certo*. The 23:01 has room in a sleeper car."

Five minutes to go. Trent could run and make it.

"Great." Trent shoved a handful of euros at the ticket window, grabbed his ticket, and ran for the platform, arriving only to find the train already departing.

He ran toward a railway worker on the platform.

"What happened? The train left early?" He pointed to the clock, 11:00 PM, and to his ticket, 23:01.

"*No. No. Non si preoccupi, signore.*" Don't worry! "That was the 20:00 train. The 23:01 will be here at two o'clock. You have plenty of time." The man gave Trent a kindly smile and a reassuring pat on the shoulder.

Fuck. He had three hours to wait. Thankfully, the 23:01 arrived slightly earlier than expected. The journey—mostly uneventful—culminated in an interesting train-to-ferry transfer between the Italian mainland and the Sicilian gateway port of Messina, where the train drove right onto the ferry and off again when it arrived in Sicily. It was well past noon before Trent managed to get to his final destination: the harbor in Milazzo, on the north coast of Sicily.

He hadn't slept a wink overnight and had to make his exhausted way across town from the train station to the ferry.

Trent lucked out, because the day's last hydrofoil to the Aeolian Islands hadn't yet departed when he eventually arrived at the port. He'd resisted the urge to call Reed to give him another warning—or just to hear his voice—because his cell phone or Reed's might be bugged. Could they do that? Trent had no idea, but he wouldn't take the chance. He'd tell Reed everything once they were together in person so no one could intercept his messages.

He still had to take a slower ferry from Lìpari to the final destination of Panarea. At least he was closer.

The clerk who sold him the ferry ticket suggested a private hydrofoil would be much faster than the ferry. While Trent most definitely was in a hurry, he needed to avoid making such a big splash on arrival. Michael Westen would advise arriving like a local so as not to draw particular attention.

The journey to Lìpari, the largest of the set of volcanic islands, took a little over thirty minutes, past the closest island, Vulcano, as late-season tourists rushed to the port side to get their first glimpse of the magical scenery.

After another awe-inspiring journey Trent was too worried to enjoy, he finally arrived on tiny Panarea. He glanced at the guidebook, too keyed up to take in anything but that Panarea was famous because years ago, Ingrid Bergman and her director-lover Roberto Rossellini had lived here during the filming of *Stromboli* and started a famous love affair. Of course, the romance of the place would be lost on Reed.

Trent would tell him all about it later on. After everyone was safe and sound.

Trent had no problem believing the actress and director could fall in love in this locale. It was lovely, or so he thought as the ferry approached the dock at one end of the tiny island. As soon as he got off, he promptly reversed his opinion, at least of the degree of peacefulness.

A small crowd of noisy touts shouted at the passengers, offering them food, rooms, transportation, and perhaps other entertainment and amenities, in a variety of languages.

Would Reed have let one of these people take him to a room? Probably not. Should he look for Reed now or play it cool, take a room, then hope to "run into" Reed later on? He didn't remember the details of whatever cover story Reed was using. All he knew was Michael Reade was traveling here, and Trent wasn't the only one looking for him, given what he'd overheard Caterina tell her co-conspirator.

What a great word, Trent thought, the writer in him edging out the would-be spy persona. He'd write it down and use it in a book soon. Just the word itself—co-conspirator—gave him plot ideas, and he forced himself to focus on the present.

"You want a room, signore?" A small child with short-chopped dark hair and huge brown eyes, not obviously a boy or a girl, tugged at his elbow.

"Trent!"

He turned at the sound of his name to see Reed rushing toward the harbor area.

Trent's pulse raced, then slowed to a more normal rhythm. Thank God Reed looked okay. At least Caterina and whomever she had called hadn't found him yet. Trent was in time. He grinned at Reed, hoping to see a glimmer of his own relief and joy mirrored in Reed's expression.

A scowl spread over Reed's face.

He certainly didn't look happy to see Trent. Not happy at all.

14

"TRENT, what are you doing here?" Reed pulled Trent aside, away from the little throng at the pier and over toward the ferry ticket office.

He'd been expecting Peter to arrive on Panarea by now, and hoped he'd be on this ferry. Trent showing up was the absolute last thing Reed needed right at the moment. He glanced at the final few passengers straggling from the ferry. No sign of Peter. Reed wasn't sure whether he was relieved—or more concerned. He turned his gaze back to Trent.

"I had to warn you, Reed. But at least you're okay."

"Warn me about what?" Reed stopped before he let loose what he'd really been thinking. Trent could be sensitive, and after what had happened in Rome, Reed was on eggshells.

"Not here." Trent's shoulders sagged a little, and Reed could see the strain at the corners of his mouth. That cute little smile had been an act on Trent's part, but Reed realized Trent was afraid.

Trent looked around, eyes darting from one direction to the next. Now Reed felt uncomfortable and had to restrain himself from looking around too.

"I'll tell you somewhere private," Trent said softly.

"Fine. Come to my hotel."

Reed turned on his heel and headed in that direction. He'd gone a few steps before he realized Trent wasn't right behind him. He looked back to see Trent struggling with his suitcase over the rough cobbled surface of the small harbor area. The sight brought back memories of an almost identical moment in Thailand, and despite his annoyance at Trent showing up in the middle of this job, Reed felt his heart tighten.

He went back and took the suitcase from Trent, brushing his fingers across Trent's in the process. He could see the immediate reaction as Trent's drawn face brightened and one corner of his mouth turned up. Reed wanted to put his arms around Trent, but that wasn't such a good idea just yet. He hadn't sized up how this little town would take that, nor had he figured out where Trent fit into his cover.

It took only five minutes along the main path to get the hotel. Trent looked around at the place, a small, fairly modern one-story building, not quite as glamorous as the enormous Best Western—undoubtedly the most beautiful in the hotel's chain—around the corner, but still holding its own on the chic and expensive island, and followed Reed to the last room, farthest from the front desk.

Once inside, Trent waited for Reed to shut the door behind them and rushed up and squeezed him in a smothering bear hug. Reed didn't attempt to break loose until he needed to breathe. He hadn't realized how much he'd craved Trent's touch until just this moment.

"I'm fine. Just fine." Reed turned around so Trent could see him from all sides. "Nothing's happened. But what's got you so spooked?"

Trent stepped back and took a deep breath. A torrent of words erupted, and Reed experienced Trent's pent-up emotion as if he'd been blown across the room by a bomb.

"Whoa. Trent, slow down. You're not making any sense." Reed took Trent's arm and led him to the bed. "Sit down. Let me get you some water. It's going to be okay. Really, it is."

Trent chewed on his bottom lip and looked up at Reed from the edge of the bed. Reed's stomach knotted. This was not good. Trent wouldn't have come here except for something deadly serious, no matter how upset he was with Reed for taking a mission in the middle of their vacation. Seeing Trent in this state didn't help Reed focus on work. It tore at him to see Trent so upset. No, scared. Trent was *scared*.

Reed grabbed a bottle of water from the refrigerator located behind a bar in the far corner of the room. He didn't even care how much they were going to charge him for the water.

"Drink this, then talk." Reed tossed the bottle to Trent.

Trent opened his mouth to talk, but Reed waved his hand dismissively. "Water first."

Trent nodded and cracked open the bottle, then drained it in two huge swigs. Reed watched Trent's Adam's apple bobbing as he sucked down the cool liquid. When Trent finished drinking, one shiny wet droplet clung to his chin, and Reed fought off the urge to brush it away. He sensed Trent had to talk, and it would be important. But touching him now, in Trent's state of distress and Reed's sudden need to comfort Trent, would certainly lead to more than just a conversation, and there simply wasn't time to indulge in that at the moment.

Reed sat down near Trent on the bed, close enough that Trent would feel comfortable, but not so close to be distracting.

"What happened in Rome? You were supposed to be at the safe house White arranged, not coming after me here."

"There's a mole."

"A mole?" Reed took a slow, deep inhalation. Trent's little obsession with spies had gone past being quirky and cute. As much as it pained him, Reed was going to have to put his foot down now or risk Trent interfering in everything. But something had happened, however innocent, and Trent must have blown it out of proportion. Reed bit his own lip to stop from saying what he thought and decided to let Trent explain first. Just in case.

"Yes. It's Caterina, the woman from the Carabinieri art team."

"And what makes you think she's a mole? A mole in the Carabinieri?"

"No. In White's team. It might be bigger than just her." Trent unleashed another stream of words.

"How about if you start from the beginning?" Reed checked his watch. It was hours before dinner, and he wasn't hungry. He suspected Trent hadn't eaten anything that day. "Let me just call the desk and see if they can bring us some food."

"Food. Yeah. Food." Trent let out a sigh.

Reed walked to the small battered desk and picked up the phone. It was immediately answered, somewhat of a surprise given the tiny hotel and the laid-back atmosphere of the island. Still, it was luxury accommodations, and Reed got what he paid for.

"Can we get something to eat here in Room 8? I don't care what. Enough for two people?"

"*Sì, signore*. Some nice fish or local seafood? Pasta?"

"Sure, that sounds good. And some beer, please?"

"*Sì, signore*. About twenty minutes?"

"Thanks. *Grazie*." Reed put the phone down and returned to Trent on the bed. "Twenty minutes. Why don't you get started while we're waiting?"

Trent nodded. His eyes still looked dark and hollow, but he seemed to have relaxed.

"I went to the safe house, which is really a suite in the Grand Hotel on Via Veneto. A really nice suite. Two bedrooms and a big living room. Oh, Reed, it was even nicer than our room at the d'Inghilterra. They had this gorgeous Carrara marble in the bathrooms. And Bulgari bodywash."

"Trent, this isn't an interview for *House Beautiful* or a Conde Nast magazine feature article."

"Ooh, I didn't even know you'd ever heard of Conde Nast. Or *House Beautiful*, for that matter." Trent gave a brief smile. "Bulgari bodywash, Reed. Imagine."

Reed relaxed a bit. If Trent could joke around, it couldn't be that bad. Trent was the only guy Reed knew who could get a hard-on talking about bodywash. Reed fought the urge to look in the direction of Trent's dick.

"Well, the suite happens to be important, if you'd let me explain," Trent said with more snark than Reed expected.

"Explain." Reed made an encouraging gesture, hoping he wouldn't have to hear about marble or bodywash again.

"So they took me to the hotel. Caterina and some FBI guy called Felton."

"Jim Felton? I know him."

Trent looked away for a moment, examining his shoes, then the doorknob before turning his gaze back to Reed.

What was that about?

"So, Caterina is the Carabinieri contact?"

"Yeah. The mole."

"One step at a time."

"Fine. We got to the hotel suite. I was really mad because I didn't want to have some babysitters watching me." Trent looked a little guilty at his admission, but it wasn't exactly news to Reed. Or to White. Or to Felton and Caterina, most likely. "And she orders some dinner and some expensive wine."

"I'm still not seeing any suspicious activity unless she ordered red wine with fish or something."

"You're not taking this seriously!"

Reed refrained from mentioning Trent's bodywash tangent. "You haven't said anything that worries me."

"You're the one who said one step at a time, and then when I do, you complain." Trent got up and crossed his arms over his chest, then started pacing the room.

Reed watched him go back and forth and around the end of the bed, then back and forth and around the end of the bed. Damn, that was annoying. Reed liked to pace, but he hadn't realized how fucking irritating it must be to everyone else. He'd have to stop doing that.

Trent stopped pacing and stared at Reed. "And while I was in my room, pretending to write, I was listening to Caterina and Felton talking. And Felton—" He stopped and put a hand to his mouth.

Reed waited to hear what Felton did or said, because now maybe it was getting good.

Trent pulled himself up his full height and sat back on the bed. "They were just talking, and Felton was drinking wine, and then he fell asleep. Only it was because she drugged the wine."

"Trent, seriously?"

"He shouldn't have been drinking, and they were making out, and he fell asleep in the middle of it."

"Wait. You skipped over the making out part before. Get back to that."

"Sure, *now* you're interested."

"Trent, calm down. You're not making sense."

There was a soft knock at the door. "*Signore*, your meal."

Reed glanced at Trent and put a hand on his shoulder as he stood to open the door, hoping to calm Trent down.

He took a heavy tray from the young man at the door and put it inside on the desk, then fished in his pocket for his wallet. "How much is it?"

The man handed him a scribbled restaurant bill that said "20 euro," and Reed paid him, plus another two five-euro notes. "One for you and one for the restaurant. Thank you." The man nodded and smiled as he accepted the money.

"Twenty euros for all this. Is that a good price?" Reed asked as he closed the door.

Trent was just lifting the lid off the tray to discover it was certainly worth the price. There was a platter of pasta heaped with shrimp and calamari rings in a light sauce with chunks of tomato and flecks of fresh herbs. It smelled divine. Reed's stomach rumbled in anticipation.

The second platter was grilled fresh fish, and a third held herb-covered grilled vegetables. Two large bottles of Patruni e Sutta, probably a local Sicilian beer, completed the meal.

Reed watched Trent scoop forkfuls of pasta and seafood into his mouth and make little sounds of pleasure and appreciation as he chewed. Normally a polite and careful eater, Trent practically shoveled pasta in, another sign of his anxiety.

"When was the last time you ate?"

"Dinner last night."

No wonder he'd scarfed down the pasta.

"Caterina ordered some huge Roman feast. I couldn't even think about food until about ten minutes ago."

Reed didn't feel quite so bad about Trent's ordeal after all. He'd been eating better than Reed.

Only after Trent had eaten about half the food on his plate did Reed open the beer. He needed Trent with a clear head, but he admitted he really wanted some of that ice-cold beer himself.

Trent carefully wiped the mouth of the bottle on his sleeve before he took a sip. Now that was back to normal. Reed smiled.

"That was good. Really good. How do they take such simple ingredients and make it taste so incredible? I wish I could cook like this."

Reed wished Trent could cook like this too. They'd save a lot of money at overpriced LA restaurants if he could. Trent did love to eat well, and Reed had recently discovered how much he enjoyed going to restaurants with him, as much for Trent's enjoyment as his own.

Trent gulped down some more beer then looked around the room. "This is some place you've got here."

"I'm undercover as a crook with a huge bank account. Room's part of the cover." Reed followed Trent's gaze as he took in the bright, spacious room filled with top-quality modern furnishings. Trent got up and wandered over to the floor-to-ceiling windows and let himself out onto the balcony.

"Holy fuck!" Trent was clearly at a loss for words at the exquisite view. Reed followed him out and let himself again be delighted at the panorama of teal-colored waters, dotted here and there with deadly volcanic rocks and eye-blindingly white-sailed boats. This was the playground of the rich and famous, and the even richer.

"What do you think of that?" Reed pointed toward a massive smooth black mountain rising out from the ocean to the north.

"Stromboli." Trent's voice held more than a note of awe at the sight.

"Stromboli," Reed echoed. He had to admit, the sight was incredible no matter how many times he saw it. There was a thick plume of white smoke floating out of the crater. It was the most active volcano in Europe, and only about twenty kilometers away. But he didn't have time to enjoy the scenery or the room right now. "Feeling better?"

"Yeah. Okay, let me get back to why I'm here in the first place." Trent took another long glance at the view and let out a sigh as he went back inside and resumed his seat on the bed. Reed sat on the armchair a few feet away.

Trent swigged some more beer and let out an uncustomary belch. His cheeks reddened slightly. "Oh, sorry. Excuse me."

Reed wanted to laugh but knew Trent wouldn't appreciate the amusement. "Sure, you left off at the making out…."

"Right. So Felton and Caterina were on the couch." An odd faraway look came over Trent's features again for a split second, but he continued. "She was kind of, you know, whispering in his ear. I couldn't hear what, but being all come-hither."

"Trent, you write erotic romance. Why are you getting all shy with describing this scene?"

Trent shrugged, then laughed. "I don't know. I guess when I write it's about strangers where I'm making it up. I don't usually watch real people do this stuff. Unless it's porn, with you."

Reed felt his own cheeks heat up a bit. Trent could talk about porn more easily than he could handle belching in front of Reed. Poor guy was absolutely mortified if he farted.

"So why were you eavesdropping in the first place?"

Trent took on that deer-caught-in-the headlights look again. *What on earth did he overhear?*

"I wasn't originally eavesdropping. I went to go get some more food to bring into my room, but I saw what they were doing, and just sort of watched." Trent slowly twirled pasta on his fork and skewered a shrimp before plunging the whole thing into his mouth. He chewed carefully, probably trying to keep Reed from asking more embarrassing questions. Finally, he stopped chewing, swallowed, and continued. "She kept refilling his wineglass but barely sipping at her own."

Reed nodded, silently begging Trent to get to the fucking point.

"Then Felton just fell asleep."

"And what makes you think she drugged the wine?"

"Reed, he was all over her. She's really…." He made curvy gestures around his chest. "I mean, there was no way in hell Felton was gonna drink too much and miss out on whatever Caterina was whispering about…."

Reed chuckled. "Still, you saw him drink a lot."

"No. I only saw him take a few sips. Then she kept saying, 'Finish this and we can go to bed.' He took one sip and boom."

"Boom?"

"But that's not the important part."

"It's not? After all the lead-up, you haven't even gotten to the important part?" Reed picked up his bottle of beer so he wouldn't be tempted to grab Trent and shake the words out of him.

"It's what she did after he passed out."

Reed stared at Trent, afraid speaking would interrupt this painfully drawn-out and seemingly pointless tale.

"She didn't try to wake him up. Didn't ask if he was okay. She grabbed her phone and called someone. She told the person that you were on your way here."

"What?" Now Trent had Reed's full attention.

"She called someone and said 'He's traveling to Panarea.' And she said your name. Michael Reade. I couldn't understand the rest of it, 'cause she was speaking Italian."

"How do you know you understood that much?"

"Because I can understand those words. And I can understand your name. And when you put those together, right after a guy passes out, it can't be good."

"No argument with you on that."

"Finally." Trent crossed his arms again and glared at Reed.

"I'm sorry I doubted you." Reed put his hand on top of Trent's and squeezed it. "But why didn't you just tell White?"

TELL White? Reed's oversimplified suggestion made Trent's blood boil. He wanted to knock Reed over the head with that damned beer bottle. Reed's prodding about the eavesdropping made it worse. Why hadn't Trent just mentioned Caterina's mysterious warning phone call and skipped over the rest? He would rather die than admit what he overheard Felton tell Caterina about Reed and Peter back when they were partners.

Worse, Trent wanted to know more of that story, but he couldn't ask Reed about it. And Reed would be embarrassed not just that Trent knew, but that Felton was flapping his gums about Reed's personal life.

"So you got away?" Thankfully, Reed tried another tack when Trent didn't reply.

"Yeah. I overpowered Caterina and tied her up. Then I ran like hell out of that hotel."

"You overpowered Caterina?" Reed's tone bordered on incredulity, and he made a sound that might have been the start of a laugh.

"Yes, I did."

"A trained Carabinieri soldier? You do know that's the military police, not the library squad."

"She had the gun with her in the bathroom. It helped. But I could have done it anyway. She was naked."

"Naked? You overpowered a naked woman with her own gun? In the bathroom? Good work."

Trent squinted as he assessed Reed's remark. Had he meant it ironically?

"Fuck you, Reed. I could have been in danger. I wanted to get away to warn *you* that you definitely were in danger."

"No. I meant that. It's how they train us, get people in vulnerable situations and use whatever you can find against them. But how did she end up naked? Did you offer to take Felton's place? Because that would probably earn you a commendation if you did." Reed was grinning.

"Ha-fucking-ha. Don't you care about her being a mole?"

Reed stopped laughing. "Yes, Trent, I do care. But I'm still not convinced it's as serious as you've made it out to be.

"Well, what could she be up to?"

"First off, she was talking in Italian, right?"

"Yeah...."

"So she was talking to someone Italian, or she'd use English."

"Okay. But how does that change anything?"

"I'm still thinking it's got to do with the auction and the antiquities. The Carabinieri enforce the export restrictions, make sure everything has a permit, or recapture items illegally exported, in cooperation with other governments, like the US."

"And?"

"She may only be guilty of working with someone to get around the permit system, and she's warning them."

"But she said you were coming here. So the person is here."

Reed inhaled slowly, clearly turning the thought over. Trent waited patiently.

"Okay. Those are good points."

Mentally, Trent did a little touchdown dance. He hoped he didn't actually wiggle his butt, but he sure felt like doing it for real.

Reed continued. "But there's one key piece of information you don't have: I'm not traveling as Michael Reade here."

"You're not?"

"No. White gave me a new cover. I'm Richard—Rick—Allen now. So don't forget that." Reed gave Trent a serious stare.

"Rick Allen." Trent nodded, returning the stare.

"But his concern about cover identities only serves to reinforce the conclusions you so easily jumped to. He suspected a mole."

Trent fought the urge to "humpfh" by reminding himself Reed believed the theory of a mole, even if he didn't take it as a personal threat.

Reed got up and started pacing. "Something isn't right about this whole mission."

"Like what?"

"I haven't figured it out yet. I'm still not clear why White let you come here instead of contacting me himself or through another agent? Is he worried the regular channels have been compromised?"

"I didn't talk to White. I was afraid to talk to him again. Caterina's the local liaison, so they were supposed to run everything through her and her department, right?"

Reed nodded.

"So she could have been giving away details about Peter and Brett. But it might also involve someone on the US side. Or maybe she bugged White's phones or office. I couldn't take the chance White would be in danger too."

"So you just ran away and came here?"

"I didn't run away. I *escaped*." Trent wanted to make the distinction abundantly clear to the ever-skeptical Reed. "But yeah, directly here. I took the train because I know they check your passport when you fly. Caterina would be able to track my movements. So I took the train—and I used cash—so she can't trace me, right?"

"Right." Reed cocked his head slightly and stared at Trent.

Trent smiled. Had he done something right this time? Reed's expression held more respect than it had when he'd first shown up. Trent had been so worried and hungry that nothing he'd said made sense. No wonder Reed had doubted him.

He'd come here to make sure Reed was okay.

And maybe those little niggles about Reed and Peter had something to do with it, but Trent hoped not much.

"So now what?"

"You passed the message on, and I'll figure out how to get in touch with White. But you're getting right back on the next ferry or hydrofoil leaving this island."

That wasn't what Trent wanted to hear.

"You just came here to tell me I was in danger, right?"

"Yeah."

"So what makes you think I want you around for that? I want you as far away from danger as possible."

"And that safe house with the babysitters was so fucking safe? What could happen to me here?"

"You don't want to know. I'll admit the safe house wasn't a good idea, but White had your best interests—and those of the mission—in mind when he suggested it."

"Now you see why I think he might be involved?"

Reed took a deep breath, and Trent steeled himself for an unpleasant response.

"Yes. I understand what you must be thinking."

Not all of it, thankfully. Trent didn't think Reed had guessed at his concerns about Peter. As long as he could keep what he'd overheard from Felton secret, maybe Reed never would. He hated himself for questioning Reed's motives now. But he couldn't stop wondering. Only Reed could set his mind—and heart—at ease.

"Reed, there's one more thing." Trent gnawed at the inside of his mouth. He was afraid for Reed or he wouldn't bring it up.

"What?"

"What if Caterina's working with Peter?"

"How did you come up with that one?"

"Well, he's supposed to be working on this case, right? And he disappears and his own partner doesn't know where to find him."

"I'm not following you."

"Then he turns up after White contacts you. Like he knows he has to make an appearance to keep White from getting suspicious. And he says, 'I'm fine, going off to some hoity-toity island near Sicily to talk to some collector,' and White's fine with that even though Peter didn't give him any details at all. *You* had to figure out who he was going to meet, because he disappeared again." Trent was out of breath when he finally forced the last words out. He stared at his plate and pushed a few stray pieces of pasta around rather than look at Reed and get the killer stare he expected.

"I guess when you put it that way it sounds kind of suspicious."

"So?"

"But that's how these missions are, Trent. White—or whoever the boss is—trusts the guys in the field to do their job with little or no support. Sometimes no progress reports unless they need something or some backup. Remember in Thailand?"

"What about it?"

"I worked on my own. White didn't keep track of my day-to-day activities, and he didn't want to. He knew when the sale went down the locals would be in place because of the agents we had planted."

"Are there other agents planted here?"

"Not as far as I know. But Peter didn't know what he was going to find either."

"So, did you get a lead on him?"

"Not exactly. He told Brett to wait for him here. Supposedly he's on his way from the mainland. I've been meeting every ferry and hydrofoil that arrives."

That explained why Reed was at the harbor when Trent arrived. He tried not to take it personally that Reed had been hoping to see Peter step off the boat. But Reed had brought Trent to his hotel room and fed him. He wasn't trying to avoid Trent in order to find Peter.

"When was he supposed to get here?"

"Brett didn't have specifics. Peter might have taken a private boat, and then I'd have completely missed him. I'm expecting a message from Brett later, one way or the other."

"Where is he?"

"On the island somewhere. We exchanged messages using a drop location. I can't afford to risk meeting him and breaking my cover. He's green and I can't be certain he followed the correct protocols."

Trent nodded. He was dying to ask how they could set up a drop location without prior communication, but he held his tongue.

"It's the tail end of the high season here, and there are plenty of Americans in and out of the area. I asked around after Peter—very carefully—but remember we're supposed to blend in and be unobtrusive. No one should even notice me or anything I do unless I want them to. If either another tourist or a local had noticed either of them, *that* would be more of a problem."

"So how do you find missing agents if you can't ask about them and they are undetectable by the human eye?"

Reed laughed and Trent relaxed a bit. At least Reed hadn't bitten his head off for suggesting Peter was involved. He also hadn't convinced Trent otherwise. He hadn't actually addressed the topic at all. Bad sign. It might mean Reed was suspicious, or he knew more than he wanted to tell Trent. Or he just didn't want to talk to Trent about Peter.

None of those was a good thing as far as Trent was concerned.

15

"So you're going to see this guy who was selling the amphora I bid on in Rome, Milano? Was that his name? How does he fit in?"

"Milacio. I'm not sure yet about him. I've made the first contact, and I'm waiting for him to decide whether or not to meet me. He's probably checking me and my story out. He was on Peter's radar because he's the owner of a few of the suspicious pieces Brett's program flagged."

"Not all of them?"

"No, but several came from the same art dealer, a guy with a shop in Rome and another in Palermo."

"Ah, so that's where Peter was going when he said 'Sicily'?"

"He'd already seen the Palermo dealer, based on his credit card activity. He bought a ferry ticket out of Messina, which is why I'm a little worried he hasn't shown yet."

"But Brett is here? Did he contact Milacio?"

"Not as far as I can tell. And he didn't have any charges here on any of his aliases. But he had notes about Milacio and a few other collectors. This guy just happens to be the most likely, given the last place Peter checked in."

"So tell me about this Milacio guy?"

"He's from a very old Sicilian family. I don't know for sure, but I think their name came from the port town of Milazzo."

"The town where you get on the ferry for these islands?"

"Yeah. His family made its money generations ago with a shipping business. They've expanded over the years, but now Elvio Milacio owns most of it—"

"Elvio?" Trent scooted next to Reed, glancing over his shoulder as he read notes off his phone. "Elvio? Like Elvis?"

"No, like 'Elvio'. I don't know what it means. And he's older, so he couldn't possibly be named after Elvis."

"Sure about that?"

"Even if he was named for Elvis Presley, it has nothing to do with this case, does it?"

Trent shrugged and shook his head.

"So Elvio Milacio still runs the shipping company, with some cousins and a younger sister as minority shareholders. He controls the board but doesn't have much say in day-to-day business. Instead he spends his time in these islands or traveling the world to expand his impressive art collection."

"What kind of stuff does he own?"

Reed flipped through a notebook. "It's pretty broad, and there's not much public information about what he owns, just what he's purchased or sold at public auction. Nothing about his private transactions. But he's well known in the art world and often allows fellow art enthusiasts—especially the rich ones—to view his collection."

"What's the angle for our visit?"

"There is no 'our'. I'm visiting him and you're leaving."

"Oh, please let me come along too? I just got here. I'll be good. Please?" Trent batted his eyes a few times. Sometimes that actually worked.

"Why would I let you come with me?"

This wasn't one of them.

"Because I know a lot about art too. I might see something suspicious you don't notice because you mostly know about Asian art."

"How do you know his collection isn't mostly Asian?"

"Because the piece in Rome was an amphora of the type common to the Roman empire for exports to its colonies. It supposedly came from a wreck lost off the Sicilian coast around 300 BC."

"You read that in the catalog."

"Yes, I did. But I also remembered it and impressed you with my expertise, didn't I?"

"No comment."

Trent grinned in triumph. He was almost there. Now he really did want to meet this Milacio guy.

"How am I going to explain you showing up like this?" Reed asked, shaking his head. "Milacio is only expecting me. He invited me."

"Just tell him I showed up unexpectedly. It's the truth."

Reed turned a low-powered glare on Trent.

"Isn't it best when you're lying to tell at least part truth?" Trent grinned, bordering on smugness. Another gem from Michael Westen and *Burn Notice*.

Reed let out a frustrated noise that might have been a sigh—or a curse word in a language Trent didn't understand. He suspected the latter, but it didn't deter him.

"I'm right…."

"Yes, that's true. He thinks I'm a gallery owner from California who wants to get an idea of his collection to give advice to some of my clients. But just who are you supposed to be?"

"Why can't I be me? The truth is best. I'm just a writer here for some… I don't know, research? I decided to come to these gorgeous islands when you said you were coming. And I'm a huge art fan. I wanted to see his collection too."

"I can't just show up with my boyfriend—"

"Why not? Are you pretending to be straight?" Trent didn't know why that plan annoyed him so much.

"No, Trent. I'm pretending to be a drug dealer pretending to be an art collector."

"Huh?"

"We suspect they're smuggling something—most likely drugs—inside the antiquities. My outer cover is I'm looking to buy art, but I'll throw out some hints that isn't all I'm interested in buying."

"Oh." Maybe there was more to this undercover stuff than Trent thought. It wasn't all that different from what Reed had done in Thailand. Now he understood why White wanted him on this job. "You're going to feel him out to see if he's selling drugs?"

"Yeah, but it has to be low-key, throwing in a specific phrase or jargon a dealer will pick up on. He'll be on his guard if I show up with you. He won't be frank with me. Won't let on he'd like to do business, assuming he's smuggling something."

Trent wasn't ready to give in just yet. "Or… he might relax because you brought me. He'll feel safe, knowing you aren't here to kill him or something. You're shopping, even if it's for drugs—or illegal antiquities—and he won't feel threatened."

Reed lowered the glare to an almost-normal gaze, but he continued to shake his head, muttering under his breath as he paced the room. "Let me think about it."

Trent's mood brightened.

Reed shook his head. "Don't get too excited yet. I haven't made up my mind. I still don't know where this guy fits into the picture. He may be an innocent collector caught in a smuggling scam, or he may be part of it. He may be very dangerous, especially if he detects any hint that I'm an agent."

"I think you'd look a whole lot less like you're investigating anything if you show up with your boyfriend." Trent shrugged and flashed Reed an innocent grin.

"I hate to admit it, but you're right. Where'd you come up with all this common sense all of a sudden?" After a beat, Reed added a soft chuckle, but it was too late.

Trent threw down the backpack with a thud and turned to Reed. "I guess around the time you perfected the backhanded compliment. Which, by the way, you're a real champ at."

Reed had the good sense to look sorry, which he was also pretty good at. "Trent, I didn't mean it that way. Just that lately you seem to have some strange insight I can't explain. Finding me at the auction, getting away from Caterina, coming down here." Reed sat next to Trent on the bed and stroked the back of his arm.

Trent looked away. He wasn't about to admit he'd been boning up on spycraft from *Burn Notice*, but so far it seemed to be a pretty good resource. He stared at the ceiling, letting Reed caress his arm, giving him a chance to make up for the implied insult.

"I'm so glad you wanted to warn me, but after those guys chasing you in Rome and coming to your hotel, I'm worried. We're going to need a cover ID for you too. You can't go in there as Trent Copeland."

"Yeah, I can."

"Trent, Marconi's guys and everyone at the auction house has your name. Whether Caterina is the mole or not, they must've told Milacio you won the amphora. You'll be a dead giveaway and destroy my cover."

"I didn't use my real name at the auction house."

"What?" Reed's eyes widened. Damn, but Trent loved surprising him.

"No. I figured if you could go around being someone else, so could I. I went as J.T. Dallas." Trent suppressed the urge to gloat.

"Your pen name? What about the banking info?"

"J.T. has his own bank account, so I gave that information. If they looked it up the name and account would match."

Reed shook his head, but a smile played across his face. "Good thinking, but they still came to your hotel room."

"I did put that as my local address, but they probably didn't check to see who the room was booked to."

"Let's hope not."

"And no one followed me away from the hotel after Caterina, or from the other hotel. I didn't see anyone tailing me on the ferry. I'm sure you're overreacting."

"I hope so. But with Peter missing and this being the last place he said he was going, you can understand my apprehension."

"I just wish I kept Caterina's phone so we'd know who she was talking to."

"Whom."

"What?"

"'Whom', not 'who'. And it should be 'to whom she was talking'." Reed grinned. "You never get that one right. I'm losing confidence in your writing skills."

"Well, Mr. Critic, you should know by now that dialog is rarely grammatically correct. It doesn't sound natural if you try to make it correct. People talk differently than they write." Trent hated when Reed corrected him, but didn't have enough energy for a full-on lecture about the topic.

"See?"

"See what?"

"You don't like it when I try to tell you how to do your job, do you?"

Trent turned toward Reed and gave a grudging smile. Reed had him on this one. "Touché."

"That's got one of those little accents on the 'e'."

"Fuck you." Trent glared. "And I knew that." He did. Really, he did.

Reed pulled at the fabric of Trent's sleeve, just behind his bicep, where a moment ago he'd been stroking Trent's arm.

Trent let Reed pull him close, and Reed kissed Trent. He let go of the sleeve and slid his hand up until it was at the back of Trent's neck, and pulled Trent in closer, deepening the kiss. Trent's instinct was to pull away because he was still a little annoyed with Reed's attitude, but Reed was such a good kisser that Trent decided to give him the benefit of the doubt.

"Is there time for this?"

"For what?"

"For whatever you're going to do about this." Trent pulled Reed's other hand into his lap and gave him a handful of hard-on.

"Oh, Trent, you are far too easily excited."

"Maybe you're just too exciting. You started it. You kissed me."

Trent turned the pleading look with the raised eyebrows on Reed.

"This is Italy, after all," Reed said. "No one's on time."

"That's *amore*."

16

LATER, after being suitably reunited, Reed took Trent out for dinner, making a short detour to a souvenir shop where he browsed through postcards, selecting one from the lowest section on the rack.

"Who you gonna send that to?" Trent asked as they headed to the restaurant.

"No one." Reed tossed the card away in a trash can once out of sight of the shop.

"I don't get it."

Once seated at the restaurant, Reed explained. "Decker left me a message. Stuck to a postcard on the lowest rack."

Trent gaped.

"Hasn't heard from Peter, though he's been leaving messages in other spots for him. I'm worried something's happened to him."

"What are you going to do?"

"About Peter? Nothing yet. I'm here to meet Milacio. But if I get wind something happened to Peter, I'll have to make a call whether to risk breaking cover to help him."

Despite Trent's quizzing, Reed refused to explain any more about Decker or how they could possibly find each other's messages without speaking or meeting.

Back at the hotel, they discovered Milacio had called and left a message for Reed—rather, for his cover identity—inviting him to lunch at Milacio's residence, and Reed called to confirm.

THE next morning they took quick showers—separately so as not to create additional delay—and dressed for the visit to Milacio's.

Elvio Milacio lived on the other side of the island. Even though Panarea was small, it wasn't an easy matter getting from one area to another. The spectacular mountainous scenery served to make travel as the crow flies an impossibility. Reed called the front desk to arrange a taxi—which turned out to be a golf cart—to take them up the narrow winding road and over the peak to Milacio's home.

"No cars on Panarea," the desk clerk had said. "Except for one or two owned by the 'royalty'."

Apparently, Elvio Milacio was Panarea royalty. That said a hell of a lot, considering Giorgio Armani, Leonardo diCaprio and Madonna were frequent visitors to the island.

The road uphill was steep and curvy. "It's kind of hard to enjoy the beauty of the place when I feel like I'm gonna be carsick." Trent leaned against the backseat of the golf-cart taxi and held onto the safety rail to steady himself.

Their driver seemed more intent on dislodging them than he did on providing a pleasant ride. He sped around hairpin curves that threw either Trent or Reed across the seat, smashing the other against the doors, which creaked and threatened to open and deposit both of them on the side of the forest-lined roads.

The scenery—what Trent was able to take in when he ventured a glance out the window—was spectacular. Punished by the strong sea winds, the trees grew at an angle, their trunks bent like old women.

Reed and Trent emerged from the taxi, with Trent a bit unsteady on his feet as they approached the turquoise-blue wooden door, echoing the jewel-toned waters surrounding the island. The house looked like a larger version of the white cubes he'd seen in the village, again reminding Trent of the rustic homes of the Greek islands. He certainly expected Milacio, some über-wealthy art collector, to have a much grander and more spectacular home, especially up here on what appeared to be a private road at the top of the mountain.

"Let me explain you, okay?" Reed gave Trent a cold glance that did nothing to improve Trent's frame of mind, so he just nodded and then wished he hadn't. "You all right?" Reed's voice softened.

Trent nodded again, giving Reed a silent thumbs-up and a half smile.

"Trent, if you're not okay, you need to let me know and we'll—"

Reed didn't have a chance to finish his thought, because the door opened. Standing inside was a man in his sixties, short, at least compared to Reed and certainly compared to Trent's six feet three-plus inches. He had thick, wavy black hair that made him look younger than his age, though the weathered wrinkles gave away more than the thick hair concealed.

Elvio Milacio had an impressive set of sideburns. Trent mouthed "Elvis!" to Reed, who frowned, but Trent detected a hint of a smile in Reed's thundercloud eyes.

Milacio wore a dark-tan suit and a crisp white shirt, everything impeccably tailored, even his shoes, elegant tan suede flats that Trent recognized as the work of a top Italian designer. He'd been attracted to a similar pair in Rome that cost about six hundred euros. Hand-stitched....

"Signor Milacio, I'm Richard Allen. Call me Rick." Reed's voice broke through Trent's loafer-induced daydream.

"Signor Allen—Rick—how nice to have you visit my home." The man's voice was rich and resonant, full of the slightly higher-pitched tones Trent had grown accustomed to since arriving in Italy. Milacio began to put a hand out toward Reed, then stopped as he noticed Trent on his doorstep.

"I hope it won't be an imposition, but this is—"

"Trent. Trent Copeland," Trent blurted, forgetting he was supposed to use a fake surname. He studiously avoided looking over at Reed's face because he knew the expression he'd find there.

"—my, uh, companion." Reed barely missed a beat in the introduction.

Damn, he was unflappable, Trent thought. But he knew he'd catch hell later, when they were alone.

Milacio held out his hand to Trent. The handshake lasted a few beats longer than entirely necessary as Milacio gave Trent a thorough appraisal that made his skin crawl. He wished Reed had said "boyfriend" or something more indicative of their relationship. Now he felt like some kind of paid escort, and he didn't want Milacio to think he was a hooker or something.

"Ah" was all he said for a moment, and he continued to stare at Trent before finally letting go of his hand.

Trent fought off the urge to wipe his hand on the back of his pants. He usually liked when other men gave him a once-over, but this time he felt a little violated. Even worse, Reed hadn't said anything or indicated he sensed Trent's discomfort. *Jerk!*

"Nice to have you both here. Come on, let's not spend the afternoon on the portico." Milacio gave a gracious smile and beckoned them inside.

Trent wondered whether Hansel and Gretel felt the same frisson of apprehension, but the worry evaporated once he got inside.

The house had been built into the side of the mountain, so the upper level where they had entered proved to be only the tip of the proverbial iceberg. A few steps down from the entry level sprawled the next layer of house, almost completely white, with walls that curved to meet the ceiling as if they had been hewn out of the mountain itself. The ceiling to the entryway was low, like a pale cave, but opened out to an impressive area just a few feet lower.

"Our local architecture is quite unique, is it not?" Like an experienced tour guide, Milacio waved his hand in the direction of the spacious room.

"Wow." Trent's facility with the English language disappeared as he took in the incredible room.

"Amazing," Reed added, only slightly more articulate than Trent.

"The house is built from the lava rock, *pomice*, or as you call it—"

"Pumice," Trent said. He liked the Italian word for it better, though: *pomice*, pronounced po-mee-chay. It sounded so much more romantic than the English word.

"Yes." Milacio turned his dark eyes on Trent and gave a thin smile. "Puh-mees," he said in his charming accent. So far, it was the only charming thing Trent had found about the man, though his home was spectacular. "Shall I show you around my 'ouse?"

He led them through a series of comfortably furnished rooms, all containing white furniture, with floors of painted tiles in exquisite shades of blue, again mirroring the close connection between nature and the island architecture. Each room contained one or two pieces of sculpture, mostly of ancient Greek or Roman origin, with a scattering of more modern work. The overall impression was of warmth and light and a symbiotic link with the natural setting.

Finally, he led them out onto a spacious back patio with hanging shady plants and bougainvillea and lovely sea vistas with an impressive view of Stromboli's massive single peak.

Milacio waved a hand toward a table set with three place settings of delicate blue and white china and cut crystal. "Tessa is just finishing preparing our lunch. Let us sit outside enjoying some local wine until it's ready."

"We'd love to see your collections...," Reed ventured. He'd been mostly silent until now, just making small talk and admiring noises as Trent asked about the house and the island.

"Signor Allen, have you spent much time in Italy?" Milacio asked as he again indicated the white cast-iron table near the edge of the veranda.

Reed settled onto a chair before replying. "Not really. Just under a week on this trip so far."

"Ah." Milacio seemed to like this word. "We don't tend to rush around here, not like you *Americani*. One thing at a time. Especially we *Eoliani*. This place is ancient, our customs thousands of years old, our islands perhaps millions of years old. The art will be there after we enjoy lunch. Unless you have a special appointment this afternoon? Perhaps a ferry to catch? For there is nothing else to do here on Panarea but to relax."

Trent fought the urge to laugh. Milacio was right. There was absolutely nothing on Panarea but a bunch of houses, a tiny fishing harbor, some chic hotels, and a handful of restaurants, some of which had already closed. There wasn't even another ferry for a day or two.

"Of course, you are right, signore. Please forgive my ignorance of local customs."

"It is forgotten." Milacio waved a hand like a magician making his assistant disappear. "But you can certainly learn from your... companion... how to enjoy life." Milacio turned his gaze on Trent again.

Trent noticed Reed's shoulders tense up, though he managed to convey nothing in his expression. Training, Trent thought, recalling another *Burn Notice* tidbit. On the other hand, Trent found himself liking the word "companion" less each time he heard it. He glanced over to Reed, who narrowed one eye slightly. Less of a wink and more of a warning not to react. Why wouldn't Reed explain exactly who Trent was?

A young woman wearing a white apron over a red-and-white striped dress brought out a tray containing a foggy carafe of chilled white wine and three wine glasses, which she placed on the table in front of Milacio. She made a gracious curtsey, treating Trent to a shy smile before she rushed back into the house, her thick black ponytail bobbing behind her and her sandals flapping along the flat stones lining the veranda.

"This is produced locally over on Salina, just to the west of Panarea." Milacio poured wine into the glasses and handed one to Trent and Reed. "It's made from ancient grape varietals but produced using modern winemaking techniques by a man who moved to the islands from the mainland. Tell me what you think." He raised his glass in a toast to his guests.

Reed sipped the wine and glanced over at Trent, who took in a mouthful and rolled it around his mouth as he'd learned from Marc.

"Bright. Minerally. Good balance of fruit and herbs." Trent grinned at Reed, who hated it when Trent acted like a wine snob.

Milacio nodded. "You have an educated palate. And a lovely way of expressing yourself."

"Thank you. I am a writer…." Trent caught Reed's "shut the fuck up" warning glare too late, and the words were already out of his mouth. He hoped he hadn't messed up whatever Reed had going for their investigation today. Not that Reed had let Trent in on anything, and this was precisely why he shouldn't leave Trent in the dark.

"A writer? You didn't mention that." Milacio made a little tsk-tsk sound and chided Reed. "Not just a companion, then."

"Much, much more." Trent said and drank more wine. It was actually very nice wine. "Tell me more about this wine. I might like to buy some of it to take home. Or do you think it's exported to the US?"

REED listened to Trent chitchat with Milacio about wine, books, and all sorts of BS as he pretended to drink. Maybe he was being too suspicious, but he could never be too careful about anything someone gave him to eat or drink—as Trent's recent experience reinforced, even if he'd imagined half of it. Therefore, he was less than thrilled Milacio wanted to serve lunch before they got a chance to look at his artwork. At the rate Milacio and Trent were going, they'd be three sheets to the wind before the main course. But Reed couldn't afford to let himself get tipsy. From the amount Milacio poured himself, it was unlikely he'd drugged the bottle, though possibly the glasses had been dosed with something.

But the girl who served them would have had to arrange the glasses in a particular way for Milacio to avoid drugging himself, and the girl seemed natural and guileless. One thing he'd learned on the job: accomplices could give the whole thing away.

Given Trent's behavior right now, it wasn't just accomplices but partners. *Companions.* Whatever. Reed should have made Trent stay in the hotel. What had he been thinking to let Trent talk him into coming along here today?

Trent never seemed to shut up for a minute. Reed had almost no opportunity to ask Milacio anything or to make the usual overtures when trying to size up a new mark. Reed needed to feel Milacio out about the smuggling operation, play up a potential new market for his goods. Reed still didn't have a grasp on precisely what was being smuggled, which made approaching Milacio even more of a gamble.

Bringing Trent along only made Reed's task more difficult. Or did it? After Reed's initial interest in the art had been so spectacularly snubbed, Milacio might not have opened up had Reed stuck to his original plan to cut straight to the chase and started questioning him about how pieces from his collection had gotten mixed up with the fakes at the auction house in Rome.

By the time they had finished the bottle of wine, lunch was ready. They moved to another table on an even grander balcony, this one set with another dazzling display of crystal, heavy silverware, and porcelain plates so thin Reed thought he could read a newspaper through one. This table also looked out over the water, where sailboats fought against the early afternoon breezes as they zigzagged between Panarea and nearby Salina, sails glowing white against the backdrop of turquoise seas.

The meal was incredible. Even Reed had to admit that. He was impatient to get to business and started off depositing forkfuls of delicious food into his mouth, while Trent and Milacio took small, measured bites and heaped praise on the delicate flavors and freshness of the ingredients. Reed forced himself to slow down, careful not to appear too anxious and set off Milacio's radar.

Trent asked about several dishes, sounding as if he intended to try making them back in LA. Los Angeles. Reed wondered when they'd be back and what life would be like when they did go home. Was LA his home? Could he go back with Trent? If only Reed could even contemplate that as a possible future for himself. For them.

But first, Reed had a mission. He had to find Peter. And only after he found Peter could Reed begin answering these questions. The mission came first, he told himself. He'd never had to remind himself about that before. Before Trent.

Finally, after several courses, lunch was over.

"Since you enjoyed the wine so much, you must try our local Malvasia. A lovely sweet wine, still made in the ancient way. The nuns on Lìpari produce it. I'm a patron of their order, and they provide me with a portion of their annual production. It's unlike anything you've had before."

"I wouldn't want to pass that up," Reed said through gritted teeth. He made fists under the table, where Milacio couldn't see his impatience. Squeeze. Relax. Squeeze. Relax. Inhale. Exhale. Reed practiced some of the Zen techniques he'd neglected during the lazy months in LA. Now he needed them more than ever.

"Tessa, *il Malvasia, per favore*!"

The young girl brought a tray with a heavy crystal decanter filled with thick caramel-colored wine and the tiny glasses that signaled this wine was going to be sweet enough to give him a headache. He glanced at Trent, who had a look of divine anticipation on his face. The expression resembled his "about to come" look too closely for Reed's comfort.

Milacio poured and passed the dollhouse-sized glasses.

Reed really needed a drink at this point, but he was just getting to his main reason for this visit. He had to ask Milacio a lot of questions about his collection, why he had sold the pieces he'd sold, and his connection to the broker and the auction house. Could this guy really be involved? Reed wondered as he listened to Trent and Milacio discuss the wine's characteristics. Was Milacio just a rich guy caught in the middle of something? Maybe it had nothing to do with him.

But Peter had gone missing after he'd left Palermo for Panarea, intending to meet one of the collectors whose items had been auctioned at Rossetti's. There couldn't be a coincidence. Reed never believed in coincidences.

Trent praised the wine but sipped sparingly, which Reed took as a very bad sign.

Reed had put off tasting the stuff as long as possible, but when Milacio turned to him with a look of expectation, he couldn't refuse. He steeled himself as the thick liquid encountered his tongue, but found it wasn't as tooth-shatteringly sweet as he'd expected. He didn't exactly love the stuff, but he didn't have the urge to spit it out immediately either.

Milacio took only one glass of the sweet wine himself, though he offered his guests a second glass. Reed immediately refused, but Trent shook his head a bit forlornly. Apparently he had enjoyed it. Reed made a mental note to pick up a bottle of this wine for Trent before they left Italy. It wasn't at all to Reed's taste, but he'd learned that suffering through something Trent loved most definitely had its rewards. Reed grinned to himself, thinking about how Trent might reward him for buying a bottle of—*what was this*? Reed glanced at the bottle: Malvasia.

"We must have coffee before we discuss business or I show you my art. I need to digest my lunch, how about you?"

Now coffee was something Reed rarely refused, but he wanted to steer the conversation to the reason he'd come: determining whether Milacio was part of the antiquities and drug smuggling. With all the food chitchat, he'd had little opportunity to set the stage for any of the usual veiled references to the "merchandise" he was interested in obtaining.

"The perfect ending to this incredible meal. Then we can move onto discussing your collection and whether I might be able to entice you to part with some of it."

Milacio narrowed his eyes and looked between Trent and Reed again but remained silent. Tessa returned to clear the table, then brought in a tray of coffee.

Reed took the offered cup—the typical tiny *tasso* used for espresso—and waited for a moment to see whether his host added milk or sugar, which Tessa had set on the table with an awkward glance in Trent's direction. At home Trent preferred both in his coffee, though since coming to Italy he seemed to have adopted the local habit of strong black coffee after meals. At breakfast, however, he indulged in a caffe latte or macchiato. That had at least been his habit for the few days they'd enjoyed a proper vacation together before Thomas White had called Reed.

Milacio took his coffee black. He eyed first Trent, then Reed, waiting for his guests before taking a sip of his own cup.

"I think I'm really hooked on espresso," Trent said after draining the tiny cup in two healthy swallows. "I'm going to have to start making it at home. Get one of those special machines."

Reed hoped Trent didn't. Not only did they make a lot of noise, but Trent really didn't need regular doses of caffeine. He could be edgy enough without it.

"We don't use those machines at home, you know." Milacio smiled. "Only in the cafés."

"Really?"

"No. We have a special device to make espresso at home. Tessa, *portami la caffettiera per l'espresso*," he shouted in the direction of the kitchen.

A moment later Tessa reappeared with a silver-colored pot that had two chambers separated by a narrow band in the middle. Even Reed's curiosity was piqued, since he'd never seen anything like it.

Milacio unscrewed the top portion of the device from the bottom. "One puts the coffee grounds in here." He indicated a little basket. "Then water in this lower section. Twist together, then boil. When the water is hot, it vacuums up to the top, ready to drink. *Eccolo!*" Milacio finished off with the Italian version of *voilà* and handed the coffeemaker to Trent. Tessa watched as Trent took it apart and inspected the pieces.

"That's it?" Trent glanced at Reed, opened his mouth, then shut it again with a pained look in his hazel eyes.

Reed knew—or suspected from the familiar glance—that Trent had been about to suggest they buy one for their place, but he'd hesitated after Reed had admonished him about revealing too much about their true relationship.

"More coffee, Rick, Trent?" Milacio asked.

"I'd love some," Reed replied, surprising himself. "It's very good."

"It's from my own plantation." He flicked a hand at the waiting girl, who nervously took the pot from Trent and hurried back toward the kitchen.

"Is that so?" Reed's own curiosity kicked into high gear now, leading him to ask more questions than Trent for a change. "Do they grow coffee in Italy?"

Milacio shook his head. "No. It's from… Kenya."

Reed wondered if he'd imagined Milacio's hesitation and filed the information away. Trent opened his mouth again, but Tessa arrived with more coffee and interrupted whatever he was about to say.

"We should get started on the rest of your tour," Milacio said as soon as Tessa had poured out more coffee for everyone.

The cups were small and quickly drunk. Milacio rose and beckoned Trent and Reed back into the house.

They spent the next two hours visiting the galleries, comprising half a dozen rooms of Milacio's expansive home. The collection had been organized by either geographical region or time period. He had items from every continent and important period of history among them.

The rooms were laid out on several levels to take advantage of the natural shape of the hillside. Nearly every room led out onto its own veranda, with a shady bower holding flowing garlands of bougainvillea or other leafy flowering plants Reed couldn't name. As subtly as possible, Reed made an offhand remark about the difficulty of maintaining security given the layout of the house and the large windows, none of which appeared to be alarmed.

"There is little need for such security measures here, Signor Allen," Milacio replied.

Did that mean there was no security or simply that Milacio employed other measures? It wouldn't do to be more inquisitive at this stage.

As they continued through the collection, Reed peppered the conversation with leading comments about how his clients back in California would be interested in several of the pieces. He used specific words, trusting that Milacio would understand the nuance of his suggestions, hoping the language barrier wouldn't prevent Milacio from comprehending just what Reed was suggesting: the clients were his partners in a West Coast drug enterprise and they weren't interested in works of art but what might be smuggled inside them. At first, Milacio waved away discussion of selling anything in particular, but he gradually warmed up to Reed as they progressed through the rooms, perhaps catching on to the real meaning of Reed's comments.

Throughout this elaborate ruse, Trent threw Reed a few inquisitive looks but thankfully didn't say anything to disturb the tenuous rapport Reed was building with Milacio. In fact, to Reed's surprise, Trent kept his own comments on the art itself, which lent a veneer of truth to Reed's outward appearance of a man interested in acquiring some new pieces for his collection. They made a good team once Trent settled in and followed Reed's lead.

One of the last rooms they visited held a collection of African art. Reed had spent no time at all on the continent and had little exposure to its variety of art styles and techniques.

"This is fascinating, but kind of creepy." Trent stood face to face with a large carved mask displayed on one wall. It appeared to be made of wood and might possibly contain real human teeth. Reed didn't want to ask more about it, but Milacio gave a quick summary of its provenance.

The teeth were real. A shiver ran up Reed's spine, and he could tell from Trent's wide-eyed response he wished he hadn't mentioned the mask.

"Have you got anything from Kenya?" Trent moved to a display where several exquisite carved wooden masks were protected by a glass case.

Milacio looked around before replying. He moved toward another display and indicated a carved wooden bird with two smaller birds affixed to the back. "This one was made in a village near my coffee plantation. It's a modern version of a very old tradition."

Now Reed was curious. He moved closer to examine the object. He noted a card next to the carving: "Senufo." He'd have to look it up later at the hotel.

"Shall I remove it from the case for you?" Milacio had been very generous as they moved through his home, allowing either Trent or Reed to examine any piece more closely.

"No. That's okay." Trent peered at the object. "You know, I've seen some work by modern Kenyan artists, but I don't think I've ever seen anything quite like this. It almost reminds me of a piece from an exhibit in Abidjan."

"Abidjan?"

"It's the capital of the Ivory Coast."

"Yes, I know." Milacio's tone had turned impatient, and Trent nearly flinched at the words. "You have been to Africa? To Abidjan?"

Trent glanced over at Reed before replying. "I have not, but a… former companion—" he narrowed one eye and looked pointedly at Reed before turning back to Milacio "—a former companion of mine organized an extensive gallery show of African art and…." Trent paused. "Perhaps I was mistaken."

"Perhaps." He led them out of the room. "I hope you don't feel you've wasted your time coming this far to see my humble collection." He pronounced it "umble."

"Far from humble." Reed still didn't have the answers he was looking for, but he needed to tread lightly. "It's been a pleasure, and I—"

"You know, Signor Milacio, I didn't notice any amphorae like the one at Rossetti's auction house in Rome. I was hoping to see more, especially as if I remember correctly, it was found not far from here."

Reed was ready to strangle Trent and his big fucking mouth. They'd gone over this, though Trent had so far played his part well. How could he have forgotten Reed's admonishment not to mention the amphora unless Reed brought it up himself?

"Ah, yes?" Milacio seemed confused. "You are interested in acquiring something similar?"

"Definitely."

"I don't have another one of that era here, but I expect to fairly soon."

"Have you got a broker to purchase another for you?"

"No. I am funding an underwater archeological dig in our local waters."

"Really?" Milacio had more than piqued Trent's interest. And Reed's. Milacio's access to shipping was a vital connection in any smuggling operation.

"Yes, in fact, from the recent reports, they have likely found another cache of similar items, perhaps to be recovered within the week."

"Oh, wow, that sounds fascinating." Trent was nearly salivating. Reed couldn't exactly blame him. It all sounded a little suspicious, though. He'd have to do some additional research on the guy, because Reed suspected he was hiding something.

"Would you care to take a visit to the operations?" Milacio's gaze moved from Trent and settled on Reed.

Reed hadn't expected such an invitation. So far Milacio had been a gracious host but not particularly forthcoming with information about anything of substance, even about his collection. Either Milacio really was just a reclusive collector, or Reed's overtures to a business deal had hit pay dirt. Otherwise, if he was up to something shady, he certainly wouldn't invite them out to see the dig site.

"That would be an imposition…."

"Nonsense. You've traveled this far to see my collection, and since Trent has such a keen interest in amphorae, it's the least I can do. Besides, I know you will enjoy seeing the details of our recoveries." His eyes settled on Reed for a significant fraction of a second.

Trent looked like a kid who was allowed to stay up late for the first time. He ventured a wary look at Reed, who shrugged.

"I'd love to see the operation." Reed was more interested in the "recoveries." Looked like Milacio had taken the bait.

"Allow me to arrange it and contact you with the details. If possible, I will attempt to arrange our visit for the day they intend to raise the next group of artifacts, including some amphorae, such as Trent had asked about."

Whew. If Milacio was part of the monkey business at Rossetti's, he hadn't connected Trent and Reed with what happened the other day. And inviting them to the midocean dive site meant he was starting to trust Reed. Despite Trent's faux pas—Reed wondered what the plural would be—Milacio had warmed up to Reed and his overtures to provide a US market for the export of his "cargo."

With that, Trent and Reed took their leave of Milacio, who had another one of his servants, a man of about fifty, perhaps Tessa's father, drive them back to their hotel in his pearl-white Mercedes.

They were barely inside the room before Reed let loose.

17

"TRENT, you ignored nearly every single thing I told you. And what the fuck were you doing using your real name? We talked about that and I told you it was too dangerous."

"Maybe you should stop telling me what you want me to do and start asking." Trent pushed his chin out a few extra centimeters and turned away, watching Reed just out of the corner of his eye.

Reed glared at him for a moment until Trent's meaning sank in.

The words had the necessary effect.

"I'm sorry. You're right. It's just—"

"It's just nothing. I'm not your *partner*." Trent had to keep from spitting the word out. He still hadn't confronted Reed with what he'd overheard from Felton or about why Reed hadn't let on what the true nature of his relationship with Peter had been. "I'm your boyfriend." He paused to calm himself down. "And it just sort of slipped out. But I said I was a writer, so if he checks me out he'll see that's true."

"That's why I don't want them to know who you really are. Just in case...." Reed moved in close, just a few inches away, and put an arm around Trent's waist. "You *are* my partner." His tone was low and clearly trying to distract Trent rather than really apologize.

Trent wasn't ready to give in to any of Reed's tricks yet. He would, eventually, but not till he said his piece. He gently plucked Reed's hand off his waist, stepped away, and sat at the desk on the opposite side of the room.

"That guy was lying."

"Milacio?"

"Of course, Milacio. Who else would I be talking about?"

"You two seemed to be so cozy."

"Can it, Reed." Trent smacked the surface of the desk and felt a twinge of satisfaction as Reed jumped at the sound. "Look, you said yourself this is serious. So stop joking."

"You're right." Reed had been sufficiently castigated. He sat on the bed and turned his full attention to Trent. "He was lying about something, but I couldn't quite put my finger on what."

"The coffee and the art."

A laugh burst from Reed's mouth. Trent wasn't sure, but it might have been a "guffaw," though he didn't know quite what one might sound like. Onomatopoeia aside, he just stared at Reed and waited for the laughter to subside.

"I'm sorry." Reed was still grinning. He swiped a hand across his mouth and took on a serious look. "Go on. I'm listening." He smiled again but didn't laugh.

"That coffee...." Trent noticed Reed's grin taking over his face again. He paused until it was gone. "That coffee was not from Kenya."

"I'm not even going to ask how you know that. But what does it matter?"

"Kenyan coffee is pretty expensive. Kenya AA is what it's called, and at home it's about five bucks more a pound than blends from South America. And the flavor profile is much lighter. It's never dark-roasted for espresso like what he served us."

"Your coffee esoterica impresses me, but I still don't understand why it matters."

"That's not how that word's used."

"Fine, Professor Copeland. Explain it."

"The word or the coffee?"

Reed sat up a little bit straighter and stared at Trent. "The coffee. Please."

"I don't know what it means. I just think it's suspicious."

"So, he's a guy who wants to impress us. Impress *you*, more like it. So, he lies about owning a coffee plantation."

"No, I don't think that's what he lied about."

"You've lost me again."

"Well, that's the other strange thing." Trent got up from the desk and sat near Reed on the bed.

Reed didn't edge closer, but he gave Trent his full attention, eyes soft and curious.

"The artwork. That stuff he said was from Kenya, I swear it looked just like some pieces Marc had in a show a year or so before he died." Trent paused.

He took a breath and waited for the weight to descend on his chest the way it always did when he talked about Marc. This time it didn't. Nothing happened. He had mentioned Marc almost casually, as if he were any other person in the world and nothing happened. Was Trent completely free of his shadow?

"Trent?" Reed reached out a hand and shook Trent gently by the arm. "Trent?"

"Sorry, I forgot what I was going to say."

Reed waited. Trent had seen that look in his eyes. The resignation, the understanding. The hope that Trent could mention Marc without reliving anything. And he had. But a wave of guilt swept over Trent, at least as powerful as the last vestiges of grief had been. Trent shook his head slightly, dislodging Marc from his thoughts.

"There were a few pieces from West Africa, a guy from the Wee tribe, who incorporated a similar style. I didn't spend enough time with the art to learn how much was traditional and how much was his particular style, but it was pretty distinctive. Those bells, for example. And the real teeth used on the mask. That's nothing like Kenyan art."

Reed took in a breath through his nose and exhaled out his mouth. He did that when he was thinking, and Trent didn't disrupt his thoughts.

"Taking your observations as fact, why would he lie about that? What would he gain by saying the art was from Kenya when it wasn't?"

Trent liked the way Reed said "fact." Did Reed believe him, then?

"Well, maybe Milacio didn't know it was wrong. He could think that stuff is really from Kenya and he bought it from another collector or broker to bolster his 'I have a farm in Africa' routine." Trent mimicked Meryl Streep's accent from *Out of Africa*. "Could there be some African art forgery ring?"

Reed shook his head. "Milacio was incredibly knowledgeable about every piece in that collection. You asked him plenty of questions, and of the items I have any experience with, he was spot on. It doesn't make sense that he wouldn't know as much about his African art as his European or Asian pieces."

"So, he's probably involved with whatever's going on, right?"

"But what is going on?" Reed moved closer to Trent on the bed and took his hand. "That's good information. I just need to figure out how it fits in with what we know so far. It's all still foggy around the edges."

"Now what?"

"We wait."

"Here? In the room?" Trent had ideas about how they could make the time pass.

Reed shook his head. "I'm an international criminal, remember? I have to act like one, play the role. Our visit to Milacio is only the beginning. He'll want to check me out, maybe even have us followed. We have to do what a smuggler and his *companion*—" Reed winked at Trent. "—would do. See the sights, maybe spend some money." Reed took Trent's hand and pulled him toward the sliding door that led to the balcony. With his free hand he slid the door open, then pulled Trent outside, leading him to the balcony railing. "Where would you like to go?" Reed waved a hand—in a particularly Milacio-esque manner.

Trent looked out at the harbor and town spread out below, and across the water toward the looming presence of Stromboli, its desolate black slopes in stark contrast to the white cloud of steam and ash floating from its crater. He smiled at Reed and turned his gaze back to the magnificent volcano. "I want to go there."

With another imperial wave of his hand, Reed bowed. "And so you shall." He tugged Trent's hand to bring him close and wrapped both arms around him.

Trent's pulse quickened and he relaxed against Reed's body. They brushed lips, letting the kiss last, chastely, neither seeming to want to let it end. Trent felt a little like an overactive volcano himself, ready to erupt—

A shrill ringing from the phone on the patio table put a premature end to the romance. Reed pulled away from Trent and answered the phone. A moment later he replaced it on the table.

"Who was that?" Trent asked.

"My alarm. Time to go check for a message drop from Decker—or Peter. He may have taken a hydrofoil rather than the ferry."

Peter. Trent had forgotten about him. Hearing his name cooled off everything Reed's embrace and kiss had heated up. Desire fizzled and he let out a sigh. Reed turned away and gazed out at Stromboli, silent.

"You have to go now?"

Reed turned around. "No. I don't."

He lay down on the lounge chair and held a hand out toward Trent, who settled himself against Reed's body on the thankfully oversized furniture. Reed curved one arm around him, and grabbed for the phone with the other. He pushed a button.

"This is Rick Allen in Room 8. What's the fastest way to get to Stromboli?"

Trent could hear snippets of the voice on the other end of the call but not enough to get the full gist of the discussion. He waited silently until Reed had disconnected.

"Well?" Trent asked.

"How tired are you?"

"That depends on what you're expecting."

"Apparently the most amazing way to see the volcano is a night hike. It erupts about five times an hour and it sounds incredible. Up for that?"

"Hike up Stromboli, at night? While it's erupting? Is that safe?"

Reed shrugged.

Usually Reed tried to drag him away from any hint of danger, but not this time. Trent grinned. "When do we leave?"

18

THE hotel concierge arranged seats for Trent and Reed on a special evening excursion to Stromboli, where they'd be part of a small group hiking to the top just before sunset. They were walking through the town square, toward the harbor, when a blond guy with a large green backpack smacked into Reed and spun him around. He hadn't been watching where he was going and didn't even apologize. Trent glanced back to see him wander over to a trash can and start digging around in it before pulling a ripped paper cup from the garbage and shoving into his backpack.

The hotel's launch took a party of seven the twenty kilometers toward the most famous island in the chain. The sun stretched out low toward the horizon, making the jutting peak appear even more formidable, and Trent wrapped his jacket more tightly around his shoulders as sea spray and breeze whipped his hair into his eyes. Reed stood next to him at the ferry's rail, close enough for intimacy without an overt display of their relationship.

A local guide met them at the harbor, took them to a tiny square in front of a low church, and reminded everyone how strenuous the climb would be. An Australian couple in their twenties had come equipped with hiking boots, and a pair of young German students also appeared more than capable of the climb. The seventh member of their party was a lone Italian man in his early forties wearing sturdy shoes, Chinos, and a long-sleeved button-down shirt under his tan jacket. He seemed to be arguing—and gesturing wildly—with the guide, who eventually shrugged in apparent acquiescence. Everyone signed the now ubiquitous liability waiver before the guide led them along a narrow street that soon deteriorated to a dirt trail. Within five minutes, they'd left the tiny harbor and church square below them and begun to make their way up.

The first hour wasn't any more difficult than other trails Trent had climbed, as they followed the switchbacks up the side of the mountain. Then things changed. The last portion of the hike was practically straight up what seemed to be sheer rock, except where a few tenacious plants grew from the cracks between enormous black boulders. Everyone was grabbing at the vines for support and leverage, helping each other up the steep hillside, any semblance to a trail far behind them. The Chino-wearing loner trailed the rest of the group, and it seemed the guide wanted him to return to the harbor, but he insisted, and with the help of the others, he struggled up the most difficult sections.

Trent's chest heaved and his heart pounded as they climbed. The air was fresh and salt-tinged, but the sulfurous scent of the volcano grew thicker as they ascended. He sucked black sand and sulfur into his lungs with each gulp of air. Reed grinned and took every opportunity to prolong the touch as he helped Trent up the hill. By the time they reached the edge of the volcano's crater, the small group had become a team, the shared exertion and exhilaration of their climbing bonding them. All but the single man who eyed everyone suspiciously, especially Trent and Reed.

"He is Italian," said one of the Germans, a grad student from Munich named Dieter. "Perhaps he has an animosity against homosexuals." His tone was cheerful and supportive, despite his formal-sounding English. Dieter smiled and nodded.

For once, Trent hoped that was the reason. He glanced at the odd man when his attention was elsewhere, wondering why he'd come up on the hike. He'd just appeared at the harbor and paid the launch captain. Maybe he was worried they'd find out he wasn't staying at their inn. Reed didn't seem worried by the guy, and as the sun slipped below the horizon and dusk overtook the group, he reached for Trent's hand and interlaced their fingers.

"Don't go too near to the edge," the guide warned. He gave everyone a flashlight and the group fanned out, exploring the strange surface near the volcano's rim.

The ground was black sand and pebble, with the occasional wide, flat hole that couldn't be natural.

"You can sit in those holes, and cover up with the tarps. Good shelter from the winds," Thomas, Dieter's friend, explained. "They used to let people stay up here over night, and they slept in the shelters. Now you get big trouble for that!"

A loud popping gave way to deeper rumble as the volcano groaned in greeting to its visitors.

"Look!" Reed pointed as a bright splash of molten lava was flung into the air, deteriorating into a series of large orange drops that pinged to the surface twenty feet away. "Incredible."

Trent just stared. He'd never seen anything like it. The natural fireworks continued for perhaps twenty minutes, alternating between throwing out large splashes of lava and a series of heavy black rocks, and a continuous rain of ash, some of which was still warm as it settled onto Trent and Reed's hair and skin. The guide had given them special protective ponchos, and they huddled as close to the source of the lava as they dared, Trent between Reed's knees, under the safety of the material.

Reed held Trent tight and kissed his ear, giving him a squeeze with each new eruption. "I'm glad you're here, Trent."

"Thank you for bringing me here tonight. Rick." Trent could feel Reed's laugh echo through his own body. "I love you, whoever you are."

Reed's reply was cut off by the sound of a loud wailing. The lone man in their group began shouting and raced toward the edge of the crater, but their guide rushed after him and dragged the man away. They had a noisy interchange and the man broke down crying. The guide put an arm around him and took him far from the rest of the group, settling him into one of the dugout shelters.

"Wonder what was that about?" the Aussie woman asked, startling Trent by coming up from behind.

Her husband arrived a few minutes later. "My Italian's pretty rough, but it sounded like he had some problem with his wife. Couldn't get much more than that."

Trent's heart skipped a few beats. He'd been afraid the man was following them. Reed said Milacio might tail them, to make sure they were on the up-and-up. Well, for a guy who wanted to smuggle drugs back to the US. Now he just felt sad for whatever had made the man so upset he'd been about to jump into the volcano. He shivered, and not just from the chill of the night wind. As if reading Trent's mind, Reed tightened his grip around Trent under the poncho.

"I've got you and I won't let go." Reed brushed his lips against Trent's ear and cheek.

The mountain rumbled and shook as Trent leaned back into Reed's warmth.

Another plume of lava shot out of the crater, reaching far up into the night sky, followed up by an even higher shaft of glowing light. The rest of the group let out gasps and sighs of delight.

"This is the most incredible place I've ever been," Trent whispered. Soot and acrid smoke burnt his eyes and he blinked back tears.

"Better than the Vatican Museums?"

"Beats the living hell out of the Vatican," Trent replied.

THEY got back to the hotel around three a.m., and despite their excitement from the night's amazing sights, fell into bed and asleep before they had a chance to resume the intimate activity they'd begun on the balcony hours earlier.

By the time Reed woke, the sun was shining into the room, announcing the start to another nearly cloudless perfect day. Trent snored softly and sprawled over three-quarters of the spacious bed. Reed shifted out from under an arm and sat up against the padded headboard. He played his fingers through Trent's hair and debated waking him up just to fool around.

His dick said yes, but his brain reminded him he had more digging to do on Milacio. He wondered whether he should call him up today or wait for Milacio to make the next move. A groan from Trent as he rolled over made Reed forget about everything else.

Trent stretched his arms over his head, giving Reed a perfect view of all the best parts. One glance at Trent's cock, morning-hard and curving toward one hip got Reed half-hard as well. Only the sight of his bite marks inches from Trent's left nipple kept him from immediately following through on every deliciously filthy thought that flashed through his mind.

REED ordered breakfast from room service and they ate on the balcony, watching the activity of the harbor below them. Trent fought off one particularly aggressive sea bird which apparently thought he deserved one of the sweet pastries even more than the humans.

They spent the day exploring the island, taking another hike—this one much shorter than the trek up Stromboli—to investigate the ruins of Bronze Age huts scattered along a curving promontory at the extreme end of the island. After lunching at one of the chic cafés—Trent swore that was Johnny Depp at a table in the back—they spent the afternoon at a beach with confectioner's sugar sand and crystal-clear water like turquoise silk, where they exhibited extreme self-restraint as they helped each other apply sunscreen in the most platonic of appearances.

Women wrapped in exquisitely tailored but narrow ribbons of jewel-toned silks and other luxurious fabrics seemed to turn and stare as they walked past Trent and Reed at the idyllic sunning spot. One woman gave her male companion a sidelong look before turning a predatory gaze on Reed. Trent knew just how she felt. He tried not to act too territorial, and only uncertainty about what might be permitted stopped him from exercising clear ownership rights to Reed.

"Don't worry, I promise not to run off with any rich housewives." Reed pulled down his D&G sunglasses—*when the hell had he bought those?*—and winked at Trent.

"Is anyone following us?" Trent asked, careful not to blatantly stare at everyone within eyeshot.

"Can't tell."

"I thought you were a professional." Trent was disappointed. Michael Westen could spot a spy with his eyes closed. Well, not quite, but pretty damn close. Reed didn't seem to be paying attention to anything.

"I am. Just can't tell which of the suspects is watching. Could be all of them."

"Who's watching us?" Trent fought the urge to swivel his head and stare. He glanced at Reed, whose eyes were closed. "How can you see anything?"

"That guy at ten o'clock, the one with the yellow swimsuit and the green watch?"

"What?" Trent glanced in that direction as subtly as possible. There was a guy with a yellow swimsuit, but… he couldn't see the watch. Yes, it was green. How had Reed *seen* that, with his eyes closed? "He's following us?"

"He keeps looking over at the woman with the red hair. But an hour ago he was at the café. Wearing wire-rimmed glasses and a different watch."

"He's spying on us for Milacio?"

"Either that or he's too shy to talk to the redhead. She was at the same café."

"I didn't notice her."

"Of course not. You were looking at me." Reed grinned without opening his eyes.

Trent punched his shoulder but got no reaction. He punched a little bit harder until Reed looked up at him. He rubbed the spot where Trent had socked him. "Hey, I'm still healing from the other day."

Trent felt his stomach knot. He traced the pale yellow spot on Reed's face where the bruise was fading. "I'm sorry, Reed. *Rick*." He leaned down to kiss the shoulder before he remembered not to touch Reed like that in public. "Aw. Sorry. Damn."

"Don't worry. But I think it's probably the redhead who's keeping tabs on us. Or the guy in the dark gray pants sitting on those rocks to your left."

Trent didn't look, because now he took back his criticism of Reed's abilities. Maybe he could give Westen a run for his money after all. Trent grinned and rolled over.

LATER, in the room, they rinsed each other off under the cool spray in a shower large enough for an orgy. Reed turned off the water and sudsed up his hand before backing Trent up against the floor-to-ceiling glass wall and thoroughly washing salt and sunscreen away, paying extra attention to the parts of him that had been covered up by the swimsuit. And that was perfectly fine with Trent.

Reed leaned in close to kiss Trent as his strong hands made their way along Trent's upper body, stopping now and then to pinch a nipple into a tight bud that sent shivers of pleasure throughout his body. Trent let a moan escape and pushed his thickening erection against Reed's wet, soapy skin, enjoying the slippery feel of him.

Reed stepped back half a pace and took hold of Trent's cock, then squeezed along the length until Trent begged for more. After soaping his own hands, Trent started in on Reed and they took turns pulling and stroking each other, alternating deep needy kisses and adding enough moaning to produce the soundtrack for a dozen pornos.

Trent leaned back against the glass, head flush with the cool surface, and with half-closed eyes watched Reed stroking away at him. Tendrils of ecstasy twirled their way to his balls, and when Reed slipped a hand down to tug and fondle his sac, Trent couldn't keep his eyes open. Then, Reed let go of his balls and put both hands on Trent's cock. He had to watch this, as Reed slid his fists up and down, adding extra pressure here and there, and twisting at the head until Trent thought he'd fall over with need.

"I could really use a third hand right now," Reed said, then angled his head to suck at a nipple and that's when Trent lost it.

His balls tightened and his cock spasmed, shooting out a surprising quantity of pearly strands. Trent watched his come streak Reed's formerly clean chest and abs as he braced himself against the shower wall and let his body take over.

Trent's heart was still pounding as he pulled Reed in for a kiss and turned the water back on to splash over their heads. He stepped away to rinse them both again, with an occasional tug to keep Reed hard. Then he turned off the water and took Reed's hand to lead him out of the shower.

"Forgetting something, aren't you?" Reed gripped his cock and pointed it in Trent's direction.

"No. Let's finish in bed."

"I like the soap and the warm water on when I come."

"I'd like you to be in me, when you come."

Reed stopped and Trent turned back toward him. "No, Trent. Not yet."

"I'm fine. I want it."

"You're not too sore after… the other day? That hurt you. I know it did." Reed looked at his feet.

Trent knew Reed meant he'd hurt Trent. He didn't care about the other day, but he knew what he needed right now. Reed wouldn't make love to him since that day in Rome, just handjobs or blowjobs—and some incredible frottage when he'd first arrived on the island. He pulled Reed over to the bed and lay down, then held out a hand for Reed to join him.

"Trent, I don't—"

Trent grabbed Reed's dick and squeezed, just hard enough to remind him he hadn't come yet. Then he let go and rolled away from Reed.

"Trent…."

Trent grinned. He knew he had him now. He felt Reed's weight on the bed behind him then Reed's heat as he pressed himself against Trent's back, cock rock hard and angled down between Trent's ass cheeks. Trent pushed his hips back a little so the tip of Reed's erection brushed his balls and let out a little moan.

Reed made an even needier sound in response.

"Lube's on the table."

Reed rolled away as he grabbed for the tube and Trent heard him squirt some into his hand. The next thing he felt was a slippery finger—not Reed's cock—circling his hole. It still felt damn good. When the tip slid inside Trent let out a little noise to let Reed know he was fine, then he squeezed the finger and wiggled his hips.

"Okay so far?"

Trent nodded. "It'd be more okay with your cock in there."

Reed leaned down to kiss Trent's back. Trent wanted more, but he felt a little extra tingle—in his heart, not his balls—knowing Reed was being especially careful for Trent's sake. Then Reed slipped in a second finger and moved them in and out agonizingly slowly. Trent felt the stretch and it was sharper than usual, and he was thankful Reed had slowed this down after all.

"Maybe more lube?"

Reed pulled the fingers out and when they slid in again Trent felt only delicious pressure and no hint of pain. Reed played around in there much longer than necessary, tickling Trent's gland just enough that it built desire and heat up and Trent's cock began to stiffen again. He groaned and pushed his face into the pillow and his ass against Reed's fingers.

"I think we're both ready, now."

The fingers slipped out and Trent heard more squishy lube sounds and Reed fisting himself.

Trent began to roll onto his stomach but Reed stopped him, keeping him on his side and sliding back up behind him.

"Lift your leg up a bit?"

Trent complied and felt just the tip of Reed's cock against his entrance. Once he lined up, Reed hooked his hand under Trent's knee and lifted it as he slid deep inside.

Trent couldn't stop the hiss that slipped out between his lips. It had been too long since Reed was here, inside, filling him up this way. Reed shifted position so he could kiss Trent's back and suck at the skin, while he adjusted the position of Trent's knee to ensure maximum penetration. Relaxing, Trent let Reed control the speed, angle, and depth of the thrusting, though he could tell Reed was being particularly careful. Hot breath against his back and Reed's increasingly incoherent moaning sent shivers of heat and bliss all the way to Trent's toes. It got even better when Reed dropped Trent's knee and wrapped his arms around Trent, whispering his name.

Reed's rhythm went to hell as his thrusts grew shorter, and Trent tugged at his cock a few times. The angle of Reed's cock changed again so it hit Trent's sweet spot and he felt his body tremble and shudder as orgasm took over before he knew it was happening. He gulped a few times as his cock spurted and he felt Reed's climax overtaking him. He felt the jets of come filling him up inside, hot and wet and satisfying. He loved that they'd stopped needing condoms.

Reed moved his hand to give Trent's cock an affectionate squeeze then spread Trent's come around on his chest, palm flat. He pulled the hand back and licked it then flattened himself against Trent's back again. Trent squeezed around Reed's dick inside him.

They lay like this in silence until they fell asleep, Reed still filling Trent up.

THE phone rang and startled Trent. He leapt an inch or two off the surface of the bed. Reed leaned toward the phone on the night table, keeping hold of Trent's hand.

The sun was low and the room was only half lit. Trent had no clue what time it was. He rolled over to face Reed.

"Hello? … Oh, yes, please connect him."

"Milacio," Reed mouthed to Trent. "Signor Milacio, thank you so much for a lovely afternoon and—"

Trent leaned into Reed, getting his ear as close to the phone as possible.

Reed pushed him away with a tiny frown.

"Yes, that would work just fine…. Eight o'clock? Yes… yes…. Yes… thank you. See you—"

Reed made a moue of annoyance and put the phone back on the cradle.

"Well?" Trent couldn't contain his curiosity or impatience. "What was that about?"

"He's arranged for us to see the underwater dig tomorrow." Reed didn't sound very excited.

"And?"

"It's too soon." Reed shook his head slowly, staring at the phone. "He's rushing things. I don't like it."

"Maybe he just wants to see me again." Trent grinned and cocked his head, but Reed wasn't amused by any of it.

He got up and paced around for a couple of minutes. "I don't like it. It all feels off."

"What's the plan?"

"He'll meet us at the harbor at eight and we'll take his private hydrofoil to the ship that's the base of the operation. It's located west of here. I don't know exactly where. I'll have to get GPS readings for White, so we can find it again."

"You think something's going on with the ship or the dig?"

"Yeah, I do."

"Then we'll find out something else tomorrow, I bet."

"Tomorrow."

"Tomorrow, tomorrow, you're always a day away...." Trent belted out part of the chorus from the Broadway tune.

Reed ran his hand through Trent's hair, pulling slightly. "You're such an idiot sometimes." He kissed Trent's mouth, a half-open, wet kiss that ended far too soon.

"Tomorrow," Reed repeated.

THEY strolled down toward the harbor and found a little hole-in-the-wall for dinner. No sign, just a menu framed near the doorway to indicate it was a restaurant. The proprietor greeted them as they entered, and served them a delicious meal of fresh local specialties. Trent didn't know what half the dishes were. They hadn't ordered off the menu, just let the chef serve them, which was apparently fairly typical down here.

After dinner they wandered around the sleepy little town, holding hands and braving the brisk autumn winds. They got a few looks from locals who walked hunched against the chilly breezes, but mostly of curiosity and not of hostility.

Reed showered first and waited for Trent in bed, tapping away at Trent's laptop, continuing his deep background check on Milacio. He hadn't done enough before their visit to his home, and now Reed chastised himself. He'd taken it all too casually, but if what Trent said was true, there was more to Milacio than his smooth, confident exterior. Reed needed to buckle down and find what he was hiding if he wanted to break open this smuggling ring and find out what happened to Peter.

The bathroom door opened, and steam from the shower billowed toward the ceiling. Trent's hair was wet, droplets of water gliding down his throat and chest. He had a towel loosely wrapped around his waist.

Reed sucked in a breath. Even after nearly a year with Trent, Reed still wondered how he'd managed to end up with someone this physically perfect. Not that Reed was all about looks. He would have loved Trent no matter how he looked, but Reed's art background led him to appreciate beautiful things. And Trent certainly was a beautiful thing. Sometimes it was all about the physical.

But this wasn't one of them. Reed mentally held back the burgeoning excitement he felt at the sight of Trent's physique and reminded himself there were bigger issues to deal with. There would be plenty of time to ogle Trent and enjoy his masculine bounty.

Trent slipped the towel off and tossed it over the desk chair.

Maybe now could be the time, Reed's cock argued, but he ignored it.

Trent slipped under the sheet and slid up close to Reed.

Reed took a deep breath and held out a hand to keep Trent from getting too close. It had to be done. "Trent, you can't come with me to the dig tomorrow."

Trent sat up slightly, a pained look in his warm brown eyes. "Why not?"

"You ask too many questions, Trent. You don't get how this is done."

"You hardly asked Milacio any questions. How do you find anything out if you don't ask?"

"Use your eyes and your brain more than your mouth."

"You've never said that to me before." Mischief flashed in Trent's eyes, and he kissed Reed softly on the lips before leaning down, moving his mouth in the general direction of Reed's cock.

"Trent, no. Listen to me."

Trent pulled back the sheets until Reed was completely uncovered, cock flaccid against one thigh, and moved his mouth closer.

"Trent…." It killed Reed to stop this.

"Naw, you're right. I won't use my mouth. Let's see if I can make you come by using my eyes and my brain."

"You idiot." Reed shook his head and let out a laugh. At least Trent had eased the tension. He thought about what it would be like not to have Trent's mouth on him again. Damn, he'd miss that. Miss his mouth on Trent's body. And that was what could happen if Trent went along on the dig. Trent could get seriously hurt and—he didn't want to think about the possibilities. Reed wouldn't risk it.

"So you do want me to use my mouth?" Trent teased. He blew cool air over Reed's cock, which had taken a definite interest in the proceedings.

Blood rushed away from Reed's brain, and he heard the laptop slip off the bed. He'd sort it out later. Finish that research after Trent fell asleep.

"Well, just this once, here tonight, feel free to use your mouth as much as you want." Reed spread his legs and patted the bed near his hip.

Trent cocked an eyebrow and gave Reed a very bored look. "Maybe you're right. It's getting late, and you have a big day ahead of you with Milacio on his underwater dig." He sat up and rolled the sheets back over Reed, then settled back against his pillow. "Good night." Trent reached for the lamp on the night table, but Reed took hold of his wrist and pulled Trent over on his side so he was facing Reed.

"You bastard!" Reed was only half-annoyed at Trent's little game. At least his brain felt that way. His cock had a different opinion.

"Before you go to sleep, Trent, let me just remind you why I want you safe and sound. Both of us safe. Because if something happened to one of us, you'd never again get to feel this." Reed brushed his lips against Trent's. When Trent didn't protest, Reed licked at the lower one before sucking it into his mouth. He loved the taste of Trent, even mingled with minty toothpaste. Trent's mouth softened slightly, yielding, opening up to Reed. As soon as his tongue touched Trent's, Reed was hard, and when Trent's tongue swirled against Reed's cheek, it sent shockwaves through his entire body. Trent's arm came around, circling Reed's waist, and they were chest to chest. Reed's nipples tingled as they hardened against Trent's muscular torso.

"Reed." Trent's voice was part whisper, part groan, and Reed's entire body responded, energy and heat thrumming through him in time with his racing heartbeat. "I'm sorry."

"Shhh." Reed took over Trent's mouth again as his fingers traced familiar territory, the curve of Trent's throat, one prominent collarbone. He took one nipple between finger and thumb and pinched, pulling it until Trent arched his back and pressed into the sensation. The groan escaping Trent's lips inflamed Reed's excitement. "What would you like?" Reed whispered against Trent's lips.

"This." Trent pulled Reed close, their bodies melding together, chest to chest, hip to hip. Cock to cock. Trent reached out and held Reed's ass, pressing Reed tightly against him, and he thrust his hips just enough that the sensation of Trent's cock against Reed's was pure magic.

Trent rolled onto his back, pulling Reed on top, keeping him close.

Reed wrapped his arms around Trent and thrust, cock sliding along Trent's slightly damp skin, brushing up against Trent's.

"Some lube?" Trent asked.

Reed nodded and slipped off Trent, who pulled a tube from the night table and applied some to one hand. He reached out and took his cock and Reed's together and stroked up, both cocks in one huge hand. Reed's hand wasn't big enough, so he used both when they did this. He let Trent stroke them a few times till they were both rock hard and slicked up and precome started to dribble out of both cockslits.

Reed enjoyed watching Trent's concentration, seeing his gaze unfocus as his hand squeezed and turned. And the sensations overwhelmed Reed's senses. He lay on top of Trent and fucked against the groove of his hip. His cock slid smoothly on Trent's skin, brushing against Trent's cock, electricity zinging through Reed's entire body at every touch.

Trent cupped Reed's ass, squeezing his cheeks, fingers playing along his hole and tickling his perineum and balls.

It had been a while since they'd made love like this, and Reed wondered why they didn't do it more often. He loved having every inch of Trent pressed close, face to face so he could see every sensation through Trent's ever-changing expression, feel Trent's heart beating, hear and feel each breath against his face.

"Reed, slow down."

Reed forced his hips to obey, though he wanted so badly to dig his cock against Trent's body. His nipples ached, and every time they brushed against Trent's chest, pleasure rippled through to every limb.

Trent opened his mouth, and Reed kissed him, hard at first, thrusting his tongue inside till Trent grunted softly and slowed the kiss. He shuddered with every stroke of Reed's cock, and Reed could feel how slick they both were, precome flowing.

Without breaking the kiss, Trent rolled over so he and Reed were on their sides, still face to face. He slid one hand between them and took hold of both cocks again. Reed groaned at the pressure of Trent's fingers. The ache in his balls expanded upward, deep inside. He wanted to keep kissing Trent, but he also loved to watch Trent's hand, see their cocks rubbing together, see pleasure overtake Trent, so he opened his eyes and pulled away.

Trent's chest heaved, and his hand worked, squeezing and stroking, thumb sliding back and forth over both cockheads, putting a little twist at the top of each stroke to maximize friction against the hoods.

As good as that felt, tension building inside Reed, he held himself back from the edge. He fucked into Trent's hand, harder but not faster, keeping Trent's rhythm.

"Ready?" Trent said, more of a gasp than anything else.

"Yeah."

Two firm strokes and Reed's orgasm started, muscles fluttering, and as thick, creamy ropes shot out of him, Trent was coming too. Their come mingled and painted both their chests. Reed reached out and, with a fingertip, drew circles in the slick warmth, enjoying the feel of their joint pleasure. Trent reached out and took Reed's finger into his mouth and sucked it clean. Reed scooped up more and Trent licked that off, and they repeated the motions until they were both relatively clean.

Reed's body was still hypersensitive, and whenever his cock brushed against Trent, aftershocks of pleasure rippled through him as he held Trent tightly and wondered what tomorrow would bring.

19

THE next morning they woke early, giving them plenty of time for another slow lovemaking session before they needed to meet Milacio at the harbor. Reed had reluctantly given in to Trent's wishes to come along, realizing it was necessary for the cover he'd fabricated. Not bringing Trent might spook Milacio at a delicate stage in Reed's investigation.

If he'd laid the groundwork properly, this was Milacio's way of taking their relationship to the next level. It was often the trickiest of the steps in an investigation. If Reed said too much at first, Milacio wouldn't trust him, suspecting him either of being law enforcement or being a rival out to learn the details of his operation, rather than a potential partner. Reed knew the day was a make-or-break opportunity for him to make headway with Milacio with regard to the suspected smuggling. He'd barely nibbled at Reed's overtures at lunch, but the invitation to the dive boat was a step in the right direction.

"Sounds kind of like dating," Trent observed. "Don't make the first move or act too needy."

"This isn't one of your damn books; this is real."

"I know, but it's a lot more similar than you think from what you've explained."

"Dating is a waste of time. I'd much rather have a quick fuck and get this whole thing over with." And get Trent somewhere safe.

"Gee, thanks." Trent got that injured puppy look.

"Damn, Trent. I didn't mean you. I mean Milacio."

"You want to fuck Elvis?" Trent's eyebrows shot up, and he moved away from Reed on the bed.

"Yes, at least as far as the contraband is concerned. Not real fucking."

Trent didn't say anything. Practically a first.

"Not like with you. Not like what we just did." Reed shut up. He could see from Trent's pursed lips he'd stepped in it again. Why couldn't he remember not to use sex metaphors? Trent could be dangerously literal.

Reed put an arm around Trent and kissed his ear. It was all he could reach because Trent had buried his face in the pillow. "Trent, you're the only one I'm fucking, okay?" Reed cursed under his breath. "Making love to. You're the only one."

"Really?" Trent asked into his pillow. Or that was what it sounded like.

"Really. Promise." Reed kissed Trent's shoulder softly and drew a heart on his back. "See?" The stuff he did for this guy. He drew another heart and kissed the middle of it.

Trent rolled over with a big smile and the makings of a new hard-on.

"We don't have time, Trent. Or you won't get any breakfast."

Trent figured out how to do both.

They stopped for espresso at the bar of the café across from their hotel, and even though they arrived at the harbor ten minutes late, Milacio was nowhere to be seen.

"I told you there was no big hurry." Trent rarely let an "I told you so" go by when it had to do with sex. He ducked into a little pastry shop and came back with a bag full of *bomboloni*, Italian-style donuts made of soft fried dough filled with rich vanilla custard.

"Mmmm." Reed swallowed the first one nearly whole and savored a second.

"Look at you!" Trent brushed stray sugar from Reed's cheek with a gentle touch, then handed him a napkin.

Reed's body had just begun to respond when he heard Milacio's voice over his shoulder.

"Signori, forgive me my tardiness." He made a gesture Reed interpreted as apologetic. "I had an urgent call from a colleague in Roma." He focused his gaze on Reed for a moment before turning toward Trent, who was wiping sugar from his hands.

"*Buon giorno*, Elvio!"

"*Buon giorno*, Trent. Let's get started, if you are both ready?"

"Of course." Reed followed Milacio down the nearest pier, where a small power yacht equipped with a hydrofoil idled loudly.

"Come aboard!" Milacio waved a hand and strode up the gangplank.

"Did I just walk into a James Bond movie?" Trent asked. "This is like a mini version of the *Disco Volante*...."

Reed hoped the engine noise drowned out Trent's comment, however apropos. He'd been thinking precisely the same thing.

The boat was spectacular, luxurious, and built for speed.

"You like boating?" Milacio asked Reed as the captain, another of Milacio's seemingly endless staff, piloted the boat slowly out of the harbor, careful to avoid the numerous fishing boats and sailboats. Trent stood at the rail while Reed and Milacio sat at a table near the bow.

"Love it." Reed raised his voice over the engine. "Need to get one of these for myself."

"The speed is very handy in the right circumstances," Milacio said cryptically.

"So, what's the captain waiting for?" They were still traveling little faster than a snail's pace.

Instead of answering, Milacio pointed toward a large boat idling just outside the harbor. "Local maritime police. This area is full of protected reefs. They monitor speed and course of all boats here, and if you break the law, the fines are deadly. Of course, so are the reefs if you hit one."

Reed nodded. The dangerous local reefs were the reason the area was full of shipwrecks that spanned thousands of years of maritime carelessness.

"Let me give you two a tour of the boat."

Milacio proceeded to show Trent and Reed the main areas of the boat, including the control room, the luxurious passenger cabins, and the tiny galley where he assured them his cook—a man this time, not Tessa—would prepare a sumptuous lunch from whatever he caught during the morning.

Reed could see Trent's eyes light up at the thought of fresh-caught seafood. Milacio also brought them below deck to see the engine room, where the equipment gleamed from attention and diligent maintenance.

Once they had cleared the reefs surrounding Panarea and the nearest island, Salina, Milacio had the boat brought up to cruising speed. Trent moved back toward the bow, the wind whipping his hair wildly as he held onto the rail. It wouldn't have surprised Reed in the least if Trent had stepped onto the rail, held his arms out, and shouted "I'm king of the world!"

Reed felt a little like the king of the world himself at the moment, enjoying Milacio's hospitality and watching Trent bask in the fresh sea air and sunshine. It was by far the cushiest undercover gig he'd had. He shifted in his chair as he waited for the sudden pain flaming across his back to subside. Was it this job that gave him the prickles, or did it have to do with Peter's proximity?

Peter. Reed had conveniently put him out of mind for the last twelve hours. The pain and the memories reminded him this was a mission for White and it included locating Peter. Reed had to use Milacio if he could provide the answers. He hadn't yet asked the correct questions.

Once the boat hit warp speed, as Trent called it, the journey to the dive boat took little more than an hour. The location was in the middle of the Tyhrrenian Sea, the portion of the Mediterranean between the toe of Italy's boot, Sicily to the south, and the island of Sardinia to the west.

The captain of the *Venere d'Oro* anchored, and the chef served lunch on the deck as a small Zodiac from the dive boat brought a lone passenger who was welcomed aboard and invited to join their meal. Milacio introduced the dive captain, a grizzled German named Uwe who spoke good English. He updated Milacio on the day's progress while Reed and Trent listened and enjoyed another exquisite meal of fresh fish, grilled vegetables, and black pasta made from squid ink.

After lunch, the Zodiac ferried Reed, Trent, Milacio, and Uwe over to the recovery vessel. This boat was industrial strength. Nothing fancy or luxurious about the accommodations here. "Here's what we filmed earlier." Uwe played a video for Milacio on his laptop. "This was shot by the remote camera."

Reed watched schools of silvery fish flee en masse as the camera moved smoothly through the dense water on its way toward the sea floor. He glanced over to see Trent entranced by the images on the screen. It wouldn't do to give this his full attention, Reed understood, and only half listened, focusing instead on what his peripheral vision told him about the activity on the rest of the boat.

Trent asked questions, his usual MO, and for the first time, Reed was grateful. While Uwe and Milacio discussed the dive and explained in detail to Trent, Reed wandered toward the railing to watch the crew in action.

Two men controlled the remote camera from near the bow while another two men zipped up wetsuits and checked their dive gear. They spoke to each other in German, which Reed had once studied, though he didn't let on. The discussion was innocuous enough, about air mixtures and depths and schedules. Every now and then Reed caught a word he didn't understand, but from the context he understood it to be either dive or archeological terminology.

From a cursory view, Reed saw only a genuine archaeological dig. Of course, with smugglers, what one saw on the surface was nothing like what lay beneath, just as for scuba divers. An operation like this was perfect for smuggling. No one questioned Milacio or his crew about what they retrieved from the water. And with a supply of fairly unique antiquities, Milacio had access to the perfect vessels to get his drugs out of Italy to his buyers in Europe and New York. All Reed had to do was to convince Milacio he needed another partner on the West Coast and he'd have enough to bring the bigger guns in on the mission.

If he bit. Reed half hoped he'd misread Milacio. He'd love to eliminate him from suspicion and get the hell out of here to continue on his regularly scheduled vacation with Trent. They'd enjoyed the luxury of Panarea, but Reed sensed Trent needed closure on this mission as much as Tom White did.

And there was still Peter Isett.

20

IT TOOK an hour for the divers to reach the sea floor, several hundred feet below the surface. Once at the bottom, they attached special cables to four amphorae. The entire operation was filmed live, with Uwe in nearly constant contact with his men. Winches on the boat deck hauled the delicate cargo up slowly, one at a time, and plunged each amphora into a vat of seawater on the deck. Once all four were safely on deck Uwe would give his divers the order to surface. Returning to the boat would take another two hours.

Reed had little patience for the long waiting game, though Trent wanted to stay on deck the entire time. With the divers' activity keeping everyone occupied near the bow, Reed took the opportunity to break away as discreetly as possible from the rest of the group as soon as the second one surfaced, while the crew's attention focused on stowing it properly.

"I'm getting a headache. Maybe sunstroke. I'm feeling a little dizzy."

"Ree—!" Trent came rushing in from the monitor and stopped himself just in time. "Rick! What's wrong?" He put a hand on Reed's arm. "Rick?"

One of the crew narrowed his eyes and gave Reed a look he'd seen far too often. Usually it ended with the other guy bleeding. Today the homophobic bastard was lucky Reed was working.

"I'll have you taken back to the *Venus*, Rick. Paolo can look after you." Milacio snapped his fingers, but Reed waved his good intentions away.

"No. It's not so serious. I just need some shade…."

"You can rest in the crew's quarters," Uwe said. He pointed aft and made a downward motion.

Milacio frowned. "The *Venus* is very comfortable."

"Let me take a little rest and see if I feel better." Reed started in the direction Uwe had indicated.

"I'll go with you." Trent was immediately at his side.

"Go back to the front of the boat."

"Forward. You mean go forward."

"Trent." Reed flashed a look that Trent understood immediately. For the first time. Reed would mark this day in history.

"Oh… I get it." He winked. "I'm going back—er, forward—to watch the divers…." He left Reed at the crew's quarters and moved toward the displays on the forward deck.

Reed opened the door and flipped on the light. The room held built-in bunks for six men. He lay down on the nearest lower bunk and collected his thoughts.

He could hear the winch on the foredeck hauling something up and shouts between Milacio, Uwe, and the crew. He also heard other sounds, aft. Something else was happening on the back of the boat.

From a hook near the door, he grabbed a brown hat like the rest of the crew wore, and went back into the hallway, looking for a bathroom. Head. He found it and went inside, splashed water on his face and smoothed back his hair. The mirror was made of shiny metal bolted to the wall, not regular mirrored glass, and his reflection was warped and almost alien. The nearly black hair made the face looking back even more unrecognizable. He was on his third identity in the past week, and he barely remembered who he was supposed to be. He had to focus, finish this mission, determine whether Milacio was behind the smuggling, find Peter, and get out. He would be so glad when this job was finished.

He heard Trent shouting, though he couldn't make out individual words. Reed peered out the door to see if anyone was looking for him, and when satisfied the coast was clear, he moved farther aft.

Two men were at the back of the boat with a computer almost identical to the one Milacio was overseeing in the front. Keeping close to the walls, Reed stayed out of sight in case either of them turned around. He heard the sound of a second winch drawing something else out of the blue depths. These men spoke Italian, and Reed couldn't understand much of what they said. From their animated appearance and the ubiquitous gestures, he knew when the winch's cargo had nearly reached the surface.

One of them ran toward the railing and pulled a white container from the water. This was no ancient artifact. It might have fallen off a ship, but only because someone wanted it to. They had retrieved some of their contraband.

Reed silently thanked whoever was looking down on him and stepped back out of the men's line of sight. They collected the box and brought it back in his direction before one of them descended the metal staircase to another level below the deck. Reed heard a knock and the sound of a door opening, then clicking shut again.

The man came back up the stairs and headed for the winch. He put the hook back in the water and lowered it.

There was more where that white box came from.

Reed had to see what it contained. How long before the next box would surface? Did he have time to go downstairs before the man retrieved another piece of cargo to stow? He had to take the chance.

As quietly as possible, Reed stepped onto the metal staircase. It squeaked softly, as it had under the other man's weight. He didn't want to alert anyone to his movements, so he bent lower at the knee and peered between the steps to get his bearings in the lower hallway. A man leaned against the wall, one knee bent, as he smoked a cigarette.

Not just any man. A thickset black man, possibly African considering the shabby military-style uniform and red beret he wore.

This couldn't be good. Reed glanced toward the front of the boat, where Trent and Milacio waited for the divers to surface.

The smuggling had nothing to do with fake antiquities or auction bid rigging.

The African man had a semiautomatic rifle slung over one shoulder, sure sign of a mercenary. No one used that sort of firepower or soldiers-for-hire to protect Greek antiquities.

This was deadly serious. This was definitely drugs.

While Reed's brain came to these conclusions, the African stomped out his cigarette butt and opened the door he had been guarding. Voices carried to Reed's precarious position on the metal staircase.

The African grumbled, shrugged, and walked down the hall toward Reed.

Reed sucked in a silent breath. He had two choices: stay where he was and risk being seen or move up and risk the African hearing the staircase creak.

Neither was particularly good. Fifty-fifty. But a 100 percent chance he'd be dealt with if he was discovered. Semiautomatics made a mess of a man at this range.

Reed threw his luck with the guard not seeing him.

The African was ten feet away and closing. Reed had his pistol in a back holster, and he slid a hand under his shirt until he felt the metal and gripped it. He had it halfway out of the holster when the African was directly below him.

The man stopped, and Reed froze. He knew how to stay as still as the dead.

The African turned back toward the door and shouted in a language Reed didn't understand, waited for a reply, then continued toward the back of the boat, passing under Reed without seeing him.

He went through a doorway and came back out with a box. As he passed below, Reed could see the box contained broken fragments of pottery like the amphorae Milacio's divers had brought to the surface. The African took the box into the room. He hadn't shut the door, and the next thing Reed heard sounded like two men in boots stomping on pottery.

They were destroying the amphorae?

Then the pieces of Milacio's smuggling process fell into place.

He heard the African shouting again, and more quickly than he thought possible, Reed was back in the top deck bathroom.

He slid the pistol back in its holster and turned the water on again. This time he filled the sink and plunged his entire head into the icy liquid. He stood and felt little rivulets trickle down his back. Damn good thing too. His scars were acting up again. The cold water lessened the throbbing under his skin, but that headache he'd faked now became a painful reality.

Milacio was into serious smuggling. And Reed had just offered to be his partner. He counted to ten and back down and performed two of the most useful breathing techniques. All he could think about was Trent. Nothing scared Reed about his job. Not Milacio, not a roomful of drug smugglers, and not even an African mercenary with a machine gun ten feet below him.

But the idea of what any of those men might do to Trent terrified Reed.

He had to see the next phase of the game through without a break in his cover or his façade. He splashed more water on his face. His shirt was dark enough that even though it was wet, the holstered weapon wouldn't be detectible.

He took one more deep breath and opened the door.

"Rick? Are you feeling better yet?" Milacio nearly collided with him in the narrow hallway.

"Yes. Just needed some cold water."

"Cold shower?" Milacio grinned. "I am monopolizing your—how you say?—companion. Forgive me. He asks such charming questions, you know?"

"I know." Reed smiled. "He's a charmer, that's for sure."

"Come and see what my divers have recovered. Two exquisite examples and two more common types."

Reed remembered almost too late he was supposed to be interested in the antiquities.

"I know that is not the cargo which most interests you." Milacio's smile widened, giving him the appearance of a shark.

Reed fought the urge to gulp as he was devoured.

"Of course, you have been very circumspect, and I appreciate that. I took you today as a little test. I see the bounty of the shipwreck has no real appeal for you, not like it has for Trent. He loves beautiful things, yes? And you wish to provide them for him?"

"You got that right."

"I think we can do business. Let's talk on the way back to Panarea. For now, let's not leave Trent alone for too long. I suspect he might have yet another admirer on board."

Reed didn't want to know what Milacio meant by that, but as soon as he spotted Trent, he discovered one of the dive controllers flirting with him, letting him maneuver the underwater camera as it followed the divers back to the surface. He had one hand over Trent's on the joystick that operated the machinery.

Trent looked up to see Reed approaching, and a pale-pink glow spread over his cheeks. He quickly pulled his hand off the equipment and looked away from Reed.

Either Trent was giving an Oscar-worthy performance, or he really was flirting with this guy. Reed didn't care as long as no one thought Trent had seen anything he shouldn't have.

"Rick? You don't look so good." Trent rushed toward him, throwing a quick glance at his new friend before reaching for Reed's hand.

"I'm fine."

"Why are you all wet?"

"I splashed cold water on my face. I'm fine. Show me what you've been up to."

"Look at what the divers brought up!" Trent dragged Reed over to the huge vats on the foredeck. Reed listened as Trent explained in detail what each was. Basically, he tuned everything out but Trent's tone. He'd genuinely enjoyed himself.

If only Reed could give Trent such beautiful things. He thought about the shirt he was wearing. Trent had bought it for him. How could he hope to keep someone like Trent happy?

Well, for today at least, he was going to be a West Coast drug dealer.

So let's make a deal.

21

As the *Venere d'Oro* sped back toward Panarea, Reed and Milacio touched only briefly on business while Trent admired the tanks of amphorae Milacio had transferred to his hydrofoil before the Zodiac brought them back.

Milacio opened a bottle of Dom Perignon for the three of them to toast the day's success. Trent refilled his flute and wandered back toward the loot.

Milacio grinned in his direction. "Let's talk specifics tomorrow. It's been a long day, and it would be inconsiderate of us to exclude Trent from too many conversations. I presume he knows of your business, soon to be our business?"

"He knows a little, but I prefer to keep him safely out of it."

"A good practice."

When Salina came into view, the hydrofoil slowed down to navigate the treacherous reefs.

"This has been a lovely day with my two new friends." Milacio gave Reed a significant glance Trent didn't seem to notice. "I would like to make it even more special. Trent, would you accept one of these amphorae as a gift? To commemorate what I hope to be a long friendship?"

Trent glanced toward Reed, seeking permission, but Reed could see the excitement welling beneath the surface. That bastard Milacio. He really did want to do business with Reed, and he was using Trent to convince him.

Reed nodded, knowing he would regret the decision. Once this mission was over, who knew where the amphora would end up.

"I'd be honored, Signor Milacio." Trent showed remarkable self-restraint by not hugging the man to death though he did put his arms around Milacio and give him a solid squeeze. Reed would have to wash him down before bed later on. "But I can't really accept something like this."

"Yes, you can. And let it be the first of many beautiful things to come from our meeting."

"How do we get this out of Italy?" Reed chimed in. "Don't they keep all the good stuff here?"

"And that is part of the secret to my success. I have a friend in the office which issues export licenses. Together we can take anything out of Italy. Even things which were never here in the first place." Milacio nodded.

Another piece fell into place for Reed.

"I'll have this preserved by one of the scientists at the museum on Lipari. Then my art dealer in Palermo will arrange the paperwork and shipping. Just let me know where to have it sent. We can finalize all of that tomorrow. Yes, Rick?"

Trent looked at Reed, and Reed glanced over at Milacio. "Yes. We'll take care of everything tomorrow."

"Splendid. As I know you are free tomorrow, I would like to suggest another little excursion, not so far this time. For a luncheon—how you say?—'peek-neek'?"

"Picnic?" Trent's ears perked up again. "Where?"

"There is a magnificent vineyard and winery over on Salina, the next island." Milacio pointed to the mass of land they had just passed. "You will join me for a tour of the vineyard. Now the grapes are fat and sweet, just waiting to be picked next month. Afterwards, we'll settle the details of the amphora."

"Rick?"

"Of course, we'd love to join you." Reed knew any other answer was futile.

"*A domani.* I will meet you at the harbor at ten?"

"Sounds perfect."

They had time to finish the bottle of Champagne as the captain maneuvered the hydrofoil up to the pier, and then Milacio helped Reed, then Trent, to disembark.

MILACIO had dropped them off at the main harbor and continued on in his boat to a private harbor closer to his home.

"That was quite an eventful day." Trent's grin had at least as much to do with the Champagne they'd drunk as with Milacio's gift of an amphora.

"Yeah, it sure was."

Trent suspected he understood why Reed seemed to be in a bad mood. "I know I can't keep it. The amphora. It's just fun to pretend for a while that it's mine."

"Yeah, I'm sorry about that. I wish you could keep it, but it's not up to me."

"I know. Don't worry about it. Let's not worry about anything tonight."

"I love that idea." Reed seemed to shake off his worries—or try to for Trent's sake—but his shoulders still appeared to sag. Trent wanted to take that weight off Reed's mind.

"Let's take a little walk. Milacio told me there's a pretty little house up here for sale...." Trent paused, then let the words tumble out. "I know it's crazy, but let's just pretend we could buy a house here."

"I'd love to see it."

Trent gazed at Reed's expression and actually believed Reed meant it. Trent's heart felt heavy, a bittersweet ache that made him want to put his arms around Reed and not let go for a very long time. Trent believed that if Reed could, he'd make all of Trent's dreams come true.

Right now, Trent's only dream was to keep Reed's work ethic and sense of duty from overwhelming him. Reed was so hard on himself, and he denied himself so many little joys of life.

Tonight Trent wished to take Reed away, even if just for a few more hours of fantasy. Keep their illusion going that they had lots of money and time and lived lives filled with art and beauty. Later, he'd find out what Reed learned on the dive boat.

"Near the top of this little street, I think."

Trent moved closer to Reed, aching to put an arm around him. Whatever Reed had found out when he'd gone snooping on the dive boat appeared to upset him even more than Trent not being able to keep the amphora.

They walked in silence for a few minutes, the street narrowing as they ascended. Trent looked around before he slipped an arm through Reed's. He hadn't dared do this near the harbor, but he also hadn't noticed anyone treating them badly or calling them names. The island might be traditional, but there must be plenty of wealthy gay couples—Italians and foreigners—who vacationed here. No harm in being a little affectionate, but not a good idea to flaunt their relationship either.

The sun was dipping toward the horizon, and the light gave the stone street a reddish-golden glow, a fairy-tale path beckoning between the familiar white-washed, cube-shaped houses dotting the island.

Reed craned his head toward the little path that sloped up the hill, then glanced back in the direction of their hotel. He gazed directly at Trent. "Let's go."

TRENT gave Reed's hand a squeeze and Reed squeezed back, understanding Trent's simple touch.

They turned off the main road, away from the water, and went exploring, weaving between the houses. It felt almost normal to be together, arm in arm, putting aside the concerns of trying to figure out what happened to Brett or Peter and whether Milacio had anything to do with their disappearances.

Save that for later. Trent had to know, but Reed would indulge his request to see the house Milacio had mentioned. The man seemed to read Trent like a book, and that worried Reed. He reminded himself that no matter what Milacio said, there was no proof he was involved in anything. Reed hadn't seen drugs on any of the boats, and it would take hard proof. Presumably he'd get that tomorrow, when he and Milacio finalized their deal. He'd have to see the merchandise before they could discuss specifics.

"This is the prettiest street on the whole island." Trent stopped and pointed back toward the water.

Reed turned to take in the view. They'd climbed enough that the whole harbor lay like a crescent below them, a hive of activity as sailors and fishermen cleaned their craft and prepared for another day tomorrow. Gulls drew giant circles in the reddening sky, squawking and zeroing in on dinner.

Reed wondered if he could ever live in a place like Panarca. He'd settled into Thailand but never made it home because he'd been there on missions. It always represented work, not paradise. But Panarea, once the mission was finished—could he relax enough to feel at home?

"Prettier than Milacio's house?"

"It's so big and… white. I'd be afraid to touch anything in there. It doesn't feel lived in. It's too clean and neat. Like something in a magazine. I can't really see a guy like him having a nearly all-white house."

"He's got good taste in clothes, doesn't he? You're the expert, but it seems he knows quality and enjoys it."

Trent shrugged. "Since when have you been paying attention to clothes? Where's Reed?" He peered into Reed's eyes, examining him, confirming his identity.

"I'm right here. Just noticing things differently. Part of my cover."

"Yeah, right." Trent folded his arms across his chest. "Prove you're Reed."

Reed let out a breath. He pulled Trent's arms away from his body so he could get close and maneuvered him against a wall, next to a spray of trailing bougainvillea that effectively hid them from anyone lower on the slope. He pressed his lips to Trent's and parted them with his tongue. He deepened the kiss for a lingering moment, then pulled back.

"Convinced now?"

Trent grinned, a hint of desire twinkling in his eyes. More than a hint visible at his crotch. "No. I think you need to try harder to convince me."

"I think you're already too hard, at least for the moment."

Trent made a few adjustments to hide his condition, and they continued walking.

The houses here were close together. Dusk set in, and delicious aromas emanated from most of them through half-open windows. It had been hours since their sumptuous lunch on Milacio's yacht, with only some fancy tidbits with the Champagne. Reed's stomach awakened and rumbled softly.

"Don't tell me you're hungry, Reed."

"I am now. Someone's dinner smells amazing."

"*Everyone's* dinner smells amazing."

"You know, you could—" Reed cut himself off. This pleasant stroll made him complacent and forgetful of what they were really up against here. He'd been about to suggest Trent take some cooking lessons while he was here. What was Reed thinking?

"Could what?"

Reed didn't answer. He stopped in his tracks, staring up ahead at the house at the top of the small hill they'd been climbing.

"Reed? What could I do?" Trent tugged at Reed's arm. "Reed, you're scaring me. What's wrong?"

"I don't know." He let go of Trent and raced toward the house. From the street it looked just like every other house: a white-washed cube with a window box overflowing with greenery and bright-red flowers. But this house screamed for Reed's attention: a strand of vine wound along the ironwork near the window. Reed reached up to examine the vine and it fell away in his hands. A dead piece of vine tied around the window. Was he imagining it?

Trent came up behind Reed. "What's that?"

Reed dropped the vine, and a shiver went down his spine. "Go back to our hotel and lock the door."

"Why?"

"Trent, just go, okay?" Reed hated doing this, but he didn't want Trent around when he checked, especially if... well, he wouldn't speculate just yet on what he might find if he'd read the signal correctly. "Go!"

Trent opened his mouth but closed it again without speaking, correctly reading Reed's change in mood. He turned on his heel and went back downhill, not turning back toward Reed.

Reed walked around to the front of the little house. It was in a lane of several nearly identical structures with a sign on the first one indicating they were rentals. There was complete silence save for the ubiquitous sound of seabirds proclaiming they'd discovered a tasty meal either on the dock or swimming near the surface of the sea. Reed's senses heightened and he became aware of every little movement, a curtain flowing in the breeze at the house two doors down and a white kitten trotting along in the shadows near the end of the lane. But there was no movement or sound at all from the little house with the dead vine on the window.

That vine was one of the signs he and Peter had used to mark their location for the other if they got separated or needed to work alone while on a mission. The signal needed to blend into the environment while still providing a clear indication of an element slightly out of normal. Something the casual passerby would never question, but that was undoubtedly placed on purpose. Peter had used a vine like this before.

Reed took a deep breath before knocking softly on the front door of the house. Like nearly every other one on the island, the door was a cheerful bright blue, flanked with blue-and-white tiles set into the stucco. A pretty touch that Reed barely glanced at as he waited. No response. He knocked again, this time with more force. The door moved slightly under his knuckles. He pushed against it with his fist and it whispered open.

He took a tentative step inside.

The room was dim, curtains drawn, but enough light came in that he could easily see within a minute. There were signs of a struggle in the front room and beyond that a door left ajar, leading into what might be a bedroom. An unpleasant but unfortunately familiar smell assaulted his nostrils as he got closer to the bedroom, and he hesitated.

He didn't want to look, but the odor told him he needed to know what lay inside.

The vine told him either Peter or Brett was staying here and had left a sign for the other, so they weren't together.

Reed didn't know why that thought struck him as important when he had much bigger concerns than whether the two men were sharing a room—or a bed. He was inches away from the door, and he reached out to push it open.

22

RED splashes stood out against the stark whiteness of the walls of the small bedroom, and in the bed lay a lump covered by red sheets. The metallic smell stung Reed's nose but was quickly overpowered by the unmistakable stench of decomposing flesh.

His throat tightened and he stood staring at the body, the vague outline still mostly hidden by blood-soaked sheets that had dried with a brownish crust.

"Oh, God. Peter…," Reed whispered under his breath and moved forward. He pulled back the sheet just enough to see a part of the face, but the head had been smashed in. All he could make out was lots of blond hair, most of which was also blood soaked.

Should he touch the body or just get the hell out of there and call the local authorities? He needed to know if it was Peter or Brett. He lowered his gaze toward the bed and saw a gray-skinned foot visible below the edge of the sheet. The angle of the foot and its location told Reed it was no longer attached to the leg. A large brown mole covered part of the ankle.

Reed let out a sigh. Peter didn't have a mole on either ankle. Or anywhere else, for that matter.

This had to be Brett Decker.

Still, Reed's heart beat an erratic rhythm, and he realized he hadn't breathed since he'd come into the house, and not just because of the overwhelming stink of death.

"Oh my God, Reed!"

It was Trent. Reed spun around to face him and saw his own horror mirrored in Trent's expression: open mouth, eyes gazing almost unseeing at the carnage.

"You were supposed to go back to our hotel."

"Reed, who is it?" Trent's voice trembled.

"It's Brett."

"He's dead?"

"Yeah, he's dead. You should go. Don't look at this." Reed wished Trent could unsee this mess. He just hoped Trent didn't get any closer than he already was.

But it was too late.

"Aw, Jesus. Where are his arms?"

"Trent, go away. Please. I don't want you to see this."

"Reed, his arms are gone."

Reed wanted to run like hell, and he couldn't understand why Trent wouldn't leave.

"Go back into the front room and please stay there? Then we'll go back to the hotel together. I just need to check things out here first. Please, do as I ask."

Trent didn't reply, just stared at the body and slowly backed out of the room, clearly in shock but still unable to look away from the horrible figure on the bed. Reed's heart ached to see him so upset. He wished he hadn't seen any of this either. It was a sight neither of them would forget anytime soon. Even Reed, who had seen—and experienced—what one man could do to another, was appalled and shaken to his core.

Whatever Peter had stumbled upon, it was bad news. And it was getting worse.

As quickly as possible, Reed unwrapped the body on the bed. It wore pale-blue boxers but nothing else. Apart from the bashed-in skull and the missing limbs—cut off just past the elbows and ankles—the body hadn't been damaged.

In one corner sat a small suitcase and a green backpack. The suitcase held only a few pieces of dirty clothing, a pair of comfortable walking shoes, and a small gift-wrapped box. Reed slid his hand into the pockets and other nooks and crannies in the suitcase but found no papers, notes, or other identifying materials. Same with the backpack— just a guidebook and some random receipts. Reed slid the box into his own pocket and moved to the closet, but he discovered nothing about what Brett had been up to or any clue indicating Peter's whereabouts.

Reed started looking around the room to see if Brett or Peter had left any other clue or message. He looked under the bed, behind the furniture, while Trent paced around the front room of the small house, as far away from the body as possible.

The body had been here for at least a day, perhaps two, so a delay in notifying the local authorities wouldn't jeopardize their investigation. He just needed to make sure whoever did this didn't see him or Trent here.

Reed went into the bathroom. Nothing in the small medicine chest or on the counter except a few dirty towels. Reed returned to the bedroom to see Trent inching closer to the body on the bed, revulsion fighting curiosity in his expression. When Trent looked up to see Reed watching, he stood up straight and moved back toward the door.

Whoever had done this.... Reed didn't need to be a rocket scientist to figure it out. Trent had come up here at Milacio's insistence. Had that been an innocent suggestion or a subtle nudge in the direction of a sinister warning?

Reed's mind reeled with possible interpretations, but he could ponder such weighty issues later. In safety.

Time to get the fuck out of here and take care of Trent.

As Reed walked back toward the front room, he heard the crinkle of paper under his left shoe. He bent and retrieved the piece of paper, half of a restaurant tab. He turned it over as he left and saw the familiar jumbled letters on the back .

Another coded message.

It took only a moment to decipher the words, but the meaning eluded him.

"ICE NOT ROCK"

Peter's handwriting. Reed's vision blurred temporarily as his heart raced at the familiar block scrawl. A punch to the gut, unlike the cold, impersonal printout White had shown him of the earlier message. He fought for control of himself.

No time to dwell on the message's meaning now, either. He took hold of Trent's arm and led him out of the little house, then pulled the door firmly closed behind them with a handkerchief wrapped around his hand. He purposely hadn't touched anything inside with his fingertips so there was no risk of leaving prints, and he wanted to preserve any prints that might have been left by the killer.

"Jesus fuck. Oh fuck, oh fuck, oh fuck." Trent started to rant, and Reed needed to get him away *now*—before he completely lost it. And before he made enough noise that someone might hear and come to investigate.

"Trent, come on. We have to get out of here before whoever did this knows we know." He grabbed Trent's arm and pulled him away from the house, inhaling sea-tinged air, glad to be out of the heat and awful stench of that room. "Act like nothing happened." He steered Trent down the little path between the houses, using his peripheral vision to determine whether anyone had seen them leave.

Thankfully, though it was past dusk, the moon hadn't yet lit up the sky enough for anyone to see them. They'd been quiet and hadn't been in the house long at all. Instead of racing back toward the harbor, Reed insisted they continue their stroll as nonchalantly as possible.

"Right. Act like everything's just normal and no one will notice, right?" Trent asked in a low monotone.

"Nothing happened?" Trent's voice rose. He sucked in a few lungfuls of fresh air, then grabbed at Reed's arm and squeezed it with all the power contained in his well-developed muscular build.

Reed tried not to flinch at the viselike grip. "We're almost at our room. Stay calm." He could feel Trent's fear telegraphed through the hand clutching his arm, and he led Trent toward the vista point and its near 360-degree view of the area. He'd be able to see anyone suspicious from the vantage.

"What the hell did they do to him, Reed?" Trent had stopped babbling, but he looked like he might possibly vomit. He still gripped Reed's hand like a kid who didn't want to go to the first day of school, and Reed didn't blame him one bit. Reed might still lose his own lunch after what he'd seen and smelled.

"I don't know." Reed did know, though he had no intention of telling Trent the horrors he'd witnessed. He'd never seen anyone who'd been hacked up quite like that before, with both arms severed below the elbows. "I've never heard of such a thing. Not in Asia, except maybe years ago, in Cambodia. Before my time." *Pol Pot*. No one would forget what he did to his own people. But who would do that to Decker?

At least Trent was speaking. It would be worse if he clammed up. But he clasped Reed's hand tightly and walked on unsteady legs. At the end of the lane, Reed turned and steered Trent back in the direction of their hotel, making an extra effort to smile and wave at the friendly locals they passed on the way.

It seemed like the walk took forever, not the usual five or seven minutes.

"Nice day with Signor Milacio?" asked Giulia, the afternoon desk clerk.

"Yes, lovely," Reed replied as she handed him the room key. Trent waited outside the tiny office at Reed's request so she wouldn't notice his odd demeanor. Usually he was smiling and chatty, but his current pallor and silence would draw unwanted attention.

They walked to the room, but Reed didn't open the door. He had one important task to perform first.

He leaned close to Trent and whispered, "I need to make sure our room is not bugged. Don't mention what we just saw until I let you know the coast is clear."

Trent just nodded. Reed opened the door and flipped the light on while Trent lay down on the bed and closed his eyes.

As quickly as possible, Reed scanned the usual spots a bug would be located, using the sensor embedded in his cell phone. He detected nothing. He considered changing rooms or even hotels but decided it was best to act as if they hadn't spotted Brett's body.

"It's clear."

Trent opened his eyes, but he didn't speak. His gaze followed Reed around the room until he sat down on the bed and put a hand on Trent's shoulder.

"Trent, it's going to be okay."

"How is what we just saw okay?"

"It's not. But as ugly as that is, it's part of my job. My world. I just hoped you'd never have to see that side of a mission."

"You've seen things like that before?"

Reed looked away. "Not exactly like that, but bad. I've seen things I'd rather not talk about."

"I'm sorry." Trent sat up and slid an arm around Reed's waist.

Who was supposed to be comforting whom here? His respect for Trent shot up a few more notches for thinking of Reed and not just of himself.

"What did that message mean?" Trent took the paper out of Reed's pocket. "It's in code."

"Ice not rock," Reed said. He said it almost like a question. "What *does* it mean?" Reed repeated Trent's question, though he didn't expect an answer from Trent.

"Don't they call diamonds 'ice'?"

"Maybe in seventies heist films, Trent. This is real life."

Trent's shoulders sagged. Reed hadn't realized how sharply he'd spoken. As upset as he was about Brett—and with Peter still missing, possibly in the same shape—Reed could not take his fears out on Trent.

"Sorry."

Trent focused on the paper in his hand, ignoring Reed's lame apology. "What's rock?" He looked around as if searching for rocks in the small room.

Reed shook his head and stifled a laugh. "Drugs. Cocaine."

"You're laughing at me because I don't know drug slang?" Trent's voice rose.

Reed acknowledged the point. He should be glad Trent didn't know much about drugs. That was a good thing. He might be one of the few whose lives were untouched by them—at least until today. "Sorry." It sounded even lamer this time around.

"So this definitely *is* about drugs? I was hoping Milacio's ring is only smuggling antiquities. Or selling fake ones. That's why he lied when I asked about where those pieces came from."

"No. Not fake antiquities. Smuggling something inside the *real* antiquities he's auctioning through the broker. I realize now, that's how they're moving the drugs."

"You do?"

"Yeah."

"Why didn't you tell me how dangerous they were?" Trent nervously twisted his fingers, his gaze alternating between the door and watching Reed.

Reed's chest ached as he saw the fear in Trent's eyes. He had warned Trent, but it took seeing Decker's body for the truth to sink in. "Would that have changed anything?"

"I might not have come here after you if I knew for sure it was drugs. Or gone rushing right into Milacio's house like that." Trent blinked a few times in thought, then shook his head. "No. I still would have come after you, but I would have been a lot more afraid. For you. And for me."

"Good."

"Good that I'm afraid?"

"Yeah. But not good that now you're involved even deeper than before."

"How?"

"Because you're here and you've seen the body."

Trent looked sick again, and he lay down on the bed. "I saw him, Reed. Decker. I saw that blond guy a couple of times around here."

"You did?"

Trent nodded. "I thought maybe he was with Milacio—spying on us."

"Trent, you have got to get off of Panarea. I'm putting you on the next boat leaving this island. Go back to Naples or Rome. Get on the next plane back to LA. This is no place for you." Reed's heart pounded until he could barely hear his own words over the sound. He wouldn't let anything happen to Trent. He'd never forgive himself if Trent…. The thought he might end up like Brett brought bile into Reed's mouth. He fought back the bitterness and fear. He couldn't let Trent see how fucking terrified he was right now.

"Only if you come with me."

"Trent, I can't go with you. I have to do this job. Peter—"

"Peter? He's why you're staying? To make sure *Peter* is okay?"

Reed couldn't leave Peter in danger despite their past, but he couldn't explain to Trent, at least not yet. He barely understood it himself. But Reed's decision was just about this mission. Wasn't it?

"Yeah. I have to find him. Even if I can't get enough evidence to figure out what the hell Milacio is really up to, I have to find Peter."

"You're going back to Milacio's, aren't you?"

Reed was torn between relief that Trent had recovered from the discovery of Brett's body and frustration that Trent continued to question his motives and duties. "Yes. He's going to show me his operation tomorrow, the whole thing, and give me the proof I need—"

"What if he kills you?"

"He won't kill me."

"I'll bet that's what Brett thought too. He was wrong."

"Look, Brett has been dead a day or two at most. We were with Milacio all day yesterday. He couldn't have done it."

"He must have henchmen."

Henchmen. Normally Trent's colorful imagination and vocabulary made Reed chuckle. He was right, though. Milacio could have had it done while he was with Trent and Reed in order to give himself an alibi. Maybe Trent had learned a few things from all those thrillers he'd been reading and watching lately.

"Well, if you know I'm with Milacio, he's hardly going to kill me, or he'd be the prime suspect."

"That means you need me to stick around so he thinks someone is paying attention to your movements." Trent paused and stared at Reed as if waiting for him to acknowledge this superior reasoning.

"You don't have to be here. Just so he thinks you're here." Reed countered Trent's logic, though he suspected he would lose the battle. Plotting wasn't his forte, it was Trent's. Reed was outgunned here. "It's not worth the risk. You are still leaving on the next boat." Reed would have put his foot down in emphasis if he didn't think it would make him look like a character in one of Trent's books. But now he understood what made people in books do such things. "Did you see where I put the ferry schedule?"

"No." Trent's voice wavered, and Reed knew he was lying. Trent was a terrible liar. Damn, but Trent's crappy lying so he could stay here to help keep Reed safe made Reed love him all the more.

"I think I saw it in the desk when I was searching." Reed stood. Before he could take two steps toward the desk, Trent leapt out of bed, raced for the desk, and leaned against the front drawer. Reed pushed him away gently and Trent swiveled his hips, knocking Reed's hand out of the way—such a flirty motion that any other time would have made Reed grab for him and pull Trent's clothes off so they could screw each other's brains out till they exhausted themselves.

But now…. Well, it was all so wrong. He smacked Trent's hip until he moved, then pulled the schedule out of the drawer.

Trent sat back down on the bed, shoulders sagging, and leaned his chin on his hands, elbows propped on his knees. He looked so defeated. So deflated and crumpled. A remnant of the confident, excited, and determined man who strode through town a few days ago, ready to help Reed.

Reed flipped through the ferry schedule, a mix of Italian and English, squinting at the tiny print to decipher the abbreviations. He sat down next to Trent and let out a long breath. Trent looked away.

"Unfortunately, there isn't a hydrofoil until Friday, but the next ferry leaves tomorrow around noon."

Trent's head whipped back around, and Reed saw the glimmer of a smile.

"Trent, this is nothing to be happy about. It means you're not safe till you get on the ferry, and maybe not even then if Milacio sends someone after you. One of those henchmen. Remember them?"

"In the meantime, you're safer, because we'll stay together. He won't try to kill both of us. If he thinks you're after him, the last thing he needs is for your boss to be looking for two missing guys, right?"

"There's some logic to that, but after what they did to Brett...," Reed left the thought unfinished, wishing he didn't have to remind Trent of the horrific state of the body. Trent's smile melted away and his frame sagged again. "These people aren't too worried about what anyone thinks of them. You saw Milacio's house. He's filthy rich, and people will do anything to protect what they've got."

"Yeah. I know." Trent took in a deep, meaningful breath and stared at Reed. "Anything to protect it."

"Me too. I'd risk you hating me if it meant getting you to a safe place."

"Oh yeah, safe. Like that safe house."

"Aw, fuck. I forgot completely about Caterina. I wonder how she's involved."

"That's right. If she's in cahoots with Milacio, then nowhere is safe. She could find out what flight I'm on and have me stopped or killed. So I might as well be here with you."

"Trent, this is not negotiable."

"Do we have to discuss it now?"

Reed looked at Trent. His tanned skin looked drawn and sallow in the room's artificial light, and the corners of his mouth and eyes sagged. He needed to rest. There would be time enough to hash this out later. "No, you're right. Let's go out for some fresh air and maybe some food."

Trent shook his head. "I don't want to eat anything. I don't ever want to eat anything again."

Reed understood. Another man's blood had that effect on nearly everyone. "A salad, maybe? Some cheese? You have to eat something."

They wandered listlessly around until they found a small shop serving *panini* and pastries. Reed ordered cheese *panini* for both of them. He had no stomach for meat tonight either.

Trent ate a few bites of his and picked at the toasted crust, leaving a pile of cheesy crumbs on his plate. Reed managed half his meal. Neither spoke until they got back to their room.

Trent took a quick shower and got into bed while Reed showered, going over the day's events in his head. He'd learned nearly everything he needed to know, and Milacio should willingly hand over the last pieces of the smuggling puzzle the following day. As soon as Reed had enough to report to White, he could focus on locating Peter. He also needed to let White know what had happened to Decker.

Once Trent had safely left the island.

Reed toweled off and climbed into bed.

Trent was still awake, and he immediately snuggled up against Reed, smelling of toothpaste.

Reed wrapped an arm around Trent. "You'll be fine for a few days while I wrap this up."

"That's what you said in Rome. *Twice*."

"You're the one who kept finding me again."

"I just cain't quit you." Trent exaggerated his soft Western drawl.

"Shut up. This is serious."

Trent grinned, then nodded. "I know. I'll listen. In the morning."

"Just be careful not to go anywhere you'll need to give your name or show your passport. Disappear into Italy somewhere. Wander around. Hang out with some backpackers who'll stay off the beaten path. Please?"

"Let's figure this out tomorrow. Don't waste tonight." Trent gave Reed a crooked grin, eyes glinting.

"I'm still going to want you to leave tomorrow. No matter what you do to me in bed."

"We'll see." Mischief flashed in Trent's eyes.

Fear and desire blended in Reed's gut.

This was a battle he wouldn't mind.

23

TRENT reached down and played with Reed's balls, rolling them around in his hand while completely avoiding his cock. It drove Reed crazy, and he bucked his hips, seeking contact and friction, but Trent deftly moved his hand. "Let me suck you awhile; then I want you to fuck me."

Reed's pulse accelerated at Trent's words. He loved when Trent asked to get fucked. That was how they'd gotten together in the first place: Reed "instructing" Trent in fucking, as opposed to making love. Now Trent was a huge fan of fucking, and Reed couldn't be happier to oblige. If only he could control himself now. His cock might not survive even a minute of Trent's skillful mouth, but they'd have to take that chance.

"Mmm. I like that plan."

Trent laid another long, deep kiss on Reed, then kissed his way lower, nibbling at one nipple until Reed ground his cock against Trent's thigh, reminding him it was feeling very much neglected at the moment. Reed didn't need any more foreplay at this point or he'd explode.

Trent slid down Reed's body and lay facing him, mouth again only inches away from Reed's aching cock. Reed silently begged Trent to take hold of him, but instead of speaking, he reached out toward Trent, whose cock was now conveniently situated not far from Reed's face. He wrapped his hand around Trent's cock, enjoying the way it grew harder and thicker as his fingers closed around the hot, rigid flesh. Reed slid his hand up and down the length, sending palpable shudders through Trent's body.

"Hey, I can't concentrate if you keep doing that!" Trent reached to pluck Reed's hand off his cock, but Reed wouldn't let go.

"It's not like you're actually doing anything down there right now."

"I'm pacing you." Trent chuckled.

"Don't pace me. I'll pace myself."

"Okay." Trent leaned forward, and Reed felt Trent's hair brush against his thighs and fall over his sorely neglected cock. Then it was gone, replaced by Trent's mouth enveloping him and sucking hard as Trent fondled his sac and teased along his perineum.

"Oh fuck, I hate you." Reed nearly hissed as Trent's mouth went into overdrive. He was going to come in about three seconds if Trent kept up at this level of intensity. "Okay, okay, you win."

The Hoover high-power suction stopped, and Reed almost wished he'd kept his fucking mouth shut. Damn Trent, the guy was a perfect example of topping from the bottom. Reed was powerless when Trent wanted something, even if it was how he wanted to blow Reed.

Trent pulled his mouth off Reed. A moment passed, and Reed thought Trent had completely given up on the blowjob. Then the flick of a tongue against just the head of Reed's cock. And another. A long stripe from the base of his shaft all the way to the sensitive bundle of nerves just below the hood. He let out a groan as Trent tortured him with tiny catlike licks, now and then teasing the tip of his tongue into the slit. Each contact jolted down his cock, gathering into an ache that settled into his balls. His hips thrust involuntarily as he needed more of Trent's mouth.

This delicious agony continued for what seemed like a year or two. All the time, Reed kept his hand on Trent's cock, holding it but not stroking. He could feel the blood pumping, the shudders as Trent's own pleasure increased. Reed never got this into sucking Trent off, though he would whenever Trent wanted. But Trent took cocksucking to a whole new level, and Reed wondered what he was missing out on. Tentatively, he ventured a lick on the head of Trent's cock, trying to mirror what Trent was doing to him.

"Ungh." Trent groaned. "Mmmuhng. Mmmm."

Reed smiled. Trent hadn't asked him to stop. He flicked his tongue up and down Trent's length and discovered how much he enjoyed the salty tang and the musky essence. Every stroke brought a different reaction from Trent: a shudder or grunt and a steady stream of precome Reed sucked away. It didn't even matter that at some point Trent let go of Reed and just lay there groaning and babbling about how good everything felt.

Reed wrapped an arm around Trent's leg to get better leverage and took in as much of Trent as he could, using his other hand to stroke Trent's six-pack or play with his balls. He alternated licking and sucking, bringing Trent to the edge of orgasm but not taking him over, not just yet. It was too much fun. The muscles in Reed's jaw and neck ached, but he loved the feel of Trent's shudders and the sound of his grunts too much to stop. The taste and feel of the hard flesh against his lips and tongue kept Reed hard.

And when Trent came, it felt like a volcano erupting. Reed hadn't been prepared for Trent's intensity as he clutched Reed's head and thrust while spurting what seemed like a gallon of come. He swallowed some, but most of it ended up on his face and hair.

He held Trent close as the last shudders wracked his body; then he switched position to lie face to face with him.

Trent's eyes were shut, but he opened them when Reed stroked his cheek and planted a soft kiss on his lips.

"Wow." Trent gasped for air. "Wow."

"That's my boy, always a way with words. No wonder you're a best seller."

Trent mouthed, "Fuck you," clearly still too out of breath to waste any speaking.

Reed laughed and ran a hand through his hair, realizing what a mess it was. He started to get up.

"That… was unexpected."

Reed turned as he stood and looked down at Trent. "If you think you might like one of those again, then you know you better be on that boat tomorrow."

Trent opened his mouth, but Reed preempted any comment.

"Nonnegotiable." He walked into the bathroom and wet a towel. His cock, red and swollen, stood out from his body, bobbing painfully as he moved. He'd clean Trent up and see about getting that taken care of, even if he did it himself. Trent sometimes fell asleep after a really powerful orgasm, and after a stressful day like today, Reed didn't have the heart to expect anything more from him.

But to his surprise when he got back to the bed, Trent had recovered and was ass-up on the bed, busy with a tube of lube. Little tremors of excitement ran through Reed's body at the sight of Trent's round butt in the air, one hand reaching between his legs and slicking his ass for Reed. And it was all for Reed, because there was no way Trent was coming again anytime soon.

"That looks good enough to eat. Or fuck. Or both."

Trent craned his neck to grin at Reed and shook his ass, letting his balls sway. "Ready for action!"

"Stay just like that." Reed came up behind Trent and rubbed his cock against Trent's ass. "A little lower."

Trent widened his stance until his ass was just the right height for Reed. "That's good." Reed squeezed Trent's right buttock, then caressed him, smoothing his hand over the skin, marveling at how lucky he was to have this gorgeous man all to himself. Trent trusted Reed and gave himself up so freely—body, heart, and soul. Reed wondered how he deserved Trent, who had put himself in danger for Reed more than once.

"Lube me up a little more, Trent." Reed moved so Trent could give him a couple of strokes.

"I'm good like this." Trent didn't like it too slippery, said he liked the friction, feeling Reed inside him, so Reed left it.

He put one hand on each of Trent's cheeks and squeezed, pulling them apart, and massaging Trent's ass. The pink pucker was shiny from lube—watermelon, from the aroma. Reed leaned down and licked at Trent's ass. Yup, watermelon. Until now Reed hadn't even known there was such a thing as watermelon lube, but he liked it. And he loved Trent for buying it. He rewarded him with a few extra licks, then nibbled at one buttock as he kept kneading at Trent and rubbing himself against Trent's sac. Reed was so hard as he lined up the head of his cock to Trent's hole. With only a little thrust, he pushed inside just an inch or so, then eased into the tight heat, feeling Trent take him and squeeze, enveloping his shaft.

There was nothing in this world like being inside Trent Copeland bareback. Trent widened his stance again to take Reed deeper, pushing back and letting Reed in all the way up to his balls, which tickled against Trent's. Reed had used condoms with every other partner he'd ever had, and that made sex with Trent even more amazing. He barely had to move to feel the ripple of Trent's muscles stroking him, the pressure so intense Reed could probably come just from thinking about it, but that would take half the fun away.

He slipped nearly all the way out again, then took a few short shallow dips inside, occasionally a long, deep stroke. All the while, he moved his hands across Trent's ass and back, now and then reaching down to play with his balls. He knew Trent's cock was supersensitive after the blowjob, and he would only stroke him lightly unless he got hard again from being fucked.

"You call that fucking?" Trent teased.

Reed's reply was a deep thrust that left Trent gasping.

"Oh, yeah. More of that."

Reed complied, feeling Trent push back at every stroke, squeezing him hard. He went back to shallow thrusts, tickling against Trent's gland. He reached down to find Trent hardening again, so he gave Trent's cock a little tug and pounded deep inside a few more times. Trent thrust his head back and groaned.

Reed reached forward with one hand and grabbed hold of Trent's hair for leverage. He pounded away, plunging in, twisting his hips with each stroke, intensifying each thrust. He lost rhythm and let his body take over. Electricity coursed through him, heat building up at the base of his cock and turning into a tingle that flushed his skin like he was in a sauna. His breath was short and ragged, echoed by Trent's groans, and Reed let go, allowing the pleasure to expand and overtake every inch of him. He pounded into Trent, who squeezed as Reed poured his release.

Later, after they had showered and were back under the sheets, Trent spooned behind Reed and put one arm across his chest to hold Reed tight against him. "So, back to our regularly scheduled programming. What were you saying about my mouth?" Trent planted soft kisses along Reed's neck.

"You're like a broken record. So I'll say it again, you are not coming with me to Milacio's today. Period."

"Why?" Trent paused. "Why not?"

Reed smiled at Trent's grammatical correction. "Because as I was saying when you so rudely interrupted me and then didn't even finish that BJ, you ask too many questions. That works great for a writer who's interviewing someone, but for a spy it's a red flag. We have to be more subtle. Watch and listen more than talk."

"Don't you think if I ask all those questions it's just proof I'm harmless and not a spy?"

"Trent, after what they did to Brett, I don't think that even matters to these people. I think whatever they're up to, they don't care who they hurt."

"Oh, God. Brett." Trent pulled away, and Reed rolled over. He put his arm out and felt shivers overtaking Trent's body.

"Trent, the time for games is over. This is deadly serious, and we're both in danger. You get that?"

Trent nodded wordlessly. Reed wished he hadn't needed to scare Trent like this, but it was the only way to get the reality to sink in so Trent would leave for safety.

"THE boat goes at noon. I won't be back by then, so you have to promise me you'll be on it."

"I promise." Trent looked away as he spoke. He did promise, but he didn't want to go. He wanted to help Reed, but he acknowledged Reed was right. Reed was always right about these things. Reed had the real spy training and the experience. Nothing Trent had seen on *Burn Notice* could equal what Reed had personally been through.

He thought about Brett. Trent didn't want to end up in a bloody puddle with no arms or feet. He hoped like hell Brett was already dead when they cut him up. Reed refused to answer when Trent asked, which only confirmed Trent's worst fears. Not only did he not want to endure excruciating pain, he didn't want Reed to come back to find him chopped up. Trent's stomach roiled at the thought, and his knees went a little wobbly.

"You okay?" Reed's voice strained with concern.

"Yes." Trent looked Reed directly in the eye. "I will be on the boat at noon. I promise you. I will call Beth when I get to a safe place and leave a message for you where to find me. How's that?"

"That's a great plan. Stay in touch with her so I can find you later. It's safest for everyone."

"Be careful, Reed. I want another blowjob like last night, and I'll kill you if you die and can't do it again."

"Splendid logic."

"You know what I mean."

"Yes, I do." Reed looked at Trent with a forced smile. Even Trent could see Reed was scared now. "Trust me, I want to be around to give you as many more of those as you can handle."

"Reed, maybe you need to get some backup. Leave with me, then come back with someone else?" Who? Trent wondered. Surely not Felton, that oversexed ass who allowed a fucking hot Italian double agent to drug him because he let his guard down. "White must have some other available operatives."

"I don't trust anyone, not after what you told me about Caterina. White's office may also be compromised. Even contacting him could blow my cover."

"You could go through Beth for that too…."

"I can't use Beth as a go-between for a classified mission!"

"I know about it."

"Because you walked right into the middle of the fucking thing. A—" Reed stopped in the middle of the word.

Trent knew exactly which word: *Again.* Trent had walked right into the middle of the fucking mission again. Just like he had in Bangkok when they first met. He almost got Reed killed then, and it could certainly happen again here in Sicily.

"Look, I have to get going. Pack up and get the hell out of this hotel. Wait by the docks, out in the open, talk to lots of people, foreigners, backpackers, whoever. Just make sure you are not alone."

Trent nodded.

"You have enough money?"

"Yeah, plenty."

"No credit cards, okay?"

"Oh, in that case I'll stop by the bank at the square."

Reed glared a warning at him.

"I'll take a backpacker with me. You want me to hook up with some hippie chick as cover? Would that make you feel better?"

"Believe it or not, it would. Do what you need to while they're busy with me."

"I got it."

"See you when this is finished." Reed reached out a hand toward Trent's face but stopped a few inches away. "I love you."

Tears stung Trent's eyes. Reed almost never said that. Now Trent was terrified. He sniffed and blinked a few times, avoiding Reed's gaze. "Me too." It came out as an embarrassing croak. He closed his eyes as hot tears rolled down his cheeks. When he opened his eyes a moment later, he was alone.

24

"WHERE'S your companion?" Milacio asked with a grin when Reed arrived alone at the pier.

"He got a call from his editor about some changes to be made right away on one of his manuscripts. They gave him a pretty tight deadline to turn it around." Reed hoped the excuse didn't sound too suspicious.

"I had no idea publishing had such time-sensitive emergencies."

"Something to do with printing and release dates. There's a PR tour set up and...." Reed had to stop from babbling details. He had been trained better than to run off with irrelevant specifics that only dug him more deeply into a lie.

"It's such a shame. I think Trent would really have loved today's little jaunt. We have our own business to conduct, but perhaps we should postpone the trip until he's free to join us."

Reed wondered whether Milacio was more interested in seeing Trent than in doing business with Reed after all. He'd gotten all sorts of mixed signals from Milacio, but he thought Trent was joking about Milacio's intentions and degree of interest.

"I'm learning to enjoy mixing business with pleasure." Reed smiled, hoping he could pull this off.

"Good. There is something on Salina which I would like in particular to show you, Rick. Something perhaps Trent would not be so interested in...."

Does Milacio store the drugs at the winery? Reed would have to make careful mental notes of everything Milacio showed him. There was little room for mental fuckups today. *Concentrate!*

They were on the dock, about to board the *Venere d'Oro* for the short trip to Salina, clearly visible from Panarea through the early morning haze. Reed didn't want Milacio delaying today's business or even their departure. What if Trent showed up with his suitcase while they were waiting to leave? Could he think on his feet and come up with a suitable explanation for leaving?

"You would still like to see the winery, even without Trent?"

"Of course. I love wine." Reed put himself in Trent's shoes as he lied.

Milacio boarded the hydrofoil and offered Reed a hand to steady him as he stepped off the pier, but Reed waved away the offer of assistance.

They took seats near the rear of the boat—aft, Trent would point out—and the steward handed them both insulated travel mugs.

"Some of my coffee." Milacio smiled as he took a sip. "Let Enrico know if you want some sugar or cream."

"I'm fine." Reed tentatively sipped at the mug. He knew better than to drink anything from a suspect, even one as gracious and hospitable as Milacio. And the situation had altered dramatically from the previous day. Finding Brett's mutilated corpse put a damper on accepting anything from this man.

Milacio, however, acted exactly as he had on their previous meetings. He did nothing to arouse Reed's suspicions. Of course, he might not know Reed had found the body. Reed had gone over and over Milacio's reasoning and still had no clear explanation for why he would send them in the direction of Brett's corpse unless he suspected Reed of working with Brett. Thus Reed chose not to call the authorities to notify them of the body. It would prove to Milacio there was a connection.

But Milacio *had* sent Trent up that street, and Reed did not believe in coincidences. It must have been a test. Letting on he knew anything about Decker proved Reed was connected to the agent. Anyone else would have reported it, but unless Reed was an agent searching for Decker, he never would have gone into that particular house. Who would show up for a picnic with a man who might be a killer? Only a man intent on finalizing a business deal.

Or a reckless agent. Coming alone was against protocol unless your partner or backup knew and could take precautions. Reed chose to protect his cover, hoped that getting closer to Milacio, earning his trust, might lead the man to let something slip about Peter. But how to approach the topic without spooking Milacio?

Reed looked over at the man, who was sipping coffee as the morning breeze caused the side sections of his ridiculous hair to flap slightly. Had this man ordered Brett's murder and mutilation just a day or two earlier? If Milacio were responsible for killing Brett, it was impossible to tell from his demeanor.

It was the true sign of a sociopath, Reed recalled: not reacting in the face of horrific events or even recognizing something terrible had happened. They rarely thought they had done anything wrong, which was how they were able to evade detection—their outer behavior was unchanged.

Reed shivered, partly from the chilling breeze of the early morning but mainly at the thought of what Milacio was involved in. He was glad Trent was safe and sound back at the hotel, packing his suitcase and soon to be on the ferry, far out of harm's way.

"We're going to Salina. Very close to Panarea but very far from the mainland in distance and time." Milacio's description gave the place a sense of mystery, romance, and foreboding. "There's a very old churchyard there, and an old winery."

"The one where your wine is made?" Reed scanned his brain for the name of the dreadful stuff. Trent would remember.

"No, no." Milacio chuckled amiably. "The Malvasia is grown on Lìpari, hence the name. Malvasia delle Lìpari."

"Oh, right." Reed gave a suitably self-deprecating laugh but cursed his memory lapse.

"This one is no longer in service, but it's a fascinating historical site. I had planned a little picnic for the spot." He waved a hand in the direction of Panarea as if invoking the spirit of the absent Trent.

The day was agonizingly long. Reed had no interest in learning the intricacies of growing grapes on the unforgiving slopes of Salina, nor the comparison to the ancient techniques used to produce the world-famous Malvasia wine. He didn't want to taste another glass of the sickly sweet stuff, but he put on his best smile and faked it as if his life depended on it.

Because he knew now that it did. He didn't know just how Milacio was involved, but he knew Brett had been killed within a mile of Milacio's home, and that was no coincidence.

"This has been truly fascinating," Reed lied. "Now I will say I'm looking forward to that picnic you mentioned."

"Just one more stop; then we'll head back to the boat, where I'm sure Enrico has arranged our repast."

They trudged around the far side of the old building to a ring of ancient stones.

"As you can see, the weather here in the islands is very unforgiving." Milacio pulled on an iron handle and a door opened, exposing a set of stone steps leading underground. "We do not bury our dead at the surface or risk the wind and sea reclaiming them. This is the ingenious local solution." Milacio indicated whatever lay beneath them.

Reed took a small step toward the stairs and leaned closer.

"Shall we take a look? It's incredible." Milacio reached into the breast pocket of his jacket, and Reed considered tackling him. Had Milacio brought a gun? What was he planning?

Before Reed's brain processed an answer, Milacio brought out a flashlight and flicked it on, then directed the beam downward.

"Take a look, Rick!"

Reed edged closer, even more aware of the danger he was now in. Milacio could clobber him and dump his body here. Why had he come alone?

Mainly so he could occupy Milacio while Trent left the island. And for a chance to process everything he had learned over the course of the past few days. But his brain still refused to assemble the pieces into anything coherent.

Time was running out.

"What do you think?"

Reed peered down, angling his head to see what the flashlight beam illuminated: a pile of skulls and bones lay near the bottom of the stone steps, but farther along the passageway, Reed could see other bones arranged in intricate patterns.

"Our local *catacombe*. Did you visit them in Rome? Very popular with tourists."

Reed took a breath. Yes, they were supposed to be tourists, doing touristy things. Thankfully, that was one site they'd managed to hit before White's fateful phone call.

"Yes, we did. Eerily magnificent." Trent had absolutely hated the place. He'd wanted to leave five minutes into the tour, and Reed talked him into staying with promises of elaborate sexual delights.

So far, Trent hadn't gotten his reward because White had called that afternoon. *Soon*, Reed promised silently. *Once we're both somewhere safe.*

As Reed went through the motions, he thought about how much Trent would enjoy every moment of Milacio's tour and lectures. It was precisely the kind of excursion Trent loved. Spending the day without him, doing something Trent enjoyed, only made Reed's job more difficult. But putting Trent on that ferry was the right thing. He only hoped he'd been able to get away safely. That knowledge made Reed's job easier.

Already he had a good idea of Milacio's level of resources. The man could control a fleet of ships on three continents. His shipping routes included Europe, Africa, and parts of Asia. While luxurious by local standards, his magnificent home remained quite modest for the fortune he'd amassed over the years. Since most Italians managed to avoid paying at least some of their taxes, Reed suspected his true net worth totaled several times the amount on public record, making him a very formidable, exceedingly dangerous foe.

A man with so much money at stake would be ruthless. But what had Brett discovered that got him killed?

Reed still had no clue what had become of Peter.

Reed refused to believe Peter could be collaborating with Milacio. No matter what Reed knew of him, he could not imagine Peter would let his partner get slaughtered like Brett had been. Would he?

The scars on Reed's back throbbed as he recalled the man who put them there. And what had happened on the long-ago mission with Peter. Despite their history, Reed refused to believe Peter was a dirty agent.

Could Peter have changed so much?

As they rode the hydrofoil back to Panarea, Reed took in the lush beauty of the island, the desolate but immense power of Stromboli in the distance. Could this much wealth turn someone like Peter into a killer, or at least into looking the other way? If Peter's relationship with Brett was even a fraction as close as his partnership with Reed, the answer had to be "no."

What man could sleep with a partner and knowingly let him be hacked to death?

Reed hoped like hell Peter hadn't descended that far.

25

Chi non risica non rosica.
He who never takes risks, can't win.
  —Italian proverb

AFTER Reed left to meet Milacio, Trent sat on the bed, staring at his suitcase through a veil of tears. He sobbed, and this time he didn't try to hide his fear. He had a sick feeling in his gut that something would happen to Reed, that he'd end up like Brett or missing like Peter. Trent didn't hate Peter; he just didn't understand how he fit into Reed's life. Why hadn't Reed mentioned him before they got to Italy?

He threw the few things he'd taken out back into the suitcase, not even bothering to fold them properly. Glancing at the clock on the nightstand, Trent tried to imagine where Reed was at that moment. What was he doing? Was he thinking about Trent?

Probably not.

Is he safe? That was more important.

As much as that hurt Trent, he knew it was for the best. Reed had to focus on Milacio, figure out what he was up to and where he might have taken Peter. If they'd killed Peter, the body would have turned up, like Brett's. Then Trent realized that they hadn't seen or heard any cops over at the house where Brett had died. They hadn't heard any sirens or gossip from the front desk clerks. The entire little town was still operating as usual. Maybe Peter was lying dead and undiscovered in another room somewhere on Panarea.

Trent shook off the idea of doing any snooping around on his own. The last thing he wanted was to find another dead body. Or worse, *become* another dead body. He got his things together and resigned himself to getting on the ferry like he'd promised Reed.

At the door, he turned back and looked at the bed, still rumpled from where he and Reed had been together only hours earlier. He'd managed to get a few more days together, but now it was time to let Reed do his job and for Trent to play it safe. He tried not to think about Reed meeting up with Peter again. Of course Peter had nothing to do with Reed sending him away. Did he?

Trent let out a sigh and looked at the bed, willing his brain to remember how Reed had felt and tasted and how he'd touched Trent. The smell of him and the way his fingers felt on Trent's skin. The sounds he made while he slept.

One fat tear slid down Trent's cheek as he closed the door and rolled his suitcase along the broken stone path toward the road that led to the ferry.

A few locals waved at him as he passed, including the woman who ran the hotel.

"*Buonviaggio*, Signor Trent!" she called cheerfully.

The walk to the ferry mooring took only a few minutes, even with the suitcase. Trent cast an eye around the small harbor, half hoping to see Reed at Milacio's boat, but a knot of fear in his gut reminded him why he was leaving in the first place. He continued to the small building across from the ferry mooring and sat down on a worn and splintered wooden bench as a dozen or so people waited for the ferry to begin boarding. He didn't have a ticket, and no one was at the little window.

"How do we get tickets?" he asked a girl with a backpack sporting a large Canadian flag.

"Dunno." She shrugged. "If they don't open the window, I guess we buy them on the boat."

Trent pulled some money out of his wallet, waiting for some instructions. The girl watched him.

"What part of Canada are you from?" he asked just to keep his mind off Reed—and Peter.

The girl looked around before leaning in close. "I'm not really Canadian," she told him in a conspiratorial whisper.

"You're not? Then why—"

"'Cause a lot of people don't like Americans, you know? So if they think you're Canadian, they're a lot nicer. Canadians don't start wars."

Trent nodded. "Right." He realized several other backpackers had Canadian flags. He motioned toward one of them.

"Oh, he's really Canadian. He doesn't like Americans much either, turns out." The girl gave a loud sniff and wiped the back of her hand across her nose. Trent was glad she hadn't offered to shake hands.

"I wonder why," Trent replied, but the girl missed his sarcastic tone. *No wonder Americans get a bad rap*, he thought.

He pulled out his little green notebook and scribbled some notes. The girl watched as he did this, then pulled out a journal of her own and started writing. Every few minutes Trent checked his watch. Eleven o'clock had come and gone. It was nearly noon, and no one had come to open the ferry ticket window. Trent put his notebook and pen away and stood up, stretching his legs. There was some movement on the ferry itself, and he wandered outside the crowded little office to see if he could get any information from someone on the boat.

"What's the delay?" Trent asked a man standing at the railing, watching the ferry bobbing in the small harbor.

The man replied in a rapid stream of Italian.

"'E say no one knows. We are also waiting," a young Italian woman translated for Trent in halting, accented English. She had long hair tied in a ponytail and wore a pastel pink-and-blue striped jacket over jeans. She reminded Trent of Milacio's cook, Tessa. The memory led him to think of Reed until he realized the girl and the young man were staring at him.

"Oh, thanks."

A flurry of shouting erupted from the deck of the ferry as three slightly grease-covered workmen came down the gangplank, furiously gesticulating and shaking their heads. Trent glanced at the woman for a translation.

"Sounds like something is wrong with the hengine," she said. "They say they may need a part from Lìpari, so if they cannot fix it now, they'll have to wait till the hydrofoil can bring one on We-neds-day." She sounded out the last word with evident concentration, adding a charming Italian shrug. "*Mercoledì*," she said, using the Italian word with much more confidence.

Her male companion nodded, then shook his head and made a few hand gestures Trent hadn't come across yet.

"Thanks." Trent took in a breath heavy with the pungent harbor aromas of sea, fish, and motor oil, then wheeled his suitcase back toward the office.

This time there was a sign that read "14:00," so apparently the crew thought they'd have the boat fixed by two o'clock. Unless that was supposed to be 2:00 p.m. on Wednesday. The ticket window was open, and a short elderly man was selling tickets and taking passenger luggage behind the counter.

"Leave your bag and take a load off," the fake Canadian girl said, coming up behind Trent and frightening him.

He glanced at the old man, not sure he wanted to trust him with his suitcase, but he also didn't feel like standing around here all afternoon.

"It's safe. I mean, who's gonna want your dirty clothes, right?"

Trent was about to mention that plenty of people would want his designer clothes, even if they were dirty, but stopped himself in time. "Right. Dirty laundry. No one would want that! Eww."

She nodded, put the earbuds back in, and rocked herself out of the little office.

Trent handed over his suitcase and some euros and in return got a ticket with a number scrawled in red felt-tip that matched a tag the old man had attached to his suitcase. At least he didn't have to lug the damn thing around while he waited.

He wandered back out to the pier and watched the workmen argue with each other for a while. Not much chance of any progress before 2:00 p.m.

It felt like a huge waste of time when he could be doing something useful. Like helping Reed. With Milacio and Reed off for an excursion to Salina, Trent could make another visit to Milacio's to discover something incriminating in his art collection. Clearly Reed wasn't taking Trent's observations seriously. What if Trent could find some critical piece of information and leave a note for Reed? He remembered how to do the code.

Wouldn't Reed be impressed if Trent left him a vital clue in the secret code? The secret lovers' code. The more Trent thought about Reed and Peter leaving each other sexy messages in their secret code, the more his stomach hurt. An unfamiliar sting of jealousy prompted a need to outdo Peter by leaving Reed a more important message than Peter ever had.

Trent wanted to discover something to help Reed before he got on that boat.

Now where would he find an important clue?

The source of everything seemed to be Milacio, and Milacio had taken Reed to the winery on Salina for the day.

Milacio's house would be empty.

TRENT had his camera in his day pack, along with his little notebooks. If he could snap some photos of the art pieces he had questions about, then Reed could use his FBI resources to research the pieces and figure out what Milacio was up to with the art portion of the scam. So far, though, it didn't make sense, at least to Trent. He admitted he had little knowledge of art crimes beyond what he'd learned from Reed and the research he'd done when he wrote a novel based on their involvement with the Ruby Buddha in Thailand.

Reed had filled him in on some of the auction shenanigans, but how on earth was Milacio involved? Why would he lie about owning a Kenyan coffee plantation or try to pass off Ivorian art as Kenyan? What was in the Ivory Coast?

Milacio had tried to keep Trent away from the African art once he'd questioned the provenance of the first piece, so he really wanted to go back and take a closer look. Damn, he wished he had his laptop now so he could Google some of these things himself and not wait for Reed to do the research.

But Trent had to see the items before either of them could figure out what Milacio's game was.

He hired a golf-cart taxi in the village and rode up the beautiful winding roads that led to Milacio's hilltop home. Again, Trent marveled at the hardiness of the trees, some blown nearly to the ground by the relentless ocean winds. As they made their way higher up, they passed through forests on the leeward side of the island, which didn't get the same high winds. These trees were nearly vertical, almost normal in their growth patterns.

He scribbled some notes down to remember the variation in scenery in this remarkable place. Too bad he and Reed had come here under such grave circumstances and weren't able to fully enjoy the beauty and mystery of the islands. Just another place to add to the list of places to come back to when their lives returned to normal.

Normal. The word seemed alien to Trent right now. Since he'd met Reed, everything in his life had been turned upside down. Not that he regretted any of it. He wouldn't trade any of this for the time before Reed, when Trent lived a hollow shell of an existence, still mourning the loss of his lover and afraid to try anything new.

The taxi bounced in the ruts near the top of the hill, and the driver turned toward Trent as he slowed.

"*Milacio? La casa di Signor Milacio, sì?*"

"*Sì.* Milacio." Trent nodded as the cart was about to pull into the drive, then realized he didn't want to show up on the doorstep. He remembered Tessa, and the possibility of other servants. The last thing he needed was to announce his arrival. "Here is okay. Stop." He reached forward and squeezed the man's shoulder, hoping that would communicate his intent. "*Qui. Qui.*" He repeated the word for "here," and the driver slammed on the brakes, the tires screeching and echoing off the dense foliage.

He pulled some money out of his pocket and handed it to the driver, then got out of the cart. As he watched it bounce down the hill and around a curve out of sight, Trent realized he had no way of getting back down any time soon. He had a couple of hours before the ferry would leave in the best-case scenario, and until Wednesday in the worst.

If he missed the boat, Reed would be furious—unless Trent found something really important. And he wasn't going to find anything standing in the middle of the road.

He crept into the woods and traced the route of the driveway, staying far enough away that if anyone happened to drive past, he would be hidden by the trees. As he got closer to the house, the trees thinned out and he had to be extra careful as he approached the front of the boxy white structure.

He tried to recall where in the house Milacio kept his artwork. Trent moved away from the road, closer to the back of the house, and assessed the terrain. Because the house was built against the side of the hill, there wasn't much yard in the back. The upper level had the terrace where they'd eaten lunch, and the lower levels had their own verandas, but he couldn't just waltz right up to one of those. The floor-to-ceiling windows looking out on the balcony in the direction of Salina made him entirely too visible to anyone inside. No wonder Milacio had said he wasn't concerned about security.

Trent was going to have to try for entry through one of the small windows away from the wide-open verandas, but the hillside fell away sharply to the side, and it wasn't going to be easy looking into any of the windows. It appeared Milacio had deliberately situated his collection in the most inaccessible portion of the house.

Trent took a few deep breaths and thanked his lucky stars he'd been branching out at the gym. In addition to more cardio, he'd signed up for a series of rock-climbing classes, though he missed as many as he attended. It was hard enough lugging his heavy frame up and down the plastic footholds with a harness, brand-new ropes, and a trusted pal on belay to keep him from falling, but he had no safety equipment here. He wished he hadn't missed so many sessions at Climb-X. If only he'd been on his Michael Westen kick sooner, he'd be much better prepared for an all-terrain assault on a shady art collector.

The idea of it struck him, and he let out a chuckle, remembering too late to cover his mouth. The laughter echoed off the rocks and the smooth stucco surface of the house. He hoped no one was home or that someone might mistake him for a noisy bird.

This was way harder than it looked in the movies and television shows. Trent suddenly had an increased level of respect for James Bond, Michael Westen, and most of all Reed. Of course, Reed had training for all of this back when he was an Army Ranger. Unfortunately that led to images of Reed's naked body, and Trent had another momentary lapse of concentration.

He moved slowly down the slope until he was even with the first window. It was open, and he slowly peered in so he wouldn't get the attention of anyone who happened to be there. The room was Milacio's office. They hadn't been invited in here, but it was obvious from the enormous desk that looked out on the ocean through a huge, nearly floor-to-ceiling window on the opposite side of the room.

Trent assessed the size of the window and looked down at his body. Could he fit in here? It would take a lot of effort to maneuver around toward the larger window on the other side of the room, and that one appeared to be closed. Chances were good that such a large window would have an alarm.

Trent wished he'd paid more attention to what Reed had asked about security. It had been so damn casual Trent had nearly missed the question. He added another point in Reed's column for skill and subtlety. He tightened his grip on the rocks and recalculated his chances of getting into the open window.

First he poked his head in slowly, in case there was a motion detector, but nothing happened. Below the window was a chair. Good place to land. This might work. If he could get his shoulders through the opening, his hips would fit with no problem. He moved inch by inch, and angling himself, he managed to get his shoulders through the opening. He was glad he'd cut back on the weights. He'd been a bit self-conscious about losing some bulk, but now he was grateful he'd changed his workout routine. He still had sufficient upper-body strength to bench-press his body weight, so he was confident he could lower himself once he got inside.

He propelled himself through the window, and as he crashed down onto the chair—far less cushioned than it appeared from outside—he regretted the decision to go headfirst. He'd know better next time.

He brushed himself off and, as quietly as possible, righted the chair he'd overturned. No one came running into the office, and no alarms went off. So far, so good. He didn't know yet how he'd get out again, but for the time being he was on cloud nine.

He made a solo high-five and then focused on his search.

A cluster of framed photographs on the desk immediately caught his attention. Milacio and Caterina. He'd been right! She was in on this. Whatever this was. Reed would eat his words.

Nothing incriminating on the surface of the desk, but Trent hadn't expected to find anything. He didn't know exactly what he was looking for, but he thought he'd know it when he found it.

He slid open the top drawer, the skinny one that often held pens or keys or some spare change. He spotted a set of keys and grabbed it, careful not to let them jangle as he slipped them into his pocket.

The rest of the drawers were locked, and he used the keys. He wished he hadn't put them in his pocket, since it was a lot harder to get them out silently than to put them in. He made mental notes of how to do this for next time.

Like there was going to be a next time.

One drawer held a set of files written in Italian, but Trent thought they could be shipping manifests. One folder held a sheet with a schedule. He could make out dates and what might be quantities of contraband shipments.

In the last file folder, what he saw nearly made him sick. It held a stack of photos of bodies. All of them had their hands and feet cut off.

Trent fought back the bile rising in his throat, thanking Reed for not letting him get too close to Brett's body the night before. Most of the men were African. In several of the photos, men in military uniforms posed with the corpses. Even more horrific, many of those in uniform were kids. Boys and one girl, all in their teens, wearing big bright grins as they showed off their victims.

The words in the coded note came back to him with increased significance. ICE. Diamonds. He'd been right. This was about diamonds. Diamonds from Africa. All the proof was right here in Milacio's desk.

Trent glanced at one of the photos of Caterina on top of the desk. She was with Milacio on the deck of a yacht, the sun glinting off the diamonds hanging off her ears. He felt even sicker seeing her smiling face compared to the carnage in the other photographs, especially the smiling faces of the children forced to murder.

He'd landed in something far beyond what he could handle. Should he take a photograph as proof for Reed or just leave them for a real agent to discover? No. If he took one, it would warn Milacio.

He slammed the drawer shut and turned back to the window. He was going to get out of here and back to the hotel to leave Reed a note about what he'd seen, then get on the ferry. He couldn't wait to get on the ferry. He never wanted to be on a ferry as much as he did right this minute.

He placed one foot on the chair to boost himself up to the window when he heard it.

The cocking sound of what had to be a very big gun.

"*Dove vai, amico?*"

Where ya going, buddy?

"He won't get far," a second voice said. This one was deeper, with a clipped accent. African.

He heard a second gun being cocked.

Trent gulped and scrambled toward the window, knowing he wouldn't get out before they shot him, but he had to try.

He felt something hard crash onto the back of his head. At least they hadn't shot him, he thought as everything turned black.

26

Ogni lassata è pirduta.

Missed opportunities never return.

    —Aeolian proverb

WHEN Reed got back to the room, he almost wished he hadn't sent Trent away. He'd been thinking of him far too much during the day, doing so many things Trent would have enjoyed. He wanted to talk to Trent, bounce ideas off him, tell him what he thought about Milacio's role in Peter's disappearance and Brett's murder.

He lay down on the bed and closed his eyes, trying to block out thoughts of Trent so he could concentrate on filtering through what he'd learned the last few days here on Panarea. He'd seen and heard plenty, but he couldn't clearly fit the pieces together into a coherent picture. Maybe a good night's sleep—alone—would do the trick.

But Reed wasn't sleepy. He got up, grabbed a jacket, and left the room. It wasn't particularly large, but without Trent it seemed empty and silent. They hadn't spent that many nights apart since Reed had moved to LA, and he was surprised how much he missed Trent's cheerful presence and near-constant stream of dialogue.

He traced the familiar path toward the marina. Milacio's boat had returned them to the smaller private marina on the other end of the island, and Reed hadn't been here since the morning. Now, cool breezes—sure signs the weather had changed for the season—blew off the water, bringing a mix of salt tang and pungent marine stench. When Reed rounded the bend in the path and the port came into view, his stomach lurched.

The ferry was still there.

Trent should have left hours ago, but the ferry remained at the dock, completely dark. Reed broke into a run toward the little ticket booth, where he found a note scribbled in indecipherable Italian. Of course no one would be working here now, but that wasn't the point.

If the ferry hadn't left Panarea, where was Trent?

He wasn't at their hotel. Reed tried not to panic as he retraced his steps, peering into the door at each of the little cafés between the dock and their room. Trent wasn't in any of them, and if anyone had seen him, Reed's nearly nonexistent Italian made conversation impossible.

"*Traghetto?*" He managed to remember the word for ferry.

The reply was a stream of rapid-fire local dialect, the only word of which he remotely recognized: *Mercoledì*. Wednesday. It was Monday. Apparently the ferry wouldn't be leaving for at least two days.

But where was Trent?

Reed rushed back to the hotel. Trent's suitcases were gone. Maybe Reed had overreacted and that wasn't the same ferry that was there in the morning. He was about to visit the front desk to ask when a knock sounded at the door, and he jumped a good three inches off the bed.

"Trent?" He tried to keep the excitement out of his voice as he rushed to the door and nearly tore it off its hinges in his haste to open it.

"*Signore….*" The rest of the words were a jumbled mess Reed didn't even hear.

Because the man standing there had Trent's little suitcase with him.

"Where's Trent?" he asked. "Trent?" He made gesture measuring out Trent's height, hoping the man understood.

"'E leave bag *traghetto*," the man replied with shrug and waved his arm in the direction of the ferry. "*Non l'ho visto*. No see Signor Trent. *Non l'ho visto*." He shook his head and made commiserating noises that were apparently universal; then the man turned and headed away.

Reed slammed the door shut and sat back down on the bed, chin in his hands, and tried to think.

Now he was really worried.

He tore out the desk drawer, hoping to find some note from Trent. He looked in, under, and around the little night table, and all he found were the vials of lube they'd used. No note, no sign.

Feeling foolish, Reed headed into the bathroom and turned the hot water on full blast until the mirror fogged up. It was smeared, but no secret coded message. He tried to laugh at Trent's recent interest in codes and his crazy ideas of spycraft. Maybe Trent's little obsession had led him into something he shouldn't have gotten into.

Something he might not live to get out of.

Reed's gut churned again, and thankfully he was in the bathroom, because his body ridded itself of the fine meal Milacio had served him earlier. He rinsed his mouth and brushed his teeth twice, and he still tasted the bitterness.

Worse than that, he had no fucking clue where Trent might be.

Reed had two options: stay here and figure out what Milacio was up to, or head out and find Trent.

IF TRENT needed further proof of just how bad his idea to investigate Milacio was, he got it when he was tossed, bound and gagged, into the trunk of an ancient Mercedes, which was now bouncing down the hill from Milacio's house.

If he had any doubts, they were completely dispelled as the car hit another bump and he crashed against the trunk lid. With his hands behind his back, he couldn't protect himself or rub the bruise he could already feel forming on the back and side of his skull.

These guys were way worse than those Thai mobsters.

The car hit another bump, causing Trent's nose to smash against the floor of the trunk. He wasn't sure, but he suspected it might be bleeding now, and possibly broken. It hurt like fuck. He'd only been punched in the face a few times, back home in Oklahoma when some guys in high school found out he was gay. Trent had a foot and at least twenty pounds on all of them, and they came out the worse for the encounter, but their fists had still done some damage before he decided to fight back.

It was the first and last time anyone had tried to beat him up, and it won him some grudging respect from the homophobic bastards.

But the guys who'd thrown him in the trunk clearly didn't stop at a few punches. The photos in Milacio's desk might be old, but when Trent recalled Brett's recently mutilated body, he thanked his lucky stars only his nose was bleeding, at least for the moment.

He consoled himself with this meager knowledge when the car stopped short, sending him flying first forward, then against the back of the trunk. The engine cut out and Trent's stomach clenched. He was safer while the car was moving than he would be once they got to wherever they were taking him.

He heard two voices arguing in a mix of English and Italian. He couldn't make out any of the words, just the tone. He'd been in Italy long enough to realize that people often sounded like they were arguing even when they were chatting amiably with friends. Maybe it wasn't as bad as he imagined. Yeah, right. Even he didn't believe that.

A key clicked in the lock and the trunk lid flew up, letting in a cool whoosh of air. Pine tree scent mingled with sea salt. He noticed moonlight but no artificial lights. They could be anywhere on the island, Trent realized. Up on the hill, where there were lots of trees, but still miles from either Milacio's house or the hotel and Reed.

Oh, Reed, why didn't I listen to you?

Then Trent remembered it wasn't his fault the ferry didn't go. But he should have stayed at the hotel instead of running off with his little bag of spy tricks courtesy of Michael Westen, who wasn't even a real spy. And he'd been fired, so maybe he hadn't even been a good fake spy—

Trent's musings were interrupted when one of Milacio's guards grabbed his arm and pulled. Hard.

With most men a strong tug like that might lift them halfway out of the trunk, but Trent wasn't most men. He was tall and worked out a lot. All the thug accomplished was wrenching Trent's shoulder, sending lightning bolts of agony up his arm. He swallowed the resulting cry of pain. He wouldn't give them the satisfaction.

The thug let loose a corresponding stream of what must be local dialect obscenities.

The guy looked down and shouted at Trent, then punched him in the gut. Not much power behind the blow, but it wasn't a lovetap either.

Trent considered staying put and not helping them get him out of the trunk just out of spite. Then he remembered guns and knives could still do plenty of damage even if he were lying in the trunk when they decided to kill him. He sat up, and the two men hauled him out of the trunk so quickly he lost his balance and landed on his knees. Then he fell forward, nearly smacking his chin on the ground. Soft, pine needle-padded earth. It smelled kind of like Christmas.

Trent knew he'd never enjoy the smell of Christmas ever again. If he lived till Christmas.

The thugs each took an arm and pulled him to his feet, then hauled him in the direction of a building that gradually came into focus about thirty feet from the car, away from the road. He tried to look around to get some bearings, but the taller of the two thugs smacked him in the back of the head, right where they'd hit him with the gun. Bright flashes of light mingled with the pain echoing in his skull. He kept his gaze forward after that.

If he didn't know they carried semiautomatic weapons, he might have tried to make a break for it. Even with his arms tied, he had enough strength and weight that he could overpower at least one. He'd been doing his cardio diligently since he'd gotten back from Thailand, and he could run miles easily. He was supposed to run a 10K race in a few weeks' time, and he knew he was in good shape.

But he couldn't outrun a bullet.

He knew he'd made the right decision when the short one pulled him to a stop at the door to the low building and jabbed a gun into his left kidney while the other, a beefy African who matched Trent in weight if not height, unlocked the door.

The big guy pulled the door open on creaking hinges while Shorty planted a foot against Trent's ass and kicked him into the building, shouting something unintelligible in Italian before pulling the door shut behind him. A raisiny-sweet smell surrounded Trent as he heard the deadbolt slide shut with a rusty scrape.

"Who the fuck are you?"

27

TRENT was just climbing up from the filthy floor when he heard the voice. *American.* He looked in the general direction of the sound, and in the moonlight-tinged gloom, he saw the dark outline of a man standing near one of the windows at the far end of the room. Along the sides of the room, dozens of boxes were stacked, but the area in the middle was clear.

"I guess your momma didn't teach you much about manners, did she?" Trent shot back. He wasn't in a very good mood. Why didn't this guy come over and help him?

"Oh, look, we got a nice little Texas boy here."

"I'm not from Texas." Trent nearly spat out the words as he got to his feet. That was harder than he expected with his hands tied. He assessed the damage to his body. Besides his head and throbbing nose, everything seemed to work more or less as intended, though he ached from head to toe.

"Ah. My mistake," the man said. "Oklahoma, then?" The voice softened slightly, but the man still didn't make any move to help—or hurt—Trent.

Trent didn't reply. There were several large windows that let in enough moonlight that he could now get his bearings in the room. In the dimness, he squinted in the direction of the voice. It was only then Trent noticed the light glinting off something on the man's ankle, which was fastened to an iron bar attached to the wall. This guy was another prisoner.

"Are you Peter, by any chance?"

"That's on a need-to-know basis."

"That's all I need to know, I guess." Trent let out a sigh. If Peter the supposed superagent was locked up here, what chance was there of either Trent getting free or Reed finding him? Then a horrible thought hit: what if Reed didn't even know Trent was missing? If the ferry departed, Reed would just assume he was on it. He'd left his luggage at the dock when he'd gone exploring, and someone probably would have just loaded it on the boat. Now it was most likely sitting in Milazzo in some lost-luggage room—if it hadn't been stolen—and Reed would think Trent was safe and sound, zipping around the Italian countryside, enjoying the sights and scenery.

"So, you never answered my question," Peter said, reminding Trent he wasn't alone.

Trent's stomach tightened again. Unfortunately, the only way Reed was coming to get him was if he figured out where Peter was. He hated admitting that he'd only be rescued if Reed was looking for Peter. What was there still between these two that had made Reed leave their Roman holiday to come here to death and danger? Only if Reed found Peter would he find Trent, but Trent wasn't sure he could handle knowing that. He blinked a few times, hoping the thought of Reed's reunion with Peter wouldn't make him cry. After what Trent had overheard about Reed and Peter from Felton back in that safe house, Trent didn't particularly like Peter. But he had to hope like hell Reed still cared enough for his former partner to go looking for him.

"I'm Trent."

"Oh, great. You're Trent. Is that supposed to mean something to me?"

"Reed's partner."

"Reed? Reed Acton?" Peter paused. "Reed's here?"

Trent couldn't quite make out the emotion behind Peter's tone. Was it surprise, pleasure, excitement?

"Yeah, we were in Rome and—"

"Rome? How on earth did you end up here?"

"Brett's code—"

"Brett. Where is he? Did he call for you and Reed?"

So Peter didn't know.

REED had to find Trent, and soon.

Had Milacio's men come to get him while Reed visited the winery on Salina with Milacio?

No. Trent had gone to the ferry as planned, because his suitcase had been there, but for some reason he'd left the harbor and his luggage before the ferry was postponed, or he would have retrieved his bags himself.

This couldn't be one of his pseudo-spy ideas, could it? Reed reasoned out what Trent might be thinking by disappearing without his belongings. There was one way to know if Trent had decided to abandon the bag as a ruse.

Reed opened up Trent's suitcase and found his toiletries bag. What he saw inside sent another chill down his spine.

Trent's favorite bodywash.

No way would Trent willingly leave this behind. He'd pack it in his day pack and keep it with him if he left the suitcase on purpose. So he hadn't left the suitcase on purpose.

He'd been kidnapped.

Reed hoped it was just kidnapping. The more he turned over the pieces of what he'd learned, the more frightened he became for Trent's well-being.

He ticked the items off: Milacio's shipping business between Africa and Europe, his lies about owning property in Kenya when he really owned a coffee plantation in the Ivory Coast, the underwater dig operation with experienced divers, and the African men Reed had noticed on the ship. When he added that to the state of Brett's mutilated corpse, it made perfect sense.

The Revolutionary United Front—known as RUF—cut off the arms of anyone they suspected of stealing their diamonds. Impossible to steal with no hands. An excellent warning to anyone else who dared.

"ICE NOT ROCK," the note near Brett's body had said.

Ice was diamonds, just as Trent had suggested.

Blood diamonds.

Milacio must be using his shipping business and the cover of coffee exports to bring conflict diamonds from West Africa—specifically Sierra Leone, Angola, and Liberia, where UN sanctions had put strict export controls in place—into Italy, then getting them out of Italy again by smuggling them in the antiquities he sold at auction.

The elaborate bidding ruse at the auction house signaled the eventual buyers to the correct pieces, and Caterina arranged the export licenses for the Italian antiquities.

Reed let out a sigh as he closed in on an explanation that included everything he'd discovered. Everything he and Trent had discovered, he corrected himself. If it hadn't been for Trent's out-of-the-box thinking about the ice and recognizing that Milacio was dealing with West and not East Africa, Reed might not have been able to piece together this quilt of random information.

But where was Trent?

28

"SO, YOU'RE Reed's new partner?" Peter asked.

"Yes. Yes, I am." Trent was standing now, shaky on his feet, but he pulled himself up to his full height. He still had his hands tied behind him, but he wasn't about to ask Peter for help getting loose.

"Bureau must be cutting the training budget."

Peter spoke almost under his breath, but in the silence Trent heard perfectly well. He decided not to dignify the insult with a response. After the repeated blows to his head, his witty repartee wasn't what it usually was, so even if he wanted to, he couldn't think of a good reply.

An idea hit him, and slowly Trent sat back down on the floor—very slowly, so as not to jar his aching head.

"Taking a nap?"

Trent ignored that comment and rolled over onto his side. He bent at the waist, and with more twisting than he expected, he got his bound wrists past his ass and legs so they were bound in front of him. He rolled back onto his rear and got to his feet.

"Good job, junior."

Trent was never gladder for his long arms and short torso. He just hoped he never needed to do this again. He was still bound, but at least he could use his hands. "Don't you want to know where Brett is?" he asked.

"He must have gotten word to you, which is why you're here?"

"He's dead.

"Oh, Jesus."

Trent was only slightly satisfied to hear genuine sadness in Peter's reply. He should have asked about his own partner sooner instead of hurling insults at Trent.

"Tell me about it, Trent."

"We found him in a little house up the hill on the far side of the main harbor." He walked toward Peter, at the back of the room, stopping half way to glance at the nearest pile of boxes.

"I was heading to meet him when they grabbed me."

"What do you mean? You were on the island the whole time?"

"I don't know how long you've been here, but I arrived from Palermo a couple of days ago. Made contact with Decker via message drop rather than face to face since I was UC. He failed to respond to my second drop, so I searched for where he'd been staying and found the sign. I went to check on him and got jumped on my way to the cottage."

Trent had to think about that sequence of events. Peter must have arrived on the next ferry after Trent, the day they'd gone to Stromboli. Trent felt waves of guilt roll over him. Brett Decker had been killed while he and Reed had been enjoying themselves—and each other—waiting for Milacio to arrange the trip to the recovery vessel. He'd seen Decker that day at the beach. Trent voiced his suspicions. "Think someone spotted Decker and followed him?"

Peter shook his head and let out a loud breath. "Brett was a bit too eager, and he tended to forget his training once he got into the field."

"But they spotted you too."

"There was a guy on the ferry who could have been a tail…. I was pretty worried about Decker, so yeah, I might have not been as careful as I should have." Peter shook his head, eyelids at half-mast. Trent wondered what their relationship had been. No matter—Peter seemed suitably upset at Decker's death, and Trent felt like a heel for bringing up Peter's own failings.

"What about Milacio? He dirty after all? The Palermo broker didn't give up anything useful on him."

"Yeah. We're onto him." Trent thought about the photos in Milacio's desk and shuddered. He wasn't going to admit to Peter how he got caught red-handed in Milacio's office.

"Reed made the contact okay? Brett was practically begging me to let him do it. Thought maybe he made a move without authorization. Milacio got suspicious with all the sudden interest in his collection."

"He invited us for lunch, and he didn't seem particularly doubtful. Served some great food. And wine."

"Guy owns a wine business on top of the shipping. The guy in Palermo raved about the stuff. Mishmash or something. Tried to get me to drink it while I was down there, but I'm not a big wine drinker."

"Malvasia?" Trent read the top of the nearest box.

Even in the dimness, Trent could make out Peter's sneer because the moonlight glinted off his teeth.

"Yeah, something like that."

"That's what's in these boxes. That local wine."

"You don't say. Guess I should have recognized the smell."

"This must be Milacio's version of a wine cellar."

Trent wondered what Peter would think of Reed going off to the winery with Milacio. Then Trent realized Reed didn't care about the wine, he was just going to find out information. No point in mentioning any of it. Instead, he pulled the flaps open on the box—much harder than he expected with his hands bound.

Trent pulled a bottle out of the box. He was thirsty and he had no clue when—or if—those guys would be back with any food or water. "Want some wine?" He held the bottle up toward Peter.

"Yeah. I am a bit parched."

Trent glanced around, wondering what the chances were of finding a cork puller here. He whirled around and saw a small table on the other side of the room. Sure enough, there was a corkscrew on top. He couldn't manage to open the bottle with his hands tied.

He handed the corkscrew to Peter, whose hands were unbound, though his ankle was cuffed to the wall. Peter opened the wine, and they sat on the floor, taking turns. They finished the bottle off in no time.

"Another?" Trent asked.

Peter nodded, and Trent retrieved another bottle for him to open. This time they took smaller sips.

"Reed was looking for you. That's why he's still here." The wine was beginning to hit Trent's bloodstream, and no wonder. He couldn't remember the last time he had anything to eat.

"What about you?"

"What do you mean?"

"Aren't you both here looking for us?" Peter grabbed the corkscrew and tried to use it to unlock the cuff around his ankle.

"I'm not an agent."

Peter's expression turned thoughtful, though it was hard to tell in the poorly lit room. "You said you were Reed's part—" Peter paused. He put the corkscrew down and stared directly into Trent's eyes. "Ah. That kind of partner."

"Yeah. That kind of partner."

"He took you on a mission?" Peter tried the corkscrew again, angling it in various ways, to no avail.

"He didn't know I was following."

Peter didn't say anything for a minute.

"You came after him, why? How?" Peter shook his head.

Trent had nothing to lose by telling the truth. "To warn him about Caterina."

"You work for some other agency?"

"No."

"The guy that dumped you in here, he made some comment about this is where the spies belong and how you didn't fool Milacio with your act."

"My act?" Trent wondered that meant. "No. I'm a writer. A novelist." That sounded more impressive.

"A novelist?" Peter let out a laugh, but to Trent's surprise it wasn't filled with scorn. It sounded almost impressed. "You risked your life with these smugglers to help Reed?"

"Yeah," Trent said defiantly. He sat up straight again, and he might have puffed his chest out just a little.

"Damn." Peter shook his head again. "Damn." He took another swig from the bottle. "Give me your wrists."

Trent held out his hands, and Peter tried to untie his bonds.

"They usually have a thing on there to cut the foil, you know?" Trent said.

"Not on this one, but you don't want to cut the rope if you can avoid it."

"Why not?"

"Couple of reasons. One, longer rope makes a better weapon in case those guards come back before we get out of here. A garrote, for example."

Trent held back a reply, but his stomach knotted. He couldn't garrote someone, could he?

"Second, you can pretend you're still tied up and use surprise as a weapon. Can't do that if you cut the rope off."

Trent nodded. Michael Westen hadn't mentioned any of this. Trent was losing respect for him, but it made him appreciate how tough Reed's job really could be.

"I'll cut 'em off if you want, but I know that door is locked from the outside and the windows are too high up to escape. Boxes're too unstable for a big guy like you to climb up." Peter glanced around the room for a few moments and shook his head. "Even if I wasn't cuffed to the fucking wall, it would be tough to get out of here."

Trent picked up the bottle and drank. "They cut off his arms."

"What?"

"They cut off Brett's arms. Why would they do that?"

"Aw, fuck." Then Peter was silent, but his breathing was audible.

Trent almost wished he hadn't said anything now.

"The RUF—Revolutionary United Front—used to control Sierra Leone and the diamond mines. They cut off people's arms and legs. Anyone who opposed them. Real sadistic bastards. Even used a lot of child soldiers. Back then you were better off if they killed you, but they liked to make examples of people. The UN was powerless for years, but the RUF were finally defeated."

"They're here, in Italy?"

"No. The leaders are mostly in prison for war crimes. Or dead. I suspect Milacio had been working with them for years and employed some of the former soldiers as his own security forces, down in Africa and here, as he moved the diamonds on his ships."

"But you said they were in prison? Who's behind this now?"

"There are still plenty of diamonds being mined in Africa. Many of them are legit, but not all. I'd come to the conclusion that someone—Milacio, as it turned out—was helping divert stones from the regular process, circumventing international observers and export controls."

"With Milacio's boats. I'll bet he put them in the coffee. Which wasn't from Kenya."

"No." Peter smiled. "How did you know?"

"Don't ask." Trent didn't want to admit Reed had laughed at his coffee theories, but with what Peter said, the specifics made sense. The pieces fell into place. Trent smiled to himself. He couldn't wait to tell Reed.

"I was coming back here to get some additional proof about Milacio when we started working more closely with the Carabinieri agent on the international angle between Italy and the African countries."

Caterina? No wonder she knew what was up and White didn't.

"Peter, White didn't know any of this. He still thought it was about drugs. Reed thought it might be drugs, then he found a note in Brett's room. 'Ice not rock.' I said 'ice' means diamonds."

"You know White? Jesus."

"I met him in Thailand. Kind of by accident."

"Thailand? That Ruby Buddha deal?"

"Yeah. That's when I met Reed and, uh, got caught up in the deal."

"Huh." Peter shook his head. "Heard some rumors about that, but never would have seen Reed hooking up with someone like—"

"What, you think I'm not his type?" Trent got defensive again. He stood up too quickly. Between the wine and his head wound, he lost his balance and stumbled.

Peter laughed, and a moment later, Trent joined in.

"No, Trent. I think you're exactly what Reed needs."

Trent gave Peter a sideways glance, because the comment sounded more than vaguely offensive. Trent just wasn't certain whether Peter had insulted him or Reed, or both.

"I mean that in the nicest way. He needs someone like you, someone who'd come after him like that." Peter shook his head a few times and grabbed the bottle back from Trent. "Someone who cares that much about him." He drank the rest of the wine and stared off into the distance. "Not like me."

"What do you mean?" Trent's stomach lurched. The wine didn't help, but he knew Peter was going to say something Trent might not want to hear. "Never mind."

But the words were too late. Peter was already answering. "It was my fault. I left him there. I couldn't have known what would happen, but that wasn't the point."

"Where?" Trent asked, his voice barely a whisper. His gut roiled, and he thought he knew what Peter was about to say.

"Thai-Lao border. They captured him and… tortured him."

That was how Reed got those horrific scars.

29

REED knew he was outmanned, and there was no way to get any backup to the island even if he knew where Trent had been taken. Milacio had been with him all day, and he hadn't talked to anyone during their time together.

That meant there was a chance nothing had happened to Trent yet. Would Milacio's men risk harming him before consulting Milacio? Not likely.

A whisper of a plan—a crazy plan—began to form in Reed's mind. He grabbed the phone and dialed Milacio's home number without thinking. A woman answered.

"*Pronto?*"

"*Il signor Milacio, per favore.*"

"*Sì, signore.*"

Reed's heart pounded as he waited. He heard the woman speaking and male voices shouting in the background before the one voice he wanted to hear spoke.

"Milacio."

"Signor Milacio, it's Rick Allen. I wanted to thank you again for your hospitality today and—"

Milacio cut him off. "Signor Allen, I'm sorry, but this is not so good a time to talk. We've had a—how you say?—robbery here today. I'm checking the collection now before calling *polizia*."

"Robbery? Someone broke in?"

"Yes. My security guard just informed me."

Break-in? Security guard? Could the break-in have something to do with Trent? Milacio didn't *sound* like he had just killed Reed's companion, though he could be a much better actor than Reed gave him credit for.

"I'll try calling again tomorrow."

"*Sì. Domani.* Tomorrow." He hung up.

Reed raced out of the room.

Milacio was still at home, dealing with a break-in. Maybe Trent had gone snooping around and only been arrested by the local cops. Reed prayed it were as simple as that. If not, he might still be able to follow Milacio or his security men—henchmen, as Trent had called them.

He ran toward the harbor and the usual three or four taxis waiting for whoever might want a lift up the mountain.

"Milacio's house, *per favore,*" he said as he slid into the backseat. "*Rapido?*"

"*Sì, signore.*" The man started the engine and screeched out of the harbor. "Popular man, Signor Milacio, eh?"

"Popular?"

"I take your friend up there already today. Or I think maybe he goes to visit pretty maid. No want to go to front door, but no take taxi down again!" The driver let out a lascivious laugh that any other time might have been amusing.

At least Reed knew where Trent had gone. But why?

As they neared Milacio's house, Reed tapped the driver on the shoulder. "Drop me in the same place."

"Popular lady? Heh heh."

"Yes. Very popular." Reed gave the man a few bills, probably double what the fare was, but was out the door before the car came to a complete stop.

He found himself at the edge of Milacio's property. He waited until his eyes adjusted to the moonlight and he was able to pick his way through the woods, treading lightly so as not to snap a dry twig. The wind had picked up, and it whistled through the branches, an eerie sound he knew he'd never forget, no matter how tonight ended.

When he got close enough to the house to see the lights through the window, he crept low.

Could Trent be inside? Milacio wouldn't kill Trent at his house. Reed recalled how white and clean the entire house was. Milacio would never want to mess it all up with the amount of blood they'd left in the hotel room with Brett's body. His stomach roiled at the memory of the sight and the smell of dried blood.

Reed watched impatiently from the trees outside Milacio's house. A lot of vehicles were coming up the private road. He'd found a safe vantage point where he could see into the large sitting room, but he was not close enough to follow what was happening. Finally, the activity died down, and he edged toward the window to see clearly into the pure white room.

Milacio sat on a pristine white couch, again wearing a crisp white shirt with a pair of tan pants with knife-sharp creases. He'd changed his clothes from the designer jeans and pale-green rugby shirt he'd worn on their outing to the winery on Salina. All the whiteness contrasted sharply with what Reed remembered of Brett Decker's blood-spattered room and hacked-up corpse.

He spoke with animated gestures to several armed men, including the African man Reed had seen the previous day on the dive boat. At least, he wore the same paramilitary style uniform with the red cap. How many armed guards did this guy employ? Reed hoped only the ones in the room, which meant Trent might still be alive and safe somewhere.

None of the men had blood on their clothing. Another good sign. Reed glanced skyward. If he ever believed in a God, now was the time to remember how to pray.

As Reed watched, a short but solidly built man handed Milacio a small box. He opened it, pulled out a handgun, and went through the routine of checking the parts, then reassembled it and loaded it with one clip of ammo.

Trent wasn't here, Reed reasoned. There wouldn't be this much hustling around if he were. And he doubted they would kill him in Milacio's living room—or anywhere in the man's house. Any blood splatter would be a telltale sign Milacio couldn't afford to leave behind even if he abandoned the premises. Besides, the man was too fastidious to have any blood on his own hands. That was why he hired these men milling around with heavy artillery.

A sound in the distance got louder until it intruded into Reed's consciousness: another of the island's ubiquitous golf carts approached the house.

He scooted low to the ground, farther from both the road and the house, momentarily losing sight of Milacio. The cart pulled to a stop near the front door, and the driver leaped out as the passenger emerged from the back seat.

A tall blonde woman emerged from the car as elegantly as Venus rising from the waves in Botticelli's famous painting. She brushed off her skirt and smoothed a hand against her hair, which was pulled back sleekly, exposing cheekbones a model would kill for. But the sour look that swept across her face and the downturned mouth canceled out her beauty and grace.

The woman also wore a pair of dangling diamond earrings so large he could see them from twenty yards away. They reflected the pale moonlight and twinkled like stars at her ears. No wonder people killed for those things. They were beautiful, mesmerizing.

Reed didn't know fashion, but he'd absorbed enough from Trent to tell by the way the fabric accentuated her body that her clothes cost a small fortune. Trent's rambling story of his night in the safe house came back with sudden clarity.

This had to be Caterina.

30

I vecchi peccati hanno le ombre lunghe.

Old sins have long shadows.

—Italian proverb

CATERINA showing up here—now—couldn't be good. Clearly her role was larger than issuing export licenses.

She walked up to the door and opened it as if she owned the place. Milacio turned as she entered, and they had an animated conversation, none of which Reed could hear, but he guessed the content when the woman opened her purse and pulled out a silver handgun. She tossed the purse on the couch and shouted at one of the guards, who grabbed a phone off his belt and spoke into it before he rushed out the front door, right past Reed, and hopped into the same car that had brought Caterina.

Reed considered following the car and decided against it.

His best bet was staying with Milacio. If he and Caterina had their guns, they expected trouble here. If anything, Trent would be brought to them and questioned, rather than killed elsewhere. Milacio ran a far-reaching enterprise with enormous resources and seemed to have done so for years. He didn't get that by killing everyone who wandered into his sphere without finding out what they knew.

What Reed didn't want was for something terrible to happen to Trent because he didn't know anything. Trent couldn't handle pain the way Reed could. Or at least the way he once had. Now Reed wasn't certain just what he was capable of withstanding.

The car with the guard had been gone about ten minutes when Milacio and Caterina moved out of the living room area. Reed shifted position as carefully as possible in order to keep them in sight without revealing himself. They headed for the front door, but they stopped to put on coats brought to them by Tessa, the girl who'd waited on them at lunch the other day. She curtseyed obediently to Caterina, who grabbed the coat away from the girl as if she were a part of the furniture.

Milacio, however, took the offered coat and appeared to speak to the girl, perhaps thanking her. Reed noted the paradox: he could be nice to the servant girl while he had someone chop off Brett's arms and bash his head in. Milacio was a series of contradictions—from his immaculate white home to the blood and destruction he contributed to as he continued the deadly practice of smuggling diamonds out of one of the most war-torn corners of Africa.

The front door crashed open and Caterina emerged, shouting, followed by Milacio, who appeared to try to placate her. Reed wished he had paid more attention to Trent's suggestion and taken some of those Italian classes or listened to the tapes before their trip. He would love to know what those two were talking about.

The night had grown colder. Caterina shouted something and pulled her coat close around her. Reed didn't have a coat and he regretted not taking one, but he had left in too much of a hurry to think ahead. The wind whipped Caterina's hair, and at first she carefully smoothed it back, but as she grew increasingly annoyed with the weather's effect on her appearance, she gave up, shouting at Milacio the whole time.

They were waiting for someone or something.

A motorcycle zoomed up the driveway and stopped in front of Milacio. The rider parked the bike and raced around the far side of the house, then returned within a few minutes driving a dark Mercedes sedan. Milacio opened the back door for Caterina and slid inside after her, and the car tore down the hill.

Reed hesitated for a moment before taking advantage of the one break he'd gotten today. He hopped onto the cycle—thankfully the rider had left the keys in the ignition—and raced down the hill, keeping plenty of distance behind the car carrying Milacio.

They were heading somewhere with their weapons but no suitcases. They were going to take care of something and come back.

Something urgent, or Caterina wouldn't have gone along. Whatever it was she needed to do, clearly she wasn't happy about it.

The car ahead zigged and zagged down the twisting road, and its brake lights would have illuminated Reed if he got too close. He held back, hoping it wouldn't turn off out of his sight. Only when the road flattened did the car pick up speed, heading for the small private harbor where Milacio had brought his hydrofoil that afternoon.

Floodlights lit up the harbor like a Christmas tree, and activity buzzed on and around the hydrofoil.

PETER grabbed one of the empty bottles by the neck and whacked it against the wall, sending shards of glass flying. One nicked him on the cheek, leaving a crimson trail dripping along his jaw and onto his pants.

Trent felt along his own face, but he was unharmed. He grabbed the bottle from Peter.

"Careful. Don't hurt yourself."

"Does it matter?" Peter's words were slightly slurred.

"Yeah, it matters." Trent collected his thoughts. Wow, that sweet wine packed a punch. He knew he'd have one evil hangover in the morning. If he made it to morning. "We have to get out of here."

"We can't." Peter pointed to his ankle.

Broken bottles and corkscrews were no match for the thick steel.

"*I* can't, but you need to get out of here and find Reed," Peter went on.

"Yeah. Find Reed." Trent should have thought of that sooner. Why hadn't he? Why had he sat here with Peter when he could have escaped?

Oh yeah, the door was locked. He'd forgotten that part. He felt a little better. He was still trapped, but at least he hadn't missed an opportunity to escape.

"Give me your hands."

Trent held his hands out, not sure what Peter had in mind. The broken shards of bottle were within reach.

Peter grabbed the corkscrew, and with surprising dexterity for a man who'd consumed as much wine as he had, he inserted the point into the knot binding Trent's wrists. He manipulated the corkscrew for a few moments, and Trent saw the knot slowly give itself up as Peter worked one loose end until he was able to pull it through the knot. With a few more minutes of concerted effort, he had Trent's wrists completely free, and the rope fell to the floor between them.

"That was impressive."

"I needed a drink, I guess."

"Needed?" Trent didn't like the sound of that. It began to dawn on him that maybe Peter hadn't been as careful with work lately if he'd been drinking. The original job White had mentioned, checking into strange auction behavior, didn't exactly sound like anything too important. It had only turned into a higher priority when Brett thought Peter was missing. Could it be that Brett had suspected he'd gone off somewhere on a drunken binge and didn't let on to White?

"So, tell me how Reed is lately?"

"He's okay." Trent said noncommittally. What was Peter getting at? Trent waited, but Peter didn't enlighten him.

"I still don't understand how you got involved in any of this."

"White asked Reed to help with a coded message he'd gotten from Brett, apparently from you. Reed and I were in Rome on vacation, and White asked him to help."

"You don't sound too happy about that."

Trent wasn't going to admit he'd been furious not at Reed wanting to help find Peter but at discovering Reed had still been working for the Bureau.

"It was… bad timing."

"Not because of me?"

"I never heard of you until this came up."

The sky was brightening as morning approached, and Trent could see Peter's chin jerk slightly as he listened.

"Reed never mentioned me?"

"Why should he? Sounds like he probably wanted to forget working—or whatever—with you."

Peter nodded. "Yeah. Never wanted to dredge up whatever he could remember."

It was Trent's turn to start. Peter suspected Reed didn't remember everything that happened? Reed had awful nightmares that made him thrash violently around their bed, but they happened less and less frequently as Reed let go of his past. How much did Reed consciously recall? He wouldn't speak of the nightmares afterward.

He may even have muttered Peter's name in his sleep during more peaceful nights, and until now Trent had worried Reed was dreaming about Peter. Could that have been Reed's subconscious reminding him what had happened when Peter had abandoned him?

"So what did happen in Thailand? Why did you just leave him there?" Trent wouldn't mince words. He didn't care how sorry Peter was about what happened or how sorry he felt for himself. Trent wanted to know the truth—all of it—before he could decide what kind of man Peter really was.

"I left him. I told you." Peter's gaze moved in the direction of the boxes.

Trent stayed seated, not about to give the man another bottle of wine. Not yet, anyway.

"We were there to get a dissident out."

"There are dissidents in Thailand?"

"Yes. No. Not Thais. This woman was Burmese. She'd been able to get near the border and was smuggled across to a safe hiding place, but then the people who helped her were afraid to move her any farther, and our embassy got involved."

"Why was she so important?"

"She had a lot of information and some documents from Aung San Suu Kyi. You know who she is?"

"Of course I do. She's a Burmese dissident calling for democracy, and she's been under house arrest for decades, till recently."

"Right." Peter nodded. "This woman had information we could use as leverage against the Burmese government. At the time it was huge. Information that might help get Suu Kyi freed."

"So what happened?"

"We'd gone to meet her, near the border, and the Burmese troops noticed us. We shouldn't have been traveling together. Two white guys up there were suspicious. I didn't listen when Reed warned me, but I was the senior agent, and I thought I knew more than he did about the conditions up there." Peter frowned. "Reed was right. He had—*has*—great instincts."

Trent stared at Peter until he got to the key part of the story.

"I was with the woman and Reed was ahead of us, doing recon, when he was approached by a soldier. We were in the brush about twenty feet behind, watching. Reed was great with languages. He picked up Burmese and some of the local languages like he'd been living there for years, but he knew how to sound like a tourist. He just threw out a few words like 'pot' and 'beer'. The soldier seemed convinced he was just a rich white boy looking for some fun and was about to let him go. But the woman got spooked and made some noise, which the soldier heard. He was looking around but didn't see us. Then Reed started running in the other direction, drawing the soldier's attention and the three other guys with him. They chased him, and we were able to get away and to the next town, where we had transport waiting. We stayed there two days because they were searching all the vehicles on the road to see if Reed had any accomplices."

"You knew he'd been captured?"

"Word got around those villages pretty quickly, and while no one would give us up, they weren't in any hurry to risk their own lives to help rescue an American. They support the dissidents but consider American actions to be interference that would get them killed—or worse."

"So you could have left her and gone back to get Reed?"

"I could have, but I didn't. She was scared. She wouldn't let me leave her even for a few hours. The only way she'd get on the truck was if I went with her."

"So you just left him?" Trent's stomach knotted.

"That was protocol. She was the mission. Sometimes…." Peter glanced away. "Sometimes you have to accept a loss to get the bigger win."

"And she was a bigger win?"

Peter looked directly at Trent for a few seconds but tore his gaze away without replying.

Trent could see the pain in Peter's eyes. The drawn look around his mouth, the way he clenched his fists. Reed did that sometimes in his sleep too.

But none of that absolved Peter.

"Did you get the woman back to the States?"

"Yeah." The word was heavy, indicating there was much more to the story.

Trent couldn't imagine what else there could be.

"How did Reed get free? Did you ever send someone after him?"

"No."

"You could have gone once the woman was at the embassy, couldn't you? Or back in the US?"

"But I didn't." Peter paused again. "Didn't Reed tell you any of this?"

"No. He doesn't talk about it. Barely talks about anything before he met me."

Peter nodded. He let out a loud sigh and sat up straight. "He got out after a few months. He was just skin and bones. They didn't feed the prisoners much, and he had nearly stopped eating. One day he just didn't wake up, and they tossed his body onto a pile of corpses. He got away by slipping through the fence. He was so thin he could get between the posts."

"That's it?" Trent suspected there was something else Peter wasn't saying. "They thought he was dead?"

"Not exactly."

Trent waited.

"They make sure you're dead by shooting you."

31

"THEY shot him too?" Chills went through Trent's body.

"Through the shoulder, but he managed not to react. Then they threw his body away." Peter looked into the distance again, as if explaining this was even remotely as difficult as what Reed had endured.

Trent thought he would throw up. How had Reed ever survived that? What had kept him going? Trent looked over at Peter and hoped like hell it hadn't been Reed wanting to see that man again that kept him from screaming when he was shot. No wonder Reed wasn't afraid of anything. He'd practically died once. Between that and the way they had tortured him, there couldn't be much that frightened him.

But it also explained why he was so fearful that something would happen to Trent. Not because he thought Trent was stupid or incompetent. Because Reed didn't want Trent to ever have to endure anything like what he'd been through.

Pain stabbed through Trent's heart. What must Reed be going through right now? Was he looking for Trent, or at least for Peter? Trent decided to forgive Reed for wanting Peter to be safe. No matter that Peter hadn't shown as much regard for Reed when it had counted. Reed was a much better man than Peter could even imagine.

"By the time he got out and across the border, the situation had eased up, and some villagers nursed him until he was healthy enough to get to the nearest embassy. They brought him back to DC. I barely recognized him when I saw him."

"They paired you back up again, after that?"

"He wanted to see me, show me he was okay, so I wouldn't feel bad about what happened."

That sounded like Reed. The man would never stop surprising Trent.

"So, you were partners again?"

"No. I—" Peter exhaled loudly, and his jaw clenched. "I had started seeing her, the woman we'd been sent to bring out of Burma. And—" He stopped talking. There wasn't really much to say.

Trent filled in the blanks for himself. Reed had thought he'd come back to his partner and lover, only to find him with the woman who had been the cause of his misfortune and pain.

"It just happened, you know, while we were hiding in one of those villages." Peter spoke softly, staring past Trent's shoulder, probably realizing there was no way of justifying any of it and barely even trying. "And I let it happen so I could drown out the thoughts and worries about Reed…."

"You fucking bastard." Trent's usual flair with words eluded him, but that was good enough. He stood up and punched at the nearest box. It crashed to the floor, glass shattering and wine spreading into a pool that looked like blood.

He wished his hands weren't free, because he wanted to wring Peter's neck right now. Trent had to get away from him. He moved toward the door and pulled at it with all his strength, as if he were any match for a steel deadbolt.

He heard noises outside. A car backfired.

"Hurry, Trent. Come back here and grab that rope."

He didn't move.

"Trent, they're coming back. If they find out you're loose…."

Despite his animosity for Peter, Trent complied. He stood, back to Peter, and let him loosely tie the rope around his wrists again. He gritted his teeth, hating being here with this man and having to listen to his instructions.

The bolt slid open and the door crashed against the wall. Three men with some kind of automatic weapons slung over their shoulders came and glanced around at the mess on the floor. They started shouting at each other, then at Trent.

One grabbed Trent's shoulder, nearly yanking his arm out of the socket. The pain was almost welcome after Peter's revelations. Trent wanted any distraction from his thoughts, even pain.

The rope held, and Trent let himself be taken out of the storage building. He turned around and saw one of the others guard pointing his weapon at Peter as the third guard tied Peter's hands. Trent was shoved out the door and kicked into the trunk, so he didn't see what happened next.

As much as he hated Peter, he didn't want them to kill him. Peter had gotten Trent's hands free and possibly saved him with quick thinking and retying them before the guards came back.

There was more shouting, and Trent could feel someone else getting into the car and heard one of the doors slam. Then more talking and more people piling into the car, making it shake, before there were three more door slams. They must have put Peter inside the car.

But where were they going?

The car started up and careened around a series of tight turns before leveling off. They hadn't been driving very long before it screeched to a halt and Trent felt and heard the others get out of the car.

He thought he smelled the ocean, but it might just have been his imagination.

REED watched the activity at the little harbor from behind an old building that must have been used to store fish guts, based on the stench. It almost made his eyes water. Milacio and Caterina shouted at each other and took turns shouting at two of their armed guards, all in rapid-fire Italian, so Reed couldn't make out any of the words. All he could tell was that they were waiting for something.

One of the guards grabbed his pocket and pulled something out. A cell phone. He spoke into it, then relayed a message to Caterina, too quietly for Reed to overhear.

Moments later another car, this one an ancient four-door Mercedes, sped toward the water and screeched to a halt. Milacio went up to the driver's door, and the front passenger door opened. A tall African man got out. He shouted and pointed his gun—a semiautomatic, possibly an AK-47, from the looks of it—at the rear door. The driver also got out and pointed his own gun at the door.

Please let that be Trent. Reed would have crossed his fingers if he thought something like that might work. Caterina moved closer, arms crossed over her chest and chin jutting out in obvious annoyance.

Milacio opened the rear door and a man began to step out.

From Reed's position he couldn't see the man's face on the far side of the car, but when he turned around, Reed's stomach lurched.

Peter?

Peter looked awful. Gaunt, unshaven, clothes filthy, but no blood. He stumbled as he walked, prodded by the muzzles of the guards' rifles. Reed could see he'd been roughed up days ago, and the bruises stood out against his pale skin.

Where was Trent?

Reed hadn't expected to see Peter here. Should he make a move to help him and risk never finding Trent? Indecision gnawed at him. Guilt soon followed. Reed had forgotten about Peter in his concern for Trent.

"Wait. Get the other one," the African man shouted in English loudly enough for Reed to hear.

The guard near the rear of the little cluster went back to the car and opened the trunk. Milacio peered in and nodded, then shouted to Caterina in Italian. She glanced into the trunk and laughed.

What was going on? Reed waited on tenterhooks.

The guard reached in and dragged a man from the trunk, with assistance from Milacio.

Trent!

Reed's relief was short-lived. As Trent turned, Reed could see his bloody, broken nose and a mixture of fresh and dried blood splotched down the front of his shirt. Like Peter, Trent walked unsteadily on his feet, and his gaze seemed unfocused, confused.

Reed still hadn't formulated a plan. If Milacio or the guards lined Trent and Peter up to shoot them, he couldn't do much to stop it. They outnumbered Reed, and he had only his handgun—no match for the AK-47s, especially at this distance—and a knife strapped to his ankle.

"What's he doing here, James?" Caterina asked.

The African man turned toward her. "This is the American spy who broke in today."

"He's no spy!" Caterina laughed again, her high-pitched cackle echoing off the decrepit building Reed hid behind.

"He is," James said. "He almost fooled everyone, but Mr. Milacio could tell from his questions. He looks harmless, but very smart." James tapped his temple.

"Nonsense." Caterina walked up to Trent. "You're not smart, just lucky. But you can't get out of this." She waved her gun at him and Reed flinched, mirroring Trent's reaction. She laughed and then smacked the gun against Trent's jaw. She wasn't tall enough to do any major damage, but Reed could see Trent was in pain. "You caught me off guard in the hotel, but you're no match for these guards. Or our guns."

Reed sent Trent silent messages. *I'm here, Trent. I'll get you out of this.* If Trent could see him, it might provide some small measure of comfort. He remembered when Trent came to save him in Thailand, letting himself be captured by the Triad guards so he could rescue Reed. He wanted Trent to know he was here for him now.

Could he create a diversion? With three armed men plus Milacio and Caterina, Reed didn't think Trent could think fast enough to see an escape route.

"Get them onto the boat already!" Caterina growled at the men.

The boat. They were taking Peter and Trent out on the boat. Why?

To kill them and dump their bodies in the ocean? How could he stop that? Besides Milacio's sleek hydrofoil, the only other boat in the harbor was an old rowboat, even more decrepit than the ancient shack.

He had to stop them before they left the dock.

The guards shoved Peter and Trent onto the *Venus* at gunpoint and tied their ankles together. Peter wasn't even struggling, but Trent kicked at one of his captors until another guard slammed the butt of his rifle against Trent's head. Reed felt Trent's pain as he slumped into the boat.

Reed rushed for the dock, his feet pounding the hard-packed dirt as he ran out into the open, but he couldn't close the distance fast enough. The boat's engine raced, and it roared away from the dock.

"Trent!" Reed shouted, but the engine drowned out his voice.

Or so he thought, until he saw Peter turn in his direction.

32

"TRENT?"

Peter's voice broke through a haze of blood and pain and fear. Trent found himself practically in Peter's lap, spray from the boat's engines splashing him with refreshing and welcome coolness.

"Wha?" Trent fell against Peter as he tried to steady himself against the boat's forward velocity.

"Reed's at the harbor." Peter's voice echoed from far away. "He saw them put us in the boat. He'll come after us."

"Reed?" Trent's heart fluttered; then his stomach churned. Reed was here? "Where are they taking us?"

"I don't know. But Reed's coming after us. Don't worry."

The fog in Trent's head cleared as he inhaled cool, fresh sea air. Peter had been whispering so no one could hear. Reed was coming to save him. Trent had to focus. A few more gulps of air and he sat up straight.

Bad idea. His head ached and his vision swam again. How much wine had they had?

"Take it easy. Caterina and the guard walloped you pretty good. Try not to move while we figure out a plan. And watch they don't see about your wrists." Peter spoke softly almost against Trent's ear.

Like Reed used to do.

Reed.

Reed was here. Or at least on his way. Trent tried to smile, but an ache in his jaw told him that wasn't such a great idea.

"Where are we going?"

"I still don't know. But as long as the boat's moving, we're safe. If they slow down, that's when we need to worry. Okay?"

Okay. Trent could follow that. "You got a plan?"

"I'm working on it."

Trent hated to think it, but he wasn't sure how much he trusted Peter. He hadn't been much help when Reed needed him years ago, and Peter had even less incentive to help Trent.

Hurry up, Reed.

REED watched the hydrofoil leave the dock.

How far out would they go? he wondered. Despite this being the private side of the island, there was still plenty of maritime traffic and fishing activity around the islands.

A couple of bodies would turn up fairly quickly unless they were carefully weighted.

And Reed hadn't seen them bring any weights. The hydrofoil was a sleek watercraft with the minimum weight on it. No heavy chains or cement blocks.

Maybe they weren't going to kill them and throw them overboard after all.

Reed saw the hydrofoil's distinctive wake curving off in the distance—in the direction of Salina.

He'd gone that way with Milacio the day before to the winery.

To the boneyard on Salina.

He had to get to a boat and intercept them before they got to the boneyard.

Reed tried to open the doors to the old shed, but they were chained shut. He sped back to the motorcycle and rode directly into the door, breaking it down and hoping against hope another boat—a fast boat—was in there.

Nothing but a few old barrels that smelled even more like fish guts.

He turned around and zoomed back out of the shed, heading for the public harbor.

Thankfully Panarea wasn't very big, and he got there in under ten minutes. Milacio's hydrofoil had to circle part of the island, essentially backtracking, before it headed for Salina. Reed wasn't out of the race just yet.

He got to the harbor and assessed the relative capabilities of the boats bobbing against the worn pier. Only two might possibly rival Milacio's hydrofoil for speed and maneuverability.

Reed picked the more expensive of the two—still little more than half the size of the *Venus,* but much lighter—and ran for it. If he got caught, he'd explain why he was stealing it later.

Only a few fishermen were around to watch him commit grand theft watercraft, and they shouted as he raced away from the pier, his wake nearly upsetting their low boats and leaving them bobbing and gesticulating wildly as they cursed him.

He glanced down at the gauges and realized he'd made one major miscalculation.

On a scale of zero to one, the fuel-gauge needle hovered dangerously close to 0. Nearly empty.

There was no time to go back and choose the other boat or to top up the tank.

Every vehicle had some sort of reserve, even at 0, though he had no idea how much breathing room he had with this one. He'd have to trust the boat wouldn't run out of fuel before he caught up to Milacio's boat.

When he got out of the harbor area, he headed in the direction of Salina but couldn't see Milacio's hydrofoil wake.

Fuck. Had he miscalculated?

Then he remembered Milacio's caution the previous morning. The maritime patrols had strict speed limits and huge fines for those who flouted them. The fishermen had been known to report people who disrupted their favorite spots. Milacio's skipper had slowed down when he only had Reed on board to avoid the dangerous reefs. Would Milacio risk either damaging his keel or being stopped and boarded when he had prisoners? Reed counted on Milacio wanting to avoid any contact with authorities now.

He hoped he remembered the way to the other island correctly and went as fast as he dared, to avoid warning Milacio that he was following—and conserve fuel.

He sped up until he caught sight of Milacio's boat ahead. It was moving slowly, snaking between the jutting rocks Reed recalled. He edged his boat closer and noticed the familiar outline of Salina ahead and a small flotilla of fishing boats about halfway in between. He was closing the distance at a good pace. Thankfully Milacio's engines were noisy enough to hide the sound of his approach.

He was twenty yards or so behind Milacio's boat, close enough to read *Venere d'Oro* on her stern, when he heard sirens.

Reed recalled the shouts of the fishermen in the harbor as he'd roared away from Panarea. Had they called the water cops on him? He hoped Milacio and his men didn't hear the sirens closing in. He needed to reach them before the cops caught up to him.

He gunned the little boat and it leapt out of the water, then crashed down and out again, jarring Reed to the bone as it met and overcame each wave.

Behind him, the cops shouted over a loudspeaker. He couldn't understand their warnings, but he would have ignored them anyway.

Ahead, Caterina turned around—she must have heard the police boat—and saw Reed approaching. Then her gaze took in the maritime police behind him. She turned, gesturing, clearly warning Milacio of the situation.

Milacio's boat sped up, leaving a huge plume of wake in its trail.

Reed would never catch up in this thing. Already he felt its hesitation when he tried to accelerate.

The police shouted again and a moment later a single bullet shattered one of the side windows. He ignored it but crouched low over the wheel.

The fuel gauge was on 0 and flashing red.

He floored it anyway.

33

ON MILACIO'S boat, the men were in a state, shouting and staring behind them—all but Milacio, who was at the helm.

Trent saw a boat following, closing the gap.

Reed?

Yes, it was Reed. He fought the urge to shout or leap to his feet.

Then Caterina started shouting. "He's got the maritime cops after us. Kill them and get them out of here before they catch up to us."

Milacio sped up, and the acceleration knocked Caterina and two of the guards to their knees.

"Now, Trent." Peter gave the signal.

Trent moved forward, careful not to stand up or he'd lose his balance. He unwrapped the rope from his wrists and headed for the nearest guard, who was still picking himself up from the deck.

Trent lunged for the man's knees, knocked him down, and grabbed his weapon as Peter, still bound at the ankles and wrists, did his best with the other guard.

Caterina had been unable to get to her feet on the slippery deck.

The boat sped on, leaping several feet out of the water as it encountered each new wave. The chopping motion jarred Trent's head, neck, and still-bleeding nose and made every movement painfully difficult. Suddenly the boat slowed and swerved, barely avoiding one of the jagged rock formations Milacio had pointed out on their excursion.

Behind them, Reed closed the gap until his boat was just beside them.

"Now what?" Trent wasn't sure if they were supposed to shoot someone or jump onto Reed's boat.

Caterina pointed her little silver pistol at Trent. As she pulled the trigger, the entire boat shuddered.

Reed had just rammed them.

Milacio slowed.

Peter smashed the butt of the rifle into one guard's head as he lay on the deck. Trent looked away, appalled, but realized this was life or death. They couldn't play nice, because if any of Milacio's men got their weapons back, they'd shoot to kill.

Thankfully Caterina's shot had gone wide, but being shot sure beat having your arms hacked off, didn't it?

There was no time to reconsider.

Trent jabbed his rifle into the other guard's gut, then swung it around and clocked him in the head for good measure.

Where was the third guy?

Caterina struggled again to stand. She made it to one knee and dropped her gun as Reed rammed their boat again.

Ahead, Milacio zigged and zagged as he encountered the slow-moving fishermen and holiday sailors, making it even more difficult to keep balance.

Then Reed's boat was nearly even with the back of theirs.

REED was just coming up on the back of the *Venus* when he heard it.

A volley of bullets slammed into the back of his boat. Too many.

He was only a foot from the back of Milacio's boat.

He took a deep breath and dove for it.

34

TRENT saw Reed evening up with the back of the boat.

Then a guard lunged for him, and he took his eye off Reed for just one second.

Too long.

The next thing Trent saw and heard was Reed's boat exploding into a ball of fire that lit up the dawn, sending scraps of lumber, fiberglass, and glass high into the air. The force of it knocked Trent and the guard down, giving Trent a chance to knock the man out.

"Reed!" Trent screamed at the fiery floating remnants of Reed's boat.

Trent instinctively reached toward him, but Milacio veered again and Trent fell.

Then he saw one hand reaching up the side of the boat, grasping at the handrail.

"Reed?"

His head bobbed up into sight for a moment before disappearing again from Trent's view.

Oh my God, he's fallen into the water. How will he save us? Trent expected the worst.

"Reeeeeed!" Trent shouted and headed for the side of the boat.

Caterina managed to get a shot off, and it caromed off the side of the boat less than a foot from Trent. He pulled back in shock and fell to the deck.

Where was Reed? Where was Peter?

All Trent could see now was the police boat racing to catch them. Of course, a smuggler like Milacio had the fastest boat around. Even the cops probably couldn't catch him. That was the point, wasn't it?

Trent heard gunshots from the front of the boat and saw the last guard—the African man—fly overboard.

Peter stood near the railing, clutching a rifle.

Trent rushed toward him, glancing back just to see where Caterina was.

He saw her facing Peter, feet wide apart, gun aimed directly at him.

He froze in place for a moment and saw her smiling.

He thought he even saw her pull the trigger, but he steeled himself and rushed toward Peter.

REED'S fingers kept slipping off the side railing of Milacio's boat. The water was cold, and he couldn't get a good grip.

He concentrated on hanging on until he heard Trent shouting and gunshots.

He had to get on the deck, now!

Finally, he managed to haul himself out of the water—in time to see Trent lunging toward Peter just as the tiny crack of a pistol sounded two feet to his right.

There was Caterina, laughing and taking aim again. Another shot rang out.

Reed looked forward and saw Trent falling, a bright red stain spreading along his side. By the time he got there, Trent was lying on the deck, Peter, hovering over him, unharmed.

Their eyes met for the briefest fraction of a second before they both looked down at Trent.

Reed pulled at Trent's shirt, yanking it out of the way to assess the damage.

He barely heard the sirens close in or felt their boat slow down.

"Trent! Trent, can you hear me?"

Trent didn't move.

The bullet had gone in near his kidneys or liver. Reed didn't fucking know anatomy. Why couldn't he remember this stuff? Blood gushed, and all he could do was press slippery palms across the gash in Trent's side and hope no one shot him while he tried to save Trent.

Everything was a blur. A red, bloody blur. Flashing red lights and shouting in a language he couldn't understand. He wouldn't get up even when someone tried to pull him away.

More flashing lights.

"Reed, it's the paramedics. You have to let them get to him."

The voice sounded familiar. Reed looked up. What was Peter doing here?

He looked down and saw more blood. Trent's blood. Trent was still bleeding, but his heart was still beating, or that much blood wouldn't still be pouring out of him, would it?

"Reed, come with me. Let him go."

Hands grabbed at him, and he punched them away until someone pulled his hands behind his back and dragged him away from Trent.

More flashing lights. More sirens. More people shouting in Italian. Another boat and then a car.

Lots of blood. Reed looked at his hands and his clothes, and everything was covered in blood.

Trent's blood.

It's all my fault.

Trent, I'm so sorry.

35

I palori di 'nnimici fannu ridiri, chiddi di l'amici fanni chianciri.
Words from enemies make one laugh, those from friends make one cry.
   —Aeolian proverb

REED was exhausted. The journey to the hospital felt as if it took forever. The closest emergency room was on Lipari, by hydrofoil. When they arrived, Reed had refused to let go of Trent, even after being threatened by an armed guard. It took a nurse to talk sense into him.

And now he sat in the waiting room, clothes still splattered with Trent's blood. The maritime police had asked him questions, but that same nurse shooed them away, and they hovered at the edge of the waiting room, giving Reed some space while the doctors worked on Trent in the operating room.

Reed glanced around at the bright, modern interior of the hospital. From outside it looked old, run-down, and inadequate, but inside it appeared as sterile and efficient as anyplace back home. He found himself clenching his fists and willed himself to relax. He wasn't helping Trent by stressing out. He glanced across the room at two of the officers pretending not to watch him. Should he just talk to them and get it over with?

He should call White in Rome. That would at least give him a buffer from the local authorities while Interpol and the Carabinieri took over the investigation. He still didn't know why Milacio and Caterina were going to kill Trent and Peter. They must know something incriminating or there was no reason to resort to murder.

Trent knew something. Reed had information and suppositions but no proof. Trent must have some proof.

Oh, God. How did I let Trent get caught up in this whole thing? Guilt sliced through Reed's brain and heart, jolting him out of numb inertia. *Please don't let Trent die.* Reed wasn't the praying sort, but it felt like the right thing right now.

Then there was Peter. He hadn't come to the hospital. Reed expected the authorities were talking to him. Hopefully he'd called White, because Reed just didn't have the strength to talk.

"Have some water, Signor Reed." The kind nurse brought him some bottled water.

He began to wave it away. "Coffee?"

"No. Water. You do not need coffee now." She pushed the water bottle into his hand.

He took a sip. The water was cool and refreshing, soothing his dry throat. He took another sip and another, and the bottle was empty. He handed it back to the nurse. "Thank you."

"I go and ask doctors how long, okay?" She gave Reed's shoulder a supportive squeeze.

"Yes. Thank you." He managed a weak smile, and she rubbed his shoulder gently and left through a swinging door at the far end of the room.

Reed stared at the door, willing her to return with news. With good news. Telling him Trent would be fine and had been asking for Reed.

The door swung open and Reed leapt to his feet and moved toward it.

It wasn't the nurse.

It was Peter.

Reed found himself staring into Peter's bloodshot eyes.

"Any news yet?" Peter asked.

Reed didn't reply. He stared at Peter. It had been years since they were face to face. Reed had imagined this moment a million times. But now that it was happening, he didn't have a single thing he wanted to say to Peter. Instead he just looked at him.

Peter was bruised, beaten up, gaunt, his clothes torn and dirty. His hair was half gray, not the thick dark hair Reed had loved to touch. Had it only been five, six years? Peter looked like he'd aged twenty.

But Reed had died and come back to life in that same period of time. Come back to life a second time, he realized, since he'd met Trent.

Oh, God, if Trent dies, I want to die too. Reed's gut twisted, and he forgot to breathe. *I'll die again and I won't have any reason to go on. Oh, Trent.*

"Reed, you need to sit down." Peter put a hand on Reed's shoulder and steadied him onto one of the orange plastic chairs.

Reed brushed Peter's hand off, had to get the thought of Peter's touch off him. He rubbed the spot where Peter's fingers had made contact.

"Reed, I'm sorry." Peter reached a hand out but apparently thought better of it and pulled back.

"Sorry? For what?"

"For Trent getting hurt."

"That's not your fault." Reed said the words, but part of him didn't mean it. Part of him thought it was Peter's fault. But a bigger part told Reed it was his own fault. Neither part was correct.

"Yeah, it is."

"I've learned I can't tell Trent what to do. Or more importantly, what not to do." Reed smiled, finally understanding the truth of this, though he hated how it had turned out.

"He really surprised me."

"Trent surprises me all the time. Usually, I like it." Reed sucked in a sharp breath. Why was he telling Peter any of this? To make Peter feel better? Or worse?

"You're a lucky man, Reed. Trent is…." Peter shook his head and chuckled, clearly at a loss for words.

"He is." Reed nodded. "And more."

Peter nodded too. "A lot more." His expression softened, and he opened his mouth to speak again.

"Don't bother. I know that too."

"You don't even know what I was going to say."

"Yeah, I do. I've been through everything you would ever want to say to me."

"And?"

"And no matter what it is, I'd say the same thing. It's history."

"You know there's this scene in a Sherlock Holmes story."

"I know."

"Do you?"

"Yeah, Peter. I know what you're thinking. Which scene in which story and who says what."

"How could you know that?"

"Because there was a time I knew you inside and out. Knew every fucking thing about you that mattered and plenty more that didn't."

Peter just stared at Reed for a few minutes.

Reed took a deep breath. "But there came a time when you surprised me."

"Look, I know I should have—"

"Shut up and let me finish." Reed's pulse accelerated. He'd thought about this conversation a million times. He'd had plenty of time in that prison camp to think about everything that had ever happened to him, and everything he imagined might happen, and even more things he wanted to happen when he got free. He never once doubted he'd escape and make it home, back to the States. Back to Peter.

Peter looked like he'd been punched in the gut.

Good, Reed thought and then took it back.

"I should have said what you did didn't surprise me. Because when it happened, I realized it wasn't what happened that surprised me. The surprising thing was that I ever expected anything different from you than what I got. I grew up that day. It was also the day I planned my escape."

"After you decided I'd left you there? Why then?"

"Before that I wanted to escape for *you*. From that day on, I wanted to escape for *myself*."

Peter's expression changed again, like a man who'd seen his own death. Reed had experienced it himself. He knew exactly what was going through Peter's mind.

"Why didn't you say any of these things in DC after you got back?"

"It wouldn't have changed anything."

"And now?"

"It won't change you. But I'm different. Today I've just lived through nearly losing the most important thing in my life. And I'll never ever take him or anything he says or does for granted again. I don't know what you went through while I rotted and almost died in that camp, but if you experienced even a fraction of how I felt when I saw Trent's blood—" Reed paused, forcing himself to breathe and not to relive that awful moment again. "—you would have said or done something *significant* the next time you met me."

"I went to see you in the hospital when they first brought you back."

"Is that so?" Reed heard his own voice, but it sounded like another person talking, not him. Someone very far away.

"Yeah. You were sedated. Medical coma, whatever they call it."

"I woke up."

"I know."

"I don't recall seeing you after that."

Peter looked away. Guilt colored his posture. Reed wasn't entirely sure precisely what Peter felt guilty about. Because he left Reed? Or because he didn't try to patch things up later? Or both?

All Reed knew now was he didn't care.

"I forgive you, Peter."

Peter stared into Reed's eyes, his expression haunted, eyes dark and sunken. "You do? Really?"

As Reed looked at him one last time, it dawned on him forgiveness was the last thing Peter could stand to hear. Then Reed got up and walked away.

He didn't look back. He didn't need to. All he needed was to see Trent. He still didn't know whether Trent would pull through, but even one more minute with him would be worth a whole lifetime with Peter.

"Signor Reed, he's still unconscious." The nurse came up to him as he left the waiting room.

Reed's heart sank.

"But they got the bullet."

36

WHEN Trent woke up, it took him a few minutes to realize where he was.

His entire body ached but his head felt calm, almost empty.

Then he was aware of a particularly sharp pain in his right hand.

He blinked a few times, and as his eyes grew accustomed to the dim room he understood.

Reed sat next to the bed, hand clutched around Trent's.

"Reed?" Trent said.

No response.

"Reed?" Trent tried again and realized his voice wasn't quite working.

He shifted his weight in the bed and Reed sat up with a jolt.

"Trent?" Reed's head jerked up and his eyes opened.

"Yeah?" Trent croaked. God, his throat was dry. *Water*. He needed water.

Reed let go of his hand and clicked a lamp on. The bright light made Trent blink again.

"Trent? Trent!" Reed stared at him.

Reed looked like crap, Trent realized. Especially his eyes. They were puffy and red.

Had Reed been crying? Trent let out a little chuckle. Reed would never cry.

"Trent? Are you... laughing?" Reed's voice sounded kind of strangled, worse than Trent's did. Yeah, maybe he had been crying.

"Water?" Best not to ask about the crying. Reed was the kind of guy who might get upset if Trent knew.

It took a few more minutes for Trent to understand why he was in a hospital, but by the time a nurse came in, he remembered about the boat, and that ache in his side must have been a bullet.

Look at that. I got shot and Reed's crying? That sure turned everything in their world upside down.

"TRENT, you have to stop doing this fucking stupid spy shit. You're not trained for it. No amount of watching spy movies is going to change that."

"But in Thailand—"

Reed cut him off. "Thailand was nothing compared to this, compared to the people we're dealing with here. Diamond smugglers, Trent, not Thai mobsters."

"It was scarier," Trent admitted.

"At least you have enough sense to be scared. But not enough to stay out of it."

"I kept thinking about you, and what *you* would do."

"I'm trained for it. But what on earth prompted you?"

"I know you wouldn't leave someone behind. Not like Peter left you. I just couldn't leave him—or let him get shot."

"Fear is there for a reason, Trent. You should listen to it. Your instinct kicks in and tells you something your brain might not realize."

"It was kind of exciting too, though. You know?"

"*Exciting?*" Reed's icy tone sent shivers down Trent's back. Or at least it would have if the painkiller wasn't so effective.

"I liked being part of this, of stopping those guys and helping someone somewhere. Like in Thailand."

"Do you realize what you just said?"

"No." Trent wasn't feeling much pain, but he thought his brain was still working. What was Reed talking about?

"Does any of that sound familiar?"

"No." Trent shrugged and wished he hadn't. The pain meds weren't quite as good as he thought. A hot spear ripped through his lower abdomen. He bit on his lower lip until the pain in his side eased. "No," he repeated, hoping Reed hadn't noticed his reaction.

"Marc."

"Oh." Trent's shoulders sagged, and his heart ached almost as much as his side.

"Marc ran around looking for excitement, and it killed him."

Trent turned away, silent.

"You remember how Marc's death affected you?"

"Of course." Trent had been devastated. It had taken years—and meeting Reed—to get him back to normal.

"Don't you see how losing you would affect me? It would destroy me."

Trent looked squarely at Reed. None of this had dawned on him until this moment. Marc's death had nearly killed Trent too. Did Reed care for him that much?

"I thought you're used to people getting hurt or losing partners."

"You're not that kind of partner, Trent, and you damn well know it." Reed paused. "Don't you get it? I love you in a way I've never felt about anyone before. Never thought I'd ever feel till I met you. I even love how you're dumb enough to run into danger to help someone else, like Peter, even after you found out what he'd done. But I just can't take the worry."

Trent's heart pounded and his stomach knotted. "I'll stop. I don't want to do that to you."

Reed was silent a moment. "Don't change who you are for me. Just promise you'll be more careful."

Trent nodded, wishing he hadn't moved his head or neck again.

"Stay low. That's the first thing to remember with guns. Didn't Michael Westen ever give that advice?" Reed gave Trent a deadpan stare; then one corner of his mouth turned up.

Aw, fuuuuuuuuuuck. How long had Reed known about Trent's *Burn Notice* fetish? Talk about humiliating. Trent blinked a couple of times, then joined in with an embarrassed chuckle.

Damn, laughing hurts. No more laughing for about a year.

The nurse came in. Trent was torn between the anticipation of more pain meds and losing the moment between himself and Reed. She kicked Reed out, but before leaving, he leaned down to plant a kiss on Trent's cheek. The gentlest kiss Trent had ever gotten, at least from Reed.

Reed really did love him.

It gave Trent a warm feeling in all the wrong places, and he worried his skimpy hospital gown might give away how Reed's slight touch had affected him.

If the nurse noticed, she didn't let on. She adjusted some tubes, checked something, and made notes in the chart hanging from the foot of his bed before giving him a cheerful smile and departing.

Alone again, Trent turned over what Reed had said. He *had* changed a lot, but it had all been because of Reed. Trent liked the way Reed had been so worried about him. The warm feeling returned at knowing how deep Reed's feelings had grown. How had Trent misread him so badly when they'd fought in the hotel room in Rome? Why hadn't he trusted Reed enough to believe if he left it was for a good reason?

There were still things Trent needed cleared up about Peter. Was there more to the story than Peter had told? He still didn't know Reed's side of it. Trent no longer feared asking or discovering the truth. He'd given Reed space regarding his past, but Trent had earned the right to know. That bullet more than gave him the right. Even more, he could handle the truth, whatever had happened.

The real question was how Reed had handled it and whether or not he was over Peter and their shared past.

37

One week later
Casa di Milacio, Panarea

REED sat on the pristine white couch in Milacio's spacious living room, staring at a two-day-old *International Herald Tribune*, waiting for Trent to wake up. It was more than fitting, Reed mused as he glanced around, yet again admiring the possessions of a man who didn't deserve them.

The Italian authorities had seized Milacio's houses and other property, and an Interpol team was due to arrive to inventory the art and antiquities. In the meantime, the Italians had allowed Reed and Trent to stay here following Trent's release from the hospital in Lìpari. It was more comfortable—and cheaper—than any hotel in the islands, with enough space for Reed and a nurse.

"Reed? Reed!"

Reed put down the newspaper and rushed toward the bedroom.

"Reed? I've got a big problem," Trent said when Reed came through the door of the lavish master bedroom suite.

He'd been out of the hospital for four days and had slept for most of each day, leaving Reed alone far too much with his own thoughts and recriminations. But Trent appreciated the opulent surroundings and declared them even nicer than the Grand Hotel Via Veneto, despite the lack of Bulgari toiletries.

As it turned out, White had sent a special delivery just for Trent, and a large bottle of Bulgari MAN sat in the marble-and-gold-fitted master bath at the moment. Trent had been ecstatic when Reed used it for his daily sponge baths.

"What's wrong? You okay?" Reed moved toward the bed. Trent looked okay, considering what he'd been through. The bruising around his eyes from the broken nose was almost gone. Could it be a fever?

"Big problem." Trent was smiling.

Reed looked him over, and it hit him as he saw the bulge under the sheet. "Trent, that's not a problem. It's normal."

"It's huge." Trent's grin widened. "I need your help."

Reed pulled the sheet down and feigned disinterest. "Not that big. I've seen bigger." He covered Trent back up and turned to leave.

Truth was, Trent's cock was pretty damn big. And Reed liked it that way. He'd be lying if he didn't admit he'd missed fooling around with Trent, but he wasn't sure Trent was ready for anything just yet.

"Aw, come on. Reed?" The disappointment in Trent's voice surprised Reed.

"Are you sure you can?" Trent had been shot only a week ago, and the doctor had cautioned against strenuous activity. He still had stitches holding parts of his insides inside, for fuck's sake.

"I probably shouldn't, but that doesn't stop you...." Trent raised an eyebrow and pulled the sheet down again. "You know you want to... and you still owe me something."

Right. Those promises Reed had made in Rome, at the catacombs. He hadn't forgotten. If Trent was well enough to be calling in sexual favors, it was good news. He was on the mend, and he wasn't going to hold Reed responsible for what had happened to him at Milacio's—Caterina's—hand.

"I think that can be arranged." Reed grinned and walked to the dresser, then dug a few necessities out of Trent's suitcase.

He walked back over to the bed, where Trent lay on his side, a bandage covering a portion of his back and right hip, but otherwise naked. His skin was clear and smooth save for his cock, thick and dark red, bobbing slightly as Trent breathed.

Reed crouched next to the bed and reached out to stroke Trent's back, feeling the smooth, warm skin tremble under his fingers.

"Come around over here first?" Trent patted the bed in front of him.

Reed stood and laughed. He did tend to head right for the main event without putting enough emphasis on the introduction. He lay down next to Trent.

Trent leaned forward until his lips could reach Reed's, just brushing together, their only point of contact. Then Trent grabbed Reed's collar to pull him in closer. For someone only out of the hospital for a few days, he was surprisingly demanding and controlling.

Reed didn't mind in the least.

He let Trent kiss him and unbutton his shirt. When Trent's fingers slid under the fabric, Reed felt his own body tremble. God, he'd missed Trent. He reached down to take hold of Trent's hand, pulled it away from his chest, and brought the fingers to his lips. He kissed them, squeezing Trent's hand the way he had as he sat beside Trent's bed in the hospital, willing him to wake up and be okay.

But Trent wasn't okay. He'd been shot, and Reed could have prevented it. Guilt racked his body again.

"Shhh," Trent whispered before taking Reed's mouth in a hard kiss that softened into a gentle caress.

"Oh, Trent." Reed wrapped his arms around Trent, pulling him close, kissing him like it might be the last time ever. "Trent, I love you so much it hurts. I—"

"Stop talking. There are better things to do with your mouth."

Reed blinked back—well, it couldn't be a tear, could it? He didn't cry. Trent was okay, so there was no reason to cry. Not now. He liked the way Trent got back on track, back to the sex. The way Reed used to. How had their lives changed so much that Reed was nearly in tears and Trent was the one asking for sex?

Trent finished unbuttoning Reed's shirt and started on his belt and jeans. Reed had to get up to undress, and he watched Trent's gaze travel along his body, hesitating at the knot of scarred flesh on one shoulder. Of course—Peter had explained that. Reed shook off the thoughts. Plenty of time for that conversation with Trent later.

Much later.

Right now, this was about what Trent wanted.

"Let me see you. Turn around."

Reed complied, turning slowly, letting Trent look him over.

"It's even bigger now, Reed."

Reed looked down at his cock. It was only half-mast at the moment. "It is?"

"Oh, yeah." Trent tugged at his own cock. "See?"

Reed grinned. "Oh, yeah, it's enormous. I've got my work cut out for me."

"I know. But I have confidence in your abilities."

Reed got back on the bed and slid down so he was nearly face to face with Trent's hard-on. He reached out and stroked one hand along Trent's hip as he moved close and licked at the head of Trent's cock. Salty precome already dripped out, and the flesh was hot and firm under his lips and tongue.

He sucked the head into his mouth and felt Trent's body shudder.

"Mmm, yeah."

Reed licked his way down one side, then up the other, hands stroking and caressing Trent's hip, thigh, and abs. Trent curled forward slightly so he could play with Reed's hair and smooth along his back, neck, and shoulders.

Reed moved up and down Trent's cock, never taking the full length entirely into his mouth, waiting to see if Trent asked for more, but he seemed content with whatever Reed did to him. Reed licked and sucked, tasted and probed. He moved lower, licking at Trent's balls, at first rolling them around in one slippery hand before licking and taking the whole sac into his mouth, using as much suction as he knew Trent liked.

From somewhere behind him, Reed heard Trent's little moans and gasps. He also felt Trent's pleasure building as the shudders grew longer and more pronounced.

A few times Trent pulled at Reed's hair, the tugs getting rougher as Reed worked. He went back to sucking Trent's balls for a moment and reached for the lube he'd left at the end of the bed. He slicked a couple of fingers and circled his fingertips at Trent's entrance.

Quickly he slipped both inside, enjoying the welcome gasp and shudder from Trent. He pushed in deep a few times, then pulled his fingers out again. Just one inside, then two. He varied the depth and rhythm of his movements until Trent started yanking at his hair.

Reed shifted position again. Now Trent couldn't get to his head, but Reed could reach out and spread Trent's cheeks apart to expose the pink ring, loosened up by the fingers. Reed moved close, squeezing Trent's buttocks.

Above him, Trent moaned softly and writhed.

Reed got closer and licked at Trent's hole with the flat of his tongue. He licked up and down, then, with just the tip of his tongue, he circled the hole before licking flat again.

Trent groaned, making the whole bed shudder with his movements.

Reed circled the tip of his tongue once clockwise. Then one turn counterclockwise. Then Reed plunged inside and felt Trent's ass squeezing around him.

"Oh, God. Reed. Oh, my God." Trent's words were half groaned. "Deeper!"

Reed started to laugh, but it was impossible with his tongue up Trent's ass. He flicked it in and out a few times, then swiped it around, then plunged as deep as possible. His tongue wasn't long enough to hit Trent's prostate, so every now and then he pushed a finger in along with his tongue and brushed against the sweet spot before his tongue took over again.

Trent was mumbling and groaning, occasionally reaching back to grab at Reed's hair. Reed liked that, even if it hurt a little. He wished he had a few more arms so he could hold Trent and still be able to reach down here.

He managed to slip his arm between Trent's legs and grab hold of his cock. Damn, he was rock hard. Reed stroked up and down a few times. He debated finishing Trent off like this. He thought about how good that thick, hard cock would feel up his own ass, but Trent wasn't fit enough to top just yet. Reed would have to put that particular pleasure off for a while.

Trent squeezed Reed's hand, helping him stroke. Long, slow strokes. Reed continued the motion with one hand while he jabbed his tongue back inside Trent, licking and sucking and feeling the way Trent's muscles gripped and tightened around his tongue. He enjoyed the sensations, the sounds, even the taste of Trent at his most uninhibited.

"Faster," Trent gasped and reached for a handful of Reed's hair, yanking at it rhythmically. Reed mirrored the pace on Trent's cock while he kept fucking Trent's ass with his tongue.

Trent lasted far longer than Reed expected, especially given his weakened state and that they hadn't had any sexual contact for about a week. But when it happened, it happened fast and hard. Trent's orgasm started with a few tremors that erupted into a full-fledged quake, and he shuddered and squeezed Reed's tongue as his cock spasmed.

"Reeeeed," Trent moaned as his body responded. He trapped Reed's arm between his tree-trunk thighs until the temblor was over.

When the sound and fury subsided, Reed extricated himself from Trent's body and wiped hands and face on a towel before climbing back into bed with Trent.

Trent let out a contented sigh and wrapped an arm around Reed.

"Thank you," Trent said, breathing heavily into Reed's ear.

The boy was nothing if not damned polite, even postcoitally. Reed smiled against Trent's hair. He didn't even care that Trent had pulled him into the wet patch. He listened to Trent's breathing even and deepen as he fell asleep.

Reed had never rimmed anyone before Trent, and he hadn't been particularly enthusiastic about starting. But as with nearly everything else, Trent had made Reed want to do it. Trent had simply offered to rim Reed, and about two minutes into it, Reed was in such a state of delight he had to do the same for Trent. Recalling that about Trent made Reed realize that was the exact same trait that made Trent go to Milacio's to find a clue to help Reed, or that compelled him to move in front of a bullet meant for Peter. Trent just wanted to do the right thing, to make Reed happy.

Reed pulled Trent closer and inhaled deeply.

The fragrance of Trent's bodywash filled his nostrils, mingled with the scent of sex and satisfaction. A slight medicinal undernote of Trent's antiseptic cream rounded things out.

Trent whispered against Reed's shoulder, lips caressing the twisted knob of flesh where a Burmese soldier had shot Reed.

"Reed," Trent mumbled. "Love you." He slid one of his large paws down Reed's body and circled his cock, still half-hard, though he didn't mind being unsatisfied for the moment. Trent squeezed slightly, then let go as sleep overtook him again.

Reed inhaled and decided he'd never been more satisfied in his life.

38

Quannu amuri tuppulìa, 'un lu lassari 'nmenzu la via.

When love knocks, be sure to answer.

—Sicilian proverb

THEY were lying together in bed, the sound of chirping birds trickling through the open window. Reed sprawled across Trent's chest, eyes closed, the streaming sunlight turning the scars on his back into bright, over-exposed lines.

Trent inhaled, not sure how to start. He traced a finger along Reed's shoulder, feeling the smooth skin give way to scarred ridges of flesh. The sight had horrified him the first time he'd seen it back in Thailand, but had simply become a part of Reed as they'd grown closer. At first, Reed had attempted to hide the scars. As he got more comfortable with Trent, he stopped trying, but he'd never told Trent the full story of how he'd gotten them.

"I know what happened." Trent let the words burst out on their own. He bit his lower lip as he waited for Reed's reaction. He continued to stroke Reed's back, smoothing the puckered flesh, as if that might erase the memories for Reed—and for himself.

"What happened when?" Reed opened his thundercloud-gray eyes, a ridge forming between his brows.

"Peter told me everything. Or at least his side of it. About what happened after he left you."

"Oh." Reed lifted his head just enough to turn it and faced away from Trent.

Trent's heart missed two or three beats, then sped up to compensate. Surely Reed could feel that?

"Why didn't you ever tell me what you went through in that prisoner camp?"

Without turning, Reed replied, "Tell you I spent months in a camp waiting for my lover to rescue me?"

The sorrow in Reed's tone ripped at Trent's soul. He threaded his fingers through Reed's short hair, then stroked up and down the back of his neck. The muscles were hard and tense.

"That's not how Peter explained it."

Reed lifted his head and stared at Trent. "Oh no? How did he explain it, then?" The bitterness of the words surprised Trent.

But Reed didn't press for an answer. He searched Trent's expression as if he were expecting to see something specific and not believing it wasn't there.

"Why don't *you* explain it for me, Reed? Tell me how you felt about what happened. That's all I care about. I know Peter's not worth caring about now, but if the thought of him helped you survive or escape, then it's a good thing."

The storm in Reed's eyes lightened, the gray seeming to make way for a hint of fair blue. "Really?"

"Really. I wasted a lot of time wondering who 'Peter' was."

Reed's eyebrows knitted into a question.

"I realized you said his name in your sleep sometimes, but I was afraid to ask. I didn't realize it was part of—" Trent hesitated, waving a hand over Reed's back as explanation. "—what happened. At first I thought he might have done that to you. Later…." Trent's gut twisted a little as he recalled his self-doubt.

"You were worried? About what he meant to me?" Reed rolled over onto his side, propped his head up on one elbow, and peered at Trent again. One corner of his mouth turned down. He shook his head. "I should have explained more once his name came up in Rome. I'm sorry I didn't."

Trent fought off the urge to respond, sensing there was more, something Reed hadn't said yet.

Reed tore his gaze away from Trent and seemed to focus on the wall behind him. "To be honest, I wasn't sure enough how I felt about Peter to be able to explain him—or our past—to you." Reed blinked, then turned his gaze back to Trent.

"Do you know now?" Trent asked in little more than a whisper.

"Oh, God, yes."

Trent's heart skipped another beat, but this time out of joy. He wanted to hear Reed say he didn't care for Peter anymore, even if he already knew it. Reed didn't talk about his feelings, though the romantic in Trent longed to hear about them. "That's good to hear." Understatement.

Reed rolled close to Trent and pulled him in tight, then surprised him with a quick, rough kiss that crushed Trent's lips.

"You know you've risked your life twice for me, and even once for Peter. That's more than he ever did. When he told me what you did...." Reed's voice trailed off.

"So, I win?"

"It's not a competition, Trent. You've never had to compete with him for me. Compete with anyone...."

"Not even your job?" Trent definitely wished he could take that back. *Stupid*! Why hadn't he shut up when he was ahead?

Reed nodded. "You're right. I wanted to be needed."

"I need you."

"Trent, you don't need me. You're fine with your friends and your writing. The Bureau needs what I need to do. To be." Reed paused.

"That's not—"

Reed didn't let him finish. "But you know, that's the way it should be. I'd rather you *want* me in your life, not that you need me or rely on me to define yourself or something."

It was Trent's turn to blink a few times. This didn't sound like Reed at all. Wanting vs. needing? It was like he'd eaten a relationship self-help book. "I don't see why you can't still work for the FBI or Interpol. Especially if you can bring me along again."

"Again? I wasn't supposed to bring you along on either of these two missions. You just won't stay put."

"I'm not very good at following instructions. Never have been."
Trent grinned. "Would you rather be with someone who did?"

Reed shook his head and planted another near-lethal kiss on
Trent's mouth. "I sure don't want that."

"Good."

"Unless, of course, I told you to roll over and open wide."

"In that case, I just might follow your instructions."

"Good."

"Very good."

"Oh, it will be."

And Reed always made good on his promises.

EPILOGUE

Two weeks later

Los Angeles

"I'M STARVING. Let's just order some appetizers," Beth Alexander, Trent's best friend since college, said as she sipped at a heavy cut-crystal water glass and stared at the empty plate on the table in front of her.

"I feel like I'm in a Godfather movie or something." Mick Masters looked around and groaned. He was another longtime friend, a California native, currently a fairly successful producer and director of pornographic films of all flavors. If asked, Mick would say he was Trent's real best friend, though as the years went by, Trent found fewer things he and Mick agreed on. The restaurant décor happened to be one of them. "I'd heard fantastic things about this place—always wanted to come here—but no one mentioned how fucktastically ugly it was."

Trent let his gaze wander across the dimly lit dining room, furnished with heavy wood and dark red walls. Mick's comments brought an overwhelming sense of déjà vu and dread he hadn't expected, and which belied the truth about the restaurant. They were in a small family-run Italian restaurant in West Hollywood, off the beaten path. So far off, in fact, it had no sign out front. It really didn't even have a name. People just called it "Giovanna's" after the owner's wife. Trent had heard of the place but never been here. He'd been shocked when Reed made reservations for a little welcome-home get-together and invited Trent's friends and his agent, who tended to show up late for nearly everything.

Trent glanced at his watch. It was so dark he could barely make out the time. Mick slid one of the votive candles closer. "Reed should be here any minute, guys."

"At least order some wine. Hell, let's just order." Mick raised a hand to get a waiter's attention.

Trent waved the confused-looking waiter away with an apologetic shrug. "Not till Reed gets here. He said he had some sort of surprise for me."

"Yeah, for you. Why should we starve while you're waiting for your surprise?" Mick started to put a hand up in the air when Reed came coasting across the room and gave everyone a quick nod before leaning down to brush his lips against Trent's left cheek. The soft kiss sent ripples through Trent's body. When Reed squeezed his shoulder gently, Trent flirted with the idea of skipping dinner entirely and taking Reed home, but his curiosity won out. By a hair.

"Sorry I'm late. I had to take care of something."

"I didn't even see you come in and I was watching the door." Trent glanced around the small dining area. There were only about six tables, so he didn't know how he'd missed Reed's arrival.

Reed shrugged but didn't reply. "Everyone hungry?"

"Hell yeah!" Mick replied, loud enough that half the other diners turned toward him. Trent felt like hiding under the table.

A heavyset man with a thick moustache and dark hair just showing slivers of silver came to their table with two bottles of wine. He glanced toward Reed, who nodded; then the man proceeded to open the first bottle.

"*Prosecco*—Italian sparkling wine—to help you celebrate!" the man said as he poured honey-colored liquid into each glass and waited for the silvery layer of bubbles to subside before adding another inch of wine. "Enjoy!" He emptied the last of the wine into Reed's glass as Reed settled into the seat next to Trent.

"*Grazie*, Marco," Reed said and turned toward Trent.

"What are we celebrating?" Trent asked, a bit taken aback that Reed was on first-name basis with the waiter. He hadn't taken a sip yet.

"A safe return home?" Beth suggested.

"Who cares?" Mick toasted the air and drained his glass.

"Let's save that part for later. Mick's right—for a change. Let's just enjoy the wine and the meal." Reed raised his glass toward Trent and clinked glasses, then clinked with Beth. Mick poured some more for himself from the second bottle, and Reed even clinked against Mick's before taking a sip.

"We don't have any menus." Mick's hand started back into the air.

"Don't need any." Reed caught Marco's eye and gave a little nod. "I arranged everything already."

"Really?" Trent took another sip of *prosecco*, letting the bubbles tickle his nose and throat. He nearly pinched himself to see if this were all just a dream. Reed never took much initiative when it came to dinners out. Sometimes Trent had to practically drag him out to dinner.

"You'll see." Reed sipped at his glass, locking eyes with Trent and giving him a very sexy but all-too-mysterious look.

"Looks like you're pals with the waiter," Mick said with a shade too much condescension for Trent's liking. Reed was treating them to dinner, after all. Even Mick could make an attempt to be gracious.

"Actually, Marco is Giovanna's eldest son and the manager."

Trent bit his lip as he watched Mick try to backpedal. "Really?"

"Yeah. He introduced me to Steven Spielberg the other day. Nice guy," Reed said offhandedly with a pointed glare at Mick. "Now if you'll excuse me just a minute…." Reed patted Trent's knee and flashed that mischievous grin again.

And before Trent could reply, Reed shot out of his seat and headed for the back of the restaurant. Trent watched Mick do a slow burn in response to Reed's mention of Spielberg. Mick had wanted to be a legitimate director way back when they'd first met, while Trent, Beth, and Mick had been grad students at USC. It would really gall him that Reed—whom Mick had never liked—was hobnobbing with one of the most influential directors of the last hundred years.

Trent watched Reed walk away from their table, and recalled a night months ago when they'd slipped into the men's room of another restaurant for some fooling around. He wondered if that was what Reed's smoldering glance had meant. He got up and followed in the direction Reed had disappeared, toward a door near the back corner of the dining room.

Marco emerged with a heavy platter of food destined for a table near the front, the door swinging back to reveal a busy kitchen. Sounds of knives chopping, dishes clanking, and general cooking noises greeted his ears. Trent grabbed the door and just stared into the kitchen, his gaze lighting upon Reed, who was talking with an elderly woman whose hair was coiled in a sleek silver bun at the nape of her neck.

What was Reed doing in the kitchen? Clearly Trent was not expected to follow, and it had nothing to do with hanky panky. Marco nearly clipped Trent as he re-entered the kitchen, and with a last glance inside, Trent turned and went back to the table where Cassandra Rivington-Ffitch, his literary agent and close friend, had just seated herself between Beth and Mick. She was British-born and had lived in the States for years but never lost the trace of her childhood accent. Trent suspected she never wanted to. She'd been married and divorced several times, and he knew that Rivington and Ffitch were simply two of the former husbands whose names she liked the most. If she got bored, she'd rearrange her surname yet again. Cass got bored a lot.

"Cass, so good to see you!" Trent went and gave her a hug.

Her arms barely went around his waist. "Trent, I don't want to damage you. Are you well?"

"Almost good as new. Maybe better in some ways."

"Ah, good." Cass gave him the typical European double-barreled kiss, undoubtedly smearing lipstick on both cheeks. He poured a glass of *prosecco* for her, then sat back in his own seat.

"Where did Reed go?" Beth asked. She dipped the corner of her napkin in her water glass and scrubbed Cassandra's carmine kiss from Trent's right cheek.

"The kitchen." Trent turned so Beth could reach his other cheek.

"This is yummy!" Cass drained her glass and raised her eyebrows at Mick until he refilled it.

"What's he doing in the kitchen? Unless he's waiting for you… though I didn't think you guys liked doing it in public." Mick's tone was typically crude. Trent ignored him.

A moment later Reed returned, arms laden with platters of *bruschetta*, toasted sliced bread topped with chunky pieces of tomatoes and flecks of bright green basil. The tantalizing aroma of garlic wafted up from the platter.

"What's this?" Trent pointed to the other dish.

"Also *bruschetta*, with *caponata*—chopped olives, eggplant, red pepper, pine nuts, some herbs, and a few secret ingredients." Reed smiled as he served some from each platter onto Trent's plate. "Lots of chopping!"

"But... you made this?" Trent wasn't sure he'd understood what Reed meant.

"Yes."

"Oh, fantastic!" Beth grinned and sunk her teeth into the tomato version, the bread crunching as she chewed. "Heaven. Just the right amount of garlic!"

No one spoke for a few moments as they savored the tasty appetizers.

"Wow, Reed, I didn't know you could cook like this!" Cass said, licking her fingers in a very unladylike manner.

"This wasn't that difficult. Anyway, save room for dinner." Reed grinned and took a couple of bites out of his own portion while watching everyone else devour theirs.

"God, I could eat a whole platter of this myself," Beth said, then stopped herself from taking another piece. "Okay, let's slow down. I want to hear more about this whole thing with the diamonds. There were articles in the paper, and CNN did a special report on it. But I didn't quite understand the details."

"What's so confusing?" Mick grabbed the *bruschetta* away from Beth, but she fought him off.

"Where that woman—the Italian agent—fit into the whole thing. And just how were they smuggling the diamonds? I'm still confused," Cassandra added.

"Trent, why don't you fill them in. I need to check on something in the kitchen." Reed stood.

Trent craned his neck to look up at Reed. "There's more?"

"There's a whole meal. Did you think this was all I'd serve you?"

"You made the whole meal?" This was far more than Trent could have imagined. Reed had surprised him a lot while they were in Italy. Admittedly most of the surprises were of the unpleasant sort: finding out about Reed's past with Peter and then being left in Rome while Reed ran off on Peter's mission. But Reed preparing a dinner for Trent and his friends—and being nice to Mick?—even Trent's overactive writer's imagination couldn't have come up with a scenario like this.

And he liked it. Loved it. It beat the hell out of all those surprises in Italy.

"Trent?"

"Right. Caterina. I'll explain where she fit into the whole scheme of things."

Reed got up, planted a kiss on Trent's ear, and turned toward the kitchen.

"Reed?" Trent still didn't quite know what Reed had planned for the evening, their first evening out with friends since they'd returned from Italy.

"Relax, Trent. Have some more wine. I mean *prosecco*."

Trent grinned at the way Reed corrected his error before Trent had a chance to comment. He shrugged and reached for the bottle.

"Let me get that for you," Beth offered. "You're still recovering."

"I'm strong enough to pour wine."

"Maybe you shouldn't be drinking." Mick tried to take the bottle away from Trent. "Can't mix well with your meds."

"I'm not on meds anymore." Trent retrieved the bottle and filled up Beth's glass before pouring some for himself. He topped up Reed's glass too, though it had barely been touched.

"So, Mick, if you've got it all figured out, explain it to me." Beth cocked her head, chin jutting out in a challenge to Mick and his big mouth.

"It's easy. She was the one who forged the export documents. She had access as part of her job, right?"

Reed backed through the kitchen door, a platter in each hand, and brought them over, placing them as far out of Mick's reach as possible. Trent laughed as Beth reached for more.

"Save room for the rest of the dinner!" Reed said and turned back toward the kitchen.

"Reed, aren't you having any?"

"Yeah, in a minute!" Reed shouted from the kitchen.

"I just wonder what's up with this whole dinner thing. Not that I'm complaining or anything." Mick snuck a piece of *bruschetta* while

Beth took a sip of sparkling wine. "I don't exactly trust Reed in a kitchen."

"You don't?" Reed had crept up behind Mick, causing him to leap about a foot off his chair. "You don't have to stay for dinner."

"I want to see if I'm right about the woman. Caterina. I saw photos of her. Damn, she was smokin' hot!"

"She tried to kill me, Mick. She did have her goons kill the agent who died there—Brett Decker." Trent forced the words through tight lips. Why did Mick see the world in hot/not-hot terms only? He couldn't see there was more to everyone than looks and sex.

"Well, except for that." Mick had the good sense to look chastened.

"So, start from the beginning. Where did the diamonds come from?" Cassandra sat back and patted her stomach, but her tone betrayed her curiosity.

"Sierra Leone, Liberia. A few different countries in West Africa. They all have strict export controls now, and international peacekeepers and watchdogs preventing them from selling the diamonds except in very controlled circumstances." Trent spoke slowly, wanting to make sure he got the details correct. "Milacio owned a coffee plantation, and he had the diamonds smuggled in the coffee. And with his shipping line, he could control the shipping routes and schedules, making sure the diamonds made it into the coffee sacks, and they were marked so he or his workers could keep track of which sacks had the diamonds."

"That's unbelievable. He owned the mines too?" Beth asked.

"No, he just paid pennies on the dollar to the locals and took the lion's share of the profits. Well, that's what he thought was going to happen."

"But it didn't?"

"Right. He could only bring the diamonds back to Italy, because he didn't have any international shipping routes for the coffee. The Ivory Coast coffee is mainly sold to Italy and France for dark roasting and espresso-type products. The lower-quality coffee market. He couldn't get the diamonds out of Europe to other lucrative diamond markets like the US without some help."

"That's where the lovely-but-deadly Caterina comes in," Mick added.

"Yes. She grew up on one of the other islands and knew Milacio for years. She encouraged him to start the maritime antiquities recovery business. They concealed the diamonds in the items he retrieved. She arranged the export papers—"

"Told you!" Mick nearly shouted, causing heads to turn again.

"But where did the brokers and auction house fit in?" Cassandra asked.

"It would be too obvious if Caterina approved a lot of export licenses for the same type of items over and over, and the value of the item has to be documented, along with a corresponding financial transaction—so the Italian government can adequately tax the transaction—so Caterina came up with a way to hide the diamond transactions in a sea of other art and antiquities purchases. The buyers—all working with an art broker partner—purchased a group of more legitimate items, overbidding on them, so the full price of the diamonds was covered. Once they'd bought the requisite amount of art, then Milacio would sell them an amphora—a diamond-filled amphora—that was the final delivery."

"And no one questioned the high art prices?"

"Italy got taxes on it, and it was a way for Caterina and Milacio to safely launder the money, as well as for the buyers to explain the huge payments they made to obtain the diamonds. Otherwise, transactions that large would raise red flags with the international agencies that monitor financial activity."

"And you got in their way by bidding on one at the auction house in Rome?" Beth leaned forward in her chair like a kid.

Trent nodded.

"So I still don't get why Milacio needed her. I think he could have come up with some other way."

"Well, that's where Mick might explain it better…."

"He was fucking her?"

"Or the other way around. I think she was stringing him along, playing at being his girlfriend, just to have access to the supply of diamonds. She took a huge cut of the profits for her part with the export licenses, but she was the one who conceived of the overall strategy. Reed saw Milacio's financial records, and he had all the risk and expense of acquiring and moving the gems. And that underwater archeological dig, big bucks." Trent grinned. He'd never forget that day on the recovery boat. It had been amazing. He hadn't told Reed yet, but he wanted to learn to dive. Maybe they could go on a trip—once he was completely recovered—and do some wreck diving.

"So she was the mastermind behind it all?" Beth nodded and grinned. "I can't decide if she was a genius or just another conniving bitch."

"Some of both," Reed said. "The Italian justice system is a world unto itself and with her looks, she might charm a judge or jury." His tone was cool, and Trent felt the chill around the table.

"Hot. Told you how important that is, even for criminal masterminds." Mick held his glass up in a toast no one returned. He shrugged it off and drank.

"She had an FBI agent killed in a horrific way. I don't think she's worth anyone's admiration." Reed's tone grew icy, and he dropped his fork on his plate with a loud clatter.

"You two make a great team, figuring it all out and apprehending them." Cass tried to interject something positive into the conversation. "And I hope you've got some ideas for your next book, Trent...."

DISCUSSION for the rest of the meal focused on what Reed and Trent had done before returning to LA a few days earlier. And, of course, everyone exclaimed over the delicious food: Reed introduced each dish, explaining they were all specialties of the Aeolian Islands and not part of Giovanna's regular menu. He'd chosen several fish and seafood dishes, including plump mussels served in the shell with a dollop of cheese and breadcrumbs, swordfish with tomatoes and capers, and fresh mahi mahi bathed in a lemony-garlic sauce that nearly brought Cassandra to tears. Add in a fennel and orange salad, a bread salad, and plenty more good wine, and the acrimonious discussion was quickly forgotten. Even Mick praised Reed's choice of dishes.

"There's one mystery you still haven't explained, Reed." Trent scooted his chair back from the table and patted his incredibly full stomach.

Reed turned to him and raised one eyebrow.

"This dinner. How'd you arrange this? How'd they let you help out in the kitchen?"

"I didn't actually help out. I cooked. Giovanna's staff helped *me*."

"You cooked?" Trent shook his head.

The others echoed his question. "You did? But how…?"

"When you got out of the hospital and you were sleeping all day, I had a lot of time on my hands. So, I got some cooking lessons from Tessa."

"Tessa?" Beth asked.

"Milacio's cook. She stayed on to help out after he and Caterina were arrested. She ran the household and even cooked for the police and Interpol agents who catalogued the collection and shipped it out. With so many agents, there wasn't much work for me to do besides looking after Trent. And he had a private nurse for the first week. So I helped Tessa in the kitchen."

"So you got these recipes from her? The swordfish dish, it's one Milacio served us that first day we went to visit him, isn't it?"

"Yes. But it's not exactly the same. I couldn't find the right fish here."

"Look at you, worried about the recipe not being perfect." Beth gave Reed a little punch on the shoulder, the way she always did to Trent.

"I love it, no matter whether it's perfect or not. Thank you." Trent reached for Reed, pulled him close, and planted a loud kiss on his cheek. He'd offer more thanks later, once they were alone. For now, he was so touched that Reed had learned to cook new dishes for him. He didn't think he could love Reed any more than he did right at this moment.

"So, Trent, you were right about Caterina all along."

"Yeah, I was." Trent cocked his head in Reed's direction. "Wasn't I?"

"I never said you were wrong, I just said it wasn't conclusive from what happened in the hotel in Rome."

"That's not what it sounded like."

"Well, I'm sorry. You do have an overactive imagination."

"This is true. Usually you like that." Trent gave a sly grin.

"Can you guys either get a room or tone it down? There are other people here!" Mick said.

Trent ignored him and scooted closer to Reed. "You know you owe me for not trusting my judgment."

"I just made this amazing meal for you. How much more can I owe?"

"Let me count the ways." He whispered a few of his favorites into Reed's ear and could feel the heat rise to Reed's neck and cheeks. He'd tease him about that later, when they were alone and he could cash in his requests. For now, Trent wanted another plate full of Reed's delicious dinner.

"I have one more surprise for you, Trent."

"Enough with the surprises. What about dessert?"

"Shut up, Mick," everyone else chorused.

"What more could I possibly want at this point?"

"This isn't what you want. It's something I want. And White."

"Tom White?"

Reed nodded. "My boss in the Bureau," he explained for Beth and Mick.

"What?"

"You're signed up for a Bureau training session starting next month at Quantico."

"What?"

"We decided, if you keep getting in the—I mean, helping out with my cases—you should get some proper training. Michael Westen ain't all he's cracked up to be."

"But FBI training? Like for agents?"

"No, not the same training the new agents get, but a special course designed for civilian employees. It covers some of the basics of law enforcement and a pretty thorough introduction to firearms. How not to get shot, as well as how to shoot."

Trent colored a little. It wasn't his fault he got shot. He wasn't sure a class would help. "Really? Does this mean they're offering me a job too?"

"Let's see how you do on the course. If you like the rest of the work, then White said he might let you help me out on something easy.

Nothing dangerous. No more international smuggling missions for you."

"But I'm the one who figured it all out! And you're the one who didn't believe me."

"Actually Decker figured it out and you just translated it for me. But that's my point. Analysts don't belong in the field. A few classes aren't enough to do that job. There will be other ways you can contribute."

"Any dessert?"

"Mick, you can't possibly still be hungry!" Cass chided him.

"No. But I do love me something sweet." He put an arm around her shoulders and squeezed her tight against his chest.

"There is something. It's another Sicilian favorite, but I got a little creative." Reed got up yet again. He returned with a tray of cut-crystal glasses that glinted in the candlelight. Marco helped him serve a portion to everyone. In each glass glistened a pale green globe of what looked like coarse salt. It nearly glowed with a luminescence enhanced by the crystal and the candlelight.

"Pretty... but what is it?" Beth's spoon hovered over her glass.

"Granita." Trent smiled. This was another thing he'd learned to love on their trip. "Popular summer dessert, especially in the islands."

"This isn't a traditional flavor... I mixed *prosecco* with green apple. It's a special flavor for a special occasion."

"Can we eat it already?" Mick asked, surprising Trent that he hadn't just dug in.

A chorus of "mmmm" and "ahhh" went around the table.

Trent dipped his spoon in, took a small amount, and let it melt on his tongue. The tartness of the green apple added a delightful tang to the yeasty base of the *prosecco*.

Beth scooped some granita into her mouth then waved the empty spoon in Trent's direction. "One thing you still haven't mentioned is that amphora you got at the auction. What ever happened to it?"

Trent took a deep breath and turned his gaze on Reed.

"The amphora. When Trent—or J.T. Dallas—didn't come to pick it up, Marconi's men tried to steal it. They were caught on video and arrested while we were on Panarea. White had staked the place out, expecting they might come back. He'd even had the thing examined, X-rayed, the whole nine yards, but they weren't able to detect the diamonds. They were that well hidden. Had to break the thing to retrieve them."

"So poor Trent didn't get that one, or the one Milacio gave him on the boat?" Cass seemed to be turning on Reed as well. "That's not fair."

Trent whole-heartedly agreed, but he put on a brave face and didn't say anything. He and Reed had already been through this.

"You're right, but there's a silver lining to this." Reed patted one pants pocket, then the other. He finally pulled something out of his left breast pocket and placed a small box on the table in front of Trent. "Open it."

Trent glanced at Reed, who sat there with a cryptic smile on his face. Curiosity won out and he flipped the little box open, uncovering a ring set with a diamond big enough to put a smile on even Caterina's face. He stared at it as it glittered and reflected even the low light in the restaurant. *A ring? From Reed?*

Trent, for all his romantic fantasies, never thought he'd be getting a diamond ring from Reed, and it left him speechless. He looked down at the ring and then up at Reed, afraid to say anything. He'd written scenes like this a dozen times, but in real life, it just felt so—unreal.

"Oh, my, God!" Beth nearly shouted. "Is that what I think it is?"

"Yes and no," Reed replied. "It's a diamond, but it's not from me. Sorry if anyone jumped to conclusions."

"Who's it from, then?" Trent felt his lower lip tremble.

"A very grateful West African government. They wanted to reward us for helping shut the smuggling ring down. Agents can't accept gifts like this, but I told White that you're not an agent. I had the ring made, but if you don't like the setting…."

"It's gorgeous. Stunning. I can see why Caterina was corrupted by their beauty." Trent watched the fire inside the stone dance for a moment, collecting his thoughts and emotions. Had he really thought Reed would propose to him here, like this, with all Trent's friends watching? In a way, he realized, it was kind of a relief the ring wasn't anything more than a reward. Trent needed to think about that for a while.

"So put it on." Reed reached for the little box and plucked the ring out.

Trent held out his right hand and Reed moved to slip the ring onto the third finger, but he lost hold of it, and it dropped with a metallic clink into Trent's granita.

Cassandra spoke up, breaking the silence. "So that's why they call it Italian ice!"

Don't Miss the Beginning of the Story in

EM LYNLEY has worked finance, the wine industry, and high-tech, though she'd rather be writing hot man-on-man romance. She spent ten years as an economist and financial analyst, including a year as a White House Staff Economist, but only because all the intern positions were filled. Tired of boring herself and others with dry business reports and articles, her creative muse is back and naughtier than ever. She has lived and worked in London, Tokyo, and Washington, DC, but the San Francisco Bay Area is home for now.

Visit her website at http://www.emlynley.com

her blog at http://emlynley.livejournal.com

her Twitter page at http://twitter.com/emlynley

and her Facebook at http://www.facebook.com/emlynley

Also from EM LYNLEY

DISGUISES
EM LYNLEY

http://www.dreamspinnerpress.com

www.ingramcontent.com/pod-product-compliance
Lightning Source LLC
Chambersburg PA
CBHW051531260626
47170CB00003B/880